On Her Majesty's

CYPRUS MISSION

****

An IAN BLACK *Novel*

Richard *and* Barbara Osborn

RICHARD AND BARBARA OSBORN

For our family members and friends who have put up with us
while we wrote this book

Thank You for your patience

The authors of this book would like to pay honour and
respect to all the British servicemen who served and, in
some cases died, on Her Majesty's Service in Cyprus.

On Her Majesty's Cyprus Mission is a work of historical
fiction. Apart from the well-known actual people, events,
and locales that figure in the narrative, all names,
characters, places, and incidents are the products of the
authors' imagination or are used fictitiously. Any
resemblance to current events or locales, or to living
persons, is purely coincidental.

Go to pages 342-345 for Glossary, Mediterranean Map,
Characters and British Army Officer Ranks.

Britannia-American Publishing
ISBN-13: 978-0692294246
ISBN-10: 0692294244

This page intentionally left blank

PROLOGUE

For centuries, the island of Cyprus has been occupied by invading armies and conquerors. It is situated in the eastern part of the Mediterranean Sea, just 47 miles south of Turkey and only 65 miles west of Lebanon and Syria. The reason, why it has been the subject of numerous conquests by invading armies, is that it is a strategic land mass close to the Middle East. In addition, two thousand years ago, it was a major source of copper. To name just a few, Cyprus has been controlled by the Assyrians, Greeks, Egyptians, Persians, Romans, Turks and the British. The Romans valued Cyprus as a strategic military base and for the copper.

Since the 1820's, when the modern country of Greece first appeared, the idea of enosis (Union with Greece) has flourished among Greek speaking populations. In particular it was popular with Greek speaking Cypriots. There was one problem, however, in the fact that there was a sizable minority of Turkish speaking Cypriots. This movement was in some ways akin to German speaking people wanting to be part of greater Germany in the 1930's.

This enosis movement kept coming to the surface, and in 1949, the Cypriot Orthodox Church held a referendum that was not sanctioned by the British colonial government. The referendum was not with a secret ballot, but a show of hands in churches.

Finally in 1955, a terrorist movement named EOKA (Εθνική Οργάνωσις Κυπρίων Αγωνιστών, Greek for National Organization of Cypriot Fighters) was formed by a group of Cypriot Greeks wanting to force the British to grant the uniting of the island with Greece. EOKA officially started its campaign in April 1, 1955 and ended it in December 1959, after the signing of the Zurich/London accord.

ON HER MAJESTY'S CYPRUS MISSION

The EOKA military arm was headed by a Colonel Georgios Grivas and, at its height, had an estimated 1,250 followers. Of these, it is estimated that 250 were regulars and another 1,000 were active underground members. They were supported with weapons from Greece and, for that reason, one of the main goals of the British was to stop the flow of arms to this organization.

Grivas's main target was the British Army that controlled the island and, to a lesser extent, the Turkish minority. The island population was made up of 77% Greek Cypriots, 18% Turkish Cypriots and 5 % others; mainly British.

From the 1st of April 1955 to the 24th Of December 1959, Great Britain waged a war against these Greek Cypriot terrorists. During this time, a total of 371 military and 16 civilian deaths were attributed to the Emergency. The exact count has never been issued by the British Government, but it is believed that actually 104 servicemen were killed by EOKA and the rest by accidents, health or other reasons. The British used the Turkish minority to help them, since the Turks wanted nothing to do with enosis or Union with Greece. The Greeks and Turks had a dislike of each other for centuries. During the Ottoman Empire, the Turks controlled Cyprus and the majority of Greek Cypriots did not take kindly to being controlled by a minority.

The political arm of the movement was led by Archbishop Makarios III, the Head of the Cypriot Orthodox Church. He was exiled to the Mahe Island in the Seychelles in March 1956 for making inflammatory statements. He was allowed to return in March 1959 and became the first president of an independent Cyprus in August 1960.

The British Prime Ministers, during this Cyprus Emergency, were Anthony Eden (1955-1957) and Harold Macmillan (1957-1963). Queen Elizabeth II was the ruling monarch at the time and was the titular head of Cyprus, until it became independent.

This Cyprus emergency took place when Britain was slowly withdrawing from the colonies because, after the effects of World War Two, they could no longer afford to control or maintain all of them. The leaders of the Enosis movement in Cyprus sensed this change in Britain's colonial policy and decided that now was the time to force the British out of Cyprus.

All this was going on, while the British were fighting the Mau Mau in Kenya and the communists in British Malaya (Singapore and Malaysia). Britain could no longer afford a large standing army and also finance the extensive welfare state, including the National Health Service, that had been created in the late 1940's, after the war, by the Labour party.

This story is about one Englishman (half American), **Ian Black**, who tried to make a difference for the British by conducting intelligence work in Cyprus. He flew from England to the airport in Nicosia, Cyprus on the 27th of March 1958, and was **On Her Majesty's Cyprus Mission.**

Royal Artillery Badge   Intelligence Corps Badge

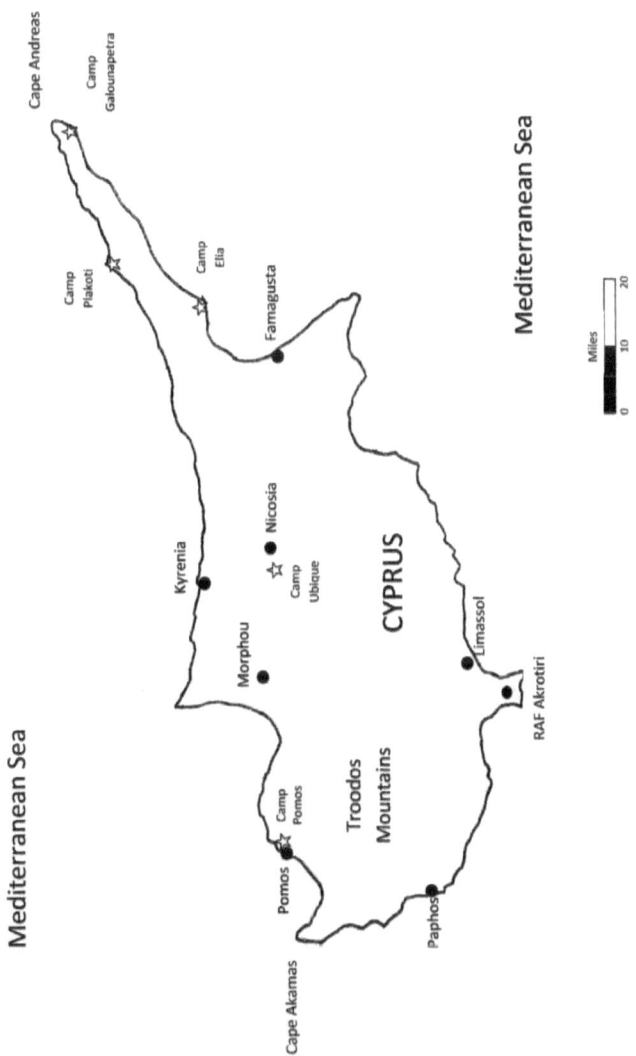

This page intentionally left blank

1

The Bridge Blows

The early afternoon sky was azure blue and full of cumulus, cotton ball clouds. This was normal for an April day in Cyprus, after a storm had gone through the night before. Squinting into the sun, a tall, lanky British Army officer stepped out of Major MacArthur's office, located at Camp Ubique, just west of Nicosia. He was the ideal image of a young British officer, a little over six feet tall, slim and had the demeanor that showed he was a leader of men. He swung his swagger stick and slapped it on his thigh, trying to hide his nervousness. Second Lieutenant Ian Black had just arrived in Cyprus, one week earlier, on the 27th of March, 1958. Since then, he had worked for the major, learning how the 188th Radar and Searchlight Battery ran its operations. Ian was also extremely useful to the CO since he was fluent in Greek. He had just been assigned to take over Camp Pomos, on the northwest coast of the island, and had been in the CO's office to receive final instructions, before starting out for the camp. He strode, still slapping his swagger stick, towards the two desert sand coloured vehicles, parked outside the Battery headquarters. His army issued Webley Mk IV service revolver was in a holster, hanging from his belt; ready in case he needed it.

Lieutenant Black walked over to the two vehicles; one was a Land Rover and the other was Bedford army lorry loaded with a driver, a bombardier in the front passenger seat and six gunners in the rear. The lorry was also loaded with mail, rations and other stores. The six gunners had standard British Army issued Lee-Enfield .303 rifles. Two of the six gunners, who had recently arrived from the U.K., were "green" recruits and were being sent to their first radar site, since their arrival. The bombardier in charge of the lorry carried a Sten gun with a loaded magazine ready for use, but not installed. The British Army had suffered several accidents with the Sten gun, because the bolt mechanism was so loose that it would accidentally load the gun and fire, when a vehicle went over a bump.

Ian went around to the back of the lorry to warn the six gunners to keep alert and be ready for anything. The major had apprised him about the possibility of snipers in the hills and bombs under the bridges. He then went to the front of the lorry and talked to the bombardier in charge.

"Remember to stay fifty yards behind the Land Rover, just in case there is some problem on the way to the camp. Also, keep your Sten gun unloaded, until you need to use it, so that you don't shoot yourself accidentally."

"Yes, sir," replied the bombardier. "Are we going to stop on the way to Camp Pomos?"

"We'll make a quick stop in Morphou to get some refreshments and satisfy any other urgent need," Ian responded.

With that, he went to the Land Rover, climbed into the front passenger seat and told the driver to head out. Then they drove out of the main gate of Camp Ubique, followed by the lorry, and headed west on Troodos Road. As a precaution, Ian checked his Webley revolver to make sure it was loaded.

He thought to himself, *I may need this before the day is out.* He had been warned of the ambushes by EOKA terrorists, in previous drives, on the treacherous mountain road to Camp Pomos.

10

Ian had been advised that it would take about two hours to go the approximate sixty miles from Camp Ubique to Camp Pomos. The trip would take them west and then north to Morphou. There they would have a short pit stop, then proceed along the coast road to Camp Pomos; travelling between the Troodos Mountains and the coast.

The most dangerous part of the trip would be the second leg from Morphou to Camp Pomos. The road was very curvy and contained many small, short bridges, under which EOKA could hide bombs. The road snaked around the Troodos Mountains and when it rained, mainly in the winter, the water coming off the mountains had to go somehow to the ocean. These small bridges were built under the road to allow for this rainwater. They also happened to be on sharp curves, where a vehicle had to slow down, to get around these curves. The bridges were an ideal place for EOKA terrorists to place a bomb. The terrorists would hide in the hills above the road. When an army lorry slowed down to go around the curve, they would blow the bomb. Then, with captured and smuggled guns, they would fire on the troops that survived the bomb blast. This is what awaited Ian and the Camp Pomos troops, if it was their unlucky day.

As they were driving west from Battery headquarters, Ian looked at the driver of the Land Rover. He appeared to be around nineteen or twenty, with a shock of red hair and a baby face.

"What's your name, gunner?" Ian asked.

"It's James Hall, sir."

"It's nice to meet you, James. Where're you from and how long have you been over here in Cyprus?"

"I'm from Leeds, sir, and I've been on the island for a little over a year."

Ian replied, "I spent a summer, three years ago, in Leeds visiting a relative. How often do you drive in from Camp Pomos to the headquarters?"

"We come once a week on Thursdays, sir. We come in

11

the morning, load up and after lunch drive back."

Upon hearing this routine from the driver, Ian became more concerned and held onto the butt of his revolver tighter. This regular "milk run" sounded ominous to him.

After travelling about seven miles, they arrived in the Greek populated town of Kokkinotrimithia. As they drove through the town, the citizens turned their backs and the fathers hurriedly took their daughters inside, for protection from those "nasty" British soldiers. At least, none of the citizens threw rocks or bottles.

They then drove on to the Greek village of Akaki, which was about four miles further. Here, the four seasoned troops in the lorry whistled at the old women who wore long black dresses, as they were walking along the road. They hadn't seen any young girls, for over a year, and were somewhat sex starved.

The two new recruits thought they were crazy, however. Little did they know that they would also be whistling a year from now, as they would not have much interaction with young Cypriot girls either. Ian could not hear the whistling by the troops, since the lorry was keeping the required distance from the Land Rover. Again, no rocks were thrown at either vehicle.

They went on westward, another three miles, and entered the Greek village of Peristerona. Here, the people threw rocks at the vehicles and shouted insults at the soldiers. Luckily, none of the stones struck the vehicles or the troops. It was a small village and they were through it within one to two minutes.

Then they drove on to the last Greek village of Astromeritus. It was just two and one half miles from Peristerona, but they didn't meet any of the hostility that they had faced in the previous village. Finally, they were out of the hostile Greek "territory" and headed for Morphou.

The town of Morphou was about six miles north from Astromeritus and it was populated, again, mainly by people of Greek descent. There was also a garrison of troops from the 1st. Battalion of the Welsh Regiment, located near the town. As they entered the town, it didn't seem as though the inhabitants were as hostile to the British troops, as some of the previous towns and villages. The few Turkish people there didn't want to see the British leave Cyprus, because they would then be at the mercy of the Greek majority.

Ian spotted a café, at the side of the road, close to the middle of Morphou and told the driver to pull in there. They parked close to the café. The lorry followed them into the parking area, but did not park too close to the Land Rover, for security reasons. They all sat outside, at the small tables, so they could keep an eye out just in case. All of them had their weapons handy. The waiter came out and, in fairly good English, asked for their order. All of them ordered a bottle of orange or tangerine drink. These drinks were refreshing, after the dusty drive from Camp Ubique.

After about fifteen minutes, Lt. Black rose and said, "Okay men, let's get going. We need to reach Camp Pomos by 1630 hours. Check your weapons, before we start."

They all rose and went to their respective vehicles, checking their weapons before they climbed into the lorry or Land Rover. As they headed west from Morphou, towards the Cyprus coast, they entered territory again populated by Greek Cypriots. The first village was Kato Pyrgos that was about eighteen miles west of Morphou.

As they entered the village, they met a hostile crowd, who hurled curse words at the British troops. Hidden, in a house on the side of the road, there was a young twenty year old Greek Cypriot, with a portable radio.

He was a member of the EOKA terrorist group and was communicating with another member, in the Troodos Mountains.

He spoke quietly in Greek into the microphone, "Η πομπή με τον τρόπο".

(English translation: "The convoy is on the way.")

This radio transmission was also picked up at a Morphou listening post, manned by the British Intelligence Corps. However, they did not know which convoy was referred to. By the signal strength, they could tell it was fairly close by, but the radio transmission didn't last long enough to get a directional fix. They alerted the Welsh Regiment, stationed near Morphou, to stand by for possible action. They had a few Ferret Scout cars and a couple of Alvis FV603 Saracen armoured personnel carriers. They also called the Royal Air Force at Nicosia airport. They requested that they send a couple of armed aircraft to the Morphou area, to determine if they could observe any danger to British troops.

Ian didn't hear any of these radio transmissions or the alert sounded in Morphou. Soon, the small convoy entered the last Greek village, before arriving at Camp Pomos and relative safety. As they entered Pachyammos, Ian noticed that there was no one on the streets. In fact, the village seemed to be deserted. He thought this was odd and it made him extremely nervous. He held onto his revolver, even tighter than he had been. They were only about three miles from Camp Pomos, when the road started to get very curvy. After leaving this village, they came around a fairly smooth bend, and then neared a sharp "U" curve in the road, that passed over a small bridge. As they approached this bridge, the hair on his neck stood up and his intuition told him that something wasn't exactly right.

The convoy proceeded toward the bridge, but unknown to Ian and his men, there were six fully armed EOKA terrorists hiding nearby. They were obscured behind some large boulders just south of the road. Five of them were in their teens or early twenties and inexperienced in terrorist tactics. Their leader was somewhat older and seasoned, and he had been involved in previous campaigns against the British Army.

When the terrorist leader had received the radio transmission from Morphou stating that the convoy was on the way, he sent two of the young terrorists down to the small bridge, located in a "U" curve of the road, with an explosive charge and a reel of twin wire. They planted the bomb under the bridge and connected the twin wires. They then ran up to some boulders in the hills, trailing the wires behind them. There they connected the wires to a mechanical detonator box, with a shaft and handle. One of the young terrorists, who was only eighteen and on his first mission with EOKA, was named Andreus Palas. He was assigned, by their leader, to blow the bridge, at the appropriate time. As he squatted behind a boulder, his hands began to sweat and shake. He placed one hand on the detonator plunger and the other hand steadied the detonator box, as he waited nervously for the convoy to pass over the bridge. When the Land Rover slowed down to go over the bridge, Andreus, who was inexperienced and nervous, pushed the plunger down prematurely. The bridge exploded about twenty feet in front of the vehicle.

The resulting force of the explosion raised the Land Rover a few feet above the road. It then crashed onto its side, spilling Ian and the two gunners onto the road. One of the gunners was unconscious. The driver was trapped in the vehicle and the fuel tank was leaking.

Meanwhile, the lorry carrying the six gunners, plus the driver and the bombardier, stopped well short of the blown bridge. Luckily, the driver had obeyed the lieutenant's order and followed fifty yards behind the Land Rover. The gunners jumped out and took up defensive positions behind the lorry. The bombardier got on the radio and called the Battery headquarters, for air and ground support.

Ian went to help the driver of the Land Rover, even though this placed him in immediate danger. He managed to free the driver from the vehicle and drag him to safety, behind it. The one unharmed gunner, from the rear of the Land Rover, managed to carry the other unconscious gunner behind the vehicle. At about this time, the terrorists started shooting at the vehicle from the hills to the south. Immediately, the troops from the lorry returned the fire.

Ian was concerned about their position, being so close to the Land Rover with its leaking fuel tank. He spotted a large boulder on the north side of the road and signaled to the gunner, guarding the unconscious soldier, to try and reach the safety of the boulder. Ian and the gunner both managed to drag the driver and the soldier to relative safety behind this boulder.

A few seconds later, Ian peered from around the boulder and saw an EOKA terrorist emerge from his hiding place. The terrorist crept towards the road and their position. He was carrying something round in his right hand. As he drew closer, Ian could see that it was a hand grenade and it looked like the man was getting ready to pull the pin. The terrorist held the grenade in his right hand and was holding the pin with a finger of his left hand.

When Ian saw this, he leapt to his feet and yelled at the terrorist in Greek, "Πάμε στην κόλαση, μπάσταρδος" (In English, this translated to, "Go to hell, you bastard!")

Andreus was so surprised to hear a British officer shout at him, in his own language, that he hesitated for a moment. This was his major mistake. Ian fired a shot from his revolver at the terrorist, hitting him in the chest; just as he was about to throw the grenade at them. When the bullet hit him, it caused him to let go of the grenade too soon. His aim was not true and the grenade went off about twenty feet in front of the Land Rover. Ian received a large piece of shrapnel in his right leg, and as he fell, he hit his head on a large rock and was knocked unconscious.

At this very moment, the two armed, RAF Hawker Hunter jets, from Nicosia, arrived overhead and drove the terrorists back into the Troodos Mountains. A few minutes later, the Welsh Guards from Morphou drove up in a Ferret and Saracen, along with a British Army Field Ambulance.

A doctor and two medics, from the Royal Army Medical

Corps (RAMC), leapt out of the British Army ambulance. They ran over to Lieutenant Black and the two injured gunners and checked them out. They placed them carefully on stretchers and loaded them into the ambulance. Then, one of the medics went over to the young EOKA terrorist that Ian had shot, felt his pulse and shook his head; he was dead. The medic then went back to the ambulance and climbed in. The field ambulance, escorted by a Ferret, raced back down the road towards the Pentayia hospital, situated on Morphou Bay. It had been built by the Cyprus Mines Corporation to treat the injuries suffered by the copper miners and had been taken over by the British military, during the EOKA emergency.   They quickly treated Ian and the two gunners and then sent them on, via Morphou, to the Nicosia British Military Hospital (BMH).

The lorry with the supplies, that was following the Land Rover, managed to slowly get around the blown bridge and get back on the road to Camp Pomos. It was only a couple of miles further down the road. They arrived there a few minutes later and told the camp sergeant what had happened. The sergeant radioed the Battery headquarters and talked with Major MacArthur. The major told the sergeant that he was in charge of the camp, until another officer could be sent out there.

2

Recovery

The field ambulance drove up to the BMH around 1800 hours.   Second Lieutenant Ian Black and the two gunners were taken into the emergency room, to be checked out and treated. Ian required an operation to remove the shrapnel from his leg and to sew it up. He, and the two gunners, also needed to be checked for concussion.

The BMH had been a general hospital, until it was taken over by the British Army in the late 1940's. It was expanded in 1955, at the commencement of the Cyprus Emergency. The staff had been told that the hospital would probably be closed at the end of the Emergency; when Britain pulled most of its troops out of Cyprus.

When Ian came to, after the operation to repair his leg, he found himself in the Officers' Ward at the hospital. An exquisite young nurse, fairly tall with an attractive figure, black hair and green eyes, was walking through the ward, checking on the patients. When she perceived that Ian was coming out of the anesthetic, she came over to his bed and started to check his vital signs. Ian looked at her name tag and noticed her name was Aphrodite Palas. She spoke in English, with a slight accent.   In fact, she was a Greek Cypriot who had been cleared by security to work in the hospital.

She asked him, "How do you feel, sir?"

Ian responded, "Fine, thank you. You can call me Ian, if you'd like."

Then, in Greek, he said, "Είναι χαρά μου να σας γνωρίσουμε. Σας ευχαριστώ για τη φροντίδα μου. Βλέπω ότι έχω ακόμα το πόδι μου"

Translated into English, "It's a pleasure to meet you. Thank you for taking care of me. I see I still have my leg."

Aphrodite looked at Ian in amazement and said in English, "You speak excellent Greek. In fact, if I didn't know you were British, I'd have thought you were a Greek. Please, let's speak in English or my superiors might have some concern about my intentions for working here. Also, regulations require me to address you as sir. I'm sorry."

"Well okay. If you must address me as sir, so be it. At least there isn't any regulation against smiling at me, is there?"

"No, sir," she said with a smile.

With that, she left the ward, and Ian drifted off to sleep dreaming about his childhood, his life and his parents.

****

He was born less than a month after World War II started in Europe, when Hitler invaded Poland. His father, James Martin Black, was English and he was drafted into the RAF as a flying officer, at the onset of the war. He had previous experience in flying planes and the RAF was desperate for any experienced pilots. He trained on the Supermarine Spitfire and fought in the Battle of Britain during the summer of 1940. He was promoted to flight lieutenant by 1941 and then to squadron leader by 1943.

After the Battle of Britain, Ian's father flew Spitfires on escort for British bombers that were going deep into Germany. Since the Spitfire had limited range, the RAF acquired American P51 Mustangs that could escort the bombers the entire round trip into Germany. Ian's father managed to fly the P51 on these trips, until he was promoted again to wing commander. He finally hung up his flying wings when peace in Europe was declared in May 1945, and he went back to being a husband and a father.

Ian's mother, Reba Ann Miles, was an American from Nashville, Tennessee, who had met Ian's father in Britain, when she was there attending university. During the War, she didn't see much of her husband, because of his RAF duties. She did an excellent job in raising Ian and sent him to school at Broomfield House, when he turned five. This was a private school close to Kew Gardens and Richmond, where they lived.

After leaving Broomfield House School, Ian became a boarder at Junior King's School in Sturry, Kent, and then, at age thirteen, he entered Harrow School, in Harrow on the Hill, after passing the Common Entrance Exam (CE). His father had attended this school and had signed him up, when he was born, to insure he could get in, if qualified. Harrow was an excellent English "public school", and Ian excelled in mathematics and languages. He loved sports, and became involved in rugby, field hockey and cross country. Both his parents were proud of him when he passed his O levels, and later his "A" level exams. He also participated in the Harrow Rifle Corps CCF (Combined Cadet Force) that gave him a taste of military life.

Ian Black was called up for National Service on October 16 1957, just after his eighteenth birthday. He was inducted into the Royal Artillery and ended up at Oswestry, a market town in Shropshire near the Welsh border, for two weeks of basic training. At the boot camp, he was assigned to the 185 Battery, 67th Training Regiment where he was kitted out, medically assessed and given intelligence tests. Ultimately, Ian was classified SG1 and declared fit for military service. After his two weeks of basic training at Oswestry, he was sent by train to Tonfanau on the Welsh coast, where the wind and the rain was almost a daily companion. At Tonfanau, he was assigned to the 55th Training Regiment. Here he received further training in marching drills and was introduced to weapons, such as the "Bren" light machine gun and heavy ack-ack guns.

While at the Tonfanau camp, which was located fairly close to the towns of Towyn and Aberystwyth, Ian, based on his education at "public school", and maybe with some influence from his father, was selected to be assessed for a commission. He passed the interview and was sent to the WOSB (War Office Selection Board) at Barton Stacey, Hampshire for further evaluation. This evaluation was a three day affair, where he had to make presentations and lead other attendees over an obstacle course. The purpose of these three days of testing was to determine if Ian was officer "material". He passed with "flying colours" and was sent to MONS officer training course at Aldershot, Hampshire, which was located 37 miles southwest of London.

At MONS, Ian spent the next four months in the Officer training course that consisted of six weeks of infantry training and ten weeks of heavy ack-ack gun training. At the end of the course, he graduated in March 1958 with a commission in the army, as a second lieutenant.

Upon his graduation from MONS, Ian's first duty assignment was to report to 188th Radar and Searchlight Battery in Cyprus. Since all ranks were needed by this outfit, they flew by plane to Cyprus, instead of going by troop ship. Second Lieutenant Black flew on a Douglas DC4, from England to Nicosia, Cyprus, via Malta. The approximate twenty five hundred mile trip took about twelve hours with a two hour, refueling stop at Valletta, Malta. Once in Nicosia it was only a short drive from the airport to Camp Ubique, the 188th Radar and Searchlight Battery headquarters.

****

While Ian was recuperating in the hospital from his leg operation, his father was making plans to visit him. His parents were concerned about his condition. Since Ian's father, James Black, was a retired RAF wing commander, he had some pull with friends that were still flying. He managed to get a lift on a RAF transport plane flying to Cyprus. As soon as he arrived in Nicosia, he went to see his son's CO, Major MacArthur, at Camp Ubique.

Showing his ID, he was allowed entry into the camp and directed to the CO's office. He went into the outer office that was occupied by a second lieutenant and a sergeant.

He went up to Lieutenant William Highwood, who was seated at a desk doing some paperwork, and said, "Mr. Highwood, my name is Wing Commander Black and I would like to see Major MacArthur." With that, he presented a card to Highwood so he could take it in to the CO's office. The officer knocked on the door that led into the inner office.

"Come In" Major MacArthur responded, loudly.

The officer vanished into the office with Wing Commander Black's card. A few seconds later, the officer came out and said to the commander, "Please follow me, sir. The major will see you now." He led him into the major's office, then turned and exited; leaving the major and the wing commander alone.

The major came from around his desk and shook the wing commander's hand saying, "Welcome to Cyprus and Camp Ubique, commander. I assume you're here to see your son, who is having a rest at the British Military Hospital?"

"Yes, major, that's correct. His mother wanted me to check up on him. I managed to get a ride on a RAF transport plane. When would be a good time for me to go and see him?"

"Well, commander, I was going to go and see him myself, in about half an hour. Would you like to join me?" asked the major.

"Yes, if that would be convenient."

"How about a cup of coffee?" the major asked. "I've a couple of reports to attend to, before we can go to the hospital."

"Yes, that would be nice. Thank you."

The major rang the bell for Mr. Highwood, who quickly entered the office.

"Yes sir?" Mr. Highwood asked smartly.

"Please get the commander a couple of coffee and show him to the spare office."

The major then turned to Commander Black, saying, "Enjoy your coffee and I'll be with you in a few minutes, and we'll go to the hospital."

With that, the lieutenant ushered the commander to the spare office and poured him a cup of coffee.

By the time the commander had finished his cup of coffee, the major joined him and led the way to a waiting Land Rover. The driver drove them to the British Military Hospital in Nicosia, about twenty minutes away from the Battery headquarters.

****

While Ian Black's father was at Camp Ubique, Ian was suddenly awakened from his dreamlike reminiscing, when a nurse, named Angela Jones, came in to take measurements of his vital signs.

After checking everything, she said, "Lieutenant. All your vital signs look good. The doctor will be here soon, to discuss your prognosis with you."

"That'll be great. I can't wait to get out of here and get back on duty. By the way, when will Nurse Palas be back on duty?"

"Sir, I'm not sure, but I believe she's on her days off and will be back in three days," replied Nurse Jones.

23

About thirty minutes later the doctor, Major Griffith, entered the Officers' Ward, followed by a retinue of nurses and aides. One could almost hear trumpets sounding, as he strode through the ward. The doctor was tall and erect, and he exuded confidence to the nurses and aides that trailed behind him. They were all in awe of Doctor Griffith who was an officer to be reckoned with.

Major Griffith looked at his charts and then said to Ian, "Mr. Black, it looks as though you're recovering well and you should be out of here in two to three weeks."

Ian responded, "That's welcome news, doctor. I want to get back to my duties, as soon as possible. Do you know how the two gunners, who were injured with me, are getting along? "

Dr. Griffith replied, "I'm not sure, since another doctor is on their cases. However, I'll do my best to find out and get word back to you." With that the doctor turned to one of his aides behind him and said, "Check into those cases and let me know today, what their prognosis is."

"Yes, sir, I'll get on it immediately," replied the aide.

With that, the doctor went down the officer's ward checking on the other patients and then exited, followed by his retinue.

Sometime later, Nurse Jones came back into the ward and told Ian that he had a couple of visitors. Ian looked up and saw two men enter the ward. Immediately he recognized his CO, Major MacArthur, and his father James Black. Ian sat up in the bed and smiled at both men.

"How are you doing, Mr. Black?" asked the major.

"Okay, sir," replied Ian. "I'll feel a lot better when I can report back to duty though. The doctor just told me that I'll probably be out of here in two to three weeks."

"Good. After you're back on duty, I would like you to work for me at headquarters. The officer, you'll replace, is due to go out to a radar site. Then, if you think you are up to it, I want you to go out to Camp Pomos, as was previously

24

planned. Just don't get into trouble this time," the major said, with a laugh.

"I'll do my best, sir," Ian said with a smile.

"Your father came all the way from England to make sure you're okay and being looked after. Your mother was very concerned about your safety, as most mothers are," said the major. "I'll leave you now with your father, so you can tell him about your adventure on the way to Pomos."

"Thank you, sir," responded Ian. With that, the major walked out of the ward, giving the two Blacks a friendly wave as he left.

"So how are you feeling, son?" asked Ian's father.

"I feel good and my leg is healing. The doctor was here a little while ago and said I could probably leave, after the stitches are taken out and they're sure there's no infection in the wound."

"Great", his father replied with a smile. "As the major said, your mother was really worried, when she heard you'd been wounded. She urged me to come to Cyprus and check on you. I called up some old RAF pals and they managed to get me a ride on a transport plane coming to Nicosia. So, here I am."

Ian and his dad chatted for about thirty minutes and then his dad said, "I'll go now and let you rest. I'll be back tomorrow, before I have to leave. The RAF plane leaves from Nicosia airport at 1300 Hours."

****

Around ten o'clock the next day, Ian's father came to see him for about an hour, and then left for Nicosia airport and his ride home.

Before his father left, Ian said, "Dad. It's has been great seeing you. Please tell Mum not to worry. I'm in good hands here and I can take care of myself."

"Okay, I'll tell her, but you know how mothers are. They always worry about their children, no matter how old they are. Cheers son."

Three days later, on schedule, Nurse Palas was back on duty. When she came into the ward, he beckoned for her to come over by his bed and talk.

However, as she approached Ian, he noticed a marked difference in her demeanor. She looked like she had been crying.

"Do you mind telling me what the matter is? You don't look the least bit happy, and you look as though you've been crying." Ian asked, looking very concerned.

"A terrible thing has happened," she replied. "My younger brother Andreus, who was only eighteen, has been killed while trying to ambush a British Army convoy. He was immature and impulsive, and somehow he became involved with the terrorist group EOKA. He was so young to die like that. Now my older brother, Minervo, swears he's going to find out who killed him and get revenge. This violence never seems to end." With tears streaming down her face, she continued, "I hate all of it."

Ian replied, "I'm so sorry to hear that. Please accept my sympathies."

"Thank you," she said, as she turned to leave and attend to her other patients.

Ten days after Ian had the operation on his right leg, the stitches were removed. The doctor advised him to be careful with his wound until it was totally healed. He also informed him that the two gunners, involved in the incident, were well and had been released for duty.

Ian was required to remain in the hospital, for a few more days, to insure that the wound was not infected and it was totally healed. Then the doctor would release him for duty.

****

Ian was released from the hospital on the 24th of April, and the major sent a Land Rover to pick him up and bring him back to Battery headquarters. There he was greeted by his CO.

"Welcome back Mr. Black. I hope you had a nice holiday at the British Army's expense?"

Saluting the major, Ian said with a smile, "It's good to be back, sir, and I'm ready to go back to work, after my holiday."

"Good. I'll see you at 0900 hours tomorrow and we'll discuss your role in my office, as you replace Mr. Highwood."

"Yes, sir," Ian Black responded, as he saluted again and then walked away to find his quarters.

3

Return to Pomos

The next morning promptly at 0900 hours, Ian Black went to see Major MacArthur, as ordered. He entered the battery headquarters and went into the outer office. There he met Lieutenant Highwood and told him he was here to see the major. The lieutenant knocked on the major's door and ushered Ian into the CO's office. The major looked up from the papers on his desk, smiled at Ian and said, "Come on in Mr. Black and take a seat."

Ian gave the major a smart salute, saying "Yes, sir." Then he sat in the chair facing the major's desk.

"I'm glad to see you're back and ready for duty. We're short of good officers and we need you. That was a courageous thing you did on the road to Camp Pomos, three weeks ago. I would like to thank you for everything, including the protection of your men."

"I did the best I could, sir."

"Well, for a fortnight, I'm going to have you take over Mr. Highwood's duties. I'm sending him out to replace the OIC at Camp Galounapetra, at the tip of the island's panhandle. This will give you time to completely recover and become accustomed to our Battery's way of operating. Then, after the two weeks, I'm going to send you out to Camp Pomos, to relieve the officer there. Lt. Severson will show you the ropes, and then he'll return back here, two days after you arrive there. For now, go out and coordinate the transfer of Mr. Highwood's duties to yourself. He knows all about this transfer, so he'll not be surprised."

"Yes, sir," Ian responded. He then stood up, saluted and left the major's office.

For the next couple of days, he worked alongside Highwood who showed him what the job involved. Mainly, he would be an aide to the CO and help him run the battery efficiently.

A few days later, after the lieutenant had left for Camp Galounapetra, the major came to Ian with an assignment.

"Mr. Black. We have here four leaflets issued by EOKA. Of course, they're all in Greek. Would you please get them translated by someone and get them back to me ASAP, with the resulting translations?"

"Yes, sir," Ian responded. "Do you want me to do it here and now, or later?"

The major looked at Ian in astonishment. "Mr. Black. Don't let's be too hasty about this. I want an accurate translation."

"Sir, I can read, write and speak Greek fluently. I'll have the translation on your desk within the hour."

The major went back into his office, mumbling to himself about how these new officers thought they knew everything.

Ian started to translate the four leaflets. The first three were standard propaganda sheets, aimed at the Greek Cypriots. They extolled the virtues of EOKA and asked the citizens to support the effort, in any way they could. They related stories of heroism by the EOKA guerrillas and, at the same time, brought up tales of British Army brutality against Greek Cypriots. For good measure, they pointed out the support the British received from the terrible Turkish Cypriots.

ʹΟ ΧΑΡΤΙΓΚ στό ἀγρόκτημά του:

— Λοιπόν Ζόρ Χιού, ἀνοιδιάτιμα.... γουρούδια
βγάτω μι' ἐσύ, ἀω' ἐμέσα πού σοῦ ἐσκείρα.

The fourth leaflet was a shocker to Ian and almost made him fall off his chair. This pamphlet contained a memoriam to an EOKA "hero" who was shot dead in cold blood, by a British soldier, near the road leading to Pomos on the 3rd of April, 1958. He was only eighteen years old and his name was Andreus Palas.

Seeing the name, Ian realized with a sinking heart that he was the man who had killed nurse Aphrodite Palas's younger brother. He felt like a man who had done a terrible deed. Of course, she had no idea that it was he, Lieutenant Ian Black, who had killed her brother. He remembered that she did say that her older brother, Minervo, was going to take revenge on the killer. Ian then decided he better be careful and, in case Minervo found out who actually shot his brother, keep a look out for any suspicious people around him.

After he recovered from the shock of discovering the identity of the dead EOKA terrorist, he took the translations to the major. Just as he had promised, it had taken Ian about an hour to translate and type out the English version of the leaflets.

Ian knocked on the major's office door.

"Come in," the major said.

Ian entered the office, saluted and addressed him.

"Sir, I've completed the translations of the leaflets, as promised, and have them here."

"Place them in my in-box. Thank you for your quick response to my request."

"Yes, sir," replied Ian. He saluted and then left the major's office.

As soon as Ian left the office, the major picked up the leaflet translations and was pleased to see how professional they were. *"Perhaps, he does know what he's doing,"* the major thought to himself.

For the next two weeks, Ian worked as the major's aide and then it became time to make the trip to Camp Pomos again.

On Wednesday, the 8th of May, Ian prepared for another trip out to the camp, and take over as the new OIC.

At around 1300 hours, Ian came out of the battery headquarters, after a last minute briefing by the major, and headed for the Land Rover parked a few feet away. Just as

31

before, there was also a Bedford lorry loaded with stores, mail and some gunners.

Ian thought, *"Well at least today is Wednesday, and not the normal Thursday milk run, so the terrorists may not be expecting us."*

Ian checked his revolver to make sure it was loaded and ready for action. As he walked up to the Land Rover, he noticed the driver was again Gunner Hall. He was the same driver as the one on the ill-fated April trip.

"How're you doing gunner," asked Ian. "Have you recovered completely? Are you ready for another go at it?"

"Yes, sir, I'm ready for anything," replied the driver.

Ian went up to the bombardier in the passenger seat of the lorry and told him that they wouldn't be stopping in Morphou this time.

"Bombardier, we're going to drive straight through to Camp Pomos today. We're not going to give the EOKA terrorists an easy target. Make sure all your weapons are loaded and ready, with the safety on; especially the Sten guns."

"Yes, sir," replied the bombardier.

With that, Ian climbed into the front passenger seat of the Land Rover and told the driver, "Let's go."

The convoy of two vehicles left Camp Ubique by the main gate and headed westward towards Morphou and Camp Pomos. The route taken was the same one Ian took approximately five weeks before. This time, all the men were on edge and ready for anything. Their fingers were not far from the triggers of their guns, except for the two drivers.

They went through the Greek Cypriot populated towns and villages of Kokkinotrimithia, Akaki, Peristerona and Astromeritus, as fast as the road conditions permitted. They then exited this area of Greek villages and headed for the larger town of Morphou.

However, they didn't plan to stop for any reason, and would continue on towards Camp Pomos, which was approximately another forty miles further west. Morphou was considered a fairly "safe" town, even though it was still mostly populated by Greeks. They passed quickly through it, heading for the coast and Morphou Bay. Once they reached the coast, they followed the road to Camp Pomos. As they approached the bridge that had been blown up five weeks before, they noticed it had been repaired. They went over it as fast as they could and then drove around the next two hairpin curves and bridges, as quickly as the road permitted, until they were only one half mile from the camp. The last half mile was fairly straight and they reached it without incidence.

The guard, at the entrance to the camp, moved the barbed wire barrier and lifted up the control arm, thus allowing the two vehicles to drive onto the grounds, without stopping. Camp Pomos was situated north of the road on a cliff overlooking the Mediterranean Sea. This location was ideal for a search radar to detect ships attempting to smuggle in weapons. To the south of the camp were the Troodos Mountains which contained hideouts for the EOKA terrorists.

Lieutenant Severson, the current OIC, came out of his office to welcome Ian. "Welcome to Camp Pomos," said Severson as he shook his hand. "I'm glad you arrived safely. Now, I can finally leave here for two weeks of rest, after I have shown you the ropes. The radio operator just sent a message to Major MacArthur telling him that you arrived here without incident."

"I'm sorry I'm five weeks late, but I was delayed," Ian replied with a grin.

The camp was manned by one officer, one sergeant and about nineteen other ranks. Some were 4 Mk 6 AA search radar operators, one was a cook, one was a signals chap and one was a REME engineer who maintained the two diesel generators and the radar. There were two Nissen huts that had been built by the Royal Engineers in 1957 and a few rectangular metal huts. In addition, there was a watch tower manned by a sentry at all times with a Bren gun. It was located above the shower stalls made of corrugated steel sheets. If you were in the shower when the sentry fired the machine gun, you would think the world was coming to an end. The deafening noise was caused by the reverberation between the steel walls.

Lt. Severson took Ian on a tour of the camp, showing him the Canadian Marconi 4 Mk 6 search radar and introducing him to Sgt. Herbert, who helped run the camp.

3 GHz Search Radar Model 4 Mk 6

Since the camp was close to the Troodos Mountains, all personnel had to be on their toes, in case EOKA attacked them. There was a beach that was good for swimming close by; however, a guard always had to be posted, in case there was an attack of some kind. The beach was wide and long enough to allow a light British Army Air Corps Auster AOP.6 plane to land and deliver mail, if the pilot didn't drop it from the sky.

For the next two days Lt. Severson showed Ian the ins and outs of running a radar site efficiently.   One night a practice "Stand To" was called, by having the sentry in the tower let off a burst from the Bren gun into the hills across the road. This simulated an attack by EOKA terrorists, and all ranks had to go to their defensive positions. Finally, on the 11th of May, Severson departed for battery headquarters and Nicosia, leaving Ian, as the OIC, with the responsibility of running Camp Pomos.

4

Plot Discovered

For the next four days, Ian acquainted himself with the camp's operation and, in particular, the operation of the radar. The radar trailer consisted of two compartments. One compartment contained the radar equipment with a scope, and the other had a radio for communicating with Maritime headquarters. There were two operators on duty at any one time, and they traded off every thirty minutes, so as to stay alert for any suspicious activities at sea or in the air.

He reviewed the camp security arrangements, in case of an attack by terrorists. He met with all twenty members of the camp, individually, to determine if there were any personnel problems. He had a strategy session with the camp sergeant to make sure the twenty four hour sentry duty timetable was as efficient as it could be.

One problem Ian had determined was that there was considerable boredom developed by the camp members. It was very hard to receive normal radio stations' signals because, every time the radar antenna revolved, the radar emitted a large burst of energy that flooded a normal radio receiver. The radar MPZI antenna revolved at 15 rpm or four times every minute. Copper shielding had been tried in the past with limited success. Overall Camp Pomos performed its required tasks very well.

After Ian had been at the camp a few days, he decided that he should go into Pomos village to determine what was going on there and introduce himself to the mayor. The village was small and had a population of about 250. Since it was only, at most, one and one half miles from the camp, it was important to know if there was any potential threat lurking there. He asked Sergeant Herbert to come to his office.

"Sergeant, I'd like you to pick out three of your best men, one a Land Rover driver, to accompany me into the village. They should all be volunteers, since there might be an element of danger. In addition, they should be well armed. I don't believe there'll be any trouble, but one never knows."

"Yes, sir, I don't believe it should be a problem getting volunteers. May I ask the purpose of the trip into the village?"

"I'm going to the village to talk to the mayor and, at the same time, assess the potential threat to this camp. We'll be in uniform and we'll present a positive show of force to the villagers."

"When will you leave the camp and how long will you be gone, sir?"

"We shouldn't be gone more than three hours, probably less. We'll leave here around 1700 hours and should be back, before dark, by 2000 hours. I'm going to leave you in charge of the camp. I suggest you have five to six men, standing by, in case of trouble and you hear some firing from the village. Even though I don't expect any problems, it's always worthwhile to be prepared."

The sergeant left Ian's office to go and recruit the three volunteers, and tell them to prepare for a trip into the village.

Meanwhile, on the 14th of May, the senior leaders of the EOKA organization had a meeting, at their hideout, in the

Troodos Mountains. The subject of the meeting was the approaching arrival of a shipment of arms and explosives from Greece. EOKA was running short of ammunition and desperately needed the munitions. They wanted to make sure there would be no obstacles to the reception of this shipment. The large fishing boat coming from Greece was made mainly of wood, so as to minimize the reflections of radar signals. It would approach the coast of Cyprus and stop about three miles out. A fast smaller boat, LCRL (Landing Craft Rubber Large), would be launched, loaded with the cargo and run quickly to the shore. These boats were available as war surplus and the arms dealer in Athens had obtained a few. The night of the 18th of May had been picked, since there would be no moon and the landing on the beach, just south of the Pomos village, would therefore be in almost total darkness. The Pomos beach was an ideal location for a landing, since the road ran alongside it and it was close to the Troodos Mountains. The arms could be quickly transported to their hideout there. In addition, Pomos was a Greek Cypriot village, where the population would not cause any problem and maybe help EOKA unload the arms. It was also decided to launch a diversionary attack on Camp Pomos, so as to draw any potential troops in the area away from the beach area. The distance from the camp to the beach landing point was approximately one and one half miles.

Two members of the group, Giannis and Neoklis, were told to go to the village the next day and make contact with the mayor, who owned a café and bar. They were both young, impressionable Greek Cypriots who joined EOKA, because they thought it would raise their esteem in their communities. They were told to stress to the mayor, who was not a supporter of Enosis that EOKA needed the support of some locals in the unloading of the arms. Also, they were to warn him not to inform the British of what they were up to, including the diversionary attack on the radar site. They were to subtly hint that non cooperation might be dangerous to his family's health.

The next day, Neoklis and Giannis swaggered into the village like they owned the place and went to the mayor's office. They were told he was at his café/bar a few streets away. They left the office and went to the café. There they found the mayor in the backroom office. They went in, without knocking, and closed the door.

The mayor yelled in Greek, "What do you mean by barging in here? This is a private office. Leave before I throw you out."

Neoklis, who was the senior of the two men, answered.

"We're from EOKA and you'd better be careful what you say. It may not be good for your health or your family's well being, if you don't cooperate."

The mayor scowled and said, "What do you want? Can't you see I'm busy, trying to balance the books? The revenue has gone down these last three years, due to EOKA driving the tourists away."

Neoklis responded with a threatening voice, "We're here to demand your cooperation for an operation that we'll carry out on next Thursday night. It'll be the darkest night of the month, just right for a shipment of arms to be sent ashore around 11:00 pm at the beach, just west of the village. We need you to supply two loyal Greek Cypriots to help quickly unload the arms into a van. You can tell the "volunteers" that the danger will be minimal, because we'll have a diversionary attack on the Pomos radar site at the same time. This'll draw any possible British troops away from the beach area, if they should come by."

The mayor responded, "Okay. I'll try to find two volunteers. Where should they meet you on the night in question and what will they get paid?

Neoklis replied, "Tell them to be at this café at 10:15 pm on the night and we'll come by to pick them up. They won't be paid but it'll place them in good standing with EOKA, if you get my meaning."

"Alright, you've said your piece. Now get out of here."

With that Neoklis and Giannis left the mayor's office, looking rather pleased with themselves. The mayor sat at his desk, muttering to himself. *What have I done to deserve this? The youth of today think they own the world.*

He wasn't too worried about the two men in his office. In his office drawer, he had a revolver. He had obtained it when he fought with the British, against the Germans, during World War II. He still had to find two volunteers, which might be a problem. *"Maybe,"* he thought, *"I'll have to pay them out of my own pocket?"*

So it was on Tuesday, the 16th of May, Lieutenant Black, the Camp Pomos OIC, and three gunners left the camp in a Land Rover heading for the village, just over a mile away.

Ian told the driver, "Let's go, but drive slowly. You two gunners in the back look out for anything suspicious."

"Yes, sir," they replied.

The driver put the Land Rover into first gear and drove out of the camp entrance, as the guard raised the gate.

Ian had his revolver in a holster on his right side and two of the gunners had Sten guns with plenty of ammunition. The driver had his Enfield rifle by his side, lying in the Land Rover. The camp sergeant, who had been in the British Army for several years, was left in charge. He was very competent and would know exactly what to do, if there was any trouble at the camp or in town.

They drove, slowly, down the narrow road that led to the village, but even so it only took about ten minutes to reach the outskirts of the village. Before he left for Nicosia, Lieutenant Severson had told Ian that the mayor owned a café, named Café Athens. Ian happened to spot a small sign, Café Athens, with an arrow pointing to the right, as they entered the village. Ian told the driver to follow the sign and they ended up right outside the café. They parked outside the front door and walked into the establishment. Ian had told the men to be prepared for anything.

They sat down at one of the few empty tables. There were actually only four tables altogether inside the café. There were a few more outside, for patrons that liked to drink in the open air. One of the other tables was occupied by the mayor and a friend.

As Ian and the gunners sat down, the friend said to the mayor in Greek, "We'd better be careful what we talk about in case they hear us."

The mayor replied in Greek, "Oh, don't worry about that. None of the British know how to speak Greek. I served with them during the war, and all they know is English and how to drink tea."

Ian smiled to himself, as he heard and understood every word they said.

The mayor continued on with the conversation, he and his friend were having, when Ian and the gunners entered the café.

The mayor said to his friend, "You know I was visited yesterday by two young men from the group. You know the group I'm talking about." His friend nodded. The mayor continued, "Well, they wanted me to round up two volunteers to help unload a cargo of arms coming in two nights from now, on the beach just west of the village. Do you know of anyone that might be persuaded to help out? If so, they must be here at the café at 10:15 pm. I understand the first boatload will arrive on the beach at about 11:00pm."

As the mayor said all this, he looked over at the British soldiers, drinking their orange flavored drinks that the waiter had served them. There was no recognition on the faces of any of them that they understood the mayor's conversation. Of course, they misjudged the British lieutenant.

The mayor continued telling his friend about the two EOKA men.

"You know they told me something else that would get them in trouble with Colonel Grivas, if he knew. They told me there would be a diversionary attack on the Pomos radar site. The idea would be to draw off any troops that might be in the beach area."

The mayor's friend replied, "I wonder where they get these young men that belong to EOKA. I hear that Colonel Grivas plays on the youthfulness and inexperience, to get them to join. Oh well, that's his problem. Our problem is to play along with them, but not get too involved. I had better go now or the missus will get mad at me, for staying out too long."

With that the mayor's friend left the café and went home, thinking about whom he could recommend to the mayor to help unload the boat. In the next twenty four hours, he would come up with two men who would be willing to help out. The mayor went to his office, in the back of the café. After the Cypriot left, Ian called the waiter over and, in English, asked him if the mayor was available.

The waiter nodded and went to the office, after knocking, to tell the mayor that the British officer wanted to speak with him. He came out of his office and went over to Ian's table.

"Good evening, gentlemen," he said in fairly good English. "I'm the mayor of Pomos, and I also happen to be the owner of Café Athens."

Ian replied, "Mr. Mayor, I'm Lieutenant Black and I'm the new officer in charge at Camp Pomos. I just wanted to meet you and to let you know that we'll not give you any trouble, if you don't give us any. We're all in a difficult period in Cyprus, but I hope it can ultimately be settled peacefully. This way we can remain friends. I understand you served in the British Army during the war. What regiment were you in?"

42

"It's nice to meet you, Lieutenant Black. I was in the Cyprus regiment put together by the British to help fight the Germans."

"I wish some of us spoke Greek so we could have a better conversation, but none of us speak your language," Ian responded quietly. "Thank you for your hospitality. You have a nice café here. We'll leave now and just drive around your village, if that is alright with you."

The mayor replied, "Of course you may go anywhere you wish to go. If I can be of any assistance in the future, please don't hesitate to ask."

"How much do we owe you for the drinks?"

"They are on the house."

"No, I insist. The British always try to pay their way," Ian said.

"Okay," the mayor said. "They are five shillings each which comes to a total of one pound."

Ian thought that was a little steep but paid it for goodwill, giving the pound note to the mayor. They then all left and climbed aboard the Land Rover. They drove around the village for a few minutes, after which Ian told the driver to go west. He wanted to look at the beach west of the village where the landing might take place. He noticed that the area contained a shallow sloping sandy beach and that the road went alongside. It would be an ideal spot to land cargo and quickly transport it up into the mountains. They then turned around and went back to camp. The guard at the gate swung it open, and they drove straight in.

"Thanks, gunners. That trip was well worthwhile," said Ian.

The gunners looked at each other and said, "Thank you, sir," in unison.

The gunners had no idea Ian had understood every word that was said between the mayor and his friend.

Ian went to his office and looked at the day calendar, which also contained the lunar calendar. He noticed that in

43

fact the 18th of May was scheduled to be the darkest night, as noted on the lunar calendar, in the next few weeks. He scribbled as much as he recollected from the two Cypriots conversation in the café. He then went to see the camp sergeant to tell him to prepare for an attack on the 18th of May around 2300 hours. The sergeant looked at this newly minted second lieutenant in astonishment. *"How could the lieutenant be so sure of himself?"* he wondered. However, he did not question the order and laid out plans to defend the camp, just in case the lieutenant was correct.

After talking with the sergeant, Ian went to the radio room and asked the radio operator to reach Major MacArthur at battery headquarters.

In a few minutes, the major came on, and Ian asked the radio operator to leave the room.

"This had better be good, Mr. Black. You've taken me away from my dinner guests."

Ian replied, "Sir, this is extremely important, otherwise I wouldn't have disturbed you. I have information that there will be an arms shipment delivered on the beach, just west of Pomos village, on the 18th of May at 2300 hours. At the same time, there will be a diversionary attack on this camp. It just happens, sir, that this will be the darkest night this month, as noted on the lunar calendar."

"Be serious, Mr. Black. How do you know all this? Did you attend an EOKA planning meeting?"

"Sir, we drove into Pomos this afternoon and went to the Café Athens, which happens to be owned by the mayor of the village. He was talking with a friend about two EOKA men that came to see him the day before. The mayor laid out the plans for the landing and the diversionary attack to his friend. I didn't let on that I understood what they said. In fact, the mayor told his friend not to worry that we were sitting fairly close by, because no British soldier can speak or understand Greek."

"Let's assume you're correct. What do you propose we do about it?"

"I've three suggestions, sir. First, I've already asked the camp sergeant to prepare the defenses of the camp for such an attack. Second, if it can be spared, I recommend that one of the AEC Matador searchlight lorries be sent to Camp Pomos together with an extra five or six gunners. We have the room to put them up for a few days and we'll hide the vehicle, until the night of the 18th. Then, when the landing is about to take place, the searchlight lorry can be driven down to an area close to the landing beach. At the appropriate time, it could be turned on, lighting up the landing zone. Then the gunners can start rounding up the EOKA people. My understanding is that there'll be four EOKA men and two Pomos village men on the beach. I can probably spare a couple of gunners to go along with the ones you supply, which should be enough. Third, I propose requesting that the Maritime headquarters send a minesweeper into the area. After the EOKA terrorists are captured on the beach, the Royal Navy can stop, board and inspect the fishing boat for contraband. Our radar may not pick up the fishing boat since it's probably made mainly of wood, but I'll tell our radar operators to watch the scope extra carefully."

"That sounds like an excellent plan, Mr. Black. Let me discuss the situation with the people here and I'll get back to you in the morning."

"Yes, sir, I'm sorry I disturbed your dinner. I'll wait for your call tomorrow. Good night, sir."

"Good work, Mr. Black. We'll talk tomorrow."

With that they both shut down the radio communication. Ian went out of the radio room, found the operator and told him he could go back in now.

Ian went to his quarters, had something to eat and went to bed.

45

5

Beach Landing

The next morning, Major MacArthur had meetings with some of his key advisers, and he also discussed the situation with his superiors, as well as officers at Maritime headquarters. Then, the major had his radio operator call Camp Pomos, so he could talk to Lieutenant Black. After contact was made, he came to the radio to speak with Ian.

"Mr. Black. First, I must ask you again. Are you sure about what you heard? There couldn't be a mistake or misunderstanding?"

"Sir, I'll stake my career in the British Army on it. What I reported to you last night, is what I heard at the café. Yes, they could have been talking just to fool us, because they knew one of us understood Greek. However, from expressions on their faces and how they spoke, I don't believe that's the case. I guess the worst case situation would be that they and I are both wrong, and there'll be no arms shipment or attack on the camp. The result would be that, we send a ship to the area and we go to the beach, for nothing. If the report is correct and we do nothing, the results could be very bad. Therefore, I suggest we go ahead with the three point plan that I outlined last night."

"Mr. Black. Thank you for your analysis of the situation and I agree in principle. I've been in touch with the Intelligence Corps and the Maritime headquarters, and we've come up with this alternate plan. First, you will remain inside the camp and take charge of the defence from the diversionary attack. Second, the Intelligence Corps will handle the actual beach landing and the arrest of the people on the beach, using the two AEC Matador searchlight lorries and gunners. Finally, the Royal Navy will send a minesweeper, named the HMS *Camperdown*, to the area, in order to capture the fishing boat. Are you with me so far?"

"Yes, sir, however, I believe the fishing boat could not travel all the way from Greece, so there would have to be a Greek freighter out there somewhere in the MED. It would need to be stopped and searched."

"That's an excellent point. I'll mention it to the Maritime headquarters. One other point, the two Matador lorries will not be coming to Camp Pomos. If their arrival was somehow spotted by EOKA, they would give away the element of surprise. Therefore, the Intelligence Corps will be handling how and when the lorries arrive in the area. You will receive, in the next twenty four hours, a visit from a Captain Phillips, of the newly formed special group of the Intelligence Corps, to coordinate activities. Is all this clear?"

"Yes, sir, it is. We'll coordinate the defence of this camp with Captain Phillips and his operation at Pomos beach."

The major ended the conversation by saying, "Mr. Black, you have done good work there. Keep it up, and I'll see if you can be rewarded. I'll talk to you later."

"Sir, thank you for your support and you can count on us," Ian replied.

With that, Ian handed the radio room back to the radio operator, telling him to fetch him immediately, if the battery CO called again.

Ian went to see the camp sergeant and informed him that there would be a visit to the camp by a Captain Phillips, in the next twenty four hours. He told him to make sure the sentry and guards were aware of this potential visitor.

Sure enough, the next morning, the 18th of May, Captain Phillips arrived at the camp in a car with a driver

47

and one other soldier, for protection. They parked the car behind a building, so it could not be seen from the hills south of the camp, and Captain Phillips was shown to Ian Black's office, by a camp gunner. He entered after knocking lightly and found Ian behind the desk, translating some more EOKA leaflets he had picked up in the village.

Ian rose and extended his hand, saying, "Welcome to Camp Pomos, Captain Phillips. I trust you had an uneventful trip."

"Yes indeed, Mr. Black. I'm sure Major MacArthur advised you of my visit."

"Yes, sir, what can I do for you?" Ian asked.

"I would like you to relate, with as much detail as possible, your visit to the village and the Café Athens, two days ago."

Ian related to Captain Phillips exactly what he had heard on his visit to the village, between the mayor and his friend.

The captain then asked, "Do you speak Greek fluently, without an English accent?

"Yes, sir," Ian replied.

"Where did you learn to do that?"

"I went to Harrow and the school had a Greek national who was a Master there. He spent a lot of time and energy, to make sure we pronounced the words accurately. He also made sure we could read and write Greek quickly, with translations into English."

Captain Phillips thought to himself, "*We need people, who can do all that, in the Intelligence Corps. Currently, we use Greek Cypriots, who may be security risks, to be translators for the Corps. I wonder if this lieutenant would be willing to join our organization. I'd better be careful and go up the chain of command to propose that idea.*"

"Mr. Black. I just received an EOKA leaflet this morning from one of my men. Would you mind doing me a favour and translating it for me? I want to make sure there is nothing in it that requires immediate action."

"Sure, captain," Ian replied. "I'll be glad to do that."

The captain pulled the leaflet out of his pocket and gave it to Ian. Ian found a pen and paper in his desk and started to write, after looking at the leaflet for a few seconds.

"Captain, why don't you grab a cup of coffee while I do this? The coffee pot is over there on the filing cabinet."

The captain poured a cup, while Ian scribbled away.

After ten minutes, Ian presented the captain with a hand written translation of the EOKA leaflet, saying, "It's a propaganda piece. I don't think any immediate action is needed."

"Thanks very much," the captain said as he glanced at it and then put it in his pocket. When he returned to his office, he would have one of his translators do the same thing for comparison. He thought, "*If this Mr. Black is as good as he appears to be, we need him and I'll talk to the Intelligence Corps CO, about getting him transferred.*"

"Mr. Black. Let's get on to the matter at hand. Are you all set to fend off the diversionary attack by EOKA?"

"Yes, I believe we are. We filled some more sandbags last night in the dark, so that any potential EOKA men wouldn't see us making preparations. We've issued additional ammunition to the men and told them to get plenty of rest today, since they may not get much sleep tonight. We've scheduled two gunners to be in the sentry tower instead of the usual one. The radar operators have been instructed to keep an eagle eye on their scope and report any blip, however small, they see. All the defense posts will be manned at 2030 hours, until dawn the next morning."

"That sounds good. The Intelligence Corps will have the Matadors with searchlights from the 188th positioned close to the beach and the lights will be turned on, as soon as we hear the LCRL boat approach the beach. I believe that we'll catch them red handed. By the way, we've alerted the

British base in Morphou to be ready, just in case we need additional support."

"Captain, you can count on us and, depending on the situation if you need additional men at the beach, we might be able to spare a few," replied Ian

"Thank you, Mr. Black. I'd better be going now, but I'll be back and, when it's all over, maybe we can celebrate with a little scotch or something."

"Yes sir, thanks for coming."

With that, Captain Philips climbed into his car, hidden by one of the huts. He drove quickly out of the camp and down the road, to have a look at the beach area, where the EOKA arms landing was scheduled take place. They then drove back to Nicosia.

****

Earlier in the day of the 18th, the Intelligence Corps, along with the 188th Radar and Searchlight Battery, had moved the two Matador lorries, with searchlights, around the southern parts of the Troodos Mountains, through Paphos. From there, they went to a location west of the landing beach, so as not to tip off EOKA that their plan had been compromised.

Since sunset at Camp Pomos would take place at approximately 1945 hours, Ian told the camp sergeant to have all the defences partially manned at 2030 hours and fully manned by 2200 hours. Ian figured the diversionary attack on Camp Pomos would start at about 2245 hours or 15 minutes before the first landing of arms at the beach, west of the village. At 2230 hours, he went around to all the defence pits, telling the gunners to remain quiet and not to shoot, unless EOKA started firing first. He also told them to keep their heads down as much as possible, as he didn't want any casualties.

At 2245 hours, nothing happened, but then, at 2250 hours, shots rang out from the hills above the camp. Ian thought to himself, *"I was five minutes early on the anticipated time of attack."* The sergeant told the sentry in the tower to return fire with the Bren gun at the spot, where he saw the flashes from the EOKA guns. The sentry sent short bursts of .303 bullets whizzing towards the hill, where he saw the flash from the terrorists' gun muzzles. The other gunner, up in the tower, reloaded the Bren magazines, as they became empty. It appeared that there were four terrorists up in the hills, since the gunfire came from four different locations. Finally, the sergeant ordered all the gunners, in the defence sandbagged pits, to open fire with their Enfield rifles and aim at the muzzle flashes in the hills.

While this was going on, Ian was in the radar compartment looking at the scope with the operator. They saw a very small blip that was probably the fishing boat, positioned offshore about two miles. The other operator in the radar trailer called in the contact to Maritime headquarters. Maritime relayed the contact information to HMS *Camperdown* that was proceeding, at full speed, towards the Pomos area. Another minesweeper, HMS *Hornblower*, was out about twenty five nautical miles to the northwest of Cyprus racing towards a large blip on their radar that might be a freighter from Greece. If they caught up with it, they were going to stop and board her, to check for any contraband cargo.

Meanwhile, within one minute of the scheduled time, a fast LCRL boat sped in from the fishing boat and landed on the beach west of the village. It contained boxes of ammunition and explosives. The four EOKA men and the two villagers rushed to unload the craft. They were half way through the unloading, when two searchlights, mounted on the Matador lorries, were turned on and lit up the landing area. A British officer in Greek shouted through a bull horn,

"Τοποθετήστε τα χέρια σας πάνω ή θα γυρίσει". In English this translated to "Put your hands up or we'll shoot."

The two men from the village put up their hands immediately, but the four EOKA men did not. They grabbed their weapons and started firing at the searchlights, trying to put them out. The firefight went on for about five minutes. Finally, one of the EOKA men was killed. The other three, as soon as they saw their comrade was dead, raised their hands and surrendered. The operation was over in about ten minutes. The arms and boat were loaded into a British army lorry that was close by. The prisoners were rounded up and put in another lorry, along with guards.

The firing from the hills at Camp Pomos went on for about a total of thirty minutes and then ceased. Whether the sentries at the camp had killed anyone they would not know, until the sun came up in about six hours. After the firing died down, the British lorries at the beach finally started up and proceeded on the road, past the camp, towards Morphou and Nicosia.

HMS *Camperdown* caught up with the fishing boat and lit up the craft with its twenty inch searchlight. The fishing boat was told to stop and was boarded by an armed boarding party. They found more ammunition, explosives and weapons down in the holds. The crew was arrested and the fishing boat was towed into Kyrenia harbour, for further inspection. HMS *Hornblower* never caught up with the freighter out at sea. It was assumed it went on to Lebanon, since it was a lot closer than Greece. An AVRO Shackleton maritime patrol aircraft was sent out to find it. The plane flew over it, as it approached Lebanon, but the pilots saw nothing suspicious.

The next morning, Ian Black sent an armed party up into the hills, to see if there were any casualties. They found a large patch of blood, but no body. It was assumed the victim either died at the spot and was carried away by his friends, or was severely wounded and died later. The amount of blood on the ground was considerable.

So the battle for Pomos beach ended, with EOKA still needing arms to continue the fight. Ian later received a congratulatory message from his CO, Major MacArthur. However, Colonel Grivas (aka Dighenis) and the EOKA leadership were still at large, and needed to be captured. Arm shipments from Greece and Lebanon would continue to be undertaken by them. Assassination attempts would still haunt Governor Sir Hugh Foot, the Queen's representative in Cyprus. The Intelligence Corps, along with MI6, would have to continue the battle against EOKA.

6

Transfer

After the battle of Pomos beach and the diversionary attack on Camp Pomos, life returned more or less to normal at the camp. Ian called a "Stand To" twice per week, just to keep everyone on their toes. The radar surveillance continued twenty four hours a day, except for occasional maintenance, and no suspicious blips were observed or reported to Maritime headquarters.

****

Meanwhile, Captain Phillips returned to his office in Nicosia after capturing the EOKA people at the beach landing. He took the EOKA pamphlet out of his pocket and asked one of his Greek Cypriot translators to give him an English translation, as soon as possible. The translator came to the captain's office about half an hour later and gave him the English translation.

"Did it take you thirty minutes to do this?" asked Phillips.

"Yes. Just under thirty minutes" replied the translator.

After the translator left, Captain Phillips then took out the English version, Lieutenant Black had given him. They were almost identical and it had only taken Ian about ten minutes to produce his version. The captain was impressed and went to see his CO, Lieutenant Colonel Baker.

"Sir, I believe that I may have found one of the individuals we've been looking for, to expand our operation.

He's Second Lieutenant Black of the 188th Radar and Searchlight Battery."

He then produced the two translations and showed them to the colonel. He was impressed.

"What do we know about him? Isn't he a little "green" to be part of the Intelligence Corps.?" asked the colonel.

Captain Phillips replied, "When I talked with him at Camp Pomos about EOKA and the planned beach operation, he seemed very bright. He attended Harrow Public School and, according to some brief research I did, his father was a wing commander in the RAF during the war. I really believe that he'd be a valuable asset to our organization."

The colonel responded, "Okay, your judgment has always been good in the past. I'll go and see Major MacArthur at the 188th and see what he has to say about him."

****

At the beginning of June, Major MacArthur received a visit from Colonel Baker. The colonel was shown into the major's office and then the major's aide closed the door.

"Colonel, it's great to meet you again. I believe that we met at the Director of Cyprus Operations conference, a few months ago. Would you like something to drink; like tea, coffee or juice?"

"No thanks, major, I'm fine. Yes, I do remember meeting you at the conference."

"What can I do for you today, colonel? I assume this isn't a social visit."

"I'll come straight to the point, major. It concerns Mr. Black who I believe is currently out at Camp Pomos."

"Yes, he is. He has only been on the island, since the end of March, and has already been involved in two actions. First, his two vehicle convoy was attacked on the way to the camp and he managed to kill one of the attackers. Unfortunately, he was wounded from a grenade and he spent the next three weeks in the BMH. During the attack, he also saved his driver from almost certain death. Then, after he was discharged from the hospital, he worked as my aide for a couple of weeks. He was very efficient and seemed very intelligent. Finally, he went out to Camp Pomos again and arrived safely. There, he found out about an EOKA arms shipment and helped organize the response. Overall, I'm very pleased with his performance and I've put him in for a promotion to first lieutenant. I'll see if I receive permission to actually promote him. I realize that normally a second lieutenant doesn't get promoted to first lieutenant for at least a year. However, he has performed exceptionally well, and I believe he deserves it."

"Well major, he does sound like an exceptional young man. Therefore I made a decision to come and discuss his future with you. As you know, our organization has three major tasks. First and foremost, the goal is to capture Grivas. The second aim is to eliminate as many of the EOKA leaders, as possible. Finally, we have to prevent as many attacks, as we can, on our armed forces, and that also includes stopping any assassination attempt on the governor. To accomplish these tasks, the Intelligence Corps needs to add a few exceptional people, who can speak and write Greek. It's very dangerous for us to rely on Greek Cypriots, as translators. From all the information I've received, Lieutenant Black would be an ideal candidate."

The major replied, "I was afraid you were leading up to that. I'd hate to lose him, but we're all on the same team, and if it makes sense, I won't stand in the way. I do need him out at Camp Pomos until I can find an officer to replace him, which will probably be by the end of June."

"Do you believe that he would be receptive to being transferred from the Royal Artillery to the Intelligence Corps?" the colonel asked.

"I don't know, however, if it's okay with you, I'll discuss the possibility with him. Since I'm his CO, I believe it would be better if I broached the subject with him. Do you agree?"

The colonel replied, "Yes, I do. Would it be possible for you to bring him in for a day, so I could meet him in your office, before you bring up the subject with him? Perhaps, I could just happen to be sitting in your office, when he comes in to see you.

"Agreed. I believe that would be an excellent idea."

"Great to see you again, major. I'd better leave and get back to the office."

With that, the colonel left Camp Ubique and returned to the Intelligence Corps headquarters in Nicosia.

****

A week later, Major MacArthur received permission to promote Ian Black to first lieutenant from army headquarters. The major had his radio operator call Camp Pomos, so he could talk with Ian.

"Mr. Black. This is Major MacArthur. How's everything going there at the camp?"

"Sir, everything is under control however, we never seem to receive enough rations for the men."

"Well, I'll try and correct that, but as you know, I can't give you any more than any other site. I would like you to come in next week to battery headquarters. I need to talk to you about a few issues. Please be careful though, as I don't want to visit you in BMH again."

"Yes, sir, I'll be in there next Wednesday around 1100 hours, if that's okay with you?"

"That'll be fine, Mr. Black. See you then."

The major then placed a call to Colonel Baker at the Intelligence Corps headquarters.

"Colonel, Mr. Black will be here in my office around 1100 hours next Wednesday, the 19th of June, if you'd like to meet him. I've received permission from army headquarters to promote him to first lieutenant for meritorious service.

"I'll be at your office next week, major. Yes, I agree, based on what I've heard, Mr. Black deserves the promotion. See you next Wednesday."

****

On Wednesday, the 19th of June, Ian left the camp at 0830 for battery headquarters, in the normal weekly two vehicle convoy. Before he left, he informed the camp sergeant that he was in charge, until he returned later in the day. The Land Rover and Bedford lorry made the trip to Morphou and then to Camp Ubique without incident. During the entire trip, Ian was on the lookout for any suspicious activities.

At 1030, Ian and the convoy pulled into the main gate of Camp Ubique. Ian told the bombardier to go and load up provisions, mail and other stores. He advised him to be ready to leave for Pomos at 1430. Ian then went to the battery headquarters office to see Major MacArthur. He entered the outer office and spoke to the major's aide, Second Lieutenant Overton.

"Lieutenant, I'm Lieutenant Black from Pomos and I'm here to see the major, as he requested."

"I'm pleased to meet you. How do you like Camp Pomos? I understand that the camp may be my next assignment."

"It's quiet most of the time, although there've been a few exciting moments," Ian replied with a smile.

"That's what I've heard. Right now, the major is meeting with a colonel from another unit, but I believe that he should be free to see you soon. Please have a seat. Would you like a cup of tea or coffee while you wait?"

58

"No thanks. I'll just be outside stretching my legs after the two hour ride. Please come and get me, when the major is available."

"Certainly, it shouldn't be long now."

About five minutes later, Lieutenant Overton came to the door and beckoned for Ian to come back in.

"He's available now. Just knock and go on in, after he answers."

Ian went up to the major's door and knocked.

"Come in."

Ian opened the door, entered the office and saluted. The major stood up and walked around his desk to greet Ian.

He saluted Ian in return and shook his hand.

He said, "Mr. Black, I'm glad you could make it and didn't have any trouble. I would like you to meet Colonel Baker of the Intelligence Corps," indicating the officer sitting in the corner of the room.

Ian gave another salute to the colonel and said, "Pleased to meet you, sir. It was a pleasure working and planning for the Pomos beach landing, with Captain Phillips the other week."

The colonel replied, "You did a good job on that operation. Thank you. Captain Phillips gave me a good briefing on the entire mission."

"Mr. Black," said the major. "I asked you to come in for a purpose. You know that, if you were in the American Army, you would receive a Purple Heart, for the wounds you suffered in the attack, on the convoy in April. Nonetheless, you're in the British Army, fortunately for us, so you do not receive a medal. We do thank you for your service, however, don't we colonel."

"Indeed we do," responded the colonel.

"You know, Mr. Black," continued the major. "It's customary for a second lieutenant to serve at least one year, and maybe two, before receiving a promotion. The army has decided though, that due to your service and dedication to duty, you're promoted, as of today, to first lieutenant. Congratulations, and here is a set of your new Bath stars (pips) that you can now add to your first one."

The major handed Ian a pair of "pips" in a small box.

"Thank you, sir. This is totally unexpected and a great honour. I didn't expect a chance to be promoted for at least a year."

"Congratulations, Mr. Black," said Colonel Baker. "I believe you deserve it."

The colonel then turned to the major saying, "I'd better depart now and leave you two to discuss battery issues. I've taken up enough of your time."

"Let me show you out, colonel. Mr. Black, I'll be back in a minute."

With that, the colonel and the major left the office, leaving Ian by himself.

When they were outside the office, the major asked the colonel, "Well, what do you think?"

"I believe he'll fit into our organization, if he wants to join us. He seems to be a very bright, young man. Thank you for the opportunity to meet him."

They saluted and the colonel climbed into his car and told the driver to return to intelligence headquarters. The major returned to his office and Ian.

"Mr. Black. Please take a seat. I want to discuss with you a couple of matters. One concerns Camp Pomos and the other concerns your future.

First, as you know we rotate personnel through the radar sites and then give everyone some R&R here at Camp Ubique for about two weeks, before sending them out to the next site. Mr. Overton, who is currently my aide, is scheduled at some point to take over Camp Pomos. I believe you've met him. The question is; what is in your future? No, don't get alarmed. I'm not going to fire you, when I have just managed to get you promoted. I don't want to lose you, but sometimes, for the good of the army and the mission, we have to make sacrifices. I've an opportunity for you, if you want to accept it. Before I tell you what it is, I want to assure you, regardless of what your decision is, it'll not affect our relationship in any way. I believe you're an excellent officer and will go a long way in this army."

"Thank you for the vote of confidence, sir," Ian replied

"Let me get straight to the point. The first goal for the army's mission, during the Cyprus Emergency, is to capture Grivas. Then, we must eliminate as many of EOKA leaders as possible and finally prevent attacks on our troops. Also, this includes preventing any assassination attempt on the governor.

The Intelligence Corps is the leader in the activities to accomplish these goals and it needs to add a few exceptional individuals, especially those, who can also speak and write Greek fluently. Currently, they rely too much on Greek Cypriots, as translators, and this is a major security problem.

How would you like to work for the Intelligence Corps? You'd be working for Colonel Baker and Captain Phillips. Both of them have high confidence in you. If you accept this mission, you'd be transferred from the Royal Artillery to the Intelligence Corps.

I have to go into the other office to talk with Mr. Overton for a few minutes. Please think about this while I'm gone and, if you can, give me a decision, when I return. The governor has set a very high mark on the capture or death of Grivas."

The major then went into the outer office to talk with Mr. Overton. In fifteen minutes, he returned to his office.

"Well, Mr. Black. Have you made a decision?"

"Yes, sir, I have. With all respect to you, I would like the challenge of trying to capture Grivas and the EOKA leadership alive. We've lost too many men to these terrorists and I'd like to help bringing them to justice. I make this decision, without any hint of disloyalty to you. You've been very good to me and I appreciate the opportunities you've given me, since I turned up here only a few weeks ago; a green, second lieutenant."

"Very well, I hate to lose you, but I believe you have made a wise decision. There could be opportunity for you over at the Intelligence Corps. Right now, I would like you to return to Camp Pomos and, as soon as I can find another officer to be my aide, I'll send Mr. Overton out to replace you. It may take two to three weeks. In the meantime, I'll request for your transfer to the Intelligence Corps be approved by higher ups. I would appreciate it, if you could write up a report with recommendations for improvements at the radar sites. This would be very useful to me."

"Yes, sir, I'll be glad to do that for you. Again, thank you for the opportunities you've given me."

"Go get yourself some lunch and I'll see you, before you leave for Camp Pomos, later this afternoon."

Ian saluted the major and left his office. He asked Overton if he would care to have lunch with him. Overton accepted.

After lunch, Ian went back to see the major and received last minute instructions, before returning to Camp Pomos. As he left the major's office, Ian saw that the Land Rover and Bedford lorry were lined up, loaded and ready to leave for the camp. The drive back was uneventful, but Ian was on high alert throughout the entire time, as usual.

They arrived at the camp before dusk and Ian had a quick meeting with the sergeant. At the end of the meeting, Ian informed him that he would be replaced in two to three weeks by a Lieutenant Overton. He did not mention anything about his transfer, deciding that would be best to wait until the new OIC arrived.

As the major requested, the next day, Ian sat down and started to write a report with his recommendations for camp improvements.

Lieutenant Overton arrived at the camp on Wednesday July 2nd in a Land Rover, accompanied by two gunners and the driver. The next day, Ian gave Overton a tour of the camp and introduced him to the camp personnel. He went over the radar operation with the lieutenant and the "Stand To" procedures currently in place.

After two days of orientation, Lieutenant Overton felt comfortable with the operation of the camp and, at 1500 hours on Friday, the 4th of July, Ian left the camp for the last time, in the Land Rover that Overton arrived in. In the back were the same two heavily armed gunners. Approximately two hours later they arrived at Camp Ubique and Ian went to meet with Major MacArthur to give him the requested report on camp improvements.

7

Salisbury House

On Saturday morning, the 5th of July, Captain Phillips drove to Camp Ubique to pick Ian up. He arrived in an older English Austin sedan with no markings on it.   Ian met the captain outside the battery headquarters with his kit. After loading the kitbag into the boot, he climbed into the passenger seat of the car. As the captain drove out of the camp towards the outskirts of Nicosia, he congratulated Ian on his promotion

"You know," the captain said, "You're lucky to get that second "PIP" so early. Most second lieutenants have to wait a minimum of a year to get one."

"Yes, I was totally surprised when Major MacArthur gave me the set of "PIPs" in a box," Ian replied.

As they drove towards Nicosia, Ian didn't realize that this wouldn't be the last time he would actually be at Camp Ubique.

Soon, they arrived at a large house, guarded by a high wall and armed guards, just outside the walled city of Nicosia. It was located northwest of the city, fairly close to the Ledra Palace Hotel.   On the wall by the main gate was a large brass sign; Troodos Mining Company. Informally, it was called Salisbury House by the people in the know. Ian noticed that the captain, after leaving Camp Ubique, took off his beret with the Intelligence Corps insignia on it. The terrorists liked to shoot anyone wearing an Intelligence

Corps beret. As they drove up to the main gate of Salisbury House, it suddenly opened and standing there were two British soldiers with Sterling submachine guns (SMGs); they weren't the inexpensive Sten guns. They recognized the car, with the captain driving, and waved them in. The gate immediately closed behind them. This was the headquarters for the Intelligence Corps Special Group, and there were also a few MI6 operatives stationed here.

The captain showed Ian to his quarters that included a bedroom and office area. He then took him on a tour of the building including the communications room, the dining hall, the entertainment room with the billiard table and, more importantly, the bar. He also showed Ian the tunnel that led from the Salisbury House to another small house across and down the street. This tunnel allowed occupants of Salisbury House to leave the building, without being spotted by anyone watching the house from the street.

There were cars available for the use of the Intelligence Corps personnel, parked in an area near the house. They were all unmarked and the license plates could be switched at a moment's notice. Every precaution had been taken to allow officers to work their trade, without putting their life in danger.

The captain then said, "Since this is Saturday and there are no immediate emergencies that need to be handled, you can take the weekend off. We'll meet at 0900 hours on Monday in the upstairs conference room, with Colonel Baker. Is there anything I can get for you, before I leave you for the weekend?"

"No thanks, I don't believe so. I'm just going to relax and take it easy for the next 48 hours. I believe right now I'll go and get some lunch in the dining room. Would you care to join me?"

"Yes, I'll do that and then leave you, to relax over the weekend."

The captain, with Ian in tow, went and had lunch. While they ate, the captain explained some of the "ins and outs" of the Intelligence Corps and what they were expected to do. He added that the colonel would explain more about their duties on Monday. After lunch, the captain left Ian, saying "I'll see you on Monday, at 0900, in the conference room."

Ian went back to his room and changed clothes into civvies. He then wandered down to the billiard room and found it empty, except for one chap who was practicing his shooting techniques.

He went up to him and said, "Do you want any competition? My name is Ian and I'm new to this building. You aren't a pool shark are you?"

The chap replied, "Well Ian, most people call me John. My real name is actually Andrew Dinglefoot, but don't tell anyone. Is your last name Black, by any chance?"

"Well yes, it does happen to be. How did you guess?"

"I've heard about you and I was told that you'd be joining the Intelligence Corps shortly. I hope your billiards game isn't as good as your performance at Pomos."

"How did you get to hear about the Pomos raid?"

"It's our job to know everything that's going on in Cyprus. Are you ready to play?"

"I sure am. I'll let you rack the balls. How long have you been in the army?"

"Oh. I'm not in the army. I'm a civilian working here."

It then dawned on Ian that he was probably one of the MI6 chaps, stationed in Cyprus.

There was a large listening station located at Ayios Nikolaos, near Famagusta. It was run by British and American SIGINT and ELINT operatives and it was an ideal place to listen in on radio signals emanating from the USSR and the entire Middle East. Ian didn't know it at the time, but John received daily reports from this station on subjects that concerned him.

"Where are you from in Blighty?" asked Ian.

As John racked up the balls, he replied, "I was born in Brighton and then we moved to Bristol, when I was six. I'll give you a head start and you can go first."

Ian had learned how to play billiards at Harrow and won handily against John.

"Sorry about that, John," Ian said.

John replied, "Maybe I need to practice more. By the way, where are you from?"

"I lived most of the time in Richmond, except when I was away at school, which was a considerable amount of the time," Ian said. He added, "Thanks for the game, John. We'll play a return game another time, if you'd like. I'm going to the reading room for a while."

"You're on. We'll play again, after I've practiced some more."

Ian went to the reading room, where the black and white television was on, broadcasting the news. In 1958, the Cyprus Broadcasting Service (later named the Cyprus Broadcasting Corporation in January 1959) broadcast in B/W three hours daily, five days a week; it had actually started TV broadcasts nine months before on 1 October 1957. Ian spent the rest of the weekend reading and resting.

On Monday morning, he went to the conference room at 0855 and found that the colonel, together with the captain, was already there; also, sitting in a corner was John.

"Good morning, Mr. Black," said the colonel. "I hope you had a restful weekend. I hear you've already met John, here. He tells me that you're quite good at billiards. By the way John, you'd better be careful when you speak in Greek, Ian here will run circles around you. He's even better at the Greek language than he is at billiards."

"That's what I've heard, colonel" replied John.

The colonel then started the meeting.

"Welcome to our small group, Mr. Black. We're attempting to add two more officers in the next two weeks, and then we'll be up to full strength. The purpose of this group is to be lean and mean. There are other Intelligence Corps units in Cyprus, but this one is Special. The other units are located at harbours and airports, and their main task is to inspect incoming cargo and people. They board ships that enter the harbours and inspect them. At the airports, they check the cargos flown in and the passengers, for any undesirables.

The three main tasks of our special intelligence group are:

1. Track down and arrest/eliminate the EOKA leadership
2. Gather intelligence, so as to prevent any assassination attempt on top British leaders here in Cyprus; especially the Governor.
3. Prevent, as much as possible, any attacks on British armed forces and their dependents.

Of course, the main objective is to eliminate the top EOKA leadership. If we accomplish this, then the other two more or less take care of themselves. The governor has set this as the primary goal, so he can inform Whitehall that the Cyprus Emergency is almost over. There is considerable pressure from the PM on the governor to end the Emergency.

In the past, we've had to use Cypriots for any meaningful translations of documents recovered during the raids, we've conducted. Ian, although we didn't bring you into our group just for this purpose, I trust you will help out in the translations, so we don't have to use these Cypriots. The potential for security problems is high when we use them.

Ian, I'm basically going over all this for your information. Captain Phillips and John have heard most of this before."

"Sir, in order to accomplish the main goal, I believe it may be necessary to go out into the general population and mingle, as if we are just plain Cypriots. This would require

68

being dressed in normal Greek Cypriot clothes; no uniforms. Is this allowed?"

"Yes, anything within reason is permissible. I'll not tolerate any torture of Greek Cypriots, however. Our Turkish Cypriot friends do enough of that already."

"Sir, may I suggest that I be allowed to have two sets of uniforms. One with the Royal Artillery shoulder flashes on the shoulders and one with Intelligence Corps shoulder flashes. It is my understanding that EOKA has announced a reward for any member that can kill an Intelligence Corps soldier. Taking the shoulder flashes off totally would not solve the problem. EOKA would just try to kill any soldier without any shoulder flashes, they would assume that they were Intelligence Corps personnel.

The colonel thought for a moment and then responded, "Ian, I believe that's a good suggestion. What do you think captain?"

"I agree, colonel. However, I believe that it would be wise to inform the regiments or batteries involved. This would prevent any confusion on their part."

The colonel replied, "It would be best if we all used the same flashes, so that I have only to contact one regiment about the issue. However, until I let you know for sure, just use your Intelligence Corps flashes, but you must be extra careful. In little less than a fortnight, on the 19th of July, the governor is holding a party at his residence and we have been invited to attend, for the purpose of checking the facility for any possible security issues. You must all wear suits and ties. This means, if you don't have one, you have only five days to obtain one. I believe a dark colored suit, with a conservative tie, would be most appropriate. Ian, you will be under the direct guidance of the captain. I also think it desirable that you, Ian, get acquainted quickly, as to how the security of this island is achieved. Therefore, it would a good idea if you flew on a Shackleton maritime plane, in order to see how they go on patrol. In addition, you should also go on a minesweeper, to observe how they stop boats and work in conjunction with the Shackleton, to patrol the coast. You can arrange those trips for him can't you, captain?"

"It shouldn't be a problem, sir. I've contacts in both the RAF and the British Navy," responded Captain Phillips.

"Good. I'll see you here at 0900 hours next Friday, a week before the governor's party, to go over the ground rules for our surveillance." With that, the colonel left the conference room.

The captain turned to Ian and asked, "Is there anything you need or require me to do for you, to help you get up to speed?"

"Yes, there is. First, if it can be arranged, I'd like to be issued a Browning Hi-Power semi-automatic 9x19 parabellum pistol for protection; just in case I go out on the town and meet some unsavory characters. Also, have I been cleared to use the passageway to the house across the road?" Ian asked.

"Yes, you've been registered with security at this facility. They are aware of who you are and will give you appropriate access. As far as the weapon, follow me and I'll take you to the arms room. I'm sure the sergeant there can issue you one immediately. I see you know your weapons. It's an excellent choice. In fact, I also have one that I carry everywhere."

The captain led Ian to the arms room and the sergeant issued him the gun, along with two holsters; one, a shoulder holster for concealment under a coat or large shirt and the other one for a belt over his uniform. The sergeant was very familiar with Captain Phillips and didn't question any of his requests at all.

8

Sea Patrol

On Thursday, the 10th of July, the captain called Ian to his office for a brief meeting.

"Mr. Black. There're three matters I wish to discuss with you. First, we've recruited two more chaps to be part of our small team and they'll be, partially, joining this organization at the end of July. One is excellent in the Turkish language and the other is an expert in communications. These are the skills we lack, so they'll complement our capability. One is a second lieutenant by the name of Roger Snell and the communications expert is a sergeant by the name of Kenneth Bingham.

"That's great. We need some help in those two areas. I look forward to them joining the team. What organizations are they from?" Ian asked.

"Lieutenant Snell is from the Wiltshire Regiment and Sergeant Bingham is from the Royal Corps of Signals. Both of them come with recommendations from their commanding officers, who were reluctant to let them transfer. Colonel Baker reached an agreement with their COs that they would work for us three days a week, until November. They'll then be on board full time."

The captain continued, "The second matter is that we've received some documents captured in a raid on an EOKA hideout, and we'd like you to translate them."

"I'll work on them today and, if necessary, tomorrow. Roughly how many pages are there to translate?" Ian asked.

"Probably around thirty pages, all obviously in Greek. Hopefully there'll be some information in them that could lead us to Grivas."

"I shouldn't have any problem translating those thirty pages by tomorrow morning, and then we can review them, if you want to."

The captain said, "Okay, here're the papers. When you have translated them, just bring them to my office and I'll look them over. If I've any questions, I'll contact you. Now the third item of our meeting today. I've made arrangements for you to join the HMS *Benton* for a seventy two hour anti-gun running patrol. It will start at 1200 hours this Saturday, the 12th of July, and end Tuesday, the 15th of July, at 0800 hours. You'll join the HMS *Benton* at Kyrenia, and you must be on the dock at 1145. A cutter will be there exactly at noon to pick you up and take you out to the vessel, anchored in the harbour. This patrol should give you an opportunity to observe how the Royal Navy tracks gun runners, and maybe you can help by interrogating any Greek Cypriots, that are picked up."

Ian responded, "Thanks for giving me the opportunity to observe for myself how the Navy works with the RAF, on patrolling the waters around Cyprus. I'll go now and start the translations on the documents."

With that, he left the captain's office and returned to his office. He spent the rest of the day, and part of the next morning, translating and typing the thirty pages of the EOKA documents into English. To Ian, they didn't provide any information on how they might locate Grivas. They did mention that EOKA was having trouble obtaining additional arms, from outside the island. They thought there might be a leak in their organization. Every time an arms shipment was scheduled, it seemed that the British were there to intercept it. There was one remark about support they were receiving from someone in the Limassol police department, but there was no name listed. Ian gathered up the original papers, together with the translation and went upstairs to give them to the captain.

He knocked on the door.

"Come in," the captain said.

Ian entered the office and gave the papers to Phillips, saying, "Here are the translations you requested, sir. I don't see anything that's extremely useful, except a Limassol police connection. However, there's no name listed."

"Thanks for the quick work. I'll call you, if I have any questions. If not, have a good cruise with the Navy and I'll see you next week. Don't forget the governor's party coming up on the 19th of July. It's important that we investigate the Government House facility and the Cypriots working there."

Ian Left the captain's office and went to have lunch in the dining room, where he met John, the MI6 chap, again. As they were eating, John mentioned, in a subtle way, that they were receiving some excellent information on the Soviet Union from transmissions, picked up at the Ayios Nickolaos listening post.

****

The next day, Saturday, the 12th of July, Ian rose at 0800 hours and prepared for his trip on the HMS *Benton*. He put on his uniform, including his Browning automatic, and placed his Intelligence Corps green beret on his head. Additionally, Ian placed a few spare clothing items in a small bag, to take with him.

The night before, he had acquainted himself with the minesweeper HMS *Benton* that was attached to the 108th squadron. It was a TON class minesweeper; 152 feet in length, 28 foot beam, shallow 8 foot draught and diesel engines. It normally carried a crew of thirty, existing of four officers and twenty six ratings. Lieutenant Commander Curtis Abney was the captain and First Lieutenant Richard Dodd was the second in command. It had a maximum speed of fifteen knots and was constructed of wood and other non-ferrous materials.

After having breakfast, Ian went downstairs to the motor pool to check out a car.

"Corporal, do you have a car I can use for three days?" he asked.

"Yes, sir, I have a white 1956 Ford Consul Sedan available. Would that be sufficient for your needs?"

"That'll be okay," replied Ian.

"For the records, sir, where will you be taking it and when do you plan to return it?" asked the corporal.

"I have to drive to Kyrenia and I'll be returning it next Tuesday, if all goes well," responded Ian.

"You'll find it parked in the covered park area just outside and to the left. I hope you have a productive trip, sir."

With that, Ian signed the log proffered by the corporal, picked up the keys and went to check the vehicle over. The car looked okay with no visible dents and it was full of petrol. He threw his bag on the back seat, climbed into the right front seat and took off his green beret, in order not to be an obvious target for EOKA. He started up the Ford and proceeded towards the iron gates of Salisbury House. The guard at the gates gave him a salute and Ian returned it, as he drove out onto the street.

Ian drove the approximate fifteen miles to Kyrenia without incident. He drove north past the Ledra Palace Hotel and on to the main road to Kyrenia. It took him about thirty minutes with the traffic and double checking he was on the correct road. He went through the beautiful Kyrenia Mountains that were shining with the bright morning sun. As he came towards the main part of Kyrenia, the traffic volume picked up with Saturday shoppers and army lorries. Since

Ian had arrived in the town early, he drove around the streets, for a short time, to get a good look at the town.

"It might come in useful later, in one of our terrorist tracking operations," he thought.

He finally ended up at the dock, which had one section cordoned off for use by the British military; mainly the Royal Navy. The guard came out of his shack, holding a Sterling SMG, and walked up to Ian's car. Ian, by this time, had placed his green beret with its Intelligence Corps badge back on his head.

"Good morning, sir. May I see your identification?" the British Army MP asked Ian. Ian handed him his army ID card and the MP looked him up on his list of personnel allowed on the dock.

The MP handed it back to Ian, saying "I hope you have a smooth patrol, sir. You may go in and park in one of the visitor parking spots. The cutter should be here in thirty minutes. By the way, for your interest, that is the HMS *Benton* out there, anchored in the harbor."

The MP saluted Ian and waved him through the gate. He drove down the quay and parked in one of the visitor parking spots, close to some stone stairs that led down to the landing position for the ship's cutter. At 1130 hours, Ian saw a cutter leave the HMS *Benton* and come towards the dock, where he was standing. It was right on schedule. They tied up and a Sub-lieutenant climbed the stone steps to where Ian was waiting. The Sub-lieutenant saluted Ian and said, "Lieutenant Black I presume."

"That's correct," replied Ian, as he gave the naval officer a salute back.

"If you'll follow me lieutenant, we'll get you to the *Benton*. We're due to get under way by 1200 hours." With that, he signaled for a sailor to pick up Ian's bag and carry it down to the cutter. Ian followed the Sub-lieutenant down the stone stairs to the waiting cutter. The sun was shining brightly and there was a slight breeze. Ian thought to himself, "*This is going to be a great day for a sea patrol.*"

They quickly boarded the cutter and it shoved off for the HMS *Benton*. It took about eight minutes, to get out to where it was anchored in the harbour. After reaching it, they quickly clambered on board using the swaying steps on the side of the ship and the empty cutter was hauled up by the shipboard davits. Ian saluted as he reached the top of the stairs, where he was greeted by Lieutenant Richard Dodd (equivalent to a captain in the British Army).

"Welcome on board, Mr. Black. I've heard good things about you from Captain Phillips. I understand you're fluent in the Greek language, and that could become very useful on this patrol. We'll be underway in a few minutes."

"Hopefully I won't get sea sick. I never have before." Ian joked.

"Well if you are, please do it in the toilet, as we try to keep the vessel ship shape. Also, we've limited space on board, so we've assigned you to share Sub-lieutenant Barwell's cabin. I believe you've already met him. I trust that's okay?" Lieutenant Dodd asked.

"Yes, that'll be fine," Ian responded.

Just then, the diesel engines started up and the minesweeper vibrated as the propellers started to rotate.

Lieutenant Dodd then said, "We're under way. I'd better get back to the bridge before the captain, Lieutenant Commander Abney, starts looking for me."

Ian went down to the cabin he was sharing with Barwell.

Right then, the sailor arrived with Ian's bag and placed it on the spare bunk. "Will that be all, sir?"

"Yes, thanks, that'll do," replied Ian.

Ian quickly unpacked his few items of clothing and toiletries. He then left the cabin and went up to the bridge. As he climbed up the ladder to the bridge, he noticed that the minesweeper was just clearing the Kyrenia harbour breakwater and heading north into open water.

"Commander Abney, this is Mr. Black of the Intelligence Corps," said Dodd, as he introduced him to the captain.

"Glad to have you on board, Mr. Black. I understand you're good with languages. You'll be extremely useful if we have to board a Greek ship". As he spoke, Commander Abney shook Ian Black's hand. "I also heard about your exploits at Pomos a few months ago."

"Thanks for allowing me to come on this patrol. Hopefully I can be of some use. What's the normal routine for a patrol such as this?" asked Ian.

The captain replied, "At the moment I have to go to the radar room. I'll let Lieutenant Dodd explain to you how we operate on a patrol." With that the captain left the bridge for the radar room.

Lieutenant Dodd explained to Ian, "Our patrol area is the whole of the north coast of Cyprus, from Cape Andreas in the east, to Cape Akamas in the west. This is approximately a distance of 130 miles and, since we'll be cruising at around ten knots (11.5 mph), it'll take about eleven hours to cover the entire north coast."

"Do you operate under a "darkened ship" routine? If so, all night or just when you believe there's a smuggler around?" asked Ian.

"Normally we operate under a "darkened ship" routine from dusk to dawn. Most of the arms smuggling takes place at night, so any action will take place in the dark. Once we've located a suspected smuggler with the radar, we'll close in on them and turn on the twenty inch searchlight to illuminate the target."

"Have the gun runners ever tried to shoot it out with you or knock out the searchlight," queried Ian?

"Not often. Generally they try to dump the shipment overboard, so there is no evidence of arms smuggling.

"Do you have any help from other resources in this hunt for gun runners," asked Ian?

"The radars operated by the 188th Radar and Searchlight Battery are key assets for these patrols," Lieutenant Dodd responded. "They can cover the entire area and report any unusual blip at night to Maritime headquarters."

The HMS *Benton* turned to the west and headed toward Cape Akamas. The ten knot speed was ideal for keeping engine performance at maximum and for conserving fuel. Since most gun runners didn't attempt a landing in daylight, there wasn't much for the crew to do but normal housekeeping duties. These tasks included polishing brass fittings and cleaning the decks. The cape was about sixty miles from Kyrenia and would take approximately five hours to reach.

At 1800 hours, they would then do a 180 degree turn and head westward towards Cape Andreas, located at the tip of the Cyprus panhandle. With the normal cruise speed of ten knots, they would be near the Camp Plakoti radar site at 0300 and arrive at Cape Andreas by 0600.

Lieutenant Dodd advised Ian, "I suggest that you go get some rest, since nothing generally happens in daylight, and you'll be up most of the night. Dinner will be served at 1830 in the wardroom (Officers' Mess)."

"Thanks for the tip. I'll go and lie down for awhile," Ian responded. "I want to be wide awake tonight and be ready for any action."

"I'll have someone knock on your cabin door at 1800 to wake you up." Dodd said, as Ian walked away from the bridge towards the cabin that he was sharing with Sub-lieutenant Barwell. Upon reaching the cabin, Ian lay down and immediately went to sleep.

Promptly at 1800 hours, there was a knock on the cabin door and a voice said, "It's 1800, sir."

"Thanks" replied Ian, as he woke up. He tidied himself up and went down to the wardroom for dinner. Out of the thirty man crew, there were only four officers. One of whom had to remain on the bridge at all times. This meant that there would be only a total of four, including Ian, dining that night. The food was excellent which reminded Ian that the Royal Navy was the "Senior Service". He had always heard that the navy food was better than the army grub.

When dinner ended around 1930, they all left the wardroom and went on deck to prepare for the night's patrol. Ian checked his Browning automatic, just in case he needed it, and made his way to the bridge.

The captain, who was already on the bridge, on seeing Ian told him, "I've assigned you to the boarding party, if one is required tonight. Since you speak Greek fluently, you'll be a great asset to the team."

"I'll be glad to be of assistance," Ian replied. "This is one of the reasons my CO sent me on this patrol."

For the next few hours, they cruised without incident, and in some ways it was becoming slightly boring. All of a sudden, at 0230, a report came in from the Maritime headquarters that Camp Plakoti radar had spotted a boat heading for the coast about ten miles away. The ships radar also picked it up at about the same time, as the report came in. The boarding party, consisting of one officer, four ratings and Ian, assembled on the deck close to the cutter, just in case they were required. HMS *Benton* went at full speed to intercept the suspicious vessel and the crew manned the Bofors 40 mm gun. As they approached the ship, the crew turned on the *Benton*'s twenty inch searchlight and fired a warning shot across the bow, using the Bofors. The ship turned out to be a large fishing trawler, and they saw the crew throwing some bags and boxes overboard. The minesweeper launched the boarding party, in the cutter, and they went over to the trawler. Climbing on board, Ian searched out the seaman that he thought might be the captain, keeping his hand on his Browning.

In broken Greek, Ian asked, "Are you the captain?"

"No," replied the seaman in Greek as he pointed out the captain further down the deck.

Ian walked down the deck to speak with the captain.

"What port are you from and what are you throwing overboard?" he asked, again in broken Greek.

"We're from Tripoli, Lebanon and we heard the fishing was good off the coast of Cyprus. We're just throwing garbage and bad fish overboard," responded the captain.

You know the fishing limit is six miles now, under the new international agreement UNCLOS 1.

"We're outside the territorial waters of Cyprus. It's not illegal to fish here," protested the captain.

"I regret that you're incorrect. You're within the six mile limit by one half mile. The three mile limit was just extended to six under this new agreement. You don't have any arms on board do you? If so, you're in deep trouble. There is an arms embargo around Cyprus that extends more than the six miles. We're going to have to search your trawler."

"You can search my boat, but you won't find anything except fish," replied the captain testily. "Our limited radar set indicated that we were outside the six mile limit."

Two of the boarding party holding Sterling SMGs rounded up the crew on the forward deck, while the rest searched to boat. Ian stood near the rounded up crew that were talking amongst themselves. He believed everything about this whole affair was too neat and tidy. Why was a trawler from Lebanon fishing around Cyprus?

As Ian stood there, just looking around while the boarding party was checking the boat, he heard the captain and a sailor talking softly. They did not realize that Ian could understand Greek perfectly. When Ian spoke earlier to the captain and sailor, he intentionally spoke slowly and made grammatical mistakes in the Greek language. He also used incorrect words.

The trawler captain and the sailor, who turned out to be the first mate, were standing by themselves, while the rest of the crew was huddled into a group.

The first mate said to the captain, "Well, this was a pretty good test of the British Navy response time. We now know what the capabilities of the minesweeper are and what their interception procedure is. We must let the freighter know what we've learned tonight. This'll make it easier for them to land the arms at Cape Andreas tomorrow night and transport them to the nearby Apostolos Andreas monastery."

"Keep it down," the captain said. "That army man might hear us. We should talk about a possible landing site near Famagusta, to draw them away from the Cape."

"Ah, don't worry," replied the first mate. "He can't speak Greek very well. He probably only understands every third word if that. However, just in case, let's talk for a short time about the possible Famagusta arms landing."

Of course, Ian heard and understood perfectly every word they said. He figured that this was a practice run for the arms shipment delivery at Cape Andreas tomorrow night. He would inform Captain Abney as soon as they were back on board the *Benton*.

The leader of the boarding party finally gave the order to return to the *Benton* and, at the same time, gave the trawler captain a warning about the new six mile fishing limit. The boarding party, including Ian, climbed into the cutter and returned to the minesweeper. The fishing trawler turned north and headed out to open sea.

When they got back on board the *Benton*, the ship continued its eastward course toward Cape Andreas. Ian went up on the bridge to talk with the captain.

"Well, Mr. Black," said the captain, "How did you enjoy that little trip? Did you learn anything useful?"

"Yes, I overheard the mate talking to the trawler captain. I believe that they were conducting a test run for an arms shipment tomorrow night at Cape Andreas. They were trying to mislead us by talking about a Famagusta landing at some length, just in case we could understand them."

"Why are you so sure the landing will be at Cape Andreas?"

"Based on what I overheard between the two Greek fishermen, it makes sense that the landing will be at Cape Andreas. For one thing, it's the closest spot to Beirut, Lebanon, where the freighter is probably coming from, rather than from Greece itself. Also, it's long been suspected that the Greek Orthodox Church has been assisting EOKA. There's a monastery near the cape, where they could store the arms."

The captain replied, "Okay, I'll inform Maritime headquarters and ask them to launch a Shackleton search plane tomorrow evening. We'll hide out away from the cape, maybe down near Famagusta, so any look out at the cape won't know where we are. We should also warn the 188th radar camp at Galounapetra to be especially on the lookout for a suspicious vessel and also be prepared to provide a few troops, in case they are required."

Ian responded, "That sounds like a good plan to me, Sir. Hopefully, we can catch them in the act."

"Good work, Mr. Black. I suggest we get some rest since tomorrow night could be a long one."

"Yes, sir, goodnight or what is left of it."

With that, Ian went down to his cabin to get some sleep. As he slept, the *Benton* cruised westward and anchored in Famagusta Bay. Ian woke up around noon and wandered up on the deck. In the distance he could see the radar set at Camp Elia that was one of the Royal Artillery 188th Radar and Searchlight Battery camps. The crew was doing a little clean up on the minesweeper.

At 1800 hours, Ian went to the wardroom for dinner. The captain and two other officers were there.

"Welcome, Mr. Black," said the captain. "You're just in time for dinner. After we've eaten, we'll discuss our plan for tonight and our future successful patrol against the gun runners."

Ian was again reminded by the excellent food that the British Navy was the "Senior Service". After the dinner was eaten and the wine finished, the captain laid out his plan.

"We'll weigh anchor at 1930 and cruise up to Cape Andreas with an ETA of 2330. A Shackleton search aircraft has verified that there is a small freighter approaching Cyprus from Lebanon. At this point, we don't know if it will enter Cyprus territorial waters, but we have to assume it will. As it reaches the horizon, the Camp Galounapetra radar should be able to detect it, when it is about twelve miles out. We'll hide around the point from Cape Andreas, so they don't pick us up on their radar. As soon as we get a communication from Camp Galounapetra through Maritime headquarters, we'll race around the point and get close to the freighter. We'll turn on the searchlight and fire our Bofors across their bow. As we do this, our boarding party will immediately go over to the freighter and board it. All members will be armed with Sterling SMGs and ready for any emergency. We don't know at this point how many sailors are on the vessel and how well they are armed. Mr. Black, I want you to go along and be available to perform any necessary translations. Lieutenant Dodd will be in charge of the boarding party. Are there any questions?"

Ian asked, "If they're running guns, what's the action we'll take? Will we take over the freighter and take it to Famagusta or do we wait for reinforcements?"

The captain replied, "If they are running guns, we'll round up the entire crew and hold them. We will place a crew on the freighter and escort it to Famagusta. Unless the freighter crew is larger than we can handle, we'll not need reinforcements. Okay, let's get going. It's time to weigh anchor."

The captain left the wardroom and went up to the minesweeper bridge, where he gave the order to weigh anchor. The engines were started and the ship left Famagusta Bay and headed east towards the cape. At dusk,

Captain Abney ordered all lights to be covered or extinguished. This was going to be a darkened patrol. At 2330, they arrived just south of the cape, as planned, and came close to land, so the freighters radar could not detect them. They dropped anchor to wait the call from Maritime headquarters. At this point in time, the Camp Galounapetra radar had not picked up the freighter.

At 0030, the call came in that the Galounapetra radar had detected the freighter and that it was about ten miles out heading for Cape Andreas. The captain alerted the minesweeper crew. The boarding party assembled on the deck and checked their weapons. Ian joined them and checked his Browning automatic. The minesweeper engines were started and the ships anchor was weighed. They then crept slowly towards the cape.

At 0130, the call came in that the freighter had stopped at three miles from the cape. Captain Abney ordered full speed and rounded the cape to where the freighter was anchored. The minesweeper crew turned on the twenty inch searchlight and the Bofors gun crew fired a shot, across the stationary freighters bow. The freighter crew was in the process of lowering some fast LCRL boats to transport the arms to shore.

The boarding party jumped into the cutter, which then sped over to where the freighter was anchored. The crew of the freighter could be seen trying to throw boxes overboard, but there were too many for them to handle expeditiously.

The cutter soon arrived at the freighter and the boarding party climbed on board. They rounded up the crew, at the front of the freighter, and most gave no resistance. They didn't however look like they were fully compliant with the demands of *Benton*'s party

Meanwhile, two of the crew remained hidden behind the boxes piled on the deck and they suddenly opened fire on the boarding party. Ian pulled his Browning from its holster but, before he could use it, the minesweeper boarding party quickly dispatched the two hidden men, with their Sterling SMGs. The rest of the crew quickly raised their hands, as they realized the boarding party meant business.

Ian isolated the captain of the freighter and covered him with his Browning. He started to question him in Greek.

"What is your name and where are you from?" Ian asked.

"I'm Captain Antonio Boutros, a Lebanese citizen and I'm from Beirut."

"Who paid you to deliver these arms and where are they located?" Ian continued.

"I am Captain Antonio Boutros and I'm from Beirut Lebanon."

"Your name sounds Greek to me," Ian replied.

The captain responded nervously, "There are many Greek descendants and neighbourhoods in Lebanon."

After this Ian did not receive any more information from the captain. He refused to cooperate.

The remaining ten crewmen of the original twelve man crew were placed in a hold on the freighter and guarded by some of the boarding party.

Captain Abney decided to move the freighter to Famagusta harbour, using some of the minesweeper crew and a few of the freighters crew under guard. It would take about four hours to get Famagusta, but another minesweeper was being sent from Famagusta, to escort them half of the way.

The boarding party asked Ian to help them separate the diehard Greeks from the normal Lebanese crewmen. They would use them to help operate the freighter, until they reached Famagusta.

Finally, after about one hour, Captain Abney was in a position to take the freighter, followed by the minesweeper, to Famagusta. They arrived there at about 0600, just after the bright, red sun had come up over the horizon. Some

British soldiers came on board the freighter, and took over custody of the vessel, along with the Lebanese crewmen.

The minesweeper boarding party, along with Ian, returned to the *Benton* for a review on the entire action by the captain. At 0800 Ian returned to his cabin and got a few hours of sleep.

The *Benton* weighed anchor at 1900, just before sunset and headed eastward for the return trip to Kyrenia, via Cape Andreas. No action was expected, although the entire crew was on edge, just in case the unexpected happened. Ian was on the bridge, most of the night, discussing with the captain and Lieutenant Dodd the previous night's action.

The captain said to Ian, "You know, if you had not overheard the trawler captain and mate talking, the freighter might have been able to transport the arms to the monastery without detection."

"Well, sir, I must admit it was fortuitous that they talked loud enough in Greek that I could hear them and understand what they were saying. Perhaps we should have the army raid the monastery Apostolos Andreas. Who knows what they would find?"

The captain replied, "That's a good idea, Mr. Black, I'll suggest it to my superior. I believe the issue will be, however, that there's a Greek religious order located in it, and the matter becomes a political problem, rather than a military one. Archbishop Makarios would not be too happy with a raid on one of his monasteries, and he could cause problems for us."

Ian nodded and said, "Even if it is not raided, the army should place a blockade around it to stop any arms being moved from the monastery, to other areas of Cyprus."

"I'll look into that idea, Mr. Black. It makes sense to at least stop the movement of arms shipments around the island. I'm going below for some shuteye. Lieutenant Dodd will you please take over and call me if any unforeseen event takes place." With that the captain left the bridge.

ON HER MAJESTY'S CYPRUS MISSION

The HMS *Benton* cruised past Cape Andreas and headed west towards Kyrenia. The sun rose around 0545 and the minesweeper "sliced" through the almost still water of the Mediterranean, with the sun glistening on it. They slowly pulled into Kyrenia harbour at 0700 and dropped anchor.

Ian went down to his cabin to pack his small bag, and then headed to the wardroom for breakfast. He was tired from the last three days and nights, but he had learned a lot about how the British Navy handles gun runners.

Since they were no longer at sea, all the officers attended the breakfast. A senior rating was left on the bridge with instructions to immediately call Lieutenant Dodd, if there was any problem.

Ian said at the breakfast, "Gentlemen, I appreciate the courtesy you have shown a lowly intelligence officer. This voyage has been very instructive and I will use what I have learned in my upcoming operations. The goal of the Intelligence Corps is to find Grivas and arrest him. I'm sure we can accomplish this, if politics does not get in the way."

The captain responded, "Mr. Black, that's a very big IF. Politics always somehow seems to get injected into military operations. For your sake and ours, I hope you succeed in bringing Grivas to justice. We have been fortunate in having you on board and your assistance in the Cape Andreas operation was extremely useful. Well done."

With that, they ate their breakfast and afterwards Ian went up to the captain, saluted and shook his hand saying, "Thank you, sir, for everything. I have to take my leave now and return to Nicosia. Will the cutter be available to take me to the landing?"

The captain shook his hand and replied, "You're welcome. Lieutenant Dodd, would you please make arrangements for the cutter to take Mr. Black ashore?"

Dodd responded, "Yes, sir, I'll personally accompany Mr. Black to the dock."

Ian returned to his cabin for the last time, picked up his bag and went on deck, towards the ladder down to the water. The cutter was lowered and moved to the ladder. Ian and Dodd climbed into the cutter and it took them towards the dock, arriving there in a few minutes. Ian thanked the lieutenant and walked over to his car. He drove through the gate waving at the MP and headed back to Nicosia. He arrived there at 1100, and immediately went to report to Captain Phillips, after turning the car in.

"How was your trip on the *Benton*? Did you have any action?" asked Captain Phillips.

"Actually, it was quite exciting and I learned a lot about how the Navy intercepts gun runners. Also, I found out that it is true, the navy food is better than the army's," Ian said with a grin.

"You look tired, Ian. Go get some rest. Tomorrow, there'll be a meeting with the colonel at 0900 sharp."

Ian nodded and said, "I could do with some shuteye. I'll see you tomorrow at the meeting."

With that, Ian went back to his room, pulled the blinds and slept for a few hours.

9

The Governor's Bed

At 0850 on Wednesday, the 16th of July, after a restful night's sleep and an army breakfast, Ian went to the Salisbury House conference room for the 0900 meeting with the Colonel Baker and Captain Phillips. Ian was the second person there. As usual, John of MI6 was seated in his corner chair by the window.

"I hear you saw some action on your minesweeper patrol," he said to Ian.

"How do you know that?" Ian asked.

"We receive all communications at Ayios Nikolaos, including some from the Soviets," replied John. "You have to be careful what you say and do, we hear everything."

At that point, Colonel Baker and Captain Phillips entered the room for the nine o'clock meeting.

"Good morning, gentlemen. We are here to discuss the upcoming reception at the Government House this Saturday and what our involvement in it will be. However, first I want to discuss a matter that was brought to my attention yesterday afternoon. I received a phone call from a Lieutenant Commander Abney of the HMS *Benton*. Mr. Black, I assume you know him," the colonel said.

"Yes, sir," replied Ian as he nodded. "I was on his ship the last three days looking for gun runners."

"Well, Ian, he was well pleased with your performance and stated that you were a great asset to his patrol. He added that, if I ever wanted to get rid of you, he would take you on. Of course, I politely turned him down. I therefore want to thank you, Mr. Black, for the honour you have bestowed on yourself and the Intelligence Corps."

"Thank you, sir, I was glad to be of service."

John, in the corner, was smiling and said, "Congratulations, Ian."

The colonel then said, "Okay. Let's get down to business. We're expected to be in attendance at the governor's reception on Saturday. The purpose, Captain Phillips and Lt. Black, is to keep a low profile all the while listening and watching for any information on the Government House staff. Some of them are Greek Cypriots and some are Turkish. Supposedly, they've all been cleared by security, but one never knows if they have been "turned". We've heard rumours, unsubstantiated, that there'll be an assassination attempt on the Governor, Sir Hugh Foot, and/or his wife and daughter. We can't allow that to happen, as it would set back the peace process for years."

Ian asked, "Will we receive special badges to allow us entry? I assume the army will have increased their guards for this event."

"Yes indeed. You'll receive your passes on Friday and they'll allow you entry into any room and facility at Government House and the grounds. Please be respectful at all times for the privacy of the governor's family. I don't think I have to remind you that the dress code will be a dark suit, white shirt and conservative tie. We discussed that at a previous meeting. Are there any questions?"

"At what time should we arrive and depart the governor's mansion?" Captain Phillips asked.

"The reception is officially from 2:00 pm until 5:00 pm. I believe it would be best if you arrive at 12:30 pm and leave at 6:00 pm. This will give you time to ask the Cypriot staff for any information you deem appropriate. Additionally, it will allow you the time to walk the premises, without being interrupted by the guests. You may mingle with the guests, as you feel necessary, but remember you are on duty; no alcohol. We'll meet back here next Monday at 0900 for a review of the reception activities."

Captain Phillips responded, "Colonel, I believe we understand what your orders are. You can count on Mr. Black and me to carry them out. John, will you be there or do you have to be at Ayios Nikolaos?"

John replied, "I may be there for an hour, but I also have other matters to attend to."

Colonel Baker then closed the meeting by saying, "I'll see you two at the reception on Saturday. That's all for today."

They all left the conference room and returned to their offices.

****

On Saturday, Ian met Captain Phillips for breakfast and then they went out to the Salisbury House parking lot and climbed into the captain's car. They were dressed in their dark suits and wore their old school ties. Ian, who had the Browning automatic in a holster under his jacket, wore his Harrow school tie which was dark blue with white and blue stripes. Captain Phillips wore his King's School Canterbury tie, which was maroon with white and blue stripes.

They drove out of the main gate and headed south from the centre of Nicosia toward the village of Ay. Omoloyitadhes and Government House. It was only two to three miles from Salisbury House to Government House, but, with the Saturday traffic, it would take ten to fifteen minutes. As they neared Government House, they entered a park like area of thick pine trees. The house and surrounding land sat near a bend in the Pedieos River, which only flowed during the winter rainy season. It was fed by the Troodos

Mountains and, in the summer, it mainly dried up, unless there had been a heavy snowfall during the winter months.

There was a check point on the road as they entered the grounds, and also as they neared the governor's residence. British Army troops carrying mainly SMG's were everywhere. Captain Phillips showed his pass both times and they were waved in. It was around 12:30 pm, when they found a parking spot in a corner of the lot and then walked towards Government House. They clipped their badges that said SECURITY to their breast pocket, so that hopefully they would not be bothered often by the soldiers guarding the house.

Government House was an imposing structure that was completed in 1937 and cost approximately seventy thousand British pounds. The general structure was built using Yerolokkos sandstone, and the grand, sweeping staircases were crafted out of harder sandstone from Limassol. It replaced a previous house that had burned to the ground in the early 1930's. The main features of the house were a massive British coat-of-arms and four gargoyle statues with human heads. The faces were supposed to be a likeness of the four major participants involved in the construction. The entrance to the house was through two oak double doors with lion head, brass knockers mounted on each door.

They walked up the long path, surrounded by a magnificent, manicured, green lawn and trimmed hedges, to the entrance of the house. They noticed armed guards on top of the building and there were two armed soldiers with rifles, one on each side of the ornate doors. One of them asked. "May I see your passes, gentlemen?"

"Certainly," Phillips said and showed him both of their passes.

"Welcome, sir," he responded and saluted, as the passes indicated they were officers in the army. "You may enter everywhere except for the governor's private quarters, at this time."

Ian and Captain Phillips saluted back, walked through the double doors into Government House and started to look around. Phillips gave Ian his pass, just in case they were separated and he needed to show it.

The captain said, "I suggest we split up to look for any security issues and meet back here at 1345. This way we can cover more ground. Ian, why don't you cover the kitchen and servants areas, since some of them are Greek Cypriots and you can understand them."

Ian responded, "Good idea, captain. I'll meet you back here before the guests arrive."

Ian wandered into the kitchen and talked with the chefs preparing the food for the reception. They all seemed friendly and he saw nothing suspicious. As he wandered down a hallway towards the servants' quarters, he heard footsteps and two people talking. Ian quickly slid into a utility room and almost closed the door. It turned out the two people were a man and a woman. The man was dressed as a waiter and the woman was obviously a maid, working at the house.

The waiter whispered to the maid in Greek, *"Alexia, you have the package, right? You know where to place it and how to arm it?"*

"Yes, Nico," she said in a hushed voice. *"I will place it between the mattress and box spring, and pull the cord at exactly 8:00 pm."*

"That's correct. Pulling the string will arm the bomb and, with the timer, it'll detonate at around 3:00 am. Be careful, and keep a good look out, while you are in the governor's bedroom."

Ian heard all this and, through the crack between the door and the frame, he managed to get a good look at the conspirators. He let them walk away, before coming out of the utility room. He wanted to see who else they conversed with. There might be other conspirators on the Government House staff.

Fifteen minutes before the official start time for the reception, Ian met Captain Phillips in the Great Hall and told him about what he had overheard.

"I thought we should keep an eye on them and see who else they communicate with," Ian mentioned to the captain.

"I agree. There's no rush, but at some point we need to notify the head of security here. The best time would be right after the reception at 5:00 pm, and before any of the staff leave for the evening. I believe it's Major Hudson. If I see him, I'll inform of what we know and our plan." Captain Phillips replied.

At exactly 2:30 pm, the Governor-General of Cyprus, Sir Hugh Foot, and his wife walked down the grand sweeping staircase and proceeded to walk through the main hall. They stopped halfway and stood under a large portrait of Queen Elizabeth II, to await the arrival of their guests, from the foyer. Not long thereafter, the first guests arrived coming through the large, double oak doors into Government House. They queued up in a reception line so they could individually shake the hand of the governor and his wife.

Ian was standing in the background watching these guests as they entered the main hall of the House. As he did so, two people walked in and shook the hands of the governor and his wife. He recognized the couple immediately. They were Doctor Griffith and Nurse Palas from the Nicosia BMH. Ian had not seen Aphrodite Palas, since he left the hospital three months earlier. She looked lovely, dressed in a pale yellow sleeveless dress, straw hat with a dark blue band and white short gloves. Her long black hair was pulled to the nape of her neck with a matching yellow ribbon. He had forgotten how attractive she was.

Ian thought, "*I wonder if she and the doctor are an item.*"

He waited until they were greeted by the hosts and then stepped forward, hoping she'd remember him. As he extended his hand, she took it and smiled.

"I hope you're feeling better than the last time I saw you" she said.

"Yes, thank you, I am." Ian replied

Aphrodite turned towards the doctor, and asked Ian, "Do you remember Doctor Griffith?"

"Of course, how are you doctor? It's great to meet you under different circumstances."

"Yes, I do remember you lieutenant. I hope you are totally recovered."

"Yes, thanks to you, doctor and Nurse Palas. I hope I'll see both of you later, before you leave. At the moment, I have to go back to work."

Doctor Griffith and Aphrodite walked off toward the main garden, while Ian went up the staircase to check out other rooms. He had to make sure no other threat existed, other than the package for the governor's bed. When he was satisfied that he had searched as many rooms as he could, he walked down the staircase into the main hall.

As he did so, he saw Aphrodite coming out of the ladies cloakroom. He walked toward her and, at the same time, she noticed him.

"Well, we meet again. Are you enjoying the reception?" Ian inquired.

"Yes, thank you," she replied with a smile.

"If you don't mind me asking and it's not too personal, are you and the doctor seeing each other?"

"Oh no, not at all, we are just good friends. My father and he knew each other for years, before my father died. Doctor Griffith has been like a father to me, since my dad's death," Aphrodite replied.

"Well then, would you mind if I give you a call and take you to dinner some time?"

"Yes, that would be nice," Aphrodite said. "I know of a smashing restaurant run by a French couple south of town on the Larnaca road, which will be a safe location from all this madness. It would be best if you call me at the hospital, if you don't mind."

"I'll call you in the next couple of days and maybe we can meet on Monday or Tuesday night. Will that be okay?"

"Certainly, I'd better go now. I see Doctor Griffith, over there waiting on me. Talk to you soon." With that, Aphrodite walked off to rejoin the doctor.

As the reception drew to a close, Ian and Captain Phillips came together again and sought out Major Hudson. He was not very hard to find. He was a tall, imposing officer immaculately dressed in a formal uniform, just right for the occasion.

"Major Hudson, I would like you to meet Lieutenant Ian Black, who works with me on intelligence matters."

Ian, although he was not in uniform, saluted the major out of deference to his rank. "It's a pleasure to meet you, sir," Ian said.

Captain Phillips turned to Ian saying, "Mr. Black, why don't you relate what you told me earlier, about the waiter and the maid."

Ian then told the major exactly what he overheard and saw upstairs, near the servants' quarters.

The major, upon hearing the details, said, "We'll first go to the kitchen area and see if the waiter is still there. They are still clearing up, but I believe some of the waiters have already left. Did you hear either of their names?"

"It was hard to hear, but I believe I heard the maid call the waiter Nico and I think he called her Alexia," Ian responded.

The major continued, "If you don't see him, Mr. Black, we'll obtain his full name from the maid. There is also a list of the workers and maybe from that we can deduce who he is. That's assuming he didn't use an alias."

"Let's go to where the waiters are and see if you recognize him."

With that, they walked into the kitchen area where most of the waiters and chefs were.

"I don't see him," Ian told the major and Captain Phillips.

The major went over to the head chef that he knew fairly well and asked him. "Do you know a waiter called Nico and do you know where he is? We'd like to talk to him."

The head chef replied, "I don't know him personally, but some of the waiters have already been sent away, as they weren't needed any more."

"Thank you," said the major. They walked back to the major's office, which was in the rear of Government House. As they went through the Great Hall to the major's office, they ran into Colonel Baker, who had just arrived at the house.

All of them then walked back to the major's security office. When they reached it, Colonel Baker was brought up to date with the details of the possible plot.

Major Hudson said, "I believe that the best approach will be to hide out near the governor's bedroom at 7:45 pm, and wait to see if the maid arrives and what she does."

"That sounds like a good strategy. Hopefully we'll catch her red-handed," responded Colonel Baker.

At 7:40 pm, all four of them left the security office and went up stairs toward the governor's bedroom. They found two closets which gave a good view of the bed and hid in them, leaving just enough of a crack between the doors and the frames.

At 7:55 pm, they heard footsteps and in walked a maid with a basket of towels. Ian immediately recognized her and carefully drew his Browning. After she turned down the bed, she reached into the basket and pulled out a package, with a cord hanging from it.

Ian stepped from his hiding place with gun drawn and pointed it at her. In Greek, he said, "Place the package back into the basket and place it on the bed. Then, put your hands up, Alexia. You are under arrest for attempted murder."

At that point, the other three men came out of their hiding places.

Alexia started to cry and said, "They made me do it. They threatened my family, if I didn't cooperate."

Ian asked her, "What's the name of the waiter who gave you the orders?"

Alexia replied, "I believe his name is Nico Petros, but I don't know if that's his correct name."

At this point, Major Hudson suggested that they all go down to his office and from there he could handle the entire affair.

They all returned to the security office. Colonel Baker, Captain Phillips and Ian felt they could not be of any more assistance. Major Hudson thanked Ian for being vigilant and saving the governor's life.

They left it up to the major to handle the situation with the maid and the waiter, and departed Government House.

Captain Phillips and Ian drove out of the house grounds feeling well satisfied that they had done their duty for the Queen and their country.

10

First Date

On the next Monday, the colonel held a review meeting, in the conference room, on the bomb affair at Government House.

"Gentleman, the EOKA waiter has finally been found and arrested. Except for the report that Ian's writing, this matter is concluded, as far as we're concerned.

Captain Phillips and Mr. Black, you both performed admirably and I've received personal thanks from the governor and his staff.

Mr. Black, I believe you're going on a Shackleton search flight on Thursday. Please make sure it's an uneventful one, and you come back in one piece."

"Yes, sir," Ian said with a grin. "I'll do my best to make sure nothing happens."

The colonel then adjourned the meeting, and Ian returned to his office. He placed a call to Aphrodite at the British Military Hospital. Ian was told that she was busy at the moment, so he left a message for her to call him back. After about half an hour, the phone rang in Ian's office.

Picking up the phone, Ian answered, "Lieutenant Black speaking."

"Ian, this is Aphrodite. I believe you called."

"Yes, I did. I was wondering if you'd like to go out to dinner tomorrow night. That is, if you're not on duty and don't have any other plans."

"As it happens, I'm free tomorrow night and I'd like that. Where would you like to meet?"

"Do you want me to pick you up at your home or shall we rendezvous at the restaurant?"

"It would be best if we meet at the restaurant. Do you have one in mind?" asked Aphrodite

Ian replied, "Not really, I've only been here in Cyprus a few months. Can you recommend a good one that's fairly quiet?"

"I've heard that the Naples Ristorante is very good, if you like Italian food. It's generally quiet and owned by an English couple, whose daughter works at the hospital. The restaurant is located in the southern part of Nicosia on the Larnaca Road."

"That sounds great. I'll call them and make a booking for tomorrow night. Will seven o'clock be okay with you?" asked Ian.

"Yes, I look forward to seeing you again. Goodbye."

Ian spent the rest of that day, and the next morning, writing a review of the affair at Government House. All the while, in the back of his mind, he was thinking about his upcoming date with Aphrodite. Later that afternoon, he took a quick shower and dressed to go the restaurant. Under his loose shirt, he wore the holster with the Browning inserted. He hoped the bulge was not noticeable, but it paid to be careful, especially at night. He had called for a taxi, and it arrived in plenty of time for him to get to the Naples Ristorante. The taxi dropped him off at the entrance. As he entered, he found Aphrodite talking to the owner's wife.

"Hello," he said to her and smiled.

"Hello," Aphrodite responded

"Have you been waiting long?" Ian asked.

"Why no, not really, I just got here a few minutes ago," she answered.

"Well, I'm glad you could come. I've been looking forward to seeing you again so I could thank you for looking after me, when I was in the hospital."

Aphrodite responded, "You're welcome. It was my job. By the way Ian, this is Margaret and she owns the place, with her husband Derek. Their daughter is a nurse at the hospital, and she's a friend of mine and my mother."

Ian turned and said with a smile, "It's a pleasure to meet you."

Margaret took his hand, smiled and said, "I'm pleased to meet you, Ian. Kindly follow me. I believe that I have just the table for you."

Aphrodite and Ian followed Margaret to a nice corner table, covered with a white and red checkered tablecloth. Turning to them both, she asked, "Will this be quiet enough for you?"

"Yes, thanks," they replied in unison.

Ian pulled the chair back so Aphrodite could sit down, and then he sat down. Margaret gave them both a menu saying, "Your waitress will be here shortly." As she walked away, she thought, *"He seems to be a nice enough young man."*

Ian and Aphrodite picked up the menus, studied them and decided what to order.

"Would you like some wine?"Ian asked Aphrodite.

"Yes," she replied. "I'd like that."

"What would you prefer, red or white?" Ian asked.

"Red would be nice," she answered.

Soon the waitress came to the table to take their orders.

Looking at Aphrodite, she asked, "What would you like, ma'am?"

Aphrodite replied, "I believe I'd like to have a cup of Minestrone, followed by the veal parmesan with spaghetti."

"And you, sir?" she asked, turning and looking at Ian.

"I'll have a small Greek salad and the meat lasagna." Ian replied. "Also, we'd like to have a bottle of Chianti."

"I'll place the orders in the kitchen and bring the wine to you right away," replied the waitress. She then walked off to get the wine and to place the order with the chef.

When the waitress was gone, Aphrodite asked Ian, "How did you get to be in Cyprus?"

As the overhead fan whirled quietly, Ian started to relate to Aphrodite his background, and how he ended up in Cyprus.

"I was born at the start of World War Two and lived in Richmond with my mother, while my father went off to war in the RAF. He was gone most of the time, and I was basically raised by my mother. We lived close to the Thames River and, at an early age, I went to a day school in Kew.

"Richmond, that's interesting? My mother originally came from Twickenham, which I believe is not very far from Richmond."

The waitress brought the bottle of wine to the table, opened it and poured small amount in one glass. Ian sniffed the aroma, tasted it and nodded, saying, "Very good." The waitress then poured some in Aphrodite's glass and some more in Ian's. "Your appetizers should be up shortly," she said, as she walked away.

Ian continued with his short life history. "When I was nine, I was sent off to a boarding school in Sturry, near Canterbury. Then, upon turning fourteen, I was enrolled at Harrow, an English public school, and did fairly well, considering I didn't study too hard.

"Is that where you learned Greek and German?" Aphrodite asked.

"Yes it was, as there was a strong language department at Harrow. Anyway, when I just turned eighteen, a letter arrived at our home stating that I was called up to serve my National Service. I applied for officer candidate school, was accepted and graduated from MONS as a second lieutenant. Upon graduation, I was assigned to come to Cyprus, and so here I am. I can't tell you exactly what I do here, but I'm in the British Army, as you're already aware."

The waitress came to the table with the appetizers and said, "Your entrées will be here soon."

They started to eat and sip some more wine.

Aphrodite said, "This wine is excellent."

"I agree." said Ian, as they smiled at each other.

Ian thought, *"How beautiful she is."* He was smitten by her dark beauty. Of course, he already knew that she was beautiful, since he saw her at the Government House garden party. He remembered the stunning yellow dress she had worn that day, and how her black shining hair had been held by a pale yellow ribbon.

"What kind of work are your father and mother involved in?" Aphrodite asked.

"My father was in the RAF during the war and became a fighter ace. It's tough trying to live up to your father's reputation," Ian said with a smile. "Now he works for a major aircraft company, as a vice president. My mother has always been a housewife, although she has helped out at the local school."

The waitress reappeared at their table with the entrées and placed the plates in front of them, after removing the appetizer dishes. "Is there anything else I can get for you?" she asked.

"No, I think that we have everything we need, thanks," Ian responded, after looking at Aphrodite who nodded.

They started to eat the food and sip more of the red wine. Both were delicious.

"This restaurant was a good choice, Aphrodite. The food and the restaurant atmosphere are both great. How about you and your family? How did your mother end up in Cyprus?"

"As I have already mentioned, my mother's family lived in Twickenham, and she came out to Cyprus, when she was twenty, to work in the Nicosia general hospital. There were ads placed in England looking for volunteers to emigrate to Cyprus. She applied and was accepted. 1932 was not a good year to look for jobs in England, even though she had just received her nursing credential. The depression was in full force in the 1930s. While she was working here, she met a Greek Cypriot. They fell in love and got married. They had three children and I was the middle one. I had an older and younger brother. During World War Two, my father joined the Cyprus Regiment and was killed during the last days of the war. This left my mother to fend for her three young children. It was tough on her, but we all survived.

"Do you remember anything of your father? How old were you when he died?"

"I don't remember much as I was only six when he was killed. This year, as I mentioned to you in the hospital, my younger brother Andreus had joined EOKA and was killed when he was attacking an army convoy near Morphou Bay. How my mother held up I don't know, but she did. She is a strong woman. I went to nursing school here and managed to get a job at the BMH, where my mother works."

Ian took a long sip of his wine and then said, "Aphrodite, I have something to tell you. As you saw my records in the hospital, you know that, in April, I was a second lieutenant assigned to the 188th Radar and Searchlight Battery. This unit has eight sites around the coast with radars which report all ship and aircraft traffic. I was travelling to the Pomos site in a convoy when ..."

At that point, Aphrodite placed a finger to her lips as though to hush Ian and she said, "I know what you are going to say, but please don't say it. I know you had no control over what happened, and you did what you had to do to survive." She then held his hand in hers, looked into his teary eyes and whispered, "I know. I know."

He then moved close to her and reached for her hand. "I'm sorry," he said.

"Don't say that," she answered. "What's done is done."

They held hands for awhile and then Ian gently kissed her cheek. Margaret noticed the exchange and thought to herself, *"This is probably more than just a one-time dinner date for those two."*

The waitress reappeared and asked, "Would you like some desert or coffee?"

"I'd like a small black coffee please," Aphrodite responded.

"Yes I'll take the same," said Ian nodding.

They drank the coffee and talked some more. The waitress reappeared and asked, "Can I get you anything else?"

Ian looked at Aphrodite and asked, "Are you ready to go?"

She nodded, "Yes, I believe so, if you are."

Ian then replied to the waitress, "No, thank you. I believe we're finished. May we please have the bill and where do we pay?"

The waitress handed him the bill and said, "You can pay it up front at the counter, on the way out."

Ian left a tip on the table and they both walked towards the exit. Ian stopped at the counter and paid Margaret saying, "That was an excellent meal. We enjoyed it very much. Thank you."

"I'm glad you liked it. Would you like me to get a taxi for you?"

"Yes," Ian replied.

"Do you want one or two?" Margaret asked.

Ian replied, "Two will be fine."

Margaret ordered the two taxis, as Ian and Aphrodite went outside into the cool evening air.

"Thank you for coming Aphrodite," Ian said. "I enjoyed it very much. Would you be interested in going out again some time?" he asked nervously.

Aphrodite moved close to him and, before he could say anything else, she whispered, "Yes, I'd like that very much." Then she added, "I really enjoyed myself." She kissed him on his cheek and said, "I'll wait for your call."

"On Thursday, I have to go on a mission for the day, but I'll call soon thereafter. Should I call the hospital or can I call you at home?"

Aphrodite responded, "Please call me at the hospital and, if I'm not there, leave a message and I'll call you back."

At that moment the two taxis arrived. Ian opened the door of the first one and Aphrodite got inside.

"Goodnight," Ian said. He closed the door and in a flash she was gone.

Ian returned to the safe house, across the road from Salisbury House, in the other taxi. He then walked under the road through the secret tunnel to the House. He was humming to himself, as he walked by the main gate and entered the building. The armed guard looked at him and thought, *"He must have had a great evening."*

Ian went up to his room and dropped off into a deep blissful sleep.

11

Emergency In The Air

On Thursday, the 24th of July, Ian arose early because an agreement had been made with the RAF by Captain Phillips that would allow him to go on a maritime surveillance flight. He dressed in his army uniform and strapped his Browning automatic on his right side. The purpose of the flight was to let Ian see for himself, how the RAF tracked suspicious ships approaching Cyprus, in conjunction with maritime naval surveillance.

He had a quick breakfast, jumped into an Intelligence Corps unmarked vehicle and drove to the RAF Squadron 38 operations centre at the RAF Akrotiri airfield, in the south. At the gated entrance to the airfield, he showed his ID card to a guard carrying the standard Sterling SMG and was directed to the RAF flight operations building. He drove over close to the building and parked in a spot, near the front entrance.

He entered the building and asked the guard, "Where can I find Flight Lieutenant Mullins?"

The guard responded, "Go down to the end of the hallway and enter the door marked *Ready Room*. You should find him in there, sir."

Ian walked down to the end of the hallway and entered the *Ready Room,* as directed. There were three RAF personnel there studying maps and flight plans. In the corner of the room, Ian saw a flight lieutenant who had a nametag on his flight suit, indicating his name was Mullins. He went over and introduced himself.

"I'm Lieutenant Ian Black from the Intelligence Corps, and I'm supposed to be flying with you today, on your coastal surveillance flight."

"Pleased to meet you, lieutenant; we're glad to have you on board. I was advised that you'd be flying with us today. We'll be leaving at around 0800 and won't be back until about 1800. I hope you're ready for a long flight. We'll have packed lunches on board and plenty of water. "

"Great, I'm here to see how you operate and how you locate suspicious boats out there," Ian responded.

Mullins replied, "I'll explain our flight procedures once we get airborne. Go grab a cup of coffee in the NAAFI and be back here at 0730. I'll then take you out to the aircraft and introduce you to the crew. We'll have to do an aircraft inspection, before we board the plane."

Ian walked down to the NAAFI and found some coffee and a roll. When he was finished, he noticed it was close to 0730 and went back to the *Ready Room* to find Flt. Lt. Christopher Mullins. Chris, who was collecting his maps and flight plans, looked up and saw Ian approaching.

"Ah, you're right on time. Let's go out to where the plane is parked. However, I want to clue you in on something first. When we're in the air, we call each other by our first name. This is normal among most RAF flight crews."

Mullins led the way out of the Operations Building and walked over the tarmac to the second nearest Avro Shackleton MR.2 (C 224), where the rest of his crew was waiting. Flt. Lt. Mullins introduced Ian to the other nine crew members that included Flt. Lt. William Jones (2nd pilot), Flying Officer Charles Higginbottom (flight engineer), two navigators (one named Donald) and five signalers. These signalers included a radar operator, sonar operator, radio signals airman, named Derek Hayward, and two spotters/gunners.

"Chaps, this is Lieutenant Ian Black from the Intelligence Corps. Let's show him how well we can search for potential ships carrying arms."

Christopher (Chris) Mullins, the 2nd pilot Flt. Lt. William (Bill) Jones and Flying Officer Charles (Chuck) Higginbottom, walked around the plane inspecting and checking for any defect that might be a threat to the safety of the plane and the crew. They found none and the crew, along with Ian, climbed on board. The crew settled into their appropriate seats, and Chris suggested to Ian that he sit in the spare seat by the flight engineer.

Chris got on the aircraft communications system and said, "Okay men, get ready. We're going to start the engines momentarily." Chris then signaled the ground crew that he was ready to start up.

He then started the first of the four Rolls-Royce Giffon 57A engines. After that, he started the other three engines in succession. The ground crew disconnected the portable generator after the flight engineer notified Chris that all four engines were operating within specification. The roar from the engines, with their contra-rotating propellers, was deafening. The Giffon engines were famous for noise, fuel consumption, oil consumption, high maintenance and being temperamental.

Chris got on the radio to the control tower, on a frequency of 122.1 Mcs., and requested permission to taxi, "Akrotiri, this is Shackleton C224 requesting permission to taxi to take off position."

"Shackleton C224, this is Akrotiri. You're cleared to taxi to the end of runway two eight and perform your engine run up. Stop just short of the actual runway."

"Akrotiri, we're taxiing towards runway two eight and will stop short."

Chris moved the throttle levers forward and the plane started to roll down the taxiway, toward the runway. In about two minutes, they were just short of the runway. Chris then set the brakes and revved up the engines. The plane shook from the vibration, and the flight engineer checked his dials to make sure all engines were in sync and running correctly.

Chuck then communicated to Chris, "Captain, everything looks fine with the engines. They're in sync and running smoothly."

"Thanks for the update, Chuck."

Chris radioed the tower.

"Akrotiri, this is Shackleton C224 ready for takeoff."

"Shackleton C224. This is Akrotiri. You're cleared for takeoff on runway two eight. The wind is out of the northwest at eight miles an hour."

"Roger Akrotiri. This is Shackleton C224 proceeding onto runway two eight for takeoff."

Chris moved the throttles forward slightly until the plane rolled onto the runway and was aimed down the concrete. He pushed the throttle controls way forward, and the aircraft proceeded down the runway. As soon as they had an air speed of approximately 120 mph, he pulled back on the control stick and the plane lifted off the ground.

When they had climbed to an altitude of 5,000 feet, he leveled the plane out and flew to the north over the Kyrenia Mountains. They proceeded out over the Mediterranean and, after they reached about twenty miles from Kyrenia, they turned eastward. They subsequently dropped down to a surveillance altitude of 1,000 feet. The flight plan called for them to cruise at 200 mph to conserve fuel and start flying the search pattern eastwards from Kyrenia to Cape Aspostolos Andreas. Once they passed the cape, they would head southwest towards Famagusta, Larnaca and Limassol. In other words, they would fly around Cyprus in a clockwise motion, about twenty miles from the shore. The Shackleton had a top speed of 300 mph and a maximum ceiling of 20,000 feet.

The twenty miles off coast search pattern was based on a complete circle around Cyprus that was about 400 miles in length or two hours of flying time, at 200 mph. They would fly approximately five times around Cyprus, before returning to base at 1800 hours.

As soon as they were at cruising speed and had started the search pattern, Chris suggested that Ian go up, through the cockpit, to the front of the plane. The bombardier used to be located there when the Shackleton was the Avro Lincoln bomber, during World War Two. From there, Ian would be able to obtain an excellent birds-eye view of the Mediterranean Sea and any suspicious ships that could be carrying arms. Ian climbed through the cockpit, past Chris and Bill, and crawled into the bombardiers spot, at the front of the plane. The bomb sight had long been removed, and Ian managed to get a great view as the plane proceeded on its search path. The noise from the four engines was reduced up front, but Ian still installed the headset so he could communicate with the pilot.

As they flew eastward, Ian saw a few fishing boats, but they did not look like smugglers. In the distance to the north, Ian could see a freighter on the horizon, but it was far enough away to be of little significance. When they reached Cape Andreas, they turned westward towards Famagusta, Limassol, Akrotiri and Paphos. Ian saw many fishing boats and two large vessels entering the Cyprus harbours. Ian reported to Chris over the headset what he saw, and he confirmed that they did not look suspicious. However, Chris had the Shackleton's radio signalman report each boat to Maritime headquarters, where they were plotted on a large board. If Maritime thought any one of them was suspicious, they would send a minesweeper to inspect them.

After one circuit of the island, Ian crept back into the main part of the plane, past Chris and Bill, and sat on the

111

jump seat by the flight engineer. Chris asked Bill to take over, and he turned around to talk with Ian.

"Are you by any chance related to James Black, the famous wing commander and ace pilot from World War Two?"

Ian responded, "Yes, in fact I am. He's my father, but obviously I was too young, during the war, to really know what was going on."

"When I was going through flight school, we heard a lot about some of the aces from the war and your father was one of them." Chris said. "Have you ever flown a plane?"

"When I was in my teens, my father, and a flight instructor friend of his, gave me some flying lessons in a de Havilland Chipmunk T10 trainer. I managed to solo in the plane, after I had twelve hours of flight time."

"Well that's great. After we've had our sack lunch, we'll let Bill take a rest, and you can take over flying this crate. He can go up in the front and be the observer."

They both ate their sack lunch, while Bill flew the Shackleton around the island for the second time. Today seemed a quiet day for sea traffic, and there was not much to report to Maritime. Ian did notice that the freighter, north of the island the first time around, was getting closer, the second time around. He mentioned it to Chris who didn't seem too disturbed, since it was still out several miles from Cyprus and their flight path.

During the third lap around the island, Bill gave the plane controls back to Chris and let Ian sit in his seat, while he ate his lunch. He then went to the front of the plane, as an observer. In a short while, Chris then suggested that Ian take hold of the controls to see how it felt.

As Ian took control of the stick, Chris said, "Okay, she's all yours. Keep her straight and level. The flight engineer will keep an eye on the four engines for you."

"This isn't as hard, as I thought it would be, to fly a large four engine plane like the Shackleton," Ian responded, after handling the large plane for a few minutes.

"Keep it at about an altitude of 1,000 feet. This'll allow us to see as far as thirty-eight miles to the horizon, depending on the haze and clouds," Chris requested.

Ian complied, using a combination of the altimeter, artificial horizon and visual flight conditions.

Chris continued, "Ian, keep flying easterly toward Cape Andreas, at a bearing of sixty-two degrees. That will keep us about twenty miles off shore."

Ian made some slight adjustments and proceeded to handle the plane, almost like an experienced Shackleton pilot. In thirty minutes or so, Bill, who was up front, came on the communications system.

"Hey chaps, there's a freighter ahead, and it looks a little suspicious to me. It appears to be heading for the Cape Andreas area. I think we should drop down and take a closer look.

Ian responded, "It looks like the same freighter I saw on the first two laps around the island. Do you think it could have arms on board?"

Chris replied, "Maybe, but that will be up to a Royal Navy minesweeper to determine. They will need to stop and board it."

Chris then asked Bill, "Are you comfortable up there in the front and would it be safe enough if I drop down to 200 feet, to get a closer look?"

"It's okay with me," Bill said. "You can go down to 100 feet if you want, since it'll give me even a closer look at the vessel."

"Okay, Ian, I'm taking over, and we'll drop down to 100 feet, to obtain a good look at this vessel. Chuck, keep a good look on the performance of the engines. We don't want to have any problems at that low an altitude. Bill, keep me informed about what you see and any potential problems. Derek, get operations on the line and tell them we are going down to 100 feet, to obtain a good look at a suspicious ship, nearing Cape Andreas."

Chris then eased forward on the control stick and reduced the speed of the plane down to 140 miles an hour. This was high enough above the stall speed of eighty-eight mph and low enough to allow Bill to get a fairly good observation on the target. Soon they were flying just 100 feet off the surface of the shimmering, blue Mediterranean.

In a couple of minutes, they flew close to the ship, and Bill, after using his binoculars, communicated, "Based on the stern, the ship is called the CRETEUS and it's out of Beirut, Lebanon. However, there are men scurrying around covering up cargo on the deck with tarps. It looks very suspicious. I recommend that it be called in to Maritime headquarters, and we should make one more pass over it, going the length of the ship."

"Bill, do you believe that it's worthwhile to go over again?" Chris asked.

"Yes, I want to get another look at what they are trying to cover up with those tarps."

"Okay Bill, you're the one with the best observation point. I'm turning around for another run at the ship. Here we go."

"Chuck, do the engines look okay?" Chris asked the flight engineer.

"Yes. All four are performing according to spec. You should be alright" replied Chuck.

Chris turned the plane around and came up to the stern of the vessel, in order to fly the length of it.

Suddenly, Bill in the front screamed into the plane's communications system, "Pull up; pull up!"

Chris pulled back on the stick as he pushed the throttles forward, but it was too late. Bullets from a machine gun mounted on the bow of the ship Creteus struck the plane, hitting Bill and Chris. Bill had seen the gun, but not in time to give a warning. He was hit by two bullets and was either unconscious or dead. Chris had been hit by one bullet and was not in condition to fly the plane.

Ian, who was still seated in the 2nd pilot's seat, took over the plane. He increased the speed of the plane and pulled back on the stick, climbing to 3,000 feet.

"Chuck, are you okay? How are the engines operating?" Ian asked the flight engineer.

"I'm fine and the engines seem to be operating normally." Chuck replied

"Good. Keep an eye on them, and let me know if there's any change. Can you get the crewmen trained in first aid up here right away? We need to take care of Chris and Bill."

Immediately, Chuck got on the aircraft communication system, "Any of you in the rear who are trained in first aid, get up here fast to help the Chris and Bill.

One of the navigators and the radar operator came up to the cockpit with a first aid kit. First, they attended to Chris who was still semi-conscious, but bleeding profusely from his stomach. They patched him up the best they could and gave him a sedative to help ease the pain.

They then went forward to check on Bill, who was not conscious. He was still alive, but was bleeding from his left leg and a chest wound. They placed a tourniquet on his leg and bandaged the chest wound, to slow the loss of blood. They then moved him carefully through the cockpit and placed him on a stretcher, in the rear of the plane.

Ian gave an order to the radio operator, "Derek, send a message to operations telling them what happened and that we're returning to Akrotiri ASAP. Also, request that they send a plane to meet us and help me land this aircraft. Then patch me in to the control tower at Akrotiri?"

"Ian, I've sent a message to operations and you can get the Akrotiri tower on 122.1 Mcs. Chuck can help you change frequency on the radio, if you need his assistance."

Ian then asked for the other navigator to come on the communications system.

"Donald, this is Ian in the cockpit. Can you give me a bearing to get us back to Akrotiri?"

"Yes", Donald responded. "I calculate that, from this location, the bearing to Akrotiri is 240 degrees."

Ian quickly turned the plane onto the desired course to get them back to the airfield.

Since Ian had used a radio in the Chipmunk T10, he needed no assistance to dial in the tower frequency.

"Akrotiri, this is a Lt. Ian Black of the Intelligence Corps calling from Shackleton C224, with a dire emergency. We need permission to land as soon as we approach the airfield. Both the pilot and 2nd pilot are incapacitated, and I need assistance in landing this aircraft. We'll need an ambulance and fire equipment, waiting for us when we land."

"Shackleton C224, what's your current location? We're scrambling a plane to meet you and help you come in."

"Akrotiri, we've just come around Cape Andreas and are headed for the airfield. We're at 3,000 feet, airspeed 200 mph and on a heading of 240 degrees. Our approximate location is twenty miles east of Famagusta, and we should be near Akrotiri in approximately twenty five minutes."

"Shackleton C224. We've sent a Hawker Hunter in your direction and it should find you shortly. Lieutenant, what experience do you have flying a Shackleton?"

"Akrotiri. I've had one hour of flying time on the Shackleton today, that's it."

The two air traffic controllers in the tower looked at each other, shook their heads and thought, "*Oh, shit, this is going to be hairy!*"

Ian continued, "However, I've had a few hours on a Chipmunk T10 trainer. The flight engineer, who is unharmed, is helping me keep the engines running smoothly and in sync. Has Maritime been warned about this vessel the Creteus? It must be stopped and boarded. It appears to be carrying arms, and it also attacked one of Her Majesty's planes."

"Shackleton C224. Maritime has been informed of the situation and a minesweeper is headed at full speed to Cape Andreas to stop and board the freighter."

By now, Ian was sweating from the strain of being responsible for the lives of ten crewmen on the aircraft. He thought to himself, *"I can't fail them and I have to get this plane down in one piece."*

A few minutes later, a Hawker Hunter came along side the Shackleton and the pilot nicknamed, The Badger, signaled to Ian with a thumbs up. The Badger then came on the radio, "Lieutenant Black, how are you doing? Follow me and I'll lead you in to the Akrotiri airfield."

"Badger, I'm doing alright. I'm going to land this aircraft safely, with your assistance. I'll follow you in. I understand the stall speed is about ninety mph. The flight engineer will keep us above that speed, until the last moment when our wheels are about to touch down."

At that moment, Ian could see the town of Famagusta below, so he figured they had about sixty miles to go to reach the airfield. He also noticed a Royal Navy minesweeper was going at full speed toward the Cape Andreas area. Ian followed the Hawker Hunter toward the RAF airfield at Akrotiri.

"Ian, this is Badger. As we approach Akrotiri, you'll need to drop down to an altitude of about 800 feet and reduce your speed to 120 mph. The wind is still out of the northwest, so you'll be landing on runway two eight. I'll lead you in on the glide path to the runway, but when I wiggle my wings, you'll be on your own to actually land the Shackleton. After I wiggle my wings, I'll peel off, go around and land behind you. We'll keep communicating through the entire process, and Akrotiri tower will be on the same frequency. They also have an expert Shackleton pilot in the tower to help you, as needed."

"Thanks for your guidance, Badger. It's good to know you're there and that there'll be an experienced Shackleton pilot in the tower. I will need both of you." Ian responded still sweating.

Ian then got on the aircraft communications system. "Hey you chaps back there, what's the current condition of Chris and Bill?"

The radar operator replied. "They're both doing alright, considering their wounds. Chris is conscious, but Bill is still unconscious and his pulse is weak. However, I believe both of them will make it."

Ian responded, "Keep me abreast on any changes to their conditions. I've asked for an ambulance to meet this plane, when we land."

When they were about ten miles out from the airfield, Badger contacted the tower, "Akrotiri, this is Hawker Hunter F231 followed by Shackleton C224. We're about ten miles out and request final landing instructions."

"Hunter F231. This is the tower at Akrotiri. The wind is out of the northwest at four mph. Use runway two eight. All traffic is being kept away from the immediate area. You're both free to land."

"Akrotiri. This is F231. We're preparing to land. Ian did you hear that message from the tower?"

"Yes I did, Badger. Akrotiri, may I speak to the Shackleton pilot on hand? I need to know where the landing gear and flap controls are located on this aircraft."

"Lieutenant Black, this is Flight Lieutenant Thistle the Shackleton pilot. The controls for the landing gear and the flaps are located in the centre console to your left. Don't forget the Shackleton, you're flying, does not have a tricycle gear. First, select the LANDING GEAR DOWN switch. Wait until all three lights, by the switch, turn green. Then your gear will be down. One of the lights is for the tail wheel and the other two are for the wheels stored in the wings. Don't forget the gear will cause drag and will reduce your speed."

"Roger, tower, I've got that. All three lights are now green. How about extending the flaps?"

"Okay, extend the flaps fifty percent using the control in the console. When you put your flaps down, the speed of the aircraft will change, but you'll be able to land at a slower speed without stalling."

"Thanks Akrotiri. I'm extending the flaps fifty percent, and I'm ready to land. The flight engineer is going to help keep us above the stall speed, until the last moment. I see the runway in the distance, and I'm following Badger in F231 down the glide slope."

"Ian, this is Badger. Follow me down. We're lined up with runway two eight. Reduce your speed to about 120 mph."

"Okay, Badger. I see the runway clearly now and am following you down at 120 mph."

"Shackleton C224. This is Akrotiri, Thistle speaking. Now extend your flaps fully to one hundred percent and hold your speed above the stall speed of 90 mph. When your main wheels touch down on the runway, pull back on the throttles to cut your speed and basically you will go into a stalled landing. Then your tail wheel will make contact. Slow the aircraft down with the foot brakes and come to a halt. The airfield is cleared of all traffic. As soon as you stop, we'll be there with an ambulance and emergency vehicles."

"Roger, Akrotiri. I understand the instructions," Ian answered, sweating profusely.

When the Shackleton reached about 100 feet above the runway, Badger wiggled his wings and peeled away, leaving Ian a clear view of the runway fast approaching.

Ian shouted at Chuck, "Reduce the speed to 100 mph."

"100 mph it is, Ian."

Ian approached runway two eight and, when the landing gear was ten feet off the runway, shouted, "Reduce speed to ninety mph."

"Ninety mph it is," Chuck answered.

At this moment, the main landing wheels touched down on the runway. The plane bounced and shuddered, but Ian managed to keep it going down the runway with the rudders. He then pulled back on the throttles, the tail wheel touched down and he applied the foot brakes. He steered the aircraft with the stick, which was connected to the rear wheel.

Ian slowed down the plane, pulled off the active runway and stopped on the taxiway. This allowed F231 to land on the same runway, which Badger did a couple of minutes later.

The ambulance and fire trucks pulled up a few seconds after Ian stopped the plane. Ian asked Chuck to shut down three of the four engines. The crew opened the rear doors and the medics in the ambulance came on board to take care of Mullins and Jones. They were both still alive, and the medics placed them in the ambulance to take them to the hospital.

Ian called the tower, "Request permission to taxi the Shackleton C224 to the aircraft parking area.

"Akrotiri tower. Lieutenant Black, a job well done. Yes, you may taxi to the Shackleton parking area. Just follow the Land Rover that's coming up right now, to lead you to the required spot."

When the Land Rover appeared in front of the plane's nose, Ian applied some power to the one engine still running and followed the vehicle to the assigned parking spot. Ian then had Chuck cut the last engine and he sat for a few moments to recover his composure,.

He then got up out of his seat and went to exit the plane. The crew was already lined up outside the rear door and, when Ian appeared, gave him a big cheer. Then individually, each crew member went up to Ian, shook his hand and thanked him for a job well done.

They all walked into the Operations building and went to a conference room for a debriefing by the wing commander. The Hawker Hunter pilot, Badger, who had also landed by then, walked into the room, to assist in the debriefing.

The wing commander was satisfied with the way the whole operation had been handled and thanked Lieutenant Black for getting everyone down safely. He then asked everyone to leave, except Ian.

After the crew and Badger left, the wing commander personally thanked Ian for his performance and stated that he would send a congratulatory letter to his boss, Colonel Baker.

"You know Mr. Black. If it wasn't for the fact that Colonel Baker would not be appreciative, I'd make you an offer to join the RAF." He then invited Ian to join him and Badger in the Officers' Club, for a drink.

As they entered the club, Badger was already there with a bottle of Glenlivet, single malt scotch. He poured the scotch, neat, into three glasses and then gave Ian a *slap on the back,* saying, "Well done, old chap." They all sipped their drinks and chatted about the day's events. When the drinks were finished, Ian said his goodbyes. He left the club and went to find his car outside the Operations centre. He climbed into it and headed back to Salisbury House in Nicosia.

Since it was still fairly early, he sat down in his room and started to write a report on his Shackleton surveillance flight. After about an hour, he found that the stress of the day had taken its toll, and he realized that he was exhausted, so he went to bed.

When he woke up the next morning, he thought about his experiences of the previous day and how lucky he had been to survive. He completed the report on the flight and then went to Captain Phillips's office to submit it.

He knocked on his door and waited for the captain to answer.

"Come in," said the captain.

Ian opened the door, saluted and said, "Sir, I've finished the report covering my activities on the Shackleton surveillance flight."

He laid it on the captain's desk and waited for a response.

The captain replied with a stern look, "Thank you for the timely report. I'll look at it later. First, I want to know what you were doing piloting a Shackleton. Had you been checked out on one? Do you realize you could have killed everyone on board, including yourself?"

Ian responded gravely, "Well, sir, it was like this............"

The captain held up hand and said, "Stop. I don't want any excuses."

Ian started again to answer him, "Sir, I didn't have any choice. Both the pilot and 2nd pilot were shot and wounded, and were not in a position to fly the aircraft. I had to take over, or as you said, we may all have died. Luckily, the pilot had let me fly the plane for about an hour, before the crisis happened. It's all in the report, sir."

The captain looked at Ian and started to smile, "Mr. Black, I've already received a verbal report on your activities, from the wing commander at Akrotiri and a pilot named "Badger". I understand you acted in a way that reflects very positively on this organization. In fact, I believe the wing commander offered you a job, but you were smart enough to turn it down. In future, please be more careful on these types of activities. The colonel and I don't want to lose you.

"I understand what you're saying, and I'll try not to get into any more trouble," Ian said, smiling.

"Good" answered the captain. "Thank you for the report and I'll read later. Good day, Ian."

Ian saluted, turned and left the captain's office, thinking *"Well, he didn't chew me out too much."*

He went down for lunch and met John, who also had heard about his flying skills.

Ian thought, *"The problem with working here is that nothing is secret. Everyone seems to know what you are doing before you have time to write a report."*

After he'd finished his lunch, Ian went back to his room and called Aphrodite, at the hospital.

The hospital operator answered the phone.

"May I talk with Nurse Aphrodite Palas?" he asked.

"She's busy at the moment, sir. May I give her a message?"

"Yes. This is Ian Black. Would you ask her to call me when she has an opportunity? She has my number."

"Certainly, sir," answered the hospital operator.

12

Getting To Know Each Other

In the late afternoon, Aphrodite received the message and returned Ian's call. He was in his room relaxing and reading a book on the troubles in the Middle East.

"Lieutenant Black speaking," Ian answered, as he picked up the telephone.

"Hello Ian, this is Aphrodite. I'm returning your call. By the way, thanks again for the dinner at the Naples Restaurant the other night. I really enjoyed it and our time together."

"You're welcome. I called to see if you were interested in going to the cinema tomorrow night. There's a new film out called "Gigi" with Leslie Caron and Maurice Chevalier. I've heard it's very good. The soundtrack is in English, but there are Greek subtitles. I'm not sure what the supporting film is, but it's probably B rated," Ian said nervously, hoping she wouldn't' turn him down.

"Yes, that would be very nice. Thank you for inviting me. What time does it start and at which cinema is it showing?"

"It's being shown at the Astral Theatre, on the west side of Nicosia, and the early show starts at five o'clock. It ends around eight, and we could go for a bite to eat afterwards, if you're interested."

"That sounds great. Is it safe to go to a crowded cinema?" she asked.

"The Astral is owned by an Englishman, and there's plenty of security there." Ian responded.

"How about if I meet you outside at 4:30?" she asked.

"That would be super. It's been nice talking to you again. See you tomorrow at 4:30," Ian replied. He then went back to reading his book, humming to himself.

The next afternoon, Ian arrived at the Astral Theatre, before the agreed upon time, and purchased two tickets for the back row, in the main section of the cinema. He waited outside for Aphrodite, but at 4:30, she hadn't shown up. He started to wonder if she had decided not to come or had a problem of some kind.

Then, at 4:35, a taxi pulled up and out stepped Aphrodite, dressed in a white blouse and a full red skirt. Ian couldn't believe his eyes; she was stunning. All the chaps around him looked at her, as she walked over to Ian.

"Sorry I'm late," she said, "but the taxi didn't arrive at my house on time, and the traffic was bad."

"That's okay," he said with a smile. "It gave me time to purchase the tickets."

They walked into the theatre and sat down in the back row. There were already quite a few young couples sitting in the back, waiting for the lights to go down. The film started and halfway through Aphrodite reached over and took Ian's hand. Many of the couples around them were kissing and did not see the film. When it ended, they all got up and walked out of the theatre, just as the sun was setting in a red glow.

"That was a great film, and I especially liked the music. Leslie Caron is a very talented actress," Aphrodite said.

"Yes, it was smashing. It will probably win some kind of award." Ian replied, and then asked her, "How about getting something to eat?"

"Yes please. I am somewhat hungry," she answered.

125

"I know just the place. It's called the Devon Café, and it's just around the corner."

They walked for a few minutes and soon they were outside the café, looking at the menu pasted on the outside window.

"Does it look okay to you?" Ian asked her.

"Yes, it seems like they have all kinds of food."

They went in and sat down at a free table. They studied the menu, and soon the waitress came over to take their orders. The food arrived fairly quickly. As they ate their meal, they discussed the day's events.

Aphrodite told Ian, "I had two wounded soldiers brought in yesterday."

"How did they get their wounds?" Ian asked.

"I'm not sure, but I understand an army convoy was ambushed near Larnaca. At least, no one was killed."

When they finished eating, they ordered some coffee and, as they were drinking it, Ian asked Aphrodite, "Are you free next Saturday, because my CO, Colonel Baker, is holding a party at this house, for some friends, and those of us who work for him. There will only be about seven or eight of us, and we are allowed to bring a wife or friend. If you met remember, you met the colonel briefly, at the Government House garden party earlier this month."

"I'll have to check my schedule, but I believe I'm off duty that day. Are you sure it'll be alright for me to come?"

"Of course, I'm sure, you'll fit right in. Both the colonel and Captain Phillips are great chaps. The colonel is married and I believe the captain's wife died in a car accident some time ago, but you can be sure he'll have someone on his arm."

"I'll let you know Monday, if I'm free." Aphrodite responded.

Ian paid the bill, and ordered two taxis. They walked outside the Devon into the clear, dark evening sky and waited for the cabs to arrive. The first one arrived, and Ian gave Aphrodite a quick kiss on her cheek and then her lips. She did not resist. He opened the taxi door and helped her in saying, "Please call me about your schedule. Thanks for coming." He closed the door and the taxi took off.

A couple of minutes later, Ian's taxi came by and he had the driver take him back to the safe house across the road from Salisbury House. As they cab was taking him there, Ian thought, "*I hope she can make it Saturday.*"

The next morning, as he was getting ready for the day, his phone rang.

"Ian, this is Aphrodite. I've checked my schedule and next Saturday is part of my three days off. If you're sure it's okay, I would love to go with you, to your CO's party."

"Of course, it'll be alright. I'm glad you can make it. I'll call you tomorrow, and let you know the time of the party and the address. "

"Call me at the hospital before ten o'clock, as I get off duty then. I look forward to your call."

The next day, after Ian had checked with Colonel Baker about the time of his party, he called Aphrodite at the hospital an hour, before she went off duty.

The operator answered the call, "This is the BMH. May I be of assistance?"

Ian answered, "I'd like to speak with Nurse Aphrodite Palas."

"One minute please. I'll put you through to her."

"This is Nurse Palas. How may I help you?"

"Hello Aphrodite. This is Ian. The party at Colonel Baker's house begins at four o'clock and will end about eight. For security reasons, he doesn't want anyone to arrive by taxi. Therefore, if it's okay with you, I'll pick you up in a car and take you there."

"That'll be fine, Ian. At some point I have to tell you where I live anyway. My mother will be working that day, so I'll have to introduce you to her some other time."

"What is your address?" Ian asked

"It's number 16 Kapella Street on the north side of town, and not far from the main road that goes to Kyrenia. What time will you be here, so I can make sure I'm ready?"

Ian responded, "How about if I pick you up at 4:30? That'll give us plenty of time, even with the Saturday afternoon traffic, to reach the colonel's house located on the west side of Nicosia by 5:00."

"That sounds great. I'll see you then. I'm looking forward to meeting your CO and the others you work with. Goodbye for now."

They both hung up, and Ian went back to work.

****

On Saturday, Ian asked Captain Phillips, "Will it be alright to use a vehicle out of the motor pool to pick Aphrodite up and then later return her home?"

Captain Phillips replied, "This once will be okay, but don't make a habit of it."

Later that afternoon, Ian drove out to Aphrodite's home on Kapella Street, to pick her up. He found her single story home, in a neat middle class neighborhood with manicured front gardens. He walked up to the front door and rang the bell.

In about thirty seconds the door opened and there stood Aphrodite. He was floored by her appearance and couldn't believe how beautiful she looked. She was wearing a light, blue, flowered summer dress with dark blue shoes and a shiny gold ribbon in her long black hair.

"I'm ready," she said, as she walked out the door and closed it. She took Ian's arm and gave him a short kiss on the cheek, as they walked to the car.

He opened the door of the car and helped her in. Closing her door, Ian walked briskly around to the driver's door, as he smiled to himself thinking, *"Boy, she looks fabulous."*

They drove around the outside of the old walled city of Nicosia and ended up on the west side, where the colonel's house was located. It was a large two story home, in an area of similar homes that appeared to have large gardens.

Ian parked in front of the house, opened Aphrodite's door and helped her out. They both walked up to the front door, and Ian rang the bell.

As they did so, Ian said, "By the way, Aphrodite, please don't ask too many questions about the work we do. It isn't wise to look too inquisitive."

"Okay Ian, I'll remember that."

The front door opened and the colonel's wife was standing there. She was a very attractive blond, probably in her middle thirties, Ian guessed.

Smiling she said, "Please come in. Some of the guests have already arrived. I'm Stephanie, Colonel Baker's wife."

Ian responded, "I'm Lieutenant Ian Black and this is Aphrodite Palas."

Stephanie replied with a smile, "I'm glad to meet you both. Aphrodite, you're gorgeous. You'd better watch out for the men around here. Come on back, we're in the rear garden, playing croquet."

She led them back through the house and entered the garden, through double French doors.

"Ladies and Gentlemen," Stephanie announced. "This is Ian Black and Aphrodite Palas, in case you haven't met either of them."

They all came over and shook hands with both of them. Captain Phillips, who was there with a long haired, strawberry blond British woman, came up to Ian and whispered, "Ian, where did you find her? She's beautiful." He continued, "Oh, now I remember, she was at the Government House party."

They all started to play croquet again. Ian and Aphrodite joined in. A waiter, the Baker's had hired, served wine and hard liquor, for those that wanted it.

As soon as everyone had arrived, Stephanie came to the double French doors, clapped her hands to get everyone's attention and announced, "Okay, everyone, it's time to eat. There's a buffet set out in the kitchen, and you can eat outside, on the tables in the garden.

After the meal, Colonel Baker came up to Aphrodite, who was separated from Ian for a moment, and said, "Do you know how lucky you are, to have Ian here today? He had to fly a four engine plane last week, when the pilots were incapacitated."

Aphrodite gasped and said, "Sir, he never told me that."

"Well I shouldn't have either. We don't talk too much about our jobs, outside the office. I can tell you he did an excellent job bringing the plane in safely, with several men on board. Let's leave it at that."

Ian then came over to join them, and the talk quickly changed to the latest cricket scores between England and India.

At around eight o'clock, the party wrapped up and people started to leave. Ian and Aphrodite thanked and bade farewell to the colonel and his wife. They walked to the car, where Ian opened the door and helped Aphrodite in.

They drove back to her house on Kapella Street and parked in front. Aphrodite reached over and gave Ian a lingering kiss on the lips.

"That's for coming back safely," she said. "Colonel Baker told me about how you flew a plane last week."

Ian blushed slightly and said, "I was only doing my duty. I'm sorry I can't tell you more."

Aphrodite replied, "Well, whatever you do, please be careful. I don't want to lose you."

"Aphrodite, there's a CSE (Combined Services Entertainment) revue being held next Friday at RAF Nicosia, and I can probably obtain some tickets, if you'd be interested. I hear Harry Secombe, Nancy Whiskey and David Whitfield will be there. Would you like to go?"

"I'd love to, if I'm off duty, which I believe I am."

"I'll call you on Monday to confirm, if that's okay?" Ian asked.

"Of course, please call me at the hospital."

She gave him another kiss and said, "I'd better go inside."

Ian came around to the passenger door and let her out. He walked her to the front door, and she opened it. She turned to say goodnight, and, before she could say anything, Ian gave her a long kiss. Then he said, "Thanks for going to the party. It meant a lot to me."

"It was my pleasure," she said. "See you soon." She then vanished into the house and the door closed.

Ian went back to the car, whistling, and drove back to Salisbury House.

****

On Monday morning, Ian called Aphrodite at the hospital, to inquire about whether she could go to the CSE revue that Friday. The operator told him she wasn't in yet, but was expected in by ten o'clock.

Later that morning, Aphrodite called Ian.

"This is Lieutenant Ian Black"

"Hello Ian, This is Aphrodite. If the offer still stands, I'd love to go to the CSE revue. It sounds exciting. I've always wanted to see Harry Secombe and David Whitfield. David has such a great tenor voice and sings "Cara Mia" so well."

"That's great, I'm so glad you can come. The show starts at 7:00 and will last about two hours. I suggest, therefore, we get a small bite to eat, before we go. There's a small café fairly close to the Nicosia Airport, where we can have dinner. Because of security, I cannot drive a car onto the base, so I suggest we go by taxi It will drop us off at the gate, and we can walk to the hangar, where the show will take place."

"What time will you pick me up?"

"How about five o'clock? That will give us time to eat and get to the show. I'll have the tickets ahead of time. Make sure you bring your BMH ID card, so there is no question about you gaining entry."

On Friday afternoon, Ian called for a taxi to pick him up at the safe house across the street from Salisbury House.

"Take me to #16 Kapella Street," Ian said to the driver in Greek.

The driver took off, and after about fifteen minutes, ended up in front of #16. Ian told the driver to wait, as he exited the taxi, and went to the door. He rang the bell, and almost immediately Aphrodite came out and closed it.

"She sure knows how to dress." Ian thought. *She looks fabulous again.*

"Aphrodite. You look exquisite. You have outstanding taste in clothes." Ian said, smiling at her.

She was wearing a medium, yellow colored dress and had on dark yellow shoes. Her long black hair was fixed in a pony tail with a yellow ribbon, holding it in place. She carried a thin white jacket, in case it became a little chilly in the hangar. Ian doubted she would need it, but didn't say anything.

He helped her into the taxi and told the driver in Greek to take them to the Olympic Café, near the airport.

"Aphrodite, I've heard that the Olympic Café offers a variety of food and the service is quick."

"That sounds good, Ian. I 'm looking forward to the show and I'd hate to miss any of it."

The taxi arrived at the café and Ian helped Aphrodite out. They entered and were immediately shown to a table. The waitress came by and took their orders.

Ian said to Aphrodite, "I understand the seats we have are close to the front so we should have a good view of all the performers."

Aphrodite replied, "I've always wanted to see Harry Secombe and David Whitfield, and I can't believe I'm finally going to see them both at one concert."

The waitress came with their food and they started to eat.

After they had finished, Ian paid the bill and had the cashier order him a taxi. It soon arrived and Ian had it take them to the RAF Nicosia gate. Ian asked the taxi driver to stop by the gate at 9:15 to take them back. He agreed he would, but Ian wondered if they would see him again.

They got out and walked to the gate, which was guarded by two RAF military policemen, armed with Sterling SMGs.

"May we see your passes, please?" one of them asked. The other one was eyeing Aphrodite up and down, as though he was undressing her.

Ian showed the guard his Intelligence Corps identification card and Aphrodite's BMH card.

The guard nodded and said, "Thank you sir. You may go in. I assume you're going to the revue."

"Yes that's correct. Is it in that hangar over there?" Ian asked pointing to a large hangar to the left, where there seemed to be a line of people.

"Yes, that's it. I hope you have a great time, sir."

Ian and Aphrodite walked into RAF Nicosia and towards the hangar.

As they did, the one guard whispered to the other, "Man, she was beautiful. The officers always seem to get the good lookers."

Ian and Aphrodite entered the hangar and were shown to their seats by an airman.

Harry Secombe started the show with some jokes and singing. Next, some good looking dancers from the UK came out and strutted around. Then came Nancy Whiskey with Chris McDevitt and she sang "Freight Train" amongst other songs. After them, Yana appeared and sang a few songs.

Finally, David Whitfield came on stage and sang Cara Mia, his signature tune, together with some other hits. At the end of the show, they all came out and sang for the audience, some British patriotic songs such as "Land of Hope and Glory".

After the show ended, Ian and Aphrodite walked off the base passing two new MPs. To Ian's surprise, the taxi driver was waiting for them. He helped Aphrodite into the rear of the cab, and then went around and entered the other door.

"#16 Kapella Street, please" Ian said to the driver.

Soon they arrived at Aphrodite's home, and they both got out. Ian asked the driver to wait.

He walked Aphrodite up the graveled pathway to the front door.

"Thank you for taking me. I enjoyed it tremendously and all the acts were great."

Aphrodite gave Ian a long lingering kiss and held him. Ian placed his arms around her and kissed her back. Ian couldn't believe the aroma coming from her perfume. It was heavenly.

"Aphrodite, next Thursday I'm coming to the hospital to visit with a Fl. Lt Mullins and a Fl. Lt. Jones. They have both been in there three weeks, recovering from some wounds."

"Yes Ian, I'm aware of them. Why are you visiting two RAF officers? Do you know them from England?"

"No, I just ran into them one time, and I heard they had been hurt by machine gun bullets. I just wanted to check to see how they're doing. If you're on duty, I'll look you up, while I'm there."

"Maybe I'll see you Thursday. Thanks again for the evening. I really enjoyed it," Aphrodite said.

With that she gave him one more kiss and then went inside.

Ian walked back to the waiting cab and had the driver take him back to the safe house, across the street from Salisbury House.

****

Three weeks after Ian's experience on the Shackleton flight, he decided it was time to visit Mullins and Jones in the BMH Nicosia. Initially, they were patients at the RAF hospital Akrotiri, but, since it was a temporary facility and available care was limited, they were transferred to Nicosia, as soon as feasible, without endangering their lives.

Ian drove to the BMH, which was only a short distance from Salisbury House, and parked in a visitor's parking spot. He entered the Reception Building and asked where he could find Flight Lieutenants Christopher Mullins and William Jones of RAF Akrotiri. After the receptionist looked in her book, she directed Ian to Ward C-4. The ward was quite a walk from reception, since the BMH was a spread out complex of many single story buildings. Finally, he arrived at the Ward C-4 building and entered, to find a matronly looking nurse guarding the door into the main part of the Ward.

"What do you want, Mr. Black?" she snapped, as she glanced at his name tag. "I'm in charge here today, since we're short of nurses."

Ian glanced at her name tag before he answered, "Captain Crachett, ma'am. I'm here to see Fl. Lt. Mullins and Fl. Lt. Jones."

"Well, Mr. Black. I've heard a few things about you, and you'd better not cause any trouble, while you're visiting them."

"Yes, ma'am, I'll try to behave myself. May I go in now?"

"Yes, you may, but be as quiet as possible, since some of the patients need plenty of rest."

With that, Ian went through the two, swinging doors into the ward to find Mullins and Jones. He walked down the ward and located them in the far right corner. Mullins was reading a book and Jones was snoozing away. Both of them seemed to have good color in their faces, which was a good sign.

Ian walked up to Mullins bed and asked with a smile, "How are you doing Chris? You look like you're getting your health back."

"I'm doing fine and should be out of here within a week.

"That's great. How's Bill doing? I don't want to wake him."

"He was in worse shape than me, but he's recovering. He'll probably be here another two weeks, according to the doctor who came around earlier."

"I'm glad to hear that. I've been worried about you two, since the incident."

Chris responded, "I'm glad you came by. I wanted to thank you for saving us and the crews lives. I understand you did an excellent job flying that four engine beast of a plane."

"Well, the one hour lesson you gave me sure helped. I don't think I could have managed it without that training experience and the flight engineer controlling the engines for me. Also, the pilot in the tower and Badger sure helped us get down in one piece."

"Again, I wanted to thank you for all of us. Maybe when I get out of here, we can meet for a drink somewhere," Chris replied.

"That sounds like a good idea. Your wing commander said he'd offer me a job, but felt my superior would not appreciate that. He'd be correct in that situation. Give my regards to Bill and let him know I'm concerned about his health. Tell him I'll try to get back in a week, if he's still here."

"I'll do that. Thanks for coming by," said Chris.

With that Ian walked out of the ward, waving to Chris as he left. He went up to Captain Crachett, who was still guarding the ward doors.

"Thank you ma'am," Ian said, as he gave her a salute. She gave Ian a stern look. "You're welcome" she responded.

Ian then asked her, "Is Nurse Aphrodite Palas on duty today?"

"I don't know. You'd have to check at the main reception area," she replied with half a smile.

Ian thought to himself, as he walked out of the building, *"She can actually smile! Maybe there is hope yet, for this man's army."*

Ian walked back to the main reception area and asked the receptionist, as to whether Nurse Aphrodite Palas was on duty. It turned out that she was, and Ian asked the receptionist to page her. Little did Ian know that Aphrodite had talked with Mullins, who spilled the beans to her, about Ian flying the Shackleton. He told her how Ian had saved their lives and the rest of the crew on that fateful day, three weeks ago. This confirmed what Colonel Baker had told her at his garden party.

Aphrodite came to the reception area and found Ian sitting there reading a magazine.

"Ian," she said. "Why didn't you tell me you were in serious trouble three weeks ago?"

"What do you mean?" Ian asked.

Aphrodite responded, "Based on what Colonel Baker told me at his garden party and what Flight Lieutenant Mullins told me earlier today, I've a good idea what you did three weeks ago."

"Aphrodite, I'm sorry, but I can't talk about it."

"Ian, maybe you can't, but that doesn't appear to have stopped other people from talking."

"Please don't be angry with me."

"Ian, I'm not angry with you. I just don't want you getting hurt. I think I'm falling in love with you, and I want you to stay in one piece," she said, with a sweet smile.

"Aphrodite. I think I'm falling in love with you too."

They stood there for a few minutes, looking at each other lovingly.

Ian was the first to speak saying, "How would you like to go to Paphos on Saturday and visit the Roman and Greek ruins there? We could talk about all this on the way. I'll rent a car and drive there. It's about a two to three hour drive, depending on the traffic, but it'll be well worth it, and we'll have plenty of time to talk."

"I'd love to do that. Can you pick me up at 8:00 am, so we'll have plenty of time, when we get there? I've never been there, even though I have lived on Cyprus all my life." Aphrodite replied.

"The time sounds good to me. I'll be there at eight o'clock. I suggest you wear slacks, so we can climb around the ruins."

"I have to get back to work now," Aphrodite said, looking at her watch.

Ian gave her a quick kiss on the cheek and said, "See you early Saturday morning."

Ian climbed into the car and drove back to Salisbury House feeling good that both Mullins and Jones were well on the way to recovering from their wounds. Also, he felt thrilled that he and Aphrodite would be going to Paphos.

****

Ian rented a car early Saturday morning and drove out to Aphrodite's home. He knocked gently on the front door, as he didn't want to wake her mother, if she was at home in bed.

Aphrodite came to the door and opened it.

"Come on in," she said. "My mother is on duty at the hospital, and I'm almost ready."

Ian entered the home, and she led him into the living room.

"Stay here. I'll be back in a moment."

138

Aphrodite vanished and, in about two minutes, came back saying, "I'm ready now."

She was wearing a white blouse and red slacks, and was carrying a wide, straw brimmed hat to keep the sun off her head.

They left her home and climbed into Ian's rental car.

"We'll stop on the way, at a café for something to eat. I assume you haven't had any breakfast yet."

The route, they had to take, took them from Nicosia to Limassol and then on to Paphos. It was just less than one hundred miles, in total.

After about fifteen minutes, Ian saw a café that looked open and some people were already there. He pulled into the parking area and they went in to have a quick breakfast. After they finished eating, they proceeded toward Paphos.

On the way, Ian broke the security rules and told Aphrodite about his flight on the Shackleton. He did not tell her everything, but enough that she understood why he had to fly the plane back to Akrotiri. She had already heard a lot of it from Flight Lieutenant Mullins in the hospital, so most of it was not new.

"Ian, I'm glad you took me in your confidence. I know the risk you're taking, breaking the rules. My lips will be sealed forever. I'll not ask you to break them again. However, I hope you'll not take any unnecessary risks, in the future," Aphrodite said.

Ian drove on and finally reached Paphos. They toured The Odeon, a well preserved amphitheatre and then toured the Roman temple of Asclepius and the Adonis Baths.

Later, they went to lunch at a café located on the outskirts of Paphos. After they'd eaten, they went to the Agios Georheos Basilica, which was an ancient pilgrimage site. There were three early Christian Basilicas and a bath located here. Next, they went to the Ayios Neophytos Monastery that was in excellent condition and had stained glass windows. Finally they ended up at the House of

Dionysos, a second century Roman villa which was a ruin, except it contained several beautiful and colourful mosaic floors. These floors, which were in excellent condition, depicted several representations of Dionysos, who was the god of wine. The house was believed to belong to a member of the Roman ruling class.

By five o'clock, they were both tired and decided to return to Nicosia. On the way back, they stopped for dinner at a roadside restaurant.

While they were eating, Ian said, "Aphrodite, I have to go away next Thursday, and I won't be back until the following Monday.

"I hope you're not going on another one of those hair-raising flights." Aphrodite answered.

"No, I'm not, but, I'm sorry, I can't tell you where I'm going. However, if you're free the following Friday, the 29th I believe, would you like to go out to dinner and do so dancing? I'm not the greatest dancer, but perhaps you can teach me a step or two."

"That sounds like a good idea. Why don't you call me, when you get back from wherever you're going to? I believe I'll be off duty that Friday, but I'm not sure, until I check my schedule at the hospital. Again, I suppose you can't tell me where you're going."

"No, I'm sorry I can't."

"Well, please be careful. I want you to come back in one piece. I don't want to find you in a BMH ward again. I've really enjoyed today. It was great to see those Greek and Roman ruins. I never realized they existed close to where I have lived for twenty years. Thanks for taking me."

They got back into the car and finished the return trip to Nicosia. They arrived back at her home around eight o'clock, just as the sun was setting.

Ian got out of the car, walked around and helped Aphrodite get out of the passenger's seat. They walked up the pathway, to the front door.

"Thanks for going with me today. I can't wait until I see you again. I think I'm in love with you. In fact, I know I am."

"I feel the same way," she answered. "I look forward to the dinner and dance, you've suggested."

Ian held her close and gave her a long kiss. He felt her returning the favour and was thrilled that she felt the same way about him, as he felt about her.

"I'll do my best to come back in one piece. I'll call you, as soon as I get back."

Aphrodite then gave Ian a kiss and said "Take care."

She opened her front door, went inside and was gone. Aphrodite went to her bedroom and knelt at her bed. She didn't do this very often. She prayed that God would take care of Ian and bring him back to her, in one piece.

Ian drove the rental car back to Salisbury House, where he parked it. He couldn't turn it in until 8:00 am the next morning, since the rental office was closed.

13

Undercover in Beirut

Colonel Baker held his next staff meeting on Monday, the 18th of August, and besides the colonel, there were four people seated at the oval shaped, oak conference table. They were Captain Phillips, Lieutenant Black, Lieutenant Snell (fluent in Turkish) and Sergeant Bingham (signals expert). As usual, John, from MI6, sat in the corner.

The colonel opened the meeting, with a call for action.

"Gentlemen, I am receiving a lot of urgent requests from my boss, General Mastin, that we must be more active in the search for Grivas and the elimination of guns being smuggled into Cyprus. He told me there is a rumour coming out of London that the PM is seriously considering negotiating a "peace" treaty with Makarios. If we don't locate and apprehend Grivas, before a treaty is signed, we may lose the opportunity to make him pay for his crimes. In addition, if negotiations are started, we can expect the level of violence to increase, so that EOKA and Makarios can place pressure on the British Government. This will allow them to get the best of possible terms in the treaty. Does anyone have suggestions they want to submit?"

"Sir, I have three suggestions that might help us to achieve the required objectives," replied Ian.

"First, subject to your approval, I plan to go on the battle – class destroyer HMS *Agincourt* (D86) that is going to

Beirut, at the end of this week. They are going to Beirut to show the flag and support for President Eisenhower's Operation Blue Bat, and the American intervention in Lebanon that started last month. My goal would be to locate the source of arms, being smuggled into Cyprus. There is a large community of Greeks there, and some of them are probably sympathetic to the Enosis campaign. I've already discussed this briefly with Captain Errol Sinclair of the *Agincourt,* and he's willing for me to go along. The *Agincourt* is scheduled to leave Famagusta on Thursday, the 21st of August, at 1100 and arrive at Beirut at 1700. It will return on Monday, the 25th of August, arriving in Famagusta around 1500. Assuming you approve the trip, I plan to spend a considerable amount of time in the Greek communities, communicating with the locals, and trying to find out how the arm shipments are organized. With the 14,000 strong American forces in Lebanon, it should be fairly safe to conduct intelligence, in the Greek communities.

Second, next month, I'd suggest that we organize, with the 188th Radar and Searchlight Battery, a raid on EOKA hideouts in the Troodos Mountains, with the purpose of seizing some terrorists and any documents located there. The main objective would be to obtain intelligence as to where Grivas might be hiding out.

Finally, I've a few Greek Cypriot contacts in Nicosia, and I propose to visit many of the hangouts in the Nicosia old town, in order to obtain any information that I can. It might be dangerous, but I'm willing to take the risk. My goal is to find Grivas and get this emergency behind us, before the treaty is signed."

"Mr. Black, your suggestions on the surface sound good. Do you believe you can achieve results with all three? Isn't there a chance you might over extend yourself?

"Yes, that could be one of my faults, but I need to give myself firm objectives to achieve results, sir. Alexander conquered much of the known world, before he was thirty," Ian replied.

The colonel continued, "Well, never mind Alexander, just be careful about making commitments. Please develop a plan, with goals, actions, risks, etc., for each suggestion and pass it to Captain Phillips. He can then discuss them with me for approval. Does that sound good to you, captain?"

"Yes, sir," Captain Phillips replied.

Turning towards Ian, the captain continued. "Mr. Black, since the *Agincourt* leaves Thursday, the written plan should be submitted for the Beirut trip by Wednesday morning, so it can be approved in time for you to go. Can you accomplish that by then?"

"It'll be on your desk no later than Wednesday morning at 0830, captain," Ian responded.

The colonel then turned to the two new, part time members of the group.

"Mr. Snell, as your time permits, I'd like you to investigate the possibility of arms being shipped to the Turkish community, from Turkey. We don't want the Turkish Cypriots arming themselves, and then have a civil war on our hands. Can you do some intelligence work in the Turkish communities?"

Roger replied, "I believe I can do that. I've some Turkish contacts, and I'll see what I can find out."

"Good," the colonel answered.

Then looking at Sgt. Bingham, he asked, "Sergeant, can you monitor local Cypriot communications traffic to see if you can pick up anything that might lead us to Grivas?"

Then the colonel, turning around and looking at the man in the corner, added, "John, can you help us in this effort at Ayios Nikolaos?"

John replied, "I'll certainly help where I can, although we generally monitor only external electronic communication traffic."

The colonel looked around the table and asked, "Does anyone have anything else to add? If not, we'll meet again next week, same time."

With that the meeting ended, and Ian went back to his office to work on the three plans of action, he needed to generate. First, he worked on the plan, for investigating the Greek link in Beirut for arms smuggling to Cyprus. He finished it by late the next day and presented it for approval to Captain Phillips. The captain glanced at it and asked a few questions. He then told Ian that he would see Colonel Baker in the morning and get his approval. If there were any questions, they would call him.

The next morning, Ian received a call from Captain Phillips.

"Mr. Black, the colonel thought the plan of action you wrote was well written, and he hopes that you succeed in obtaining some good intelligence on your trip to Beirut. Your trip is herewith approved. Be careful there, as we'd not like to lose you. With the threat of civil war between the Christians and the Muslims, it could be dangerous for all Westerners. Nasser of Egypt is trying to stir up trouble and our friends, the Americans, are in the middle. Good luck."

"Thank you, sir, for the approval. As soon as I return early next week, I'll write a report on my activities in Beirut and submit it to you."

Ian then called Captain Sinclair of the HMS *Agincourt* and was lucky to reach him.

"Captain, this is Lieutenant Black of the Intelligence Corps. If your offer still stands, I appreciate the opportunity to travel on the *Agincourt,* when you head for Beirut, on Thursday. The trip has been approved by my CO, Colonel Baker. The purpose of my Beirut visit, as I mentioned the other day, is to find out the process used to collect, store and ship arms from Beirut to Cyprus, on board Greek owned Lebanese freighters."

"Mr. Black, we'll be glad to have you on board. Please be on the Navy dock in Famagusta at 1000 sharp on Thursday, as we'll cast off at exactly 1100. So don't be late."

"Yes, sir, I'll be there right on time," Ian answered.

With that, they both hung up the phones. Ian started work on the other two plans he had to come up with for approval. He booked his car for the drive to Famagusta on Thursday and prepared his clothes for the trip. These included some civvies that would make him look like a Greek sailor.

On Thursday morning, Ian rose fairly early, so that he could finish packing and get some breakfast. He went down to the breakfast room, and found Captain Phillips and John having breakfast together.

"May I join you?" Ian asked.

"Of course, you may," both men replied.

John mentioned to Ian, as they ate, "The Yanks are controlling the Beirut airport, harbor and other important public facilities. You should have no problem while you're there. They're keeping everything fairly peaceful, at least for the moment."

"Thanks for the information, John," Ian replied. Then turning to Captain Phillips, Ian said, "I'll be back next Monday and will submit a report by Wednesday evening on my activities in Beirut."

"I hope you have a productive trip. Just be careful, as we want you to come back, in one piece," responded the captain.

After breakfast, he said goodbye to the captain and John, picked up his bag from his room and headed down to the car pool. From Salisbury House he drove to Famagusta that was about 43 miles away or just over one hour by car. Arriving at the dock area, Ian showed his army ID card to the guard, parked the car and walked down the wharf, to where the HMS *Agincourt* was tied up. He walked up the

146

gangplank and presented his identification to the officer on duty, who was there to prevent unauthorized personnel coming on board.

"Welcome on board HMS *Agincourt*, lieutenant," said the duty officer. "Captain Sinclair would like to meet with you, as soon as it's convenient. You'll find him on the bridge. Also, you're assigned to share a cabin with Sub-lieutenant Barry Thistleburt, if you don't mind. There is a crew of over 250 on board and space is tight. One of the seamen here will take your bag to the cabin for you."

"Thanks. I'll go to the bridge immediately, to find Captain Sinclair."

Ian walked up the stairs to the bridge and found Captain Sinclair, sitting in a revolving captain's chair. He was surveying the actions of the crew, making preparations to cast off.

Ian saluted the captain saying, "Lieutenant Black reporting as requested, sir."

"Mr. Black, welcome on board the *Agincourt*," replied the captain. "We're glad to have you going with us. Perhaps, what you find out in Beirut will help make our job of patrolling around Cyprus easier and more predictable. We'll be casting off in less than one hour. It's about 107 nautical miles from Famagusta to Beirut. At a cruising speed of eighteen knots, we should make it in about six hours. This destroyer can go as fast as thirty-five knots, if we have to, but we cannot maintain that speed indefinitely. I believe you've been bunked in Sub-lieutenant Thistleburt's cabin." The captain added, with a smile, "He's a great fellow and I've heard that he doesn't snore too much. He can direct you to the officer's wardroom, where meals are served."

Soon, the HMS *Agincourt* was under way cruising eastwards towards Beirut, Lebanon. The Mediterranean Sea was fairly smooth and the afternoon sun glistened on the clear, blue water. After they were underway for about two hours, the captain had the destroyer's speed increased to over thirty knots. Ian could feel the increased vibrations and went up to the bridge to get a good view. He could get a feeling of what it would be like to chase a submarine, if there was one close by. The ship knifed through the water with ease. After about fifteen minutes at almost full speed, the captain had the ship's speed reduced back down to eighteen knots. After about five and one-half hours at sea, they started to get close to Beirut and Ian went back up to the bridge, to obtain a good view of the city.

In the 1950s, Lebanon was considered the Switzerland or Paris of the Middle East, depending on one's point of view. It only had problems towards the end of that decade with the influx of more Arabs that upset the demographic balance. President Eisenhower decided to prevent a civil war by sending in the US Marines and other troops in July 1958. Beirut was the indeed the shimmering city and "Paris" of the Middle East.

Soon, the HMS *Agincourt* was tying up in Beirut harbour, alongside some American ships, of the Sixth Fleet. It was almost exactly 1700, the scheduled arrival time. After changing into civvies, Ian decided to go ashore early in the evening, just to get his bearings on the streets and buildings around the harbour. It was too late in the day to do much investigating about gun smuggling. The harbour was swarming with Americans, since the harbour and airport were considered key facilities that they needed to control. A U.S. marine at the entrance to the docks asked to see his identification. After Ian showed him his ID card and the American scrutinized it, the marine saluted and waved him through, saying, "Be careful, sir, there're some rough neighborhoods out there."

Ian didn't spend much time that evening exploring Beirut, and he returned to the *Agincourt* about an hour later.

The next morning, Friday, the 22nd of August, Ian, dressed in respectable civvies, left the *Agincourt* and took a taxi to the British Embassy. The cab drove down Rue

148

Allenby from the docks and then went west on the Rue de Georges Picot. The taxi dropped Ian off at the embassy entrance and he walked in the main door, guarded by a Lebanese policeman. Inside the main door was a British Royal Marine who waved Ian through, after he showed his British Army identification card.

"I would like to speak with the military attaché," he said to the receptionist, as he again presented his military ID card.

"Just a minute, sir," replied Angela, an attractive, auburn haired receptionist. She talked for a moment on a phone with whoever answered and then hung up. "Major Paynter will be able to see you now, for a few minutes. Please go up to the second floor, turn to the right and enter office 23."

"Thank you," Ian said, with a smile, and did as she directed.

Ian knocked on the door, numbered 23, and entered, after he heard a man say, "Come on in."

Major Paynter stood up, as Ian came in. They both saluted, even they were both in civilian clothes, and then shook hands.

Ian said, "Major, thank you for seeing me. I'm with the Intelligence Corps in Cyprus, and I came in on the HMS *Agincourt*. The purpose for my visit is to investigate the trail of arms shipments, from Greece to Cyprus. We believe that they flow through Beirut. Our information is that a ship brings them to Beirut from Greece. Then, they're stored in a warehouse and finally transported to Cyprus, generally on a moonless night. Since I'm fluent in Greek, I propose visiting a few bars/cafés, to see if I can pick up any clues. Perhaps you can give me some leads on some Greek owned cafés in East Beirut."

"Mr. Black, I'd like to help you, but I'm sorry to say I'm not too familiar with cafés, in the Greek section of Beirut. Maybe, a civilian who answers to the name of Percival can help you. He's three doors down from here, in room 26. I believe he's in this morning. Have a good day and be careful in the back alleys of Beirut."

Ian responded, "Thanks for your time. I'll go and see Percival. Good day. It was a pleasure meeting you, sir."

With that, Ian walked out of the military attaché's office and down the hallway to room 26, hoping he was in.

There was a secretary named Virginia in the outer office, according to the name plate on her desk.

Ian asked, "I'm here to see someone by the name of Percival. Is he in?"

Virginia replied, "Yes, he is. Is he expecting you?"

"No," Ian replied, "but Major Paynter recommended that I talk to him."

"He has someone with him at the moment, but they should be finished shortly. May I tell him who wants to see him, sir?"

Ian replied, "I'm Lieutenant Ian Black from the Intelligence Corps in Cyprus."

At that moment, a man, in his late twenties, walked out of Percival's office and said smiling, "Nice to see you again Virginia. You look more beautiful, every time I see you."

He looked at Ian, nodded and with a wink said, "Good luck in there."

Virginia got on the intercom and said, "Sir, there's a Lieutenant Ian Black from Cyprus here. He says that Major Paynter recommended he talk with you."

Percival replied, "Send him in."

Virginia told Ian he could go in now. Ian went up to the door, opened it and entered a large bright and airy office. Sitting behind the desk was a balding man in his fifties, scanning some documents.

Percival finally stood up and extended his hand, saying, "Please take a seat."

Ian then told him who he was and why he was there, just as he had with Major Paynter.

"Do you know someone by the name of John or Dinglefoot there in Cyprus?" he asked Ian, as he scribbled some names and addresses on a piece of paper.

"In fact, I do," Ian replied. "I see him almost every Monday at our staff meetings. When I first met him, I beat him at billiards and he accused me of being a hustler."

"John and I are old friends. Next time you see him say "hello" for me." Percival held out a piece of paper and continued, "Okay, lieutenant, here's a list of Greek cafés, with their addresses that may not be totally accurate. Any good Beirut taxi driver should be able to get you there, without the address. For your information, we believe the arms are shipped through Beirut, because the Greek Government does not want to be directly involved with the shipments to Cyprus. This allows the government to deny, either to Britain or the United Nations, it has anything to do with the arms smuggling."

Ian said, "Thanks of the list of the cafés and bars. This'll be very helpful."

Percival responded, "I'm glad to be of service, just a word of warning though. Take a weapon with you, when you visit these establishments. You never know what or who you'll run into. Please be careful. I don't want to receive a message from John asking what happened to you, when you don't return to Nicosia."

Ian shook Percival's hand and left his office. He looked at the list Percival had given him. It contained the names of three cafés/bars in the eastern part of Beirut, near the harbour and in order of preference.

The first one was the Acropolis bar and café that was situated near the harbor and east of Rue Allenby. Supposedly, it was located in a small alley called Souk El Hussein. Anyway, Ian thought, *"The taxi driver will know where to go."*

After leaving the British Embassy, Ian decided to go to the waterfront for lunch, at the St. George Hotel overlooking the St. George Bay. It was a nice spot and very English. After lunch, he walked along the sea front past the St. Georges Club, the Anglican Church and the New Royal Hotel, back to the port. He went to his cabin, on board the *Agincourt*, to prepare for the evening. He planned to go to the café/bars suggested by Percival.

Later, Ian, dressed in clothes a normal Greek merchant sailor would wear, went down the gang plank of the *Agincourt*. He made sure he had his Browning automatic with him, hidden under his loose shirt. He headed for the dock exit, and again presented his British Army card to the U.S. marine on duty.

"Make sure you're back by midnight, lieutenant," the marine said. "There's a curfew from midnight to 0500, while we're here. Our street patrols might give you a problem, if they catch you out between those hours."

"Thanks for the warning," Ian said. "I'll make sure I'm back by then. By the way, you don't happen to be from Tennessee, do you? My mother was originally from the Nashville area."

"No, I'm from Seattle. Sorry," responded the marine.

Ian wandered from the dock area onto Rue Allenby, and hailed a cab. "Take me to the Acropolis bar and café," he told the driver.

The driver drove south down Rue Allenby and then headed east on rue Weygand for a distance. Then the cab headed north, up some narrow streets and alleys that were dingy and required some new paint. Ian was glad he brought his Browning with him, as the area did not look very safe. Finally, the cab stopped in front of the Acropolis bar that didn't look too run down.

Ian paid the driver and entered the bar. It was dark inside and it took a few seconds for Ian's eyes to adjust. There were about fifteen people in the bar, most of whom looked shifty and at least half appeared to be sailors. Ian sat down at the counter, next to a scroungy looking Jack Tar (sailor), and ordered one half liter of Almaza light beer. Ian then struck up a conversation with this Greek sailor.

"Hello, my name is Daemon. This is my first time in the Acropolis. Do you come here often?" Ian asked the sailor.

"Pleased to meet you," he replied. "I'm called Takis by my friends, especially those who like to buy me a drink."

"Well, Takis. How would you like another beer?" Ian asked, smiling.

"That would be great," Takis said, as he told the bartender to bring him another beer.

"I'm looking for a ship to "sail" on that'll pay me well. I can work hard and I need money. Do you know of any shipping companies looking for some crew?" Ian asked Takis.

As Takis took a sip of the beer paid for by Ian, he said, "Shipping companies trading between here and Greece don't pay too much. However, I've heard that there are a few companies that go to Cyprus and they pay a lot, but the work is risky, if you know what I mean. I believe the man over in the corner knows something about that kind of work, so you would have to talk to him. Supposedly, his name is Bastien."

For a few more minutes, Ian and Takis talked about where they were from, the weather and other mundane items. Ian told Takis he was from Athens. Takis informed Ian that he was from Rhodes originally, but had lived in Beirut for a few years.

After they ended up with nothing much more to say to each other, Ian said, "I'll go and talk with Bastien about jobs, if you don't mind, Takis. I need to get some work and make some money."

"Nice to have met you and thanks for the beer," Takis responded.

Ian got down from the bar stool and wandered over to the table in the dark corner, where a man was sitting.

"Bastien?" asked Ian.

The man nodded, "Yes, I am. What can I do for you?"

"My name is Daemon, and Takis, over there at the bar, said I should talk to you. Can I join you?" Ian asked.

Nodding, Bastien asked roughly, "What do you want?"

"I need some work that will pay well. I've been a merchant seaman for a few years and can handle almost any task requested of me. Takis thought you might be able to help me or steer me in the right direction, if you know what I mean."

Bastien looked around to make sure no one was listening and then whispered, "The only seamen jobs that pay well involve a lot of risk. It requires one to sail to Cyprus and run the British blockade."

Acting dumb, Ian asked, "What are the risks involved?"

Bastien replied, again whispering, "I hear some of the cargo contains weapons and ammunition for EOKA. In case you don't know, they're the military arm of the ENOSIS campaign being waged in Cyprus by the Greek Cypriots. If you get caught by the British, they'll either imprison you, or worse, hang you. That's the reason the pay is good."

"Well, I certainly don't want my neck stretched, but I do need the money. Who do I have to talk to in order to sign on? Would this be a regular job or just a one-time affair?"

"I can't answer any of those questions, but I know the person who can. He's very secretive and does not give out information to anyone. Where are you from Daemon and how long have you been a merchant seaman?"

"My full name is Daemon Misko and I'm from Athens. I've been a seaman for five years, starting out at age sixteen. It's a tough life, but I enjoy it. I just wish the money was a little better."

Bastien took a pencil and a piece of paper out of his pocket, and scribbled on it. "Here's the name of a person who might be able to help you. Be careful though. He's tough and, if he doesn't trust you, watch out or you might end up in a dark alley with your throat slit."

Ian glanced at the paper. It contained the name Christos Papandreo, Olympia Shipping Company and the Modka Café.

Bastien continued, "That's all I can do to help you and don't tell him who gave you his name. This is a dangerous city. I don't think he is there tonight, but will be tomorrow night.

"Thanks," Ian said, as he rose from the table.

Bastien again reminded Ian, "Don't forget you didn't hear about him from me. I have large ears!"

Ian left the bar and walked down to rue Weygand where he found a cab. He climbed in and told the driver to take him to the Mykonos Café. It was close to Souk el Armadan. This area was a narrow alley that contained a market in the daytime. Ian looked at his watch. It was 9:30 pm so he had about two hours, at most, before he should head back to the *Agincourt*. The cab dropped him off in front of the Mykonos Café, and he entered the small dark door with a darkened window. Inside, he found several tables, a bar and a stage. On the stage was a belly dancer who seemed to know what she was doing.

Ian sat down close to another person who also appeared to be a seaman. He started to talk with the seaman who was half drunk. The conversation did not go very far, and Ian finally gave up. He tried starting a conversation with other customers of the café, but they were more interested in the belly dancer. Ian stayed at the café to watch a couple of more belly dancers, clicking their zills, and, he was so impressed, he slipped some money into the last dancer's waist band.

He glanced at his watch and decided that it was time to return to the *Agincourt,* before the curfew commenced. He walked out of the café and headed down the Souk el Armadan. It was dark and he walked briskly to reach rue de Michel Ney. There he found a cab and had the driver take him back to the dock. There he found the same marine on duty and talked to him for a few minutes. Finally, he walked up the gangplank and presented his Intelligence Corps identification to the duty officer at the top. He went to the cabin, which he was sharing with Sub-lieutenant Thistleburt, and found he was already asleep.

****

The next day, Saturday, the 23rd of August, Ian rose, after a good night's rest and went to the Officers' Wardroom for breakfast. After a hearty breakfast, he went to his cabin and wrote up a report on the first day's intelligence operation. He then took a cab ride to the western part of Beirut, just to see what it was like. On the way back he stopped by the Place des Martyrs, which was close to the police headquarters, St. George Cathedral and St Elias Church. He went to the New Royal Hotel on rue du Port for lunch. He figured the food there would be better than the RN's meal, although as he walked into the hotel, he thought, *"Royal Navy food is pretty good, better than the army or Harrow."*

After lunch, he walked down rue du Port to the dock and went on board the *Agincourt* to get some rest, before going out that evening. He wanted to make sure that he had all his wits about him. At the appointed hour, he went to the Officers' Wardroom for dinner, which was attended by all officers, except for the duty officer. Captain Sinclair seemed in the best of spirits, cracking jokes and talking about a visit he had with an American officer, from the USS *Taconic*.

After dinner, Ian headed for his cabin and changed into his Greek seaman's clothes. As before, he made sure he had his Browning hidden underneath his loose shirt. He then left the *Agincourt* and headed for the dock gate guarded by a U.S. marine. The marine on duty reminded Ian that there would be a curfew at midnight, and that he should try to be in before then. Again, Ian asked the marine on duty if he was from Tennessee.

"No," he answered. "I've never been to Tennessee. I'm sorry." It turned out he was actually from a small farming town in Vermont and had his basic training at Parris Island, South Carolina.

Ian walked off the dock and caught the first cab, waiting in a line on rue Allenby. He told the driver to take him to the Modka Café, hoping the driver knew where it was. He did and, after driving for a few minutes down some seedy side streets with mostly French names, the cab ended up outside a building with a large, red sign "Modka Café and Bar". As he entered, he noted the sun was setting, and it was starting to get dark in the dimly lit street.

He walked into the Modka Café which contained twenty tables and a bar with about ten stools. Ian noted that there was no stage for belly dancers, however. He looked around the fairly crowded café and sat on one of the empty bar stools. Like the previous night, he ordered a liter of Almaza light beer. Speaking Greek again, he tried to strike up a conversation with the middle aged man on the bar stool to Ian's right. The man didn't seem interested in talking, but just wanted to drink his dark ale.

In a few minutes, however, a younger man dressed as a Jack Tar came in and sat down on the stool to Ian's left. Ian nodded at him and asked if he would like a beer. "I'm buying," Ian said.

"You're buying?" asked the man in wonderment. Very few people ever bought him a drink, at least not in Beirut. "In that case, I'll have a dark ale."

"I certainly am," Ian replied and told the bar tender to bring the man a dark ale. After it arrived and the man had taken a sip, Ian asked him, "Do you come here to the Modka often?"

"Yes, I do. It's very friendly here. A lot better that some of the other bars, and the prices are reasonable."

"My name is Daemon and I'm a sailor from Athens," Ian said in his best Greek. "Where are you from? Are you a sailor?"

"People call me Plutus, and I'm from the island Santorini. I've been a sailor for fifteen years. It's the only life I really know. I have a wife back home, but I don't get to see her very much."

Ian then asked him, "Since you come here to the Modka often, do you happen to know a man called Christos Papandreo? I hear he comes to this café quite often."

Plutus nodded and said, "I don't know him personally, but that's him at the table, in the corner, with a liter of beer. He drinks it like it is water."

Ian glanced over to the corner table and saw a huge man in his forties. He must have been at least six feet two inches tall and probably weighed about sixteen stone or more. The man sported a neatly trimmed moustache and a short beard.

Ian thought to himself, *"He doesn't look like someone you would want to tangle with in a dark alley."*

After a few more minutes engaging in talk with Plutus, Ian rose from his stool saying, "It's been nice talking with you." He then wandered over to the corner table, where Christos was.

"May I join you, Mr. Papandreo?" Ian asked respectfully.

"Who are you?" Christos asked gruffly. "I don't think I know you."

Ian responded, "My name is Daemon Misko and I was given your name by a sailor at the Acropolis Bar. I'm a merchant marine sailor, with five years experience and I'm looking for some well paying work. My mother is sick in Athens, and I need money to help her."

"Who was it exactly at the Acropolis that told you to look me up?"

"I don't remember his name," Ian said remembering Bastien's warning. "It was some sailor, sitting on a stool next to me at the bar."

"Well, I suppose it doesn't matter, but I don't like people giving out my name. I do have a need for seamen, now and again. What shipping company did you last work for?" asked Christos.

"My last job was with the Overseas Marine Shipping Company Ltd and we took cargo from Athens to Tripoli," replied Ian to the last question. He had done some research, just in case he was asked where he worked. There was a seaman, by the name of Daemon Misko, who had worked for Overseas Shipping.

"Since you're here, I can tell you that the work is sometimes dangerous, but pays about double what the normal pay is for a seaman. Are you interested?" said Christos, giving Ian a questioning look.

"Yes, I certainly am interested in any job you have to offer. When you say it's risky, what type of risks are we talking about? Is it the type of cargo or where the ship is going to?" Ian asked.

"Maybe some of the both," replied Christos. "Think about it and, if you're still interested, come and see me Monday at this address. We can discuss some more about the opportunities."

Christos scribbled an address on a piece of paper and handed it to Ian. "This address is for a warehouse near the docks, where I have my office."

Ian took the paper, glanced at it and placed it in his shirt pocket. He asked, "What would be a good time to come on Monday?"

Christos Papandreo replied, "Any time after 9.00 a.m. will be fine. Now don't bother me anymore with your questions. We can talk on Monday."

Ian got the hint. He rose, thanked Christos for his time and walked back to the bar, where Plutus was just finishing his third beer.

He asked, "Well, how did it go? He isn't the most pleasant man, is he?"

Ian replied, "I must admit that he wasn't the most genial person I've ever met. The meeting was somewhat productive though. Thanks for pointing him out to me. It was nice to have met you, Plutus."

Ian finished his second half liter of light beer for the evening and decided to get some fresh air. He left the bar; exiting the establishment into a dark, star studded night. It was totally dark by now, and it could be dangerous in the dimly lit alleys. He decided to walk down rue Hamra, as it was well lit and full of people. He stopped now and again to look in the shops, many of which were still open. This gave him a chance to see if he was being followed. As far as he could determine, no one was following him. After he had walked most of Hamra, he looked at his watch and saw it was almost 10:30 pm. He decided he should head back to the *Agincourt*, as he had accomplished what he set out to do. He had the name and address of the shipping company that appeared to be involved in the shipment of arms to Cyprus.

He found a cab and told the driver to head for the docks. A few minutes later, he was there showing his ID card to the same US marine that he had showed it to earlier. The marine hardly looked at it, as he recognized Ian. "Good evening, sir" he said and waved him through. Ian looked around one more time to make sure that he hadn't been followed. He then boarded the *Agincourt*, went to his cabin and hit the sack.

****

Ian rose at 0800 Sunday morning, after a good night's sleep, and went to the Officers' Wardroom with Sub-lieutenant Thistleburt, where they joined most of the other officers. Captain Sinclair did not appear for the meal, but Ian saw one of the waiters take a tray of food out of the wardroom. He assumed the captain was eating in his cabin alone.

After breakfast, Ian went to the small tool room on board the *Agincourt*, where there was a sailor sitting behind the counter.

"Is it permissible to borrow a crowbar, a hammer, a Phillips head screwdriver, a flat head screwdriver and a tool bag for twenty-four hours?" Ian asked of the sailor. "I'll be taking them off the *Agincourt*, but I'll bring them back. Of course, if I lose any of them, I'll reimburse the Royal Navy."

"As long as you sign for them, sir, you may do whatever you want with them. Are you going to rob a bank or something?" asked the sailor laughing.

"Not quite, but something like that," Ian responded, smiling.

He signed for the tools, and the sailor placed them in the tool bag. Ian carried the bag back to his cabin and continued to add to the intelligence report he had started the day before. At around noon, Sub-lieutenant Thistleburt came into the cabin and went up to Ian, who was still writing.

"The captain would like to see you in the wardroom immediately, if you're available," said Thistleburt.

Ian glanced at his watch and determined it was too early for lunch. He wondered, *"I hope I'm not in trouble for requesting the tools."* He walked to the wardroom where the door was closed. This was a little unusual, so he knocked and opened the door.

"Come on in Mr. Black and close the door," commanded Captain Sinclair. He was seated at the end of the table and there was a balding gentleman seated next to him. Ian saluted the captain and immediately recognized that the man seated, next to him, was Percival from the British Embassy.

"I believe you've met the gentleman seated here, correct?" asked the captain.

"Yes, sir," replied Ian, as he walked forward to shake Percival's hand. "Glad to see you again, sir," Ian said to him.

"Please take a seat Mr. Black. As captain of the *Agincourt*, I'm responsible for all officers and sailors who are on board. Since you're a visiting officer, I am somewhat responsible, even for you. If something should happen to you while in Beirut, I'd have some explaining to do to the admiral and your CO. I'm concerned about what you are doing in Beirut. I know you're attempting to track down the source of arms being smuggled into Cyprus. There're people in Beirut, I am sure, who would not want you to find out too much. I understand you just checked out some tools from the stock room. Would you mind telling me, what you plan to do with them?" asked the captain.

"I've been trying to find out the name of the shipping company and the manager, who would be responsible for shipping arms. I believe that I've found them. The name of the shipping company is Olympia Shipping Company Limited and it's located at #135, rue de Darlan. I understand it's a warehouse in an alley, behind the dock. I'm supposed to meet with a Christos Papandreo on Monday morning, after 9:00 am, to discuss employment as a seaman. I met him last night at the Modka Café, and he gave me the address.

Percival said, "Captain, this information is similar to what I found out, after Mr. Black's visit to my office last Friday."

Ian continued, "If I may, I would like to continue answering your question, sir. Tonight, after dark, I plan to visit this address and somehow get inside. I'll then search the premises for crates and open some of them up, to determine if they contain arms. I'll copy down names and addresses of the shippers listed on the crates. When I'm finished, I'll make sure all the crates have their lids back on. I'd then exit the premises, hopefully leaving no trail that I'd even been there."

"What would you do if someone comes in the warehouse, while you're searching it?" asked the captain.

"I'd defend myself as best I could. I'll have my Browning automatic with me. I'd then flee the premises as quickly as possible," replied Ian.

"It appears to me that you may need some assistance tonight. It'd be a problem for me to break into a building, while attached to the British Embassy, but I could certainly "stand" watch for any approaching danger. What do you think captain?" asked Percival.

"Sounds like an excellent suggestion to me," replied the captain. "How would you warn Mr. Black, if trouble approached?"

Percival continued, "I have access to certain devices that are not on the commercial market. The system consists of two boxes, one is a transmitter and the other is a receiver. They're built using transistors, the latest in electronic components. I'd have the transmitter and Mr. Black would have the receiver. The receiver would vibrate, if I press the transmitter button. Mr. Black would feel the silent vibration and take appropriate action."

The captain responded, "We appreciate your offer of help, Percival. Don't we, Mr. Black?"

"Yes, sir," replied Ian.

"Good then, it's settled," said the captain.

Percival then said, "Ian, if I may call you that, I'll pick you up in my car at 8.30 p.m. by the dock gate. We can then drive to the warehouse and I'll drop you off. Then I'll park by a building and keep watch."

Ian responded, "Okay, I'll see you at 8:30 just outside the dock gate."

The captain then said, "Let's conclude this meeting. Good luck to both of you. Please don't make me have to write a report to the admiral."

Ian saluted the captain and said to Percival, "See you tonight." He then returned to his cabin, to work some more on the report of yesterday's meeting, with Christos at the Modka Café.

After being served the evening meal in the wardroom, Ian went back to his cabin and changed his clothes into a black outfit. Again, he strapped the Browning under his loose shirt and picked up the bag with the tools inside. At 8.20 p.m., he went down the gang plank and headed for the dock gate. This time there was a US marine there that he had not seen before. He showed his ID, and the marine, after checking it waved him through saying, "Don't forget the midnight curfew, sir."

"Thanks for reminding me. By the way, do you happen to be from Tennessee?" asked Ian.

"Yes, I am," said the marine. "I lived in Nashville all my life, until I joined the Marines."

Ian responded with surprise, "My mother is from just outside Nashville, but has lived in England for many years." Ian thought to himself, *"Finally, I have met someone from Tennessee."*

"Have a good evening, sir. Don't forget the curfew. The U.S. Marines can be a tough bunch," he said, with a laugh.

Ian walked out the gate and, a few yards away, found Percival parked in a black, Vauxhall Victor, sedan. He climbed in, and Percival drove off down the rue Allenby. He kept driving though some narrow streets that contained warehouses and finally arrived close to #135, rue de Darlan. Percival pulled in close to a building short of number 135 and looked around, to make sure there was no one there. They had not been followed. Percival pulled out a small box from his pocket, set the power switch to on, and told Ian to place it in his pocket. Ian complied, and then Percival pulled out

164

another box from his pocket and turned the power on. He pressed the red button and Ian jumped.

"I felt that for sure," said Ian.

"Good," replied Percival. "We're now ready for your escapade. Please be careful, as I don't want to leave here without you. Here're some items that might also be helpful. I do need them back."

Percival handed Ian a bunch of master keys for opening locks. Why Percival had them, Ian thought it was best not to ask. Ian got out of the Vauxhall and walked towards the warehouse at #135. He kept close to the walls, so he would not so visible, in case someone came along.

He reached the warehouse, marked with a brass plaque that read *135, Olympia Shipping Company Limited* on the wall, and went around the side of the building, where he found a small door. He tried all the master keys that Percival had given him and, after trying ten of them, the eleventh key worked and opened the door. He went inside, closed the door and locked it. If anyone came along to check and try it, they would believe the building was secure.

He went into the main part of the warehouse and looked around to make sure there were no lights on, indicating someone might be there. There were several large crates in the middle of the warehouse. Using the torch, he had placed in the tool kit bag, he determined that they were marked *Bottling Machinery* and they were destined for Nicosia, Cyprus. They had been shipped to Beirut from Germany, and were waiting for shipment on to Cyprus. These crates didn't seem very suspicious to Ian, since Cyprus bottled a considerable amount of wine and fruit drinks.

He then looked in other areas of the warehouse, and in a corner of the building, Ian discovered a locked cage with some more crates inside. Again, Ian tried the master keys and finally found one that unlocked the large padlock. He went inside the caged area and looked at the crates, with his torch. They were marked *Mining Machinery*, and they had been shipped from Greece. Since Cyprus had copper mines, these crates on the surface seemed to be innocent. However, Ian didn't remember Greece manufacturing any machinery equipment. Mostly it came from Britain, Germany, France or America.

He took his crowbar from the bag and started to pry off the front panel of the crate. Finally, it came loose, and he looked inside the crate with his torch. The crate was full of World War Two British Enfield .303 rifles and ammunition boxes. He then opened up another crate and it contained explosives and mines, mainly of World War II vintage. He had discovered what he came to Beirut for. He remembered that at the end of the war Churchill had made an agreement with Stalin. It was called the naughty document and, in effect, it allowed Britain a free hand in Greece, while Russia could have some of the Balkans. Under this agreement, Britain shipped huge quantities of arms into Greece to fight the communists, at the end of the war. These arms were now being shipped to Cyprus.

He quickly replaced the covers back on the crates and hammered down the nails; so that no one would know they had been opened. Using the torch, he wrote down everything that was on the crates, including the contents, name of shippers, manufacturers, crate numbers, etc.

Just when he was finished, Ian almost jumped out of his skin. The vibrator in his pocket went off. He turned off the torch and left the cage. He snapped the lock shut behind him, took out his Browning and headed for the small, side door of the warehouse. He reached it at the moment the main door to the warehouse was opened, and a man walked in. Luckily for Ian, the side door was obscured from the main door by a wall, and he didn't have to use his gun. He slipped outside and carefully closed the door behind him, without making too much noise. He locked it with the master key and quickly walked down the side alley, towards rue de Darlan.

He reached the street and noticed a car parked in front of the warehouse. It was not Percival's Vauxhall. Where was Percival? Ian looked around worried, since he couldn't see the car anywhere. He took out his torch and aimed it in several directions, turning it on and off; making sure anyone in the warehouse could not see it. Finally, Percival drove his car, without lights, up to the alley, where Ian was, from another side alley, two buildings away.

Ian jumped in and said to Percival, "Let's go, quick. That was close."

Percival, as he drove off down the rue de Darlan, asked," Did you get what you came for?"

"Yes I did, thanks to you." Ian responded.

In about ten minutes, Percival pulled up at the dock gate. It was 11.45 p.m., fifteen minutes before curfew.

Ian gave Percival the vibrator box back, together with the master keys, saying, "I couldn't have succeeded without these items. Thanks again for all your help. Can you make it home before the curfew starts?"

"Yes, I only live ten minutes from here. One thing though you must remember. I was not here tonight. You only saw me at the embassy." Percival responded.

Ian shook hands with Percival saying, "I understand." He got out of the car and walked to the dock gate. He turned and waved at Percival, as he drove off. The marine, at the gate, remembered Ian and said, "I'm glad you made it back, before the curfew starts. So your mother came from the Nashville area that must make you half an American."

"That's right, chum. Goodnight." Ian replied.

Ian walked up the gang plank and went to his cabin. He was still shaking, somewhat, from the experience in the warehouse. He was also wide awake and was not able to go to sleep for a good hour.

****

Ian awoke Monday morning tired, but happy that he had accomplished what he set out to do in Beirut. He went to the wardroom for breakfast at 0800, and the captain was there along with several other officers.

Captain Sinclair smiled as Ian entered the room, "Well Mr. Black, I'm glad to see you are up and about, and I don't have to write a report to my admiral or your CO."

All the other officers there, in the wardroom, looked at the captain wondering what he was talking about. However, all of them were smart enough not to raise any questions, as to what he meant.

Ian responded, "Sir, I believe I had a very productive and enjoyable evening. Thank you for this lift to Beirut, and all the assistance you and your men have given me."

The captain then changed the subject, and the rest of the breakfast was spent talking about the Americans controlling Beirut and Lebanon.

At 0845, the captain rose and said, "Gentlemen, it is time to get the *Agincourt* under way. We are due back in Famagusta at 1500, so we have no time to waste."

The crew had actually started the oil fired boilers about 0730, in order to get the ship ready to sail. In five minutes, Ian could feel the vibration of the engines as they started up, and the ship cast off from the dock. Ian went on the bridge and watched as they pulled away. A few Americans on the other ships waved, as the HMS *Agincourt* left the harbour.

Once they cleared the harbour, Ian went down to his cabin, collected the tool kit and took it back to the tool room. The same seaman who checked the tools out was there and checked them back in. Ian then went back to his cabin and worked on his intelligence report for Colonel Baker and Captain Phillips.

As they did when they came to Beirut, about halfway back to Cyprus, Captain Sinclair had the speed increased to maximum just to exercise the engines. He held the speed at maximum for about thirty minutes and then lowered it to half speed for the remainder of the trip.

They arrived in Famagusta five minutes late at 1505 and tied up to the dock. Ian went up to the bridge, and he thanked Captain Sinclair for the lift and for all his assistance.

The captain told Ian, "If you ever want to join the Navy, just let me know. It's been a pleasure knowing you. Perhaps we'll meet again someday."

Ian walked down the gangplank onto the dock and went to find his car. It was still parked, where he left it. He climbed in, placing his bag on the back seat. He drove out of the dockyard and headed for Nicosia. It took just over one hour, and he was soon back in Salisbury House. He reported briefly to Captain Phillips that he had returned, and that he would have a full report in a day or so.

He started to write the report, which would become an important intelligence document on the transportation of arms from Greece to Cyprus, via Lebanon.

14

Ledra Palace Hotel

On the next morning, after returning from Beirut, Ian placed a call to Aphrodite at the hospital and left a message for her to call him back.

Around noon, she returned his call.

"Lieutenant Black speaking," he said, answering the phone.

"Hello Ian, this is Aphrodite. I'm glad to hear you're back. Safe and sound I hope?"

"Yes, I'm all in one piece. I don't think anything is missing," he said with a laugh. "I called to see if you'd like to go out Friday or Saturday to the Ledra Palace Hotel? I hear they have a good band on those nights. We could have dinner and dance at the same time."

"That sounds great to me. I'm off Friday and Sunday, but I have to work Saturday. What time will you pick me up or do you want me to meet you somewhere?"

"I'll pick you up at six o'clock on Friday, in a taxi, and we can go together to the hotel. Does that sound okay to you?"

"Yes, that'll be great. I'll see you Friday evening. Goodbye till then. I love you Ian."

"I love you too. Goodbye."

Ian went back to work, writing his Beirut report. Two days later, he presented a full report, on his activities in Beirut, to the captain, but left out any reference to Percival, by name. He outlined how the arms were shipped from Athens to Greece and then on to Cyprus. He also expressed the belief, although he had no absolute proof, that the Greek Government itself, or someone in a government agency, was involved in the shipments.

The next time he saw John, he mentioned that Percival said "Hello", and somehow Ian received the impression that John was not surprised. Perhaps, Percival had already contacted John from Beirut.

On Friday afternoon, Ian prepared to take Aphrodite out to dinner and to dance the evening away, at the Ledra Palace Hotel. This hotel was located just outside the old city and was one of the popular hotels in Nicosia.

He called for a taxi and had it pick him up at the safe house, across the road from Salisbury House. For security reasons, they rarely called for a taxi to pick up someone right outside the House.

"Number 16, Kapella Street," Ian told the driver in Greek.

The British had learned not to trust all the taxi drivers. There had been cases where an English speaking person vanished, after calling for a cab. Soon the taxi arrived at Aphrodite's home.

"Please wait here, I'm picking up someone, and then we want to go to the Ledra Palace Hotel," Ian again spoke in Greek to the driver.

Ian went to the front door and rang the bell. Aphrodite came to the door, and stepped out, into the late afternoon sun, wearing a shimmering, black, calf-length dress. Just like the time she went to the colonel's party, her long black hair was pulled into a pony tail and tied with a red ribbon.

Ian gave her a kiss on her cheek and said, "You look beautiful." He then escorted her down the gravel path to the waiting taxi, holding her arm to make sure that she didn't slip.

171

Soon they arrived at the hotel, and a doorman came up to the taxi to open the door for Aphrodite. Ian quickly got out of the other door, walked around the vehicle, took her arm and entered the hotel. People, especially the men, outside the hotel looked at Aphrodite in admiration. They went inside and found the restaurant with the dance floor.

"I'm Ian Black, and I've a booking for two," Ian said to the maitre d'.

Ian thought to himself, *"This is going to be expensive but Aphrodite is worth every penny."*

He looked at his list and said, "Follow me sir."

The maitre d' led them to a table close to the dance floor. Ian was glad he made a booking, as the restaurant was filling up fast. The band started playing at 7:30, he had been told, when he made the booking.

The waiter brought menus to the table, and Aphrodite looked a little apprehensive, as she looked at the selections and the prices.

"Ian," she whispered, "This is very expensive."

"It's only one time, and you're worth it," Ian responded with a smile. My father sent me a small check the other day to help out with my army pay.

The waiter came back and took their orders. He asked, "How about some wine, sir?"

Ian looked at Aphrodite and asked, "Would you like some wine, and if so, would you prefer red or white?"

She nodded saying, "a glass of red would be nice."

"One glass each of your red house wine will be fine, thank you," Ian requested of the waiter.

The meal was delicious, and they both enjoyed it very much. The red wine was okay, but it wasn't the best. That didn't matter, because they were both having fun.

"I'm glad we came here tonight. I'm having fun, how about you, Ian?"

"Yes, this is a lot more fun than flying a plane."

"Ian, that reminds me. Flight Lieutenant Mullins was released from the hospital a week ago and Flight Lieutenant Jones was released yesterday. They both asked me to say "Hello" to you for them."

"Well, I'm glad to hear they've recovered from their wounds. Are you going to be ready to dance in a minute, when the band starts playing?"

"I can't wait for the music to start and to be held in your arms, as we go around the dance floor." Aphrodite answered.

By the time they finished their meal, the six piece band began to play. They were very good for a local band.

"Aphrodite, they're playing a waltz. I think I'm game for that, how about you?"

"I'd love to," she replied.

Ian got up and pulled back her chair, as she rose. He took her arm and led her to the dance floor, where there were several other couples dancing.

Ian held Aphrodite in his arms, and as they danced, he could smell her sweet perfume and feel her lovely body close to him. They danced, as if they had danced together all their lives.

"I love you, Ian," she whispered, as they danced. She clung onto him, as though she never wanted to let go. Finally the music stopped, and then a foxtrot was played.

So it went on all evening, the band interchanged ballroom music with more modern types of music.

At ten o'clock, Ian said to Aphrodite, "I had better get you home, since you're on duty tomorrow at 8.00 a.m."

"Yes, you're right, but I wish the evening would never end," she said.

They went back to their table and Ian paid the bill. Then, they walked outside to find a taxi. The hotel had a taxi rank, so finding one was not a problem.

Ian helped Aphrodite into the cab, and as they rode back to her home, she laid her head on his shoulder, sighing with contentment. When they reached her home, Ian helped her out and took her to the door.

"Aphrodite, I love you so much, and I'm afraid I might lose you."

"Ian, I'm not going anywhere, so there's no way you can lose me. I love you more than you know."

"Aphrodite I need to talk with you about a small trip I'm thinking of going on. Would you be available for lunch on Sunday, somewhere small and quiet?"

"It sounds mysterious. I'm off duty on Sunday morning at 8:00 am, so I can meet you around noon."

"I'll do a little research and call you tomorrow at the hospital. If you're not available, I'll leave a message."

"That sounds good, Ian. Thank you for a lovely evening. By the way, your dancing is a lot better than mine."

Ian took her in his arms and gave her a long warm kiss, and she responded in kind.

"I'd better go in now, as I have to get up early."

She gave him another kiss, and then she was gone.

Ian walked down to the waiting taxi and had him drive back to the safe house.

The next day Ian called the hospital in the afternoon and managed to reach Aphrodite.

"Aphrodite, this is Ian. I have found a small quiet place called the Pirgos Restaurant. I'll pick you up at twelve o'clock from your house and we'll go straight there by taxi. Is that okay?"

"Ian, that'll be great. I'll see you tomorrow about noon. I love you, goodbye. I have to go."

The next day Ian took a taxi to Aphrodite's home and picked her up. They then went to the Pirgos Restaurant and found a quiet corner table. They ordered from the menu that covered various types of dishes – Greek, Turkish and English.

While waiting for the food, Ian said "Thanks for coming. I've missed you."

Aphrodite replied "Me too. It seems so long ago. I go back to work and it's hard to concentrate."

Ian asked Aphrodite, "You're off duty for three days starting next Friday at four o'clock in the afternoon. Is that right?"

"Yes, why do you ask?"

Just then, the waiter arrived with the food and placed it in front of them.

"Thank you." Ian said to him.

The waiter walked away, and Ian continued with the conversation.

"Aphrodite. I was wondering if you'd like to get away for a few days. I know of a great Bed and Breakfast, run by a Swiss couple, up in the Kyrenia Mountains. It would be quiet and restful there. We could look at some of the castles and go swimming in the MED."

"That sounds delightful. I could do with a nice, quiet weekend."

"Good. I'll make a booking for two rooms at the inn, overlooking the mountains and the ocean."

"Ian. I like the sound of the mountains and the ocean, but I'd prefer one room, if it's okay with you?" she asked, looking at him with a coy smile.

"Are you sure?"

"Yes, I've never been more certain in my life." Aphrodite replied.

"Okay, I'll make a booking today and I'll pick you up on Friday, at five o'clock, in the hospital parking area. Make sure you take your bag with you that day to the hospital and include a swim suit."

Aphrodite replied, "I saw a fashionable bikini in a store window the other day and I've been looking for an excuse to buy it; now I've found one."

"We'll have a great time, I promise you." Ian said.

They finished their meal and then Aphrodite asked Ian, "Would you mind taking me home. I'm tired. I've been on duty for twenty four hours, without any sleep."

Ian responded, "Of course, how inconsiderate of me. I'll order a taxi immediately."

They went to the cashier's counter. Ian paid the bill and asked the cashier to call them a taxi.

In a few minutes a taxi arrived and they climbed in. Ian gave the driver the address in Greek. As soon as he stopped outside her home, they got out and Ian walked her to the door.

She turned to him, gave him a long kiss and whispered, "I'll see you Friday. I'm looking forward to it and don't worry about just one room. I want it."

With that, she entered her home, closed the front door and Ian had the taxi take him back to the safe house. He walked through the secret tunnel to Salisbury House, whistling to himself. He was happy.

The next day he booked one room for three nights at the Davos-Platz B&B.

15

Young Love

On the week-end of their planned outing, Ian went to pick up Aphrodite, after she got off work at the hospital. It was still warm and sunny, even though it was in the late afternoon. As they had previously arranged, he parked in a visitor parking spot and waited for her to come out. He only had to wait a few minutes before she appeared with a small, overnight case and walked towards the car. She got into the car and gave Ian a kiss. Aphrodite was glowing and appeared very happy to be going away for a few days with Ian.

They were so intent and focused on each other that they failed to notice someone watching, from the window in one of the buildings. It was Diana Palas, Aphrodite's mother. Her daughter had told her she was going away for the week-end with a friend, but she didn't say who it was. Diana was glad for her daughter, because she seemed to be very happy. She hoped he was a nice young man.

Ian backed out of the parking area and drove off out of the hospital grounds, taking the road north to the town of Kyrenia. He had reserved a room, with a mountain view, at the Davos-Platz. It was a bed and breakfast run by a retired Swiss couple, Hans and Verena Gerschwiler, and was nestled in the Kyrenia Mountains, just west of the town. It took Ian and Aphrodite only about thirty minutes to drive the fourteen

177

miles from Nicosia to the old town. It then took them another fifteen minutes to travel the three miles up the twisting, mountain road to the Davos-Platz inn.

Along the way they discussed the day's events, the weather and what they would do that week-end. They were both nervous about being with each other and, at the same time, excited.

Aphrodite glanced at Ian and thought how handsome and dashing he was. *"I hope he thinks that I'm beautiful also,"* she thought.

Ian caught her looking at him and smiled. She smiled back as they proceeded toward the inn, and they became more at ease with each other. It would be the first time for both of them, and they were filled with anticipation.

They arrived at the inn, just as the sun was setting.

Ian opened the car door for Aphrodite and said, "Well, here we are."

"It looks lovely," she replied.

The old inn was rebuilt from an ancient stone fortress and had yellow roses growing across the entrance.

As they entered the inn with their cases, Verena Gerschwiler, the proprietor, greeted them warmly.

"We have a room reserved for the week-end," Ian said. "I requested one with a view of the mountains."

"Mr. Black?" she asked.

After he nodded, she said, "Yes, I've put you in room 21. It has a lovely view of the mountains and usually has a cool breeze coming in from the ocean."

"Thank you," said Ian, as he signed the register.

"Frau Gerschwiler, do you know of a good restaurant that is close by that you can recommend for dinner?" he asked.

"Most certainly, there's the International Restaurant just one and a half miles down the road you just came up. It serves all types of food; European, Greek or Turkish. Just be careful driving, as the road twists a lot, and it's getting dark. By the way, please call me Verena."

"Thanks for the recommendation, Verena." Ian said with a smile.

He picked up their bags and turning to Aphrodite, said, "We'd better get going, while we still have some light to find our way."

They made their way up the stairs to their room, and Ian placed the bags on a shelf built for that purpose. The room was fairly large with a blue and white décor, and the double bed felt comfortable. Lace curtains that were moving with the soft, evening breeze, hung in the window. The walls were lined with a periwinkle print that matched the bedspread. Aphrodite went to the bathroom and freshened up. Then they went down stairs, got into their car and headed for the restaurant

It was fairly easy to find, and there was plenty of parking room. They entered the restaurant, and a hostess seated them at a nice quiet corner table almost immediately. The place was not very crowded since it was fairly late. The waitress came and brought menus to them. Ian and Aphrodite made their selections and waited for the waitress to return.

Ian asked Aphrodite, while they waited, "Would you like some wine?"

She replied, "Yes, please. May we have a Chardonnay?"

"Of course," Ian responded.

The waitress came to their table and took their meal orders.

Ian said to her, "We would also like a bottle of Chardonnay."

"Certainly, sir, I'll bring it right away," the waitress said, as she went off to place their menu selections with the cook. In a moment, she returned with the bottle of Chardonnay and two wine glasses.

While they waited for their food, they sipped the wine.

Ian asked Aphrodite, "How was your work today?"

She replied, "We had an emergency. Some soldier had been shot on murder mile, but luckily he survived."

Then she said, "I would ask you how your day was, but I know I wouldn't get a straight answer or any answer at all.

Ian replied, "I can't tell you what I do or else I'd be in trouble. In addition, one never knows who's listening.

The waitress finally brought their entrée choices to the table. The food was excellent, and it showed that Verena's recommendation was right on the mark.

After they finished their dinner and Ian had paid the bill, they headed back up the mountain to the inn driving very carefully, as it was now dark. Luckily they did not meet any vehicles coming down.

As they pulled into the inn parking lot, they noticed two other cars, so they knew they were not alone. They went up to their room and locked the door. Ian placed his Browning on the night stand by the bed. Aphrodite was surprised, but Ian assured her it was just a precaution.

Aphrodite picked up her case and went into the en-suite bathroom. She put on a calf length, red lacy nightgown. She looked into the mirror to make sure her hair was in place, brushed her teeth and then opened the door. Ian was sitting on the bed, with his eyes closed, wearing pajama bottoms with short legs and no top.

She sat on the bed by him.

He opened his eyes and looked at her. *"How beautiful she is,"* Ian thought. He pulled her close to him and kissed her. She had a sweet aroma about her, and she felt soft in his arms.

He released her, looked her in the face and asked, "Are you sure you want to go through with this?"

"Yes, I'm sure. I love you Ian. I don't want to wait any longer to consummate our love."

Ian got up and went to the bathroom. In a couple of minutes, he came out, pulled back the curtains, and turned down the lights. The moon was already up, and it flooded the room with a soft glow. She was a vision of loveliness, lying on the bed waiting for him.

He lay down beside her and pulled her into his arms. He began stroking her hair and kissing her. Then, his hands slowly moved down her red lacy gown until they found her small round breasts. Soon, Ian pulled the straps of her gown down, so he could see how beautiful her pale breasts were in the moonlight. He drank in her beauty, enhanced by these pale, white breasts. They were pert and firm. The honey coloured aureoles were tipped with medium brown, semi-hard nipples.

Ian bent down and kissed both of her nipples, one at a time. He then started to suck slowly on them, running his tongue over them individually. While he did this to one of them, his hand was gently massaging the other breast. Aphrodite's heart started to beat faster, as a warm glow came all over her and a low moan escaped her lips. She was in ecstasy.

Ian's penis was starting to rise, and he quickly took his pajama bottoms off, so he was completely naked. Aphrodite looked down in amazement. She had never seen a penis in full erection before. Sometimes at the hospital, she had to wash patients who were too wounded to wash themselves, but they were mostly always flaccid.

Ian slowly moved Aphrodite's red lacy gown down until it was below her feet, and she was totally naked. Ian had never seen such a gorgeous sight before.

"You're beautiful. I can't believe how beautiful you are, Aphrodite. I love you so much."

He ran his hands slowly all over her body, except on that magical patch where her legs came together. Finally, he could not resist any longer and placed one hand there. It was covered with curly black hair. It felt wonderful.

At the same time, Ian took her hand and placed it on his quivering penis. She was amazed how hard it was. *"How* was it going to feel to have that inside of her?" she wondered.

Ian felt between her legs and discovered she was very moist, at the entrance to her delightful honey pot.

He massaged her body some more and then felt down there again. It was totally moist, almost dripping with her juices.

Ian gave Aphrodite one last chance not to lose her virginity this night. "Are you sure you want to do this?" Ian whispered.

"Yes, please. I want you now." gasped Aphrodite.

Ian rolled on top of her and placed his penis at the entrance between her legs. With rigid arms, he looked down upon Aphrodite and slowly inserted his throbbing penis into her.

Aphrodite's eyes widened and, with parted lips, begged, "Yes, Ian, yes!"

Slowly he pushed into her until he felt a slight resistance. He pushed a little more and Aphrodite groaned in pain. Then he was through and his penis was inserted fully into her vagina. The pain bothered her for a few minutes and Ian just lay there, inside of her, without moving. He kissed her nipples and stroked her hair.

Finally, she whispered, "More please, more."

Ian started to slowly move his penis in and out of her. It felt wonderful, and she was also amazed how good it felt. Ian slowly upped the pace until finally he was thrusting at a fairly rapid tempo. It felt so good. Suddenly he stopped and whispered "Are you okay?"

"Don't stop" she replied. "Please don't stop!"

Ian started thrusting again and upped the rhythm even more, until he felt a stirring in his body. Then he knew he could not stop and, for the first time in his life, he had a real orgasm, spouting his hot semen into her body. It felt great to Ian, as he gasped. At the same time Aphrodite had an orgasm and moaned, also gasping for air.

Later, Ian thought, *"How different it was to the experimentation, when he touched himself as a young boy at school."*

They lay in each other's arms, kissing and whispering love words. They were savoring every moment of their first time. Aphrodite felt a little sore, but she knew it would pass. She couldn't wait for the next time and fell asleep in his arms.

Ian also soon drifted off into a deep sleep.

He was the first one to wake up, as the sun rose and poured through their opened curtained window. The cool ocean breeze caressed their bodies. Ian looked at Aphrodite who was lying naked on the bed and he thought, *"How beautiful she is."* His heart filled with love and passion for her.

He stroked her body softly, and she woke up stretching her arms and legs. She rolled onto her side and gave Ian a kiss and saying, with a shy smile, "I'm hungry! I need a good hearty breakfast this morning."

"I agree with you," Ian answered.

They both went to the bathroom individually to prepare for the day. They got dressed and went down the stairs to the breakfast room.

As they entered, Verena said, "Good morning. I trust you both slept well.

Ian and Aphrodite answered back together, "Yes, thank you."

Verena then asked, "Would you both like a full English breakfast?"

Smiling, with a glow on their faces, they both replied in unison, "Yes, please."

Verena went to the kitchen, as Ian poured Aphrodite and himself a cup of coffee. Soon, Verena came back in with two plates filled with eggs, sausages, fried bread and baked beans.

"This should fill you up," she said and placed the plates in front of them.

Ravenously, they both ate everything on their plates and then got up to go to their room. Ian knocked on the kitchen door, and Verena came to see what they wanted.

"If it is not too much trouble, could you make us a couple of ham sandwiches and also supply a couple of bottles of orange drinks? We plan to go on the hiking trail to St Hilarion Castle this morning. We will, of course, reimburse you for the added expense."

"No problem. It will be ready when you come down," replied Verena.

Ian and Aphrodite came down in a little while, ready to walk the trail. They picked up the sack lunch, that Verena had made them, and headed out into the bright morning sun. She had told them the direction in which to take the trail and said it was only about one mile away. The trail sloped upwards, as the castle ruins were at 2,400 feet on the side of a rocky crag. The trail itself was fairly easy to walk, and they held each other's hands, as they went along.

They walked for a while and then stopped to kiss.

"I love you, Ian," Aphrodite said in a low voice. "Every day, I hope you will call so we can talk."

"I love and adore you too, Aphrodite," Ian said to her. He then gave her another long kiss.

They continued on in silence, each lost in thought of what their future would be. Finally they reached the castle that had fallen into decay, starting when the Venetians ruled Cyprus, roughly five hundred years before.

After walking around the ruins and taking in the sight of the beautiful north Cyprus coast, including the town of Kyrenia, they found a grassy spot to sit and eat their lunch. One other young couple came by, but they hardly saw Ian and Aphrodite, as they were also engrossed in each other.

Ian remarked, "See Aphrodite. We're not the only ones in love."

"You're right Ian, but we're the ones that count." She gave him a long lingering kiss that caused his member to start swelling. She glanced down and saw the bulge in his pants. "Well that started something," she said smiling.

Ian replied with a grin, "We'd better begin going down before we start something else. Don't forget, we're going to Regas Beach this afternoon to swim, and I want to see what you look like in that new, bikini you brought with you. Afterwards, we're having dinner at the famous Regas Fish Restaurant before returning to the Davos-Platz."

They found the return walk to the inn easier, since it was downhill. Upon reaching the inn, they went up to their room to get their swim suits and the keys to the car.

While in their room, Aphrodite went up to Ian and gave him a French kiss, as she felt for his bulge. She then quickly stripped off her clothes, unbuckled Ian's belt and pulled his trousers down.

"Let's make love," she whispered, taking his hand and leading him to the bed. Ian went of course willingly and whispered back, "I love you Aphrodite."

As they lay on the bed, she placed her hand on his member and stroked it gently. Soon, it was as hard, and she was moist down below. Ian gently caressed her body for a short while and then straddled on top of her. He lowered his body slowly and at the same time thrust forward gently, until his member was totally inside of her.

"Oh, that feels good," she whispered in Ian's ear, as she started to move her hips in unison to Ian's thrusting in and out. He grabbed hold of her buttocks and pulled her towards him, as far as he could. They were locked in an undulating movement and this continued for a few minutes.

Then she cried out, "Now, Ian, now!" Ian moved very quickly, until they both had an orgasm together, and Ian shot his fluid into her. They both lay panting for a while as Ian continued to lie inside of her. He rolled onto his side giving her another long kiss. Her eyes were closed, and her face had a healthy flush to it.

"That was heavenly," she said, as she finally opened her eyes.

"I love you. I love your whole being inside and out." Then jokingly Ian said, "Now I know what a *nooner* is like. It was heaven."

She spanked his behind and laughingly said, "You're right."

Aphrodite rose and went to the bathroom, saying with a big grin, "Thanks for showing me that part of heaven. We'd better get going though, if you want to see me in my bikini."

They quickly put their clothes back on and headed down to the car, carrying their swim suits and towels. They climbed into the car and went back down the twisty road, each still feeling the glow and wonderment of young love, until they reached their destination – Regas Beach. It was located near Ayyorgi, just a few miles west of Kyrenia. They quickly changed into their swim suits, in the appropriate toilet areas, and placed their clothes in lockers.

When Aphrodite came out of the Ladies area, Ian gasped "You look smashing in that bikini. It doesn't leave much to the imagination, though."

"If any men look at you, I'll have to beat them up," he said laughing.

"Don't worry," she replied, "I only love you. By the way, you look pretty good yourself in that suit." Again, she looked down and saw his bulge was starting to get slightly bigger. She thought, *"It's amazing how his thing goes up and down."* Of course, she had seen her brothers', but never like this.

"We'd better get in the water," she said smiling.

They ran across the sandy beach and splashed into the blue Mediterranean Sea. It was warm, since this was September, and it felt invigorating to both of them. They swam around for awhile, splashing each other and playing like two children. Then they went and lay down on the beach in the warm, bright sun. There were quite a few people on the beach, but that didn't bother either Ian or Aphrodite. They were oblivious to them all, as they were thinking only of their love for each other. After they had lain quietly for a while in the sun, they rose and went back into the water, to cool off.

After a couple of hours, they went and changed back into their clothes. They placed their wet swim clothes into the boot of the car and then went to the Regas Fish Restaurant.

The hostess greeted them and Ian asked, "May we have a corner table with a view of the Mediterranean, if one's available?"

"Certainly," replied the hostess, as she led them to a nice secluded corner table that overlooked the beach and the ocean. She handed them the menus and said, "Your waitress will be here in a moment to take your orders."

They both ordered a local Mediterranean white fish dinner and a carafe of a French Chardonnay. They sipped the wine, as they waited for the food.

Aphrodite whispered to Ian, "Thank you for this week-end. I'm enjoying every minute of it. I wish it would go on forever."

"Thank you for coming along. I love you Aphrodite, and I hope our love for each other will go on forever and forever."

Soon the meal arrived, and it was excellent. The reviews of Regas Fish Restaurant were correct. It was the best fish that they had both tasted in Cyprus. Of course, Aphrodite was more of an expert as she had lived here all her life. After the meal, they finished off the wine and, feeling a little giddy, they made their way back to the inn.

After they made it up the narrow road and arrived at the inn, they took their wet suits out of the car boot and went up to their room. Here they laid out their suits on the small balcony to dry off.

Aphrodite said, "I think I'll take a shower to wash off the salt from the ocean."

She stripped off her clothes and climbed into the shower, which was somewhat rare, instead of a bath tub.

Ian entered the bathroom and asked, "May I join you or will that embarrass you?"

'No," she replied shyly. "Come in. It will be tight, but there is room for two; just."

Ian entered the shower and found Aphrodite with water cascading down her face and body, with droplets of water dripping from her nipples. He thought, *"She looks like a goddess and is an image of loveliness."*

"Do you want me to wash you?" he asked in anticipation.

"That would be great," Aphrodite replied.

Ian reached for the bar of soap and rubbed it with his hands all over her entire body. She stood there with her eyes closed feeling every movement of his hands. She loved it when he washed her small firm breasts and her flat stomach. Finally, he reached the soft patch of black hair, and she groaned with ecstasy. As he rubbed her in that area, her breath got quicker and quicker until she had the third orgasm of her life. It felt wonderful. *"How can it feel so good?" she thought.*

He took the shower head off the hook and rinsed her off with the warm clean water. She turned and gave him a kiss.

"Thanks for all of that," she panted and tried to recover her breath. "Okay, it's your turn now. We have to make sure you're clean."

"Alright, but don't go too far, or you may have a quiet night ahead of you," he replied.

She soaped him down and watched in amazement as his member grew longer and more rigid with every second. She rubbed him all over with the soap foam, except on the item of interest. Finally, she could resist no longer and placed her soapy hand on his member. She felt it tremble and almost vibrate. She moved her hand up and down and heard Ian starting to breath heavier.

He placed his hand on hers and stopped the movement. He whispered, "Please don't go any further, otherwise I won't be able to make love to you later."

"Are you sure?" she asked. Ian nodded.

So, she took the shower head and rinsed all the soap off of him.

They both got out of the shower and dried off. Ian put a little bath powder on Aphrodite's back and front which made her smell sweet as the yellow roses over the front door of the inn. They went and lay down on the bed totally naked, holding each other and kissing.

Ian had her turn over on her stomach and, after he knelt on the bed, started to rub her back and small firm buttocks. He ran one of his finger nails up the spine of her back and she shuddered.

"That felt wonderful," she whispered.

Ian then had her roll onto her back, and he started to gently rub her front. He ran his hands over her beautiful breasts all the way down to her patch of hair. She tingled all over from his touch. He placed his mouth over her right breast, as he softly massaged the left one. She felt like she was in heaven.

"That feels so good. Don't stop," she said, between her quick breaths. He continued alternating between the two round mounds, topped with a small nipple. As he did so, her hand slipped down to find him. It was already hard and firm.

She cradled his testicles in her hand, being careful not to be too rough. She then turned her attention to his enlarged member with its round head. She rubbed a finger over the top of it and felt it pulse as she did so. As she was massaging him with her hand, he was rubbing her between the legs with his hand, and he felt the moisture at the entrance to her wonderful honey pot. As he continued massaging her at her secret spot, she started to breath heavily.

He rolled on top of her and lay there for awhile, with his member teasing her with its presence at the opening to her moist being. As he slowly inserted the round head of his member into her, she gasped with pleasure.

The bed squeaked slightly as they started to make love. They continued moving back and forth in an undulating motion, until both of them came in a united orgasm. Aphrodite again believed that she had gone to heaven. *"How can it feel so wonderful?"* she thought. Ian was beside himself because he had made her happy again and also because he loved her so much.

They fell asleep in each other's arms and woke up ten hours later, exhilarated from their love making.

Again, the morning sun, streaming into the room, had finally woke them up. The cool breeze felt wonderful on their naked bodies.

After they had cleaned up and got dressed, they went down to another full English breakfast. Verena, after she placed the plates of food in front of them, said, "I hope your room has been comfortable for you."

"Yes, thank you," Ian replied and Aphrodite nodded with a shy smile.

They woofed down the breakfast, as they were both very hungry.

On this last full day at the mountains, they planned to drive and see both the Bellapais Abbey and the Buffavento Castle. They were east of Kyrenia, in the mountains, and could only be reached by driving up windy roads. They thought it would be best to visit the abbey first and then, on the way to the castle, have lunch in Karakum or Catalkoy.

After breakfast, they went to their room and got ready to go on their drive. As Aphrodite was in the bathroom, Ian looked out the window at the mountains and the ocean in the distance. The bright sun was shining on the water that looked very still. It was a beautiful sight.

After they were both prepared, Ian and Aphrodite descended the stairs and went out to the car. They drove off down the twisty road again, until they reached Ayyorgi, and then turned east down the coast. Ian drove through Kyrenia and took a road out of the town, toward the village of Bellapais. The abbey itself was located near the village.

They parked the car and walked amid the ruins. Actually, it was in fairly good condition; much better than the Hilarion Castle. After spending an hour or so there, they decided to go to Karakum, on the coast, for lunch.

As they drove into the village, Ian spotted a small restaurant, tucked down a side street that had outside seating.

"That looks like it might be a good restaurant," Ian said. "Let's try it, if you're game."

"Yes, it looks good and there're several people there, which means it can't be too bad," Aphrodite responded. Their guess was correct and the menu had a variety of food listed.

As they were seated there eating, two young Greek men at another table were eyeing them. One said to the other, "I believe that's the sister of Andreus Palas who was killed in April by a British Army lieutenant. I wonder if that's the officer."

The other responded, "I don't know, but I don't suppose that she would go out with him, if she knew."

The first man said, "I think we should inform Demetrio when we get back to Nicosia."

After Ian and Aphrodite ate their lunch, they got back into the car and headed east towards Catalkoy. Just past this village, they turned south up the road to Buffavento Castle. There were sign posts for the castle all the way along, so it would have been hard to get lost.

They reached the castle after a long drive in the mountains. Again, it was a ruin on top of a rocky hill, just like the Hilarion Castle. They wandered around the ruins for about an hour, drinking in the beautiful view and the inland plain in the distance.

After climbing back into the car, Ian and Aphrodite drove down the mountains and onto the coastal road. Halfway toward the inn, they stopped to rest on a green expanse overlooking the Mediterranean. The afternoon sun was reflected off the calm water. About an hour before sunset, Ian and Aphrodite returned to the Davos-Platz and walked out to a bench that was on a bluff, overlooking the mountains and the sea. Holding hands, they sat down and enjoyed the picturesque view for a few minutes.

"Aphrodite," Ian said. "Look at that magnificent vista. We don't see anything like that in Nicosia. Let me take your picture."

He got his Leica camera and had her stand with the view behind her. As he was taking the picture, Ian said, "You're the most beautiful person I've ever met, and I've fallen in love with you. Thank you for coming on this trip."

She responded with a smile, "Thank you for inviting me. I've had a wonderful time, in many ways. I love you too."

They went to their room and cleaned up for dinner.

As they drove to the International Restaurant, Ian turned to Aphrodite and said, "I hope we can do this again soon."

"I hope so too," replied Aphrodite.

While waiting for their meal to be served, Ian held her hand and looked into her eyes, he said, "Aphrodite, I wish this could go on forever. I love you so much. Thank you for being my friend and my lover."

Aphrodite looked at him and her heart welled up. She thought, "*I can see his soul.*"

"Thank you, it's been a wonderful weekend that I'll never forget," she replied.

They ate their meal as they sipped the dry, red wine. As before, the restaurant food was excellent, and the wine was superb. They lingered in the restaurant until closing time. Since it was Sunday evening, the restaurant closed early. Afterwards they drove back to the inn and rang the bell.

Verena came to the counter. "Can I help you?" she inquired.

Ian responded, "Yes, we have to leave by 7:30 am, so would you mind waking us at 6:15 am."

"Of course, I'll knock on your door at 6:15, and I'll have a quick breakfast ready for you, when you come down."

"Thanks very much. We'll appreciate that."

They climbed the stairs and entered the room for the last time. They lay on the bed and made love again. Ian went very slowly, trying to savour it as long as he could. He wanted this to be memorable for Aphrodite and, of course, for himself.

Finally, he could hold it no longer, and they both came at the same time, holding each other.

They both fell asleep, with Aphrodite on her right side and Ian pressing against her back, holding her. He didn't want to let go in case he lost her.

The next morning, at the scheduled time, Verena knocked on their door and woke them up. They both took turns in the bathroom and got dressed for the return to Nicosia. After they had eaten the quick breakfast that Verena had prepared and Ian had paid the bill, they got in the car with their bags and drove back to Nicosia.

On the way, they talked about the week-end and how much fun it had been. They also discussed what lay in their future.

"Where do you want me to drop you off, Aphrodite; at your home or the hospital?" Ian asked.

"Please drop me off at my home. I'm not due on duty at the hospital until tonight. I think you know how to get to my home but, just in case, I'll tell you how to get there when we're closer."

Ian drove on some more and then said, "Aphrodite. I'd like to see you every day, but I'm sorry, it'll not be possible for the next four weeks. I can't tell you what I'll be doing, for security reasons. However, I can assure you that I'll not be flying a plane or going on a ship. I'm going to be very busy, but I'll try to call you as much as I can. You can also call me, if I'm in my office."

"Ian, I'm sorry to hear that," Aphrodite said, with disappointment in her voice. "I hope it isn't dangerous, whatever you'll be doing. I trust you'll be faithful to me because I love you so much. Please be careful."

"Aphrodite, there's always a little danger in whatever I do, but be assured I'll take every precaution necessary to stay out of danger for you. Of course, I'll be faithful to you, and I hope you'll also be true to me."

When he said this, she took his hand, kissed it and smiled.

They drove on some more and soon they were in the outskirts of Nicosia. Suddenly, Aphrodite said, "Turn left at the next road and proceed down it about half a mile. Then turn right onto Kapella Street and go to the third house (#16) on the left."

Ian did as she said and stopped in front of her neat, single story house, which he immediately recognized. Ian got out, opened the passenger side door for her and retrieved her case from the boot. He carried the case to the front door for her and put it down. He then pulled her toward him, and she melted into his arms. He gave her a long lingering kiss and whispered, "Aphrodite, I love you and will do so forever."

She returned the kiss and said, "I love you too. Please be careful and ring me up. I'll be anxious until we can talk again."

With that, she opened the front door and went inside. She went to her room and lay on her bed, thinking about the wonderful time she had.

After awhile there was knock at her door and her mother said, "May I come in?"

"Yes", Aphrodite replied.

Her mother came in and sat on the bed saying, "Are you okay?"

"Yes, mother. I just had a wonderful week-end with the man that I love, and I'm going to marry some day. I'm just scared because he's in the military and could get hurt again."

"Aphrodite. You are my daughter, and I don't want to see you hurt in any way."

"Mother, he'll not abandon me, like some military guys. I know that with all my heart. I'm just afraid he'll get hurt or killed."

Her mother said, "My dear Aphrodite, every day I'll pray that nothing bad befalls you or him."

"Thank you mother, that makes me feel better."

Her mother replied, "If you don't mind me asking, would you tell me his name?"

Aphrodite responded, "He's name is Ian Black, and he's a lieutenant in the army."

Her mother gasped silently, but said nothing. She had already guessed that Ian Black was probably responsible for her son's death but she wasn't sure that Aphrodite knew this.

She rose, kissed her daughter and left the room. Diana went to her room and prayed silently that nothing bad would ever happen to her daughter.

16

Operation Moonshine

In an early September staff meeting, held by Colonel Baker, Captain Phillips brought up Ian's previously suggested idea of a raid in the Troodos Mountains on the EOKA hideouts. If they could catch them unawares, they might be able to catch a few of the terrorists and some documents, before they could be destroyed. This action had been tried before, but with limited success, by other units. Some SIS (Secret Intelligence Service) people had tried to infiltrate the villages located in the mountains, but since the villagers were very suspicious of strangers, this operation did not go well.

"Colonel, some intelligence has been obtained that there will be a major EOKA planning session in a hidden camp near the village of Agros, on the evening of the 23rd of September. For some time now, Agros has been a command centre for the Pitsilia area, and a considerable number of the villagers are strong EOKA sympathizers. I suggest we have a combined operation between an infantry unit and the searchlight lorries of the 188th Battery, on that evening."

"Do you believe it can be pulled off successfully?" the colonel asked. "As you just stated, the previous raids were not very successful. In fact, the raid three years ago, on Spilia, ended in disaster. Our own units fired on each other in the fog that surrounded the area at the time."

"Sir, the raid may have been too ambitious. They wanted to capture Grivas, which although a noble goal, may have caused the planners to make tactical errors," replied Captain Phillips.

"Okay, we'll try again, and the raid will have the code name Operation Moonshine. John, since it is part of your organization, will you coordinate it with SIS and other Intelligence operations.

"Certainly colonel, I'll be glad to," replied John.

"Captain, I suggest that you obtain the support of an infantry unit, maybe the Durham Light Infantry 1st Battalion. Mr. Black, you will be in charge of obtaining some Matador Searchlight lorries from the 188th Radar and Searchlight Battery, since you know them best."

The colonel continued, "We have to be quick about the organization of this raid, since the date is only about three weeks from now. We'll meet again in three days to plan this operation. I'll call in some experienced army planners, who can help lay out the plans and schedule of the attack. In the meantime, captain, besides rounding up the infantry support, I want you to arrange for aerial photography of the area. In fact, the plane, probably an Auster AOP.6, should also take pictures of other villages, in the Troodos Mountains, so it doesn't look like we're just concentrating on Agros."

Captain Phillips replied, "I'll arrange the air photography and make sure it's not concentrated just on Agros and the Pitsilia region."

The colonel ended the meeting by saying, "We've a lot to do in the next three weeks, so let's get to work. We'll meet every three to four days, to go over the plans for Operation Moonshine. Incidentally, Mr. Black that was some good intelligence you conducted in Beirut. We'll get together later to go over your report."

Ian nodded and said, "Yes, sir."

197

The colonel left the room. Captain Phillips and Ian sat discussing the upcoming raid and the tasks before them. They then both left and went their separate ways, to coordinate their individual activities.

Ian drove out to Camp Ubique, just a few miles west of Nicosia, to visit with his former CO, Major MacArthur. After showing his ID to the camp gate sentry, he was allowed to pass in and he drove to the CO's office. Parking, he went in, again presented his army identification card and asked the major's aide, if he was available. The aide went in to the major's office and, in a couple of moments, came out saying, "He'll see you now, lieutenant."

Ian knocked on the door and after hearing "Enter" went in to find the major seated behind his desk. He rose to greet one of his former officers. Ian saluted him and he returned the favour.

"Mr. Black, it's a pleasure to see you again. How are you doing at Salisbury House? I've heard of some of your exploits in Beirut, on board a minesweeper and a Shackleton. You've been busy, since you left here. You don't look any worse for the wear, even with all the problems you faced."

"The work is very interesting and I would like to thank you again, for giving me the opportunity to transfer."

"What can I do for you, Ian? I'm sure you didn't come here just to say hello and go over old times."

"We're going to conduct an operation in the Troodos Mountains, called Operation Moonshine, and we're hoping for the support of the 188th, sir. The actual operation will take place in the evening of the 23rd of September near a village named Agros. If you could provide us with six searchlight Matador lorries, it would give us enough support in the raid and also provide diversions. Initially, the trucks would fan out over six villages – Pelendri, Spilia, Kakopetria, Polistipos, Palaichori and Agros. We would then have three at Agros triangulating on the hideout, at the appropriate time. The other three would be located at three of the other villages, as diversions to EOKA. We'll have the support of 300-500 infantry and SIS"

"That sounds like an ambitious plan. What are the goals of the operation?" asked the major.

Ian replied, "We don't expect Grivas to be there. He's too crafty to be caught in a trap like this. However, we do hope to catch a few of his "lieutenants" and some documents, both of which we hope will ultimately lead us to him."

"Let me talk with my officers and determine how many searchlight Matadors, with crews, we could provide you around that date. We'll let you know within a day, as I realize your schedule is tight for the planning of this operation," responded Major MacArthur.

Ian left the 188th with the feeling that they would support Operation Moonshine, as best they could. He drove back to Salisbury House to report to Captain Phillips, about his conversation with Major MacArthur.

"The major was positive, but he'll only commit to how many AEC searchlight Matadors he can provide, after reviewing the request with his officers," Ian told the captain.

The captain replied, "By the next Operation Moonshine planning session, we should have answers both from the 188th and the Durham light infantry."

"Sir, I've done some thinking about Operation Moonshine and I propose the following tactics.

First, as proposed previously, we should have an Auster AOP.6 take photos of various villages including Pelendri, Spilia, Kakopetria, Polistipos, Palaichori and Agros. Targeting this number of villages will cause EOKA not to suspect any one specific target for a raid.

Second, we need to get support from the AAC (Army Air Corps) and have them provide four Bristol 171 Sycamore helicopters, with three men per craft. Sunset on the 23rd will be around 1845, and therefore the helicopters should have no problem identifying their hover points. At 1855, the heavily armed men would be lowered from the Sycamores, and they'd seal off escape routes from the Agros EOKA meeting place.

Third, assuming we get the six Matadors from the 188th, we'd have each of them go to a different village, listed in the first tactic, and then at the appointed hour, two would return to Agros and triangulate, with the one already in place, on the meeting hideout.

Fourth, the Durham light infantry would converge on the target building and, together, with two or three Saracens, totally seal off any escape routes, initially secured by the AAC forces.

Fifth, and this is critical, all units would be equipped with the same type of portable radios with identical crystals installed, so that all units involved could talk to each other. This way we should be able to avoid any friendly fire incidents.

Sixth and finally, I think we'd need an individual embedded, for a few days, in the area close to the building, where they will meet, to act as a spotter. He would inform us about the situation there and tell us when all the participants to the meeting have arrived."

"In general, Ian, the tactics you have outlined sound very practical. Let me think about them and we can discuss them at the next meeting with the colonel."

At the next planning meeting with the colonel, Captain Phillips outlined the tactics with the group. By the time this meeting occurred, they had received word that the 188th could supply the six Matador searchlight lorries and that the Durham light infantry was available, in a strength of 300, if required.

However, the captain changed the need for 300 infantry, down to 100. The thought was that 300 would make too much noise and would be hard to hide, on their way to Agros. Plus, since there would be only ten to twelve EOKA leaders at the meeting, according to the latest intelligence, the captain thought that the 300 would be overkill.

The colonel listened to all the pros and cons and decided it was worth the risk to go ahead with the Operation. Its aim was to help find Grivas and shut down EOKA, and that was important enough to justify it.

The colonel stated, "I'll coordinate Operation Moonshine with the AAC and insure that they will provide the four Sycamore helicopters and special troops. I'll also discuss with the SAS (Special Air Service) to see if they could provide the one embedded soldier, we need as a spotter, on the meeting place.

Mr. Black, I want you to coordinate the plan for inserting the searchlight lorries with the 188th.

Captain Phillips, you need to get back to the Durham infantry and tell them we only need 100, and coordinate their movements to the area.

John, as you agreed, please contact the SIS and make sure they'll support us in this effort. Let me know if there is any problem, or issue with them.

The colonel concluded the meeting by saying, "Okay, that's all for today. Let's get moving we've a lot to do, between now and the 23rd of September. It's only a fortnight from now."

Over the next couple of weeks, all of them contacted the various organizations that were involved in the Operation and refined the tactics and plans. Everything seemed to be coming together, without any major hitch. The weather forecast was good for the date involved and no fog was anticipated, as it had occurred in the 1955 Spilia raid. The latest intelligence gathered indicated that the planned EOKA meeting was still scheduled to start at 1900 hours, on the evening of the 23rd. The army Signals Corps provided several portable radio sets, with the same crystal installed, so that they all operated on the same frequency. All the radios were checked out to make sure all of them worked perfectly. It was critical to the operation that all units could communicate with each other.

During a break in the planning activities, Ian called Aphrodite at the hospital, but she was busy attending to her patients. He left a message for her to call him, whenever possible.

A couple of days before the raid actually took place, the colonel held one final planning session. He wanted to be sure all contingencies had been considered.

"Captain Phillips. Is the Durham light infantry ready and do the officers understand what they have to do?"

"Yes colonel, they'll arrive twenty to a lorry, at the different points around the meeting farmhouse, just after the Sycamores have dropped the men off to seal the escape routes. They will fan out and surround the farmhouse. The plan is to make sure no one escapes."

"Captain, will they have the necessary radios?"

"Yes, sir, every tenth man will have a radio that can communicate with all radios used on the raid, including the Sycamores. In addition a radio will be provided to each Matador searchlight lorry."

"Has the photography of the area been studied, and do we know what we could run into, as far as obstacles?"

"Yes colonel," replied Captain Phillips. "We've had photographic experts do a complete study of the photos and we know exactly all the obstacles around the farmhouse."

"Mr. Black, are the six 188th searchlight Matador lorries ready to roll and will they be manned with operators and troops to guard them?"

"Yes sir, Major MacArthur assures me that they'll be ready and will know what to do, according to the plan we've given them," replied Ian.

"John, have you heard anything at Ayios Nikolaos that indicates they suspect we might be planning a raid? Also, have you any new intelligence at MI6 that suggests they're cancelling the meeting?"

"No colonel, we've heard nothing that would compromise this raid. Of course, as you're aware, our major objective at Ayios Nikolaos is the listening in on external communications."

"Sergeant Bingham, has the Signal Corps picked up any EOKA radio communications that would suggest they've changed their meeting or have discovered our plans for a raid?"

"No colonel, we've not picked up any EOKA communications traffic lately. I think they're lying low, or using other forms of communication."

The colonel ended the meeting with, "Okay, to keep you all informed, General Mastin has approved this operation, with the condition that it hasn't been compromised in any way. I've made the necessary arrangements with the AAC for the Sycamores and the Special Forces, to be available and ready for the raid. The SAS is willing to provide the one embedded spotter. In fact, even as we speak, he's actually already in the area, keeping a watch on the hideout. So far, he's seen nothing that would indicate they're on to us.

We'll meet again, on the morning of the raid at 0800, to conduct a review of our readiness, and then we'll head out. I'll go in an unmarked car, with one SAS chap and one SIS agent. The SIS agent assigned was one who was on the Spilia raid in 1955, and can help insure we don't make the same mistakes. Captain Phillips, you'll go with the Durham Light Infantry and Mr. Black you'll travel with the 188th Matadors. We'll all converge on Agros and the other villages in the area, and then, just before dusk, take up positions around the farmhouse, after the spotter radios us that they're all inside. The AAC Sycamores will drop their Special Forces, a little before sunset, and they'll initially block any escape routes.

Is this all clear? If so, we'll meet here Friday morning at 0800."

All the attendees at the meeting nodded and said, "Yes sir." They all left the meeting room, to work on last minute details.

On Friday morning at 0800, the day of the Troodos Mountain raid, they were all in attendance at the brief meeting in Salisbury House. Colonel Baker was the last to arrive. He walked into the room and sat down, at one end of the table, as a hush fell over the room, except for the ceiling fan noise.

"Gentlemen, the day for Operation Moonshine has finally arrived. The last three weeks have been tedious and difficult, but the work will pay off, I'm sure. I'll go round the table asking each of you individually whether you're ready to take on your assigned tasks for the raid. If there are any issues, bring them up, as I call on you.

Okay John, let's start with you. Do you have any intelligence that would suggest that this operation has been comprised and should be stopped?"

"There isn't any information from either SIGINT or HUMINT sources, including intercepts at Ayios Nikolaos, which would indicate a leak of any kind." John answered.

"Sergeant Bingham, do you have anything to report?" asked the colonel.

"Colonel, the Signal Corps, as far as I'm aware, has not intercepted any communications between EOKA terrorists that would indicate they are aware of the upcoming raid in Agros."

"Mr. Snell, have you heard anything in the Turkish community that indicates that someone knows about the EOKA meeting or Operation Moonshine?"

"Colonel, I've checked with most of the officers and several of the men in the Wiltshire Regiment and no one has heard anything about the EOKA meeting or our Operation, in their normal patrol duties."

"Mr. Black, is the 188th Battery, with their six searchlight lorries, ready to conduct their part of this Operation?"

"Yes colonel, they're all ready and waiting for the word to head out."

"Okay, good, your call sign on the radio will be BULLDOG 3A and the other five Matadors will be BULLDOG 3B through 3F."

"Captain Phillips, is the light infantry ready to proceed in the five lorries?"

"Yes, Colonel Baker, they're ready to proceed."

"Good. Your call sign, captain will be BULLDOG 2A and the other four lorries of infantry will be BULLDOG 2B through 2E.

Gentlemen, my call sign will be BULLDOG 1. The embedded Special Forces soldier is BULLDOG 4 and the four Sycamores will be BULLDOG 5 through 8.

It appears there are no reportable problems and therefore we shall proceed immediately with Operation Moonshine. Let's go!"

They all left the conference room and, Colonel Baker, Captain Phillips and Lieutenant Black climbed into their vehicles and headed out from Salisbury House.

Ian drove to Camp Ubique to join the convoy of six Matadors, waiting to roll. When he got there, he gave the lieutenants or sergeants in charge of each Matador their call signs. He climbed into the lead Matador, after telling each of the lorries to proceed separately to their assigned location, in the Troodos Mountains. It was imperative that each lorry parked at a different point, so that it didn't look like a mass raid to the local villagers. They would then converge at around sunset on the farmhouse, where the meeting was taking place. Since the raid would not take place until sunset, there was plenty of time for the lorries to get into position.

The lorries, containing the light infantry and Captain Phillips, also headed into the mountains, some taking a circuitous route to their assigned destination. Colonel Baker drove into the mountains with the SIS agent and ended up at Spilia, a distance away from Agros and the farmhouse. There the colonel called the embedded Special Forces soldier on the radio at 1400 hours.

"BULLDOG 4, this is BULLDOG 1. Is everything quiet outside the farmhouse?"

"BULLDOG 1, this is BULLDOG 4. I haven't seen much activity yet at the farmhouse. Two men did arrive a few minutes ago, by car, and they went inside."

"Your report is received and understood. We'll contact you again at 1700 hours, unless we hear from you earlier."

While the colonel and the embedded soldier were communicating, all the others on the same frequency could hear the same report. All communications were kept as short as possible to prevent EOKA from listening in or pinpointing the location of the transmitters.

At 1700, the colonel again called the spotter.

"BULLDOG 4, this is BULLDOG 1. Have you seen any more activity?"

"BULLDOG 1, this is BULLDOG 4. Another car arrived at 1645 and two more men got out. I've seen one man come out of the farmhouse, look around and go back in."

"Thanks for the report. We will contact you again at 1900, over and out."

At 1850, the embedded soldier called the colonel.

"BULLDOG 1, this is BULLDOG 4. Two more vehicles have arrived at the farmhouse with a total of five men and one woman. Two of the men walked around the grounds and it looked like they were searching for any suspicious activities. They didn't get close enough to be of danger to me, over.

"This is the colonel, thanks for the report."

ON HER MAJESTY'S CYPRUS MISSION

"This is BULLDOG 1 calling all BULLDOGS. Everything appears to be a go and on schedule. Start preparations to converge on the farmhouse for the raid at 2000 hours. BULLDOG 1 to BULLDOGS 5 though 8, start loading the men and start up your engines. We need the Air Regiment men to be dropped, on the assigned landing zones, at 1950 precisely. There are no clouds or fog in the area and pilots should be able to locate the landing sites. All BULLDOGS confirm by number now."

They all confirmed with an, "okay understood", in order, until all had replied.

At 1930, the embedded soldier got on the radio again.

"BULLDOG 1, this is BULLDOG 4. Two more cars just arrived, with five more men in total. One of them seemed like the ring leader, since the others came out of the farmhouse and shook his hand. This means there's a total of fifteen now assembled here. They've now all gone back into the building. The sky is still clear and fog free."

"BULLDOG 1 calling all BULLDOGS. There are now fifteen EOKA terrorists in the farmhouse for their planning meeting. BULLDOGS 2 and 3 prepare to surround the building. BULLDOGS 5 though 8 prepare to drop your Special Forces, at the assigned drop zones, and then quickly seal off any escape routes from the farmhouse. The light infantry will back you up, as soon as they get there."

At 1950, the four Sycamore helicopters hovered over the drop zones, and three AAC soldiers slid down the ropes onto the ground. They fanned out around the building sealing off most of the escape routes. The helicopters were far enough away from the farmhouse so that the terrorists could not hear them.

At 2000 hours, the Durham light infantry, with Captain Phillips, arrived in the five lorries. The soldiers jumped out of the vehicles and spread out to join the AAC men, thus sealing off the entire area. Ian and the 188thMatador searchlight lorries came up, parked with their rears facing the building. They quickly started their generators and turned on the searchlights, illuminating the entire farmhouse and the surrounding fir tree covered farm.

Ian drew his Browning automatic, just in case he needed it. He jumped onto the ground and crept towards the farmhouse, using bushes as cover. At the same time, Colonel Baker arrived with the SIS man in their unmarked car. They got out and started towards the building, using the trees and bushes as cover. The colonel had a bullhorn in one hand and a revolver in the other.

He converged on the same bush that Ian was using as cover and turned on the bullhorn. He asked Ian to speak, in Greek, to the terrorists, inside the building.

Ian took the bullhorn and shouted in Greek, "This is the British Army. We have you surrounded. Come out with your hands up."

There was silence for a second or two, and then gunfire erupted from a couple of the upstairs windows. They were shooting at the searchlights, trying to knock them out. The light infantry fired at the windows from where the gunfire was coming from, and it immediately ceased.

Ian got on the bullhorn again and, in Greek, shouted, "You have one more chance to surrender, and then we'll be coming in."

There was silence again and then two terrorists ran out of the back door, heading for the trees. Unfortunately for them, the Durham light infantry had the area covered and they were cut down, before reaching the safety of the trees.

Ian got on the bullhorn one last time. "Come out with your hands up, now," he yelled in Greek.

Finally, the main door of the farmhouse opened and seven terrorists came out with their hands up, led by the lone woman. They walked towards Ian and a few soldiers who had joined him and the colonel. The infantry surrounded them and took them into custody.

As they did, a lone terrorist jumped out of a window on the side of the house and made it to the cover of the trees, just as he was spotted by one of the AAC Regiment men. The soldier ran after him but he was hit by a bullet in the leg, when the terrorist opened fire. A soldier from the light infantry was close at hand, and he dropped the terrorist with one well aimed shot. He was dead before he hit the ground.

The colonel did a quick count and figured there were three more terrorists unaccounted for. He assumed that the infantry had killed the two upstairs, who were trying to knock out the searchlights.

The colonel said to Ian, "I can only account for twelve of them. There must still be three more inside the farmhouse."

"I'll take two infantry men and go inside to check out the place," Ian said.

"Be very careful," the colonel replied. "We'll cover you the best we can."

Ian signaled to two of the infantrymen to follow him, and they ran quickly, hunched over, towards the front door of the farmhouse that was slightly ajar. The one searchlight that had been lighting up the front door area had been turned off, so as not to illuminate them. Ian kicked open the door, as he stood to one side. He started to enter the building, when there was a muzzle flash that came from a corner of the large room. The bullet flew past Ian's ear and he fired his Browning in the direction of the flash. Immediately, he heard some groaning coming from the corner of the room. As he crept towards a large, overturned chair, where the sound was located, Ian began to hear some noises above him, in the second story of the house. He beckoned to the two infantrymen to come to him.

Ian whispered to them, "I hear some noises coming from upstairs and they sound as though they are coming from more than one source. I believe that the other two men, we're looking for, are up there trying to escape. Go up the stairs and see if you can get them. Be careful, and don't be

209

heroes. I'll be up there as soon as I've looked at the wounded bugger in the corner."

Ian crept over to the corner of the room and found an EOKA terrorist in a pool of blood. He was in no condition to keep fighting, and Ian picked up his weapon, to take it with him.

The terrorists groaned in Greek, "Help me, help me."

Ian replied Greek, "We'll help you as soon as this place has been neutralized."

Ian then went up the stairs to the second story, following the infantrymen. As he rounded a corner in the stairwell, the two infantrymen, ahead of him, were met with a hail of bullets. One of the infantrymen was hit in the arm and was out of action. The other returned fire and hit one of the two terrorists.

Ian joined the unwounded infantryman and together they slowly went to the top of the stairs. Here, they were met with another hail of bullets. In the dim light, Ian was able to see one of the terrorists and he fired his Browning twice. The second shot hit the terrorist right in the middle of his chest and he stopped firing.

The other terrorist vanished into one of the rooms at the end of the hallway that ran the length of the second floor. Ian and the infantryman crept down the hallway towards the room.

When they were close, they stopped and Ian yelled in Greek, "Come on out with your hands up. You can't get away. This building is surrounded."

The gunman yelled back, also in Greek, "You won't take me alive. I'll kill you both, before you can kill me."

With that, the gunman moved towards the door, ran into the hallway, firing his automatic weapon. Luckily, Ian and the infantryman were lying prone on the hallway floor, one on each side. They both fired back hitting the terrorist in the chest and face. The leader of the terrorist group died instantly and fell on the hallway floor, face down.

Ian descended the stairs, went to the front door of the farmhouse and shouted for the colonel and the captain to join him.

"You can come in now, colonel. The building has been neutralized. There's one wounded terrorist that needs medical attention. The others, including one who I believe was the ring leader, are dead."

The colonel and captain, followed by some infantrymen, came into the farmhouse to review the damage and casualties. A medic came with them to assist the wounded terrorist, lying in the corner of the room.

Ian said to the colonel, "Well, we've disrupted their planning session, but I haven't found any documents yet. I'm sure they must have had some written plans somewhere."

Ian went outside and obtained a torch from one of the searchlight operators. He came back in and looked around the lower room, where the meeting took place. He couldn't see any papers anywhere.

"That's strange," he thought. *"There must be some hidden in here somewhere."*

He looked around the room and all he saw was some furniture, a couple of lamps and a Persian rug on the floor. In desperation, he pulled back the rug and didn't see anything.

Then he shone the torch over the floor where the rug had been and noticed some of the stones were a slightly different colour to the rest. The colonel and the captain had gone upstairs to look around.

"Colonel," Ian shouted, "I think I may have found something."

"I'm coming down," the colonel shouted back.

The colonel and the captain ran down the stairs to where Ian was standing.

Ian pointed out the different colors of a few of the stones, making up the floor. Then Ian noticed something else.

"Colonel, all of the stones have been cemented together, except for these four."

"Mr. Black," the colonel replied. "I think you're on to something."

The captain went outside and, in a few minutes, returned with a large crowbar. He placed the narrow head of the bar into the crack between the stones and levered up the stone. It came loose and Ian shone the torch down below it.

"Sir, I think we've found the papers we're looking for," Ian said.

All three of them looked in the hole, beneath the stone, and the white papers reflected the light from the torch.

Captain Phillips levered up all of the four loose stones and a large hidden niche appeared below the floor. In it was a stack of papers, all written in Greek.

Colonel Baker said, "Mr. Black, I believe you have some work to do, translating these papers."

"Yes sir," Ian replied, as he gathered up all the papers and placed them into an empty box that just happened to be in the corner of the room.

They all went outside where an ambulance had just arrived, to take the wounded back to the closest hospital.

They placed the dead terrorists in the rear of one of the Durham Light Infantry lorries, while the colonel went and thanked, as many as he could, for their participation in the raid. The prisoners were placed in another lorry, with guards, and they were taken to Nicosia for interrogation.

Then all the vehicles formed a long convoy and headed back down the direct route to Nicosia and their individual camps. Captain Phillips and Ian rode in the car with the colonel and the SIS agent.

The SIS agent said to the colonel, "Well, I believe that was a very productive raid. It was certainly better than the

Spilia raid, four years ago. At least, you had no friendly fire accidents. Let's hope we obtain some good information out of the prisoners and the retrieved EOKA papers."

"The amount of information we get out of the papers will depend on Mr. Black, correct Ian?" the colonel asked.

"Yes sir," Ian replied.

Captain Phillips said to Ian, "If you need any help, let me know. I'm sure it can be arranged."

Ian nodded and responded, "Thanks, sir."

After about an hour of driving out of the mountains and onto the plain, they arrived at Salisbury House and got out of the car. The colonel thanked the SIS agent for his assistance and then turning to Ian said with a broad grin, "Mr. Black, I expect a translation of all those papers, on my desk by 0800 tomorrow morning.

"I'll do my best, sir, "Ian replied.

"I've changed my mind, as is my prerogative. Two or three days will be fine, Ian. Go get some rest," the colonel responded.

They all walked into the building and Ian went up to his room with the box of papers and crashed. He did not wake up until ten o'clock the next morning.

For the next few days, Ian worked on the translations of the papers found under the floor at the farmhouse. On the following Friday morning, he presented Captain Phillips with the translations, who immediately took them the colonel.

After lunch, Ian's phone rang.

"Mr. Black, can you come to my office immediately?" the colonel asked.

"Yes sir, I'll be there momentarily." Ian answered.

He went to the colonel's office and entered. The captain was also in there. Ian saluted them both, as he approached the colonel's desk.

"Take a seat, Ian," the colonel said.

After he was seated, the colonel continued, "These documents contain some good information. First, it appears

EOKA is having trouble obtaining the necessary arms they need. Our embargo must be working. Second, they're worried about the Turkish community arming itself and the chance of sectarian warfare. Third, there seems to be a leak in the Limassol police department. It may be that someone fairly high up is helping Grivas to hide his whereabouts. Fourth, EOKA is worried about the negotiations going on in Europe, between the Greek Government, the British Government and Archbishop Makarios. EOKA is concerned that Makarios and the Greek Government will give away too much. Finally, Grivas thinks that EOKA must step up the terror campaign, in order to influence the negotiations. He writes about the need for indiscriminate killings of civilians. This is all excellent information that I'll pass up the chain of command. Before I do, do you have anything to add?"

"The only points, I can add, are that we need to be more vigilant about Turkish arm shipments and the danger of assassination of the governor. Other than that, sir, I believe your review of the documents covers all the major points," Ian responded

"Good. I'll send a written review to the General Mastin, along with the papers and translations, and include the two issues you just raised."

Then looking at Ian, the colonel said, "Thank you for all the time you spent on this. By the way, the HMS *Benton*, I believe you know that ship, is going on intercept patrols against suspected Turkish arm shipments. I want you to go on one of them with Lt. Snell, our Turkish language expert."

"Yes sir, I'll check with Captain Abney of the *Benton* about the possible sailing dates and times."

"Good, we'll talk more about that at our next Monday staff meeting. That will be all for now." the colonel said.

Ian stood up, saluted and left the colonel's office feeling relieved that his work was well received.

After he left, the colonel said to Captain Phillips, "Ian will go a long way in this man's army. He's bright, daring and a hard worker. Keep an eye on him."

"Yes, sir, I'll make sure he doesn't make any major mistakes. Also, you've met his girlfriend Aphrodite. She seems to be very level headed, and she'll probably keep him focused and disciplined."

17

Cyprus Heats Up

On Friday, the 3rd of October, 1958, the violence in the Cyprus Emergency came to a head. It had been going on for four years, but now the rumours of talks between the British Government and Makarios had reached Grivas. He decided his group of "freedom fighters" needed to ratchet up the violence, in order to place additional pressure on the British, so they would concede more than they wanted to.

Three British women happened to be shopping on Hermes Street in the Greek section of Famagusta. They were Mrs. Catherine Cutliffe, the wife of a Royal Artillery 29th Field Regiment NCO, Margaret, her eighteen year old daughter, and a German friend, Mrs. Elfriede Robinson, married to a British Army sergeant. Margaret had plans to get married soon and was shopping for her trousseau, amongst other things.

According to reports from the scene, the women were coming out of a bridal store, carrying Margaret's wedding dress, when two young Greek Cypriot men came up behind them and opened fire. One of the men shot Mrs. Cutliffe, a mother of five, twice in the back and she fell to the ground. The man kept firing at her two more times and she died at the scene. Mrs. Robinson was also shot in the back by the other man and he shot her again, as she lay seriously wounded on the pavement. However, she did ultimately recover from her wounds. One of the men shot at Margaret, missed and she escaped unharmed. However, she obviously did suffer mentally, seeing her mother die on a Famagusta street in Cyprus. The killers escaped and a guard was placed on the Cutliffe home, since the daughter Margaret might be able to identify the killers, if and when they were found. Ultimately, authorities identified the two men as Costas Christadoulides (the ring leader) and Kikis Constantinou. However, the police did not have enough evidence against either of them, and they were never brought to trial.

The British troops were so incensed by the shootings and the murder that they started a campaign of intimidation against the Greek Cypriots. Later that day and into the night, they went on a rampage beating up Greek locals and looting stores. Any male, over sixteen years of age, in Famagusta was rounded up for questioning and hundreds of them were held until the next day, either at an army camp or the police station. The Turkish residents were happy to help the British in this roundup and the beatings that followed.

Violence broke out with windows being smashed and general looting taking place. Grivas had achieved what he wanted; a dramatic increase in the violence to put pressure on Prime Minster Harold MacMillan. The Times of Cyprus, controlled by a liberal editor, placed the blame for all the violence squarely on the shoulders of the military, and disregarded the killing of an army wife.

While this was going on in Famagusta, Nicosia was still fairly quiet, although tensions between the Greeks, the Turks and the British had increased.

Then, a few days later, the NAAFI at RAF Nicosia was hit with a bomb that was hidden in a sofa. The resulting explosion killed two airmen and seriously wounded seven others. The bomb appeared to have been hand built and contained nails that did a lot of damage to the victims. Body parts from the two victims went everywhere. They had happened to be sitting right on top of the bomb.

The RAF Regiment personnel cordoned off the area and started to round up any NAAFI employee. Most of them were Greek Cypriots and they were questioned, sometimes with beatings and torture. Any non British NAAFI employee immediately became a suspect. They were taken to another building, where they were confined. No medical personnel came to their rescue, even though some had been severely beaten. In the end, 3,800 NAAFI employees were fired and volunteers came out from Britain, to help run the facilities.

Thus it was that October 1958 became the month in the Cyprus Enosis Emergency when violence was significantly increased. Sectarian violence between Greeks and Turks increased and gave a taste of what would happen, off and on, for the next 16 years. The Turks were vastly outnumbered, by the Greeks, so they decided it might be time to arm themselves, for what they perceived as the inevitable clash.

A future shooting on Ledra Street would be just another manifestation of this dismal situation in Cyprus. Lieutenant Ian Black was in the middle of it and was doing his best to locate and arrest Grivas, before more lives were lost.

18

Love Revisited

Ian called Aphrodite, whenever he could get hold of her, during the four weeks of the planning and conducting of Operation Moonshine. Finally, by the 7th of October, the operation had been completed, and the recovered documents had been translated. In addition, results from the interrogation of the survivors had been disseminated to the appropriate personnel.

Ian placed a call to Aphrodite at the hospital and, luckily for him, she was in and available to take his call.

"Hello, Aphrodite, this is Ian. These last four weeks have been hell, not being able to see you. How are you today?"

"Ian, it's great to hear your voice. It's been terrible only being able to talk with you on the phone. Since the shooting of Mrs. Cutliffe and all the renewed violence, we've been very busy. Several nurses have quit and returned to England. I've been working double shifts, and Captain Crachett has not been easy to deal with. She's under a lot of pressure, due to the lack of staff. I miss you and hope that we can get together soon."

"I hope so too. All of us are also under a lot of pressure, and Colonel Baker is pushing us to capture Grivas and his top leadership. The increase in violence and riots has affected us. According to the colonel, I'll finally have some time off on the weekend of the 11th and 12th of October.

How does your schedule look for those dates? I want to get together to talk about our future, and how we can see more of each other."

"It just happens that I have been promised three days off by Captain Crachett for that week end. My mother flew to England, on the 4th of October, to visit her sister and brother, and will not be back for two weeks. So I have the house all to myself."

"It must be fairly lonely, living there all by yourself. Would you like some company on the weekend I'm off?"

"I thought you'd never ask. Of course I would. Why don't you come over early on Saturday morning, and I'll cook breakfast for us. You didn't know I could cook, did you?" she said, with a small laugh.

"That sounds smashing. Then, we can talk about our future and also go to the cinema. I've heard that the film titled, "Cat on a Hot Tin Roof", with Elizabeth Taylor and Paul Newman, is highly rated."

"Okay, it's all planned then. We'll eat breakfast at nine o'clock on Saturday morning, and then we'll talk for a couple of hours. Afterwards, we can get a quick bite to eat at a café, before we go to the afternoon matinee of the film you mentioned. Later, we can come back to my home, and I'll cook us a Greek dinner. How does that sound, Ian?"

"That sounds like a great plan to me. Are you sure your mother wouldn't mind me being at her home?"

"No, she has complete confidence in me. We're very much alike, and she only wants the best for me. I believe, whenever I get married, she might return to England for good, since she doesn't see any long term future for her, here in Cyprus."

"She sounds like a great woman to me. I hope I can get to meet her in the near future. I'll arrive in time for breakfast on Saturday. I can't wait to see you again and hold you in my arms."

"See you then, Ian. I'd better get back to work. I love you."

"I love you too, Aphrodite."

****

It was hard for Ian to concentrate on his work, for the next ten days, but the colonel kept pushing for ways to find Grivas and bring him to justice. News of the negotiations in Zurich indicated that the parties were slowly getting the problems ironed out.

At last, Saturday, the 11th of October, arrived and Ian took a taxi from the safe house to Aphrodite's home, arriving fifteen minutes early. He rang the door bell and Aphrodite was soon there, opening the front door. She looked as beautiful as ever. He went in, took her in his arms and gave her a long kiss.

She whispered, "Ian, I've been looking forward to seeing you. I've missed you so much." She then pressed herself against him and returned his kiss.

Finally, they parted and she said, "Breakfast is ready to be served. Would you like to eat in the back garden? It's very nice out there and it's not too hot."

"The back garden sounds great. Can I help you carry it out?"

"Yes, that would be very helpful. I have a tray all set up in the kitchen, if you don't mind carrying it out there for me. I'll bring the coffee."

They walked into the kitchen and Ian picked up the salver, with the breakfast on it. Aphrodite, carrying the coffee pot and two mugs, followed Ian into the back garden. They set the items on the table and sat down to eat their breakfast. It was very comforting to take the meal in the garden with the flowers, green lawn and a gentle cool breeze.

After they were finished, they started to talk about many things that affected both of them.

Ian said, "I'm hoping to go back to England early in 1959, as soon as this Emergency is settled, and have a few days vacation. How would you like to go with me and meet my parents? I'm sure you'll like them. They're easy to get along with."

"That sounds great, as long as I can get time off. If the Emergency really winds down, I don't see that as a problem. I would love to meet your parents. I hope they will like me."

"Oh, I don't think you have to worry about that. They'll adore you, especially my mother. Which reminds me, when can I meet your mother?"

"Maybe, as soon as she returns from England."

"This brings up another question. If we are to be a couple, what would your mother think about someone who killed her son? This point could prove to be a very sticky wicket."

"My mother and I have not discussed the issue. However, I believe she already knows the truth. She knows your name and that you are in the army. She works at the hospital and has access to records. I would be surprised, if she hasn't put two and two together. She has been in Cyprus since before World War Two and realizes sometimes terrible things happen, beyond one's control."

"What would your mother think, if we did eventually get married and we moved to England, to Germany, or wherever the army sends me?"

"As I mentioned the other day on the phone, she has talked about returning to England, after I am married and provided for. I do not believe this will be an issue, in the long run."

"When you get married, how many children you would you like to have?"

"I believe two, and no more than three, would be enough for me to handle. Preferably, I would like one boy and one girl, but one cannot be choosy in matters like that. What about you?"

Ian replied, "I believe that three children would be plenty. I would prefer one boy and one girl, like you."

For the next two hours, they just talked about things that affected both of them, and finally at 11:30, Aphrodite said to Ian, "We had better take the dishes in and wash them, before we go to the cinema. Will you help me?"

"Of course, I'll be glad to," Ian responded.

They went into the kitchen and cleaned it up together.

Aphrodite then said, "Ian, why don't you go into the sitting room, while I go upstairs to freshen up. Then we can go out for a quick bite to eat, before we go to the cinema. I believe the matinée starts at 3:00, doesn't it?"

Ian responded, "Yes, I checked the times and it starts at 3:00 on weekends."

While Aphrodite went upstairs, Ian went and read a magazine he found in the sitting room. In about fifteen minutes, Aphrodite came downstairs and asked, "Well, how do I look?"

"You look gorgeous, Aphrodite," Ian said, as he rose and came over to her. He put his arms around her and gave her a kiss.

"I think we'd better order a taxi to take us close to the cinema. There is small café close by, where we can get a quick lunch."

Ian asked, "Would you mind calling the taxi, since you know the number?"

Aphrodite picked up the phone and asked the operator to put her through to the taxi company.

In about fifteen minutes, the taxi pulled up outside her home. Ian and Aphrodite walked out the front door, closing it behind them. She took his arm and they walked down to the taxi, where he helped her in. He then went around to the other door, climbed in and told the driver, in Greek, where they wanted to go.

Soon, they were outside the small café, located about a twelve businesses away from the cinema, where "Cat on the Hot Tin Roof" was showing. Ian helped Aphrodite out of the taxi and they both went into the café for a late lunch. After they had eaten and Ian had paid the bill, they exited the café and walked down to the cinema, arm in arm. They queued up, and Ian bought the tickets for the back part of the cinema. Luckily, they were close to the front of the queue and managed to get tickets for the row, in the back of the cinema, on the lower level.

When the lights went down, Ian and Aphrodite held hands throughout the film and kissed a few times. They did watch the film though, which some of the others in the back row did not. With the Pathé newsreel and the second film, they did not get out of the cinema until about 6:30.

As they walked outside into the sun that was approaching the horizon, Aphrodite said to Ian, "That was a great film and Elizabeth Taylor is an excellent actress."

"You're right, but she's not as pretty as you, Aphrodite."

"Well, thank you Ian."

Just then Ian saw a taxi driving by and hailed it. Soon they were back at Aphrodite's home, and Ian walked her up the gravel path. She opened the front door and they both went in.

Aphrodite said, "Ian, I'll cook a nice Greek meal for you. How does that sound?"

"Sounds great to me, can I help?" Ian responded.

"No, the kitchen is great for one cook, but not two. Thanks anyway. Why don't you go into the sitting room and read a magazine, while I get the meal ready?"

In about thirty minutes, Aphrodite came to the door and announced dinner was served. Ian rose and followed her into the dining room, where the meal was already there on the table, with a bottle of red wine.

After they had finished, Ian said, "That was excellent, Aphrodite. If you cooked for me every day, I would soon gain some weight."

"Maybe I will, one of these days," she said with a smile.

Ian got serious and asked her, "Would you really like to be married to a soldier, who has to move around a lot?"

"Well, whoever that soldier was, maybe he wouldn't be in the army forever. Anyway, if I truly loved him, I would follow him anywhere," she said, looking straight into his eyes.

We'll have to talk about this some more, Ian said. It is getting late, and I guess that I should get back to my digs."

"So you are going to eat and run," Aphrodite said, with a grin.

"Well, no, but I suppose you need to get to bed."

"You're right, but not by myself. This house frightens me, when I am here alone. Why don't you stay the night, and then I can fatten you up with another big breakfast? My bed is a double, so it's big enough for two."

"I didn't bring any pajamas or toiletries."

"Who needs pajamas? If it will make you feel more comfortable, I won't wear any either."

"What would your mother think?" Ian asked.

"My mother is not here and, as I told you earlier today, she is on my side as long as I act responsibly."

"What would your brother, Minervo, think if he dropped by the house?" Ian asked.

"Oh, don't worry about him. He lives in Limassol with his girlfriend and hardly ever just drops by, besides he always calls first."

"Well ...."

"Ian, come on, follow me upstairs."

She walked over to him, took his hand and led him up the stairs to her bedroom. They entered her room, and she closed the door. She wrapped her arms around him and gave him a long kiss.

225

"Why don't you climb into the bed, while I go into the bathroom, to make myself pretty for you?" Aphrodite said, as she left the bedroom to go into the bathroom.

Ian turned out the light and opened the drapes slightly, to let in the bright moonlight. He took his clothes off, except for his Y-front Jockey shorts, lay down on the bed and waited for her.

Soon, she opened the bathroom door and came back into the bedroom, closing the bathroom door behind her. She was dressed in a short, lacy, white nightgown that only came down mid thigh. In the moon light, she looked stunning.

As she came and lay by him on the bed, he exclaimed, "Aphrodite, you are more beautiful, every time I see you. I love you with all my heart and I'm sorry it has been so long, since we have really been together. Soon, this Emergency will be over, and we'll be able to be together forever."

He rolled over onto his side, and his hand went up under her nightgown, until it found one of her small and firm round breasts. Her nipple hardened up, as he found it, and he slowly, carefully, massaged it. She kissed him, as he stroked her, and she slowly slid her hand down his front, until she found his stiff member, hidden in his shorts.

"Let's get rid of those things," she whispered, as she slowly pulled his "Jockeys" down to reveal his long, stiff penis. Seeing it brought back to her some pleasant memories, of their long weekend in early September.

"Two can play at that game," he whispered back, as he pulled her white nightgown up and over her head, leaving her completely naked. Ian couldn't believe how beautiful she was, just as he was overcome with awe the first time he saw her naked at their rendezvous five weeks ago.

"Aphrodite, you look like a goddess, as your name suggests."

They lay there for a while, holding each other and kissing. Finally, Ian leaned over, started to kiss her nipples

226

and run his tongue over them. As he did so, Aphrodite started to breathe quicker and uttered a soft moan. Ian ran his hands over her smooth, flat stomach and finally one of his hands ended up at her soft, curly haired honey pot. At this point, she spread her legs apart, so that Ian had easier access to her moist vagina. He placed his hand there and started to massage the entrance to her being. Soon, he felt her moisture had increased and decided it was time, to fill her honey pot with his penis.

He rolled over on top of her and used his arms to support the main weight of his body. He slowly placed his member at the opening and started to push it in. She started to moan with pleasure, as she could feel his penis enter her. To both of them, it was heaven.

Ian started to move his member in and out and, at the same time, Aphrodite commenced to rotate her lower body in unison. After a few minutes of this bonding, Aphrodite had an orgasm and, at the same time, Ian spurted his semen into her body.

Ian lay there on top of Aphrodite, kissing her and whispering, "I love you so much, Aphrodite. I hope I make you happy."

"You do, you do. I love you too," she gasped, trying to recover her breath.

When his member had shrunk, he rolled off of her and lay on the bed by her side. He held her and kissed her some more. Finally, they both drifted off to sleep, feeling satisfied and fulfilled.

The next morning, daylight woke Ian up first and he lay there admiring the beauty of Aphrodite, as she slept. As he watched her sleep, he thought, *"I love her so much and I can't lose her. She'll be a great partner, friend and lover in my life. I'll marry her, if she'll have me."*

She must have sensed that he was awake and watching her. Soon she woke up and looked over at Ian. She smiled and said, "Did you sleep well? You were exhausted from all the activity last night," she said, with a smile.

"Yes, I did. I only woke up about fifteen minutes ago. How are you feeling this bright and sunny morning?"

"I feel fabulous," she said, with a grin.

Ian reached over and started to stroke her body, starting with her breasts and ending up at her thighs.

As he did so, she started to rub his chest and stomach, and ultimately ended up at his member, which had suddenly sprung to life. It wasn't long before they repeated what they'd done the night before. They were both breathing heavily, when she had another orgasm, and he filled her body again with semen. After a few minutes, he rolled onto his side and held her hands. He looked into her eyes and said, "Aphrodite, I love you with all my heart." He then gave her a long, caressing kiss on her soft, sweet lips.

Afterwards, Aphrodite said smiling, "That's a great way to wake up. I've never had a wakeup call like that before."

Ian replied, "I hope I can wake you up many times in the future, like that. Aphrodite, I love you so much that I want to be with you, for the rest of my life."

"I agree also," she replied. "But first, we have to determine what affect that would have on my mother. She will return from England next weekend. Maybe I can have you over in a week or so, and then you can meet her. In the meantime, how about some breakfast? I'm ravenous."

"Me too, all this exercise makes me hungry," he said grinning.

Aphrodite jumped out of the bed totally naked and padded to the bathroom. Ian eyed her, as she left the bedroom naked, and thought, *"Her body is beautiful. How can I be so lucky? I must take care of her. I hope she loves me as much as I love her."*

She closed the bathroom door and quickly washed herself all over. In a few minutes, she came out of the bathroom, fully clothed, and said, "It's your turn now. I'll go to the kitchen and cook us something to eat."

"I'll be down, as soon as I can, and help you," Ian responded.

About ten minutes later, Ian came down and helped Aphrodite cook a full English breakfast of eggs, bacon, baked beans and fried bread. He made the coffee, and they ate the meal in the dining room, while they discussed the film they had seen the day before.

After they washed the dishes together, they went upstairs to make up the bed.

Later that morning, Aphrodite made a small lunch for them and they went for a walk, taking it with them. They ended up at a park, a mile or so from her home. The grass was still green, but most of the flowers were on their last legs. They sat on the grass and ate the lunch that she had made. They talked about their future in the event they did get engaged, after her mother approved. They then walked back to the house, just as some light rain started to fall. They managed to make it back, before it began to rain hard.

"Aphrodite, I've really enjoyed this weekend and hope it is the start of a long relationship. Don't forget, we'll go to England in the New Year, assuming everything has settled down here. I believe it will, since the British want out of here and the new Greek Government is not insisting on Cyprus joining Greece."

"I hope so too. As soon as my mother returns from England next weekend, I'll talk to her about us and then invite you over to meet her, in a couple of weeks. How does that sound?"

"Aphrodite, I'm so in love with you, I'm afraid something will happen and I'll lose you."

"Ian, you don't have to worry, I'm not going anywhere, except with you."

"Please be careful and also ask your mother to be careful. She is English and you are half English. Since EOKA has increased the violence, you never know what might happen. Just be careful. Look what happened to Mrs. Cutliffe in Famagusta. By the way, next Friday and Saturday, I've been ordered to go an assignment, so I'll not be able to see you. It will not be very dangerous, so don't worry. The following week and weekend, I should be free and I'll call you to set up something exciting for us to do. Maybe, as I mentioned a few minutes ago, Saturday the 25th or Sunday the 26th would be an opportune time to meet your mother."

"I'll call you at your office, Ian, to touch base. When you can, please call me at the hospital, as often as your work schedule allows. Once, I have told my mother about us, you will also be able to call me at home."

"Aphrodite. Thanks for inviting me here for the weekend, and I've enjoyed every minute, we spent together. I love you so much and would do anything for you. I had better get back my digs, as we have an early meeting with the colonel, about the upcoming week's activities. Can you call me a taxi?"

"I'm sorry you have to leave, but I understand. In addition, I'm on duty at 8.00 a.m. tomorrow morning. I'll call you a cab."

In about ten minutes a taxi pulled up outside the house. Ian went over to Aphrodite, held her for a long time and gave her a kiss. "I love you and I'll be in touch. Please be careful, as I advised."

She whispered, "I love you too" as she opened the front door. Ian gave her one more, long kiss. He walked down the gravel path to the taxi and climbed in, waving to Aphrodite. She quickly blew him a kiss and then he was gone back to Salisbury House.

19

Turkish Arms Connection

At the next Monday staff meeting, all of Colonel Baker's staff was in attendance, including John of MI6 and the two newest members.

"Gentlemen, the governor and his staff are getting concerned about the Turkish minority. They've heard about the negotiations going on in Zurich and London, and they're worried that they will be victimized, if the Greeks take over control of the island. There are rumours that they are beginning to arm themselves, in order not to be outgunned by the majority. Obviously, the natural end to all of that would be a civil war, if Britain ever pulls out. The problem is that the PM is committed to pulling out of Cyprus, leaving only a few military bases here. We know of a few small arms shipments that the Turkish Cypriots have already successfully made, even with our blockade. There's a rumour that they're going to try and make a large shipment soon, between Kyrenia and Cape Plakoti. In order to accomplish the landing easily, they may be planning to knock out the radar at Camp Plakoti, so we will be somewhat blind. Our intelligence sources believe that it would be hard to do. Failing that, they will try to follow a storm front in, if one is available."

"Sir, if I may interrupt?" Ian asked.

"Yes, Mr. Black?" the colonel queried.

"I don't believe it would be that hard to knock out the radar. If I was in the Turkish minority, I would dress up like Greek Cypriots and carry out a false flag operation. The Greeks would then get the blame. All I'd require would be a bazooka, with one round from World War Two, and I could either blow up the radar or the diesel generator that provides the power. The bazooka has an effective range of 150 yards to 300 yards, depending on the model. There are only twenty men on a radar site, so a dedicated group could also overrun a site, even without a bazooka. The British camp defenders typically have one Bren gun in the sentry tower and one .303 Enfield rifle for each occupant of the site." Ian responded.

"That's interesting, but do you really think they could obtain one?" the colonel asked.

"I'm not sure sir, but the Cyprus Regiment fought on the side of the British during and after the war. I don't think we can ignore the threat."

"Well Mr. Black, please don't publish your suggestion in the Cyprus Times newspaper. Someone might pick up the idea and run with it."

"Yes sir, I'll keep quiet about it."

"Very well, we'll warn Major MacArthur at the 188th to be on alert for the next few weeks, just in case. Has anyone recently been in touch with Captain Abney on the HMS *Benton*? I believe they are again patrolling the waters, off the north coast of Cyprus."

Captain Phillips asked, "Ian, why don't you make contact with Captain Abney after this meeting? Colonel, do we have a rumoured date as to when we believe the Turks might try to land a shipment of arms?"

"The date that has been picked up by SIGINT is Saturday, the 18th of October. Obviously, this is not a firm date, but we will plan around it, just in case it's for real. Ian, I want you and Roger to go on the *Benton* and participate in the patrol. He is fluent in Turkish, so he will

232

be of a great assistance to Lieutenant Commander Abney. Captain Phillips, can you contact the 188th Battery and warn them about the possibility of an attack at Camp Plakoti?"

"Yes, I'll do that colonel," the captain responded.

"Okay, good, that's all for now. You have your orders. Let's get moving."

The colonel adjourned the meeting and left the conference room.

Ian placed a call to Captain Abney of the *Benton*, but he wasn't available at the time, so he left a message.

A few hours later, Captain Abney called Ian back.

"Mr. Black, how are you doing? It's been a while, since you helped us with the Greek smuggling vessel. What's the reason for your call?"

"Yes, sir, it's been some time. Our intelligence sources inform us that Turkey is going to try and ship in some arms, to bolster the resistance by the Turks to the Greek enosis plan."

"I've been informed of the same information. The last date, we heard, was around the middle of the month and that they will try and land the shipment, on a beach somewhere between Kyrenia and Cape Andreas."

"Our thoughts are that they will try to knock out the radar at Cape Plakoti or, if they are lucky, follow a storm front in. Either way, it would probably be hard to detect them and stop them, from landing their shipment. As I'm sure you're aware, the storms start coming through the eastern MED, this time of year. Our CO, Colonel Baker, wants Lieutenant Snell and me to go on the most likely patrol that will catch them in the act. Would you be willing to take us on the night that the latest intelligence reports indicate is the landing date? Roger is fluent in Turkish, so he could be very useful in any interrogation of the crew."

"Yes, Mr. Black, I'll be glad of your assistance. Please contact me, or Lieutenant Dodd, when you have more information on the possible date for the Turkish smuggling operation. Goodbye. I'll talk to you later.

"Goodbye, sir, it's been great talking with you again," Ian responded, as he hung up the phone.

****

On the next day, across the MED on the southern coast of Turkey, Captain Ekren of the MV *Fatma* and a Turkish Cypriot leader, Commander Sarica, were discussing the best way to land the arms, without being intercepted.

Suddenly, the *Fatma* first mate burst into the meeting and said, "Captain, we've just received word from the Turkish meteorological office that a major front is coming this way and will go through Cyprus on Friday. This is the first storm of the season with high winds and pounding rain. If we could come in right behind it, we could probably complete the task, without being discovered. The British won't be able to fly their Shackletons, and their ships will have a rough time, until the storm passes. By then, we should have been able to deliver the goods and get out of there. This will be almost like the Japanese raid on Pearl Harbor, where they approached the islands behind a weather front."

Captain Ekren replied, "That's good news, and just what we've been looking for. Now, we won't have to knock out the radar at Plakoti after all."

Looking at Commander Sarica, Ekren asked, "Do you agree?"

"Yes, that's good news indeed. I say let's go and be unloading on the Dhavlos beach near the Greek village of Kaplica at around 11:00 pm on Friday evening. Our men will be dressed like Greek villagers to throw off anyone, that's around at that time."

"I concur," said Captain Ekren. "We'll leave the port around 2.00 p.m. or just as the front passes. At around 6-7 knots, we should have plenty of time to make the seventy miles from Tasuçu to Dhavlos, by the scheduled arrival time."

****

On Wednesday, Ian received a call in his office from Lieutenant Dodd of the HMS *Benton*.

"Lieutenant Black, this is Lieutenant Dodd. I'm calling for Captain Abney who is busy at the moment. We've received word that there's a major weather front coming through in the next few days, bringing with it high winds and almost monsoon type rain. We feel that the Turks may use it to bring in their arms. They could hide behind the front, land their shipment on a beach and take off before we find them. The maritime search planes won't be able to fly in that kind of weather. In addition, the seas will be very rough ahead of and in the front."

"When is the front expected to pass through Cyprus?" Ian asked.

"The best estimate is that the major part of the front will be over Cyprus, around 1800 hours on Friday evening. Of course, the exact time will depend on the speed of the front. Based on this estimate, we'll pull out of the Kyrenia harbor on Friday evening and head east towards Cape Andreas. Another minesweeper will weigh anchor at the same time and proceed in a westerly direction. Hopefully, one of us will catch the Turks. Captain Abney suggests that you both be on board the HMS *Benton* by 1000 hours on the Friday, since it'll be very rough when the front does go through, and we're not sure exactly when we'll weigh anchor."

"Thanks for the information, lieutenant. Roger and I will be there no later than 1000 hours, as you've recommended. See you on Friday."

"See you then. We'll provide you with some oil skins, when you get here. Goodbye for now. If anything changes, I'll call you back.

Ian called Captain Phillips, told him about the plan and explained the idea of why the thought was that the gun runners would hide behind the front. He agreed that he and Roger should go on the *Benton*'s patrol.

Ian then called Roger.

"This is Lieutenant Snell."

"Roger, this is Ian. I'm calling to let you know that we're going to join the HMS *Benton* for a patrol cruise, on Friday. We need to be on board by 1000 hours, so we should leave here for Kyrenia by 0830, since the weather might be bad. Don't forget to bring your sea sickness pills, in case you need them. The sea could be very rough."

"Ian, I'm an old yacht sailor, so hopefully I won't need any. I'll see you on Friday at Salisbury House. I assume you'll have a car to get us to Kyrenia?"

"That's correct," Ian replied, as he hung up the phone.

On Friday morning, Ian and Roger linked up at an early breakfast and then went down to the motor pool. Ian signed for the usual nondescript black Ford sedan to take them to Kyrenia. He told the corporal signing him out that the car would probably be gone for twenty four hours. Ian and Roger drove out through the main gate and saluted at the guard on duty. The drive to Kyrenia took about an hour, which was longer than normal, due to the storm that was already making its presence felt. The main part of the front was still miles off shore.

They pulled onto the wharf, at the port, around 0930 and they both presented their IDs to the army MP at the gate. He checked their identification quickly and waved them through. Obviously, he didn't want to stand there by the car and get thoroughly wet from the rain that was picking up. Ian parked in a visitor spot and waited for the cutter from the *Benton*. At 0945, it pulled up at the wharf and the officer signaled for them to come on board. They both jumped out of the car and ran in the torrential rain towards the bobbing craft. They climbed down into the partially enclosed section, dripping rain water. The army issued raincoats only worked well in drizzle, but not in a monsoon type of rain.

"Good morning, lieutenants," said Sub-lieutenant Barwell.

Ian remembered him from before and said, with a grin, "This weather is slightly different from last time we met."

"Yes, it certainly is."

"I'd like you to meet Lieutenant Roger Snell, who is coming with us today. He's going to help us with any translations we need. He's fluent in Turkish," Ian said.

"I'm pleased to meet you, Roger." said Barwell.

The cutter was already under way and, in a few minutes, was tied up at the *Benton*. They all clambered up the ladder, as the craft was hauled up out of the water.

Lieutenant Dodd met them on the deck, and Ian introduced him to Roger.

Lieutenant Dodd informed them both, "Gentlemen, we'll get underway shortly, as it's generally safer to ride out the storm in the open sea, than it is being tied up in a harbour. It might be somewhat rough, and I hope you can both handle that. The front itself is scheduled to be here at 1815, if our weather office is correct. One other thing, if you are on deck in the storm, you must be careful not to be swept overboard. We may not be able to pick you up and save you. Captain Abney will be able to meet with you in the Officers' Wardroom at 1100 hours. In the meantime, Mr. Barwell will get you outfitted with the standard RN oilskins, so you don't get too wet."

Barwell said, "Follow me." He led them to the stores room on board, where a sailor behind the counter issued them both with the standard waterproof PVC type of outfit.

At 1100, Ian and Roger went to the Officers' Wardroom and found Captain Abney already seated at the head of the table.

"Good morning gentlemen," the captain said as he greeted them. "This is probably going to be a rough ride. We get this type of storm a few times a year, from October to March. We're concerned that this storm might be used, by the Turks, to land a shipment of arms for their compatriots in Cyprus. Of course, the storm could be dangerous for them also but, if they are careful, they could use it to their advantage. Right now, we plan to ride the storm out in open waters. As soon as the front has passed through, we'll patrol the coast, all the way to Cape Andreas. So, for the next few hours, I suggest that you get some rest and try not to get sea sick. If you go out on deck, please be careful. I'd prefer not to have to call your CO and tell him that we lost you overboard. We'll have meals in here at the normal times, if you feel you can keep the food down. That's about all for now."

For the next few hours, Ian and Roger tried to rest, but it wasn't easy, with the rolling of the ship. The rain and the wind made it miserable to go out on the deck. So, they were stuck down in the cabin that they had been assigned, for the length of the patrol.

At 1800, Ian and Roger went to the wardroom for dinner, although neither felt too hungry. As they entered the room, they noticed some long faces on those officers already present.

Captain Abney came in, sat down and said. "We've two major problems on our hands, concerning the interception of the suspected arms shipment from Turkey.

First, the radar antenna on this ship has been damaged, and at the moment, we're blind. We're trying to repair it but, in this weather, it isn't easy.

Second, I've received word from Maritime headquarters that the radar at Camp Plakoti is out of action. It appears flying debris from the storm has cut the power cable and shorted out the generator itself. They have a backup generator, but they don't have a spare cable. In addition, some other debris struck the radar trailer itself and the extent of the damage won't be known, until power is restored.

As you're already aware, the maritime search aircraft can't operate in this foul weather. So for now, we've no visibility of the ocean either on radar or through visual sighting, from Kyrenia to Cape Andreas."

Ian responded, "If I understand you correctly, captain, except for the radars at Cape Kormakitis and on the south side of Cape Andreas, we're completely blind. This means that any landing, east of Kyrenia and west of Cape Andreas, will go undetected."

"That's correct, Mr. Black."

"Sir, if I was in their shoes, I'd always have aimed to land the arms east of Kyrenia on one of the secluded beaches, about half way between the town and Cape Plakoti. Yes, there are Greek villages in the area, but if the Turks dressed as Greek villagers, there'd be very little alarm raised by the locals. This would be a kind of false flag operation, if you know what I mean?"

"Let's assume you may be correct, what do you suggest we do?"

"Well, sir, as soon as possible, I'd head east, as planned, and check out all the coves and beaches along the way, especially close to the half way point. Once the ship's radar is repaired, the search could be completed faster. Hopefully, we find them before the arms are unloaded. They're probably following this front in, so we don't have time to waste or we'll be too late."

"That suggestion sounds good to me. Does anyone else here have any other ideas?" the captain asked, looking at the officers around the table. They all shook their heads.

As the captain of the HMS *Benton* was trying to decide what they should do, the MV *Fatma* was following in behind the front and was only a few miles off the coast of Cyprus. They were heading for Dhavlos Beach, near the Greek village of Kaplica. By 2200 hours, the front had passed through the area, and it was safe for the Turks to land the arms. Turkish Cypriots had assembled some men on the beach, with four cars and a small lorry. The beach was located close to the main coastal highway, for a quick getaway.

The *Fatma* anchored close to the secluded beach and lowered, with their davits, two boats loaded with crates. The boats made it the last few hundred yards to the beach, where the waiting men unloaded the crates onto the sand and opened them up. They reached inside and quickly took out the guns and ammunition, and loaded the arms into the waiting vehicles.

As soon as the arms were loaded, the Cypriots took off down the highway in different directions; east, west and up into the hills. The two boats went back to the *Fatma* and were raised on board, even as the captain weighed anchor. The Turkish vessel then started back out into the MED.

In the meantime, the minesweeper's crew had finally managed to repair its radar and it proceeded out of the harbour. Since the front had passed through, it was able to detect the *Fatma* on the radar. When it reached a distance of approximately ten miles, the HMS *Benton* caught up with it and fired a shot across the bow. The MV *Fatma* slowed down and came to a halt in the open sea.

Captain Abney, of the *Benton,* sent a boarding party over to the *Fatma*, including Ian and Roger, to search the ship for arms. They came on board and Roger found the captain on the bridge.

"Captain, what cargo are you carrying?" he asked in Turkish.

240

The captain replied, "We've crates of machine tools that we're taking to Beirut."

"Aren't you a little off course?" Lt. Snell asked.

"Yes, that's true. The storm blew us off course. As soon as we realized our mistake and saw the coast of Cyprus, we turned out to sea and are now headed in the correct direction."

"I'm not sure I believe you and we're going to search your cargo, to make sure you've no arms on board."

"Go ahead. You won't find any embargoed shipments in our holds."

The boarding party searched the holds, as the captain of the *Fatma* and the first mate winked at each other. They found nothing except machine tools, as shown on the manifest.

Ian was disappointed that they hadn't found any arms, but there was nothing they could do. The search party returned to the *Benton* and informed Captain Abney about what had transpired.

"Captain, do you have a map of the area we're in, including the coast of Cyprus?" asked Ian.

The captain took Ian over to the chart table and indicated their current position. Ian looked and saw that, if you drew a line from where they were to the closest secluded beach for a possible landing, it ended up at Dhavlos.

"Sir, can we get close to Dhavlos beach, without grounding the ship and have a look with your searchlight?"

"Mr. Black, we'll do this one time, but I can't search every cove or beach, from Kyrenia to the cape."

The captain ordered the helmsman to go carefully towards Dhavlos Beach. He had the sonar man to check the depth, as they proceeded, to make sure they didn't hit a rock or ground the *Benton*. Finally, they entered the cove and anchored. The crew turned on the searchlight and, as they swept the cove with the light, lit up the empty crates on the beach.

The captain sent a party ashore, but all they found were empty crates, with no markings on them. There was no proof where they came from or who transported them there. The captain, Ian, Roger and the crew could only guess.

Captain Abney had the radio operator send a signal to Maritime headquarters, explaining what had happened and requested the army send out a patrol to the area. They all knew that it was too late. The Turks had a few more arms, with which to defend themselves, in case of sectarian violence or even a civil war.

The *Benton* weighed anchor and left the Dhavlos beach area. They headed west, patrolling the coast of Cyprus. On their ships radar, they could see the MV *Fatma* heading east towards Beirut. When it was twenty five miles away from the Cyprus coast, it turned and headed north towards Tasuçu, Turkey.

As the *Benton* passed Cape Plakoti, they received word from Maritime that the site's radar was back on the air. The rest of the *Benton*'s patrol that night was uneventful, and by dawn they were approaching Kyrenia.

They anchored in the harbour and Ian thanked the captain for the patrol, while expressing his regret over the failed interception of the Turkish arms. The captain thanked Ian and Roger for their help and bade them farewell. The cutter took them back to the wharf, where the sun was shining, drying out the rain puddles from the storm. There was some debris scattered around, but overall it seemed that the storm had not caused too much damage.

Ian and Roger found their car and climbed in for the trip back to Nicosia. They waved at the MP on duty at the gate and proceeded on the road back to the capital.

When they arrived at Salisbury House, Ian went to his room and started work on his report. In it, he outlined what had happened and how sometimes it seems problem upon problem crop up, with the result that there's no good solution.

Ian called Aphrodite at the hospital and left a message, informing her that he was back in the office again. In a few minutes, she called back.

Ian finished up the report and submitted it to Captain Phillips, for approval.

When the captain read the report a couple of days later, he called Ian and said, "Mr. Black, welcome to the real world, sometimes snafus (situation normal; all fucked up) happen. Let's hope the Turks don't use the arms, while Britain is still running Cyprus. Otherwise, we could be stuck in the middle, between two groups that hate each other."

20

Murder and Sorrow

A few weeks after her weekend trip to the Kyrenia Mountains with Ian, Aphrodite started to not feel well, especially in the mornings. She felt tired and threw up periodically. When she failed to have her period, she thought she knew what was wrong.

She thought, *"What if I'm pregnant? What will Ian think about it? Will he be happy or just vanish? I don't know what to do. I won't tell my mother yet, until I know how Ian will react. I have to call him and talk to him."*

****

Aphrodite called Ian at Salisbury House on Wednesday afternoon and reached him in his office.

Ian answers, "Lieutenant Black speaking."

"Hello, Ian. This is Aphrodite. I'm sorry to bother you. Are you free to talk?"

"For you, I certainly am, Aphrodite"

"Are you free for drinks tonight? I need to talk to you in person."

"Yes. What time and where do you propose?"

"How about 7:00 pm at the Dorchester Café. It's generally fairly quiet on a weekday and it's safe. It's located outside the old city on the west side of Nicosia."

244

"I know exactly where it is, although I've never been there. I'll see you there at 7:00."

Ian finished off the report by 4:00 and then went down to the Officers' Mess for dinner. Rather than taking a car, he ordered a taxi, since Salisbury House was not far from the Dorchester Café.

The taxi dropped him off at the café that was run by an Englishman, and he went inside. Aphrodite was already inside, sitting at a private corner table. She looked a little nervous and that puzzled Ian. Ian gave her a kiss and then sat down next to her, so they could talk. A waiter came by and took their orders. In a short time, he placed the drinks on the small round table and left the two alone.

Aphrodite started the conversation by whispering, "Ian. Thanks for coming, and I hope you take the news well. I have missed my period and I believe I'm pregnant." She was nervous when she said it, because she wasn't sure how Ian would take it.

Ian looked at her and took her hand. "That's great news, I couldn't be happier. We'll get married, if you'll have me. Are you okay with that?"

Aphrodite relaxed a little and replied, "I'll be glad to marry you, but I don't want you to do it, just because you feel obligated. I want you to marry me, because you love me."

Ian responded, with a firm and loving tone. "I do love you with all my heart, and I'd be honoured for you to be my wife."

They hugged and kissed each other. They decided that they had lots of plans to make and should meet again very shortly.

"Have you told your mother?" Ian asked.

"Not yet. I plan to tell her, after we have made some plans. I'm not sure what her reaction will be, since I'm half Greek Cypriot. I think she'll be happy for me, but one never knows. "

Ian replied "I have to inform my CO of our plans. It is an old army custom, but I've never heard of anyone being turned down. I think that we should get married fairly soon, so you don't show in your wedding dress."

"I agree. I think we should meet again shortly to discuss the various issues, involved with planning a wedding. How about meeting next Saturday at the Dakis Restaurant on Ledra Street for dinner? Say at 5:00 pm, would that be okay?" Aphrodite asked.

"That sounds great. However, do you believe it would be safe to go to Ledra Street, with all the violence emanating from the Famagusta killing?"

Aphrodite replied, "I understand the military patrols in the old city have been increased since the Famagusta incident, so it should be safe. If you'd prefer, we could meet somewhere else."

"No, the Dakis Restaurant will be great. I know the owner and it's generally very safe there. According to our intelligence, he's actually against enosis. Okay, we'll meet at 5:00 pm. Thank you for the wonderful news, my lovely and dear Aphrodite."

"I'm glad you're happy."

They hugged and kissed again, and then finished their drinks. Ian paid the bill and asked the café to order a taxi for them. He told the driver to take Aphrodite to her house and then take him back to the Salisbury safe house.

It was difficult for him to concentrate the next two days, and he could hardly wait until Saturday, to see Aphrodite again.

****

On the Saturday, Ian dressed in a pair of tan coloured pants, with a military crease and a neat loose white shirt. Underneath the shirt, he strapped on a holster with his Browning inserted into it. He thought it was wise to have it with him, just in case of any trouble. The weather was getting a little cooler now, at the end of October, so he also took with him a light beige jacket, to ward off the evening chill.

He decided to leave Salisbury House at around 2:00 pm, three hours before his date with Aphrodite. He was excited that he was going to see her again. He left this early, so he had time to shop for a present to give her.

Ian took a taxi and had it drop him off near the Paphos Gate. He then walked through the gate into the old city of Nicosia and started strolling slowly down Baf Caddesi, humming to himself. He was in no hurry, since they were not going to meet until five o'clock. He stopped and looked in several shops for a gift to purchase for Aphrodite. He saw a few items, mainly jewelry, that he thought she would like, but held off buying anything, until he went down Ledra Street.

He considered buying her an engagement ring, however he thought it would be best, if they both went shopping for it, so she could get the type of ring she wanted. At the corner of Baf Caddesi and Ledra Street, he turned right and started walking down Ledra. It was the main Nicosia shopping area that also had an infamous name – murder mile. EOKA terrorists had been active on the street.

Ian stopped at another jewelry store, where he saw an attractive gold bracelet with diamond chips embedded in it. He entered the store and asked to see the item. He was sure it would fit Aphrodite's wrist, as most bracelets came in only one or two sizes. He knew roughly the size of her wrist and compared it to the bracelet. He paid for the item and had the owner of the store gift wrap it for him.

It was now around 4:30 pm, and he thought he should be heading for the Dakis Restaurant that was further down Ledra Street. The street itself was approximately one mile in length, so it would take him a few minutes to reach the restaurant, which was just over half way down the street.

RICHARD AND BARBARA OSBORN

****

Aphrodite left her home, in the new western section of Nicosia, and caught a bus to Eleftheria Square. This square was at the edge of old Nicosia, at the southern part of Ledra Street. Ledra Street went north- south and almost divided the old city into two parts. She was happy that she was going to see Ian again and wanted to buy him a gift. She didn't make a large salary as a nurse, but she was sure he would look at the thought behind the gift.

She proceeded to walk slowly up Ledra Street, looking in the shop windows. Glancing at her watch, she realized she had plenty of time, before she was to meet Ian. She walked into several of the shops and also stopped at several of the stalls on the pavement. In the window of a jewelry store, she saw a 17- jewel Accurist watch and thought it would remind him of the good times they had together. It took a lot of her money, but she thought Ian was worth it.

She walked out of the store with the gift wrapped watch in her hand and again started to walk up the street. She failed to notice the two young, Greek Cypriot men who were following her fairly closely. As she passed a narrow alley to the right, they grabbed her and pushed her down the alley. At the same time, they inserted a gag in her mouth, so she couldn't cry out for help. One of the men held a gun in a brown paper bag and told her to do as they said or she wouldn't see tomorrow.

They opened a door half way down the alley, pushed her into a dark building, containing one small window, and sat her down on a chair in a room, lined with a large map of Nicosia. One of the men pulled the gag out of her mouth.

"You'd better not yell, or it'll be bad for you. What's your name?"

Aphrodite, shaking, responded, in a low voice, "My name is Aphrodite Palas."

"What are the names of your brothers?"

248

Still shaking, Aphrodite answered, "Andreus and Minervo. Andreus was my younger brother who died in an ambush on two British vehicles last April."

"So far, you've told the truth. We already knew the answers. Andreus was one of our youngest recruits, and he was very brave."

"You're not very brave, if you have to shoot women in the back," replied Aphrodite.

The taller of the two men slapped her across the face and said, "You'd better watch what you say, or it'll be the end of you. We don't like traitors to the cause."

"Who killed your young brother, Andreus?" the other man asked.

"I've already told you that he was killed in an attack on a British Army convoy. You should already know that anyway."

"What we want to know is the name of the British soldier who killed him; his name, rank and unit?"

"I don't know who shot my brother."

"Yes, you do. You work as a nurse at the British Army Hospital and would have privy to such information," the man shouted.

Aphrodite thought to herself, *"No matter what they do, I will not give them Ian's name. If I did, it would be like signing his death warrant."*

Aphrodite raised her voice and said, "I've already told you, I have no idea who shot my brother. I wish I did, because I would take care of him myself."

"We don't believe you. We're going to let you go but, be forewarned, we'll be watching you and your family. Maybe your mother or brother will tell us, what we want to know. You wouldn't want us to harm them, would you?"

With that, the one younger man nodded slightly to the one who had the gun, and said, "Let her go. She doesn't know anything."

The gunmen led her to the door that led to the alley, opened it and pushed her out. Aphrodite stumbled down the alley to Ledra Street. She started walking fast up the street towards the Dakis Restaurant, where she knew Ian would be waiting for her. She looked behind her, to see if she was being followed. She didn't see anyone, but she couldn't see the young Greek Cypriot hiding in a dark doorway. In the distance, Aphrodite saw Ian coming down the street, from the north, and waved to attract his attention.

Ian saw her and waved back. There were many people in the street, so the gunman could only watch as Aphrodite met Ian outside the Dakis Restaurant.

They gave each other a kiss, and then Aphrodite said, "Ian. I had a very unpleasant incident a few minutes ago, and I'll tell you all about it inside."

Ian gave her a puzzled look as they entered the restaurant, where they were greeted by the owner. He led them to a quiet table in a corner, where they could talk undisturbed.

They studied the menu and, after a couple of minutes, a waiter appeared to take their orders. After they had ordered their meal, Aphrodite told Ian about her encounter with the two EOKA terrorists.

Ian became concerned and said, "You must be very careful and look around you at all times. It's best, if possible, to stay in areas where it is fairly crowded. Most trouble comes about in isolated areas, or if one is alone walking down a street. When we leave here, we'll walk to together up Ledra and find a taxi. I'll drop you off at your house and make sure you get inside safely. I don't want you walking down Ledra Street by yourself to catch the bus. It can be dangerous."

"Yes, Ian, I understand, and I'll be very careful in the future. Thank you for the offer to take me home. I think that would be best."

"Let's talk about our plans for the wedding. There're so many questions to be answered. Is there any particular date on which you'd want to get married? Where do you want to get married? Who will we invite?" Ian asked. "Perhaps we should deal with a lot of these questions, after you tell your mother. Do you want me there, when you tell her?"

Ian and Aphrodite discussed the many issues concerning their wedding, while eating their dinner. At the end, right before they left the restaurant, Ian and Aphrodite exchanged the gifts they had just bought each other. The bracelet was the right size, and Ian sighed with a sense of relief. He thought highly of the watch that Aphrodite had purchased for him.

He smiled and remarked "Now I can keep my appointments on time."

They left the Dakis Restaurant, both happy that they were going to get married. They stood outside the restaurant for a few minutes talking and, while standing there, two British soldiers on patrol walked by, heading south on Ledra Street. However, Ian and Aphrodite didn't notice the gunman standing in the shadow of a doorway just watching.

They started walking up Ledra Street to the junction with Baf Caddesi in order to find a taxi. From the Dakis Restaurant, they walked about 100 yards or so, when Ian heard a slight commotion behind him. The noise was caused by people in the street, scurrying out of the vicinity. As Ian started to look back down the street, in the crowd of shoppers on the pavement, he saw a Cypriot with a smirk on his face.

Ian thought to himself, "*I'll never forget that man.*"

Ian and Aphrodite turned around completely to finally see what the commotion was all about, and they saw a gunman holding a revolver. He was aiming it right at Ian.

Ian pulled his Browning out of the holster, underneath his shirt, and fired at the gunman. At the same time, the gunman fired at Ian but, because he was young and nervous, his shot went wide. The bullet hit Aphrodite in the chest and she collapsed on the pavement. Ian's shot hit the gunman who dropped his gun, as he also fell to the pavement. The gunman reached for his revolver in order to shoot again, but Ian shot twice more, in rapid fire, with his Browning automatic killing the gunman him instantly. As he turned to check on Aphrodite, his eyes hastily scanned the crowd, and the smirking man was nowhere to be seen.

Ian turned to help Aphrodite and found her lying down in a pool of blood.

He yelled out in English and Greek, "Someone call for an ambulance." "Κάποιος κλήση για ασθενοφόρο."

At the same time, the two soldiers who had walked by on patrol a few minutes earlier heard the shooting. They came running up the Street, to where the victims were and stood guard. One called on his radio for an ambulance. Two other soldiers at the other end of Ledra Street also heard the shooting, and they came running down to the area and the four soldiers cordoned it off.

Ian was trying to stop the bleeding coming from Aphrodite's chest with his jacket. She was still conscious, but Ian could tell she was not in good condition.

She whispered to Ian, "I'll love you forever. Please don't ever forget me."

Ian tried to comfort her, "You're going to be alright. We've called for an ambulance, and it should be here momentarily. I love you with all my heart."

At that moment Ian heard the ambulance coming down Ledra Street. It stopped just short of Aphrodite lying on the street, cradled by Ian. They quickly loaded her on a stretcher, and a medic attended to her. The ambulance headed up Ledra, and Ian told the driver to go to the BMH. The driver didn't argue, although he normally went to the Nicosia General Hospital.

Ian got on their radio and called the BMH.

"Is Dr. Griffith there on duty?" he asked the person answering.

"Yes, he is," the BMH operator answered.

"Good. Tell him this is Lieutenant Ian Black, and an ambulance is bringing Aphrodite Palas to BMH, in critical condition. She's been shot in the chest and is bleeding heavily. Also, please inform Diana Palas, if she's on duty, about this. We should be there in five minutes."

The ambulance driver drove very fast, with the lights and bell sounding. He managed to reach the BMH without incident. They pulled up at the Emergency door, and two nurses ran out. One was Diana Palas. They quickly pulled Aphrodite out of the ambulance and rushed her into the emergency room. Dr. Griffith and another doctor were standing by, as she was brought in.

Ian went to the waiting room, where he paced the floor. Dr. Griffith would not let him accompany Aphrodite into emergency. After about thirty minutes, Dr. Griffith came out and went up to Ian.

"I'm sorry Ian, but we couldn't save her. We did our best, but she had lost too much blood."

With his face in his hands, Ian collapsed on a chair, sobbing, *"No. No. No."* and then in a low, quivering voice cried, *"My Aphrodite is gone. It can't be true. Only an hour ago, we were making plans for our future."*

At that moment, Diana Palas came out of the Emergency Room sobbing also. Although she had never met him, she knew all about him from Aphrodite. She came and sat down by Ian, and held him close to her. They held each other and cried for a long time.

When they had finally cried themselves to a point, where they had no tears left, Ian told Diana Palas he would contact her to find out about the funeral arrangements. He then had the receptionist at BMH call him a taxi.

The taxi came and took him back to Salisbury House, where he went to his room and cried himself to sleep. He was inconsolable and didn't leave his room for twenty-four hours. *"He didn't know what he was going to do without her. No one knew about the baby and he decided, for Aphrodite's sake, it would be their secret forever."*

Later, the next day, there was a knock at his door. When he didn't answer it, the knob slowly turned and Captain Phillips walked in.

He went over and sat on the bed, saying, "I know what you're going through. I lost my wife a few years ago, in a car accident in England. One has to pick yourself up and carry on. Think about it. If you were the one killed, wouldn't you want your loved one to carry on? Aphrodite wouldn't want you to be unhappy, all the rest of your life."

Finally, Ian sat up and said, "Captain, you're right. I must pull myself together, but I'll never forget her. I'll remember her forever."

The captain stood up and said, "We'll see you tomorrow at our staff meeting, won't we?"

"Yes, I'll be there," replied Ian.

"Good. By the way, shooting the terrorist with the extra two shots has been justified by the police. Witnesses came forward saying the man was reaching for his gun."

Ian attended the next day's staff meeting, but didn't remember much about it afterwards. He went around, as if in a daze, for several days always managing to do his job, but still in disbelief of what happened. Only at night alone in his room, did he think of her and the baby, and cry himself to sleep.

The funeral was held three days after Aphrodite's death, and she was buried next to her father, who died at the end of World War Two. Ian attended in a black suit, so as not to attract attention by wearing his uniform. The service was attended by almost 100 people, as she was very popular at the hospital.

Yellow was Aphrodite's favourite colour, and Ian laid a yellow rose on her coffin, as it was lowered into the ground.

She had told him that on the first weekend they had spent together. Yellow reminded Ian of Aphrodite, as her smile was like the sun shining from above. She lit up a room whenever she came in. She was buried with the bracelet that Ian had bought her on that fateful day.

****

A few months later, Ian received a telephone call in his room at Salisbury House.

"Hello. Is this Lieutenant Black?"

"Yes, it is."

"This is Diana Palas at the BMH. I would like to meet with you at the hospital this afternoon for a few minutes, if you are free."

"I can get off. What time would you like me to be there?"

"How about two o'clock?"

"That will be fine. I'll see you at 2:00."

After lunch, Ian reserved a taxi to pick him up and take him to the BMH. He arrived in plenty of time and asked the receptionist to page Diana Palas. Soon, she arrived in the lobby area and asked Ian to come with her to one of the small conference rooms close by.

"Ian," she said. "I've made the decision to return to England after all these years in Cyprus. I still have a lot of family in England who will help me get reestablished. I've buried my husband and two of my children here and the violence continues. Even with this rumoured treaty, I see no peaceful future for this island, with the Turks and Greeks disliking each other. Minervo, my oldest son and last child alive will stay here, since he has found a Greek girl he loves."

"Mrs. Palas. I'm sorry to see you leave, but I understand your reasons why. Before you leave, I must confess to you, something that I don't believe you know.

255

I loved Aphrodite very much and would have done nothing to hurt her. That fateful day, when we met at the Dakis Restaurant, she had been dragged into an alley by two EOKA men. They questioned her about who killed her brother, your son, Andreus back last April. She knew who did it, but refused to tell them. They then followed her and saw her meet me at the Dakis Restaurant. The gunman initially aimed his weapon at me, but when I drew my pistol and shot at him, his gun moved when he fired and he hit Aphrodite. His bullet was meant for me and I wish he had killed me, because then Aphrodite would still be alive. I'll bear this grief until my dying day."

"Ian. I found out some time ago that you were the British soldier who killed Andreus. I have forgiven you, because you had no choice, but to defend yourself."

They hugged each other and said goodbye. Ian took a taxi back to Salisbury House feeling a little better that he had told her the truth about the attack on Ledra Street

She moved back to England and that was the last time Ian saw Diana Palas. He heard that she died a few years later. *"Probably from a broken heart,"* Ian thought.

21

Assassination Attempt

On the Friday, after Aphrodite's death, the colonel called an urgent morning meeting, in the conference room. The meeting was attended by all of those that reported to him, including John of MI6.

The colonel started the meeting, "Gentlemen, we have received a request from the governor's security detail for assistance. The Governor-General has expressed a desire to tour Ledra Street in the Old Town on Sunday, in order to present an image that he is not intimated by the terrorists. He also wants to shake hands with as many Cypriots as possible in the area, as a sign of goodwill.

Therefore, we must perform two tasks. One is to fan out today and tomorrow in the Old Town, and see if we can pick up any information that suggests there might be an assassination attempt. He would, of course, be a prime target for some young potential terrorist to prove his worth to the EOKA leadership. Second, we must be on the street, when he does tour the area, in order to assist in the security and to watch for any attempt on his life."

"Has intelligence picked up any chatter that suggests an attempt will be made on the governor's life?" Ian asked.

"May I answer that, sir?" asked Captain Phillips.

"You certainly may, captain."

"There's been a communications intercept at our Nicosia listening post, which intimates that someone may try to eliminate the governor. However, there were few details other than it might be carried out on Ledra Street, also nicknamed murder mile," the captain responded to Ian.

"Are there any other questions?" the colonel asked, looking around the room. "If not, this meeting is adjourned. Let's get to work immediately on this."

After the meeting, Ian decided that he must snap out of his depression, as Aphrodite would not have wanted him to waste his life away. In addition, the army has just assigned him a major task that, during the execution of the assignment, he might also find the terrorist, who killed his beloved Aphrodite and their unborn child. He had already set this as the major personal objective, for the next few months.

He was going to find the other terrorist that had caused the death of his Aphrodite. He would always remember that smirking face in the crowd, on that Saturday afternoon. It was etched into his memory. He had decided the best way, to maybe find this terrorist, would be to visit the taverns, cafés and bars in the Old Town, using his fluency in Greek. At the same time, he would also be able perform in the execution of the new order from the colonel.

To accomplish both the personal and army objectives, Ian decided the best approach was to express an interest in joining EOKA to the people he met in the Old Town. This would be risky, but well worth it, if it helped him accomplish both tasks. In addition, he might also discover some information that could lead him to the whereabouts of Grivas's safe house.

Later that day, Ian took a walk into the walled city of Nicosia and started to visit the bars and taverns.

"Maybe a drink will make me feel better," he thought.

As he sat in a bar on Arsinoe Street sipping his first beer, he started talking, in Greek, to the young, dark haired Cypriot sitting next to him. Ian judged he was in his early twenties.

"My name's Nico. How are you doing tonight?" Ian asked him.

"Well, things could be better. I need a good job. My name's Spyros," the young man replied.

"I'm fed up with the way the British are running this island. I wish they'd let us join Greece. We'd be a lot better off." Ian continued.

"You'd better be careful how you talk about those things," responded Spyros.

"Maybe, I should try and join EOKA. Do you know how one goes about that?"

"Do you want to get yourself killed? Anyway, I wouldn't know how one can go about it. You'd better talk to someone else. I don't want to be involved with you. You'll get me in trouble."

Spyros then got up from the bar and walked away. He sat down at a table with one chair, taking his drink with him.

Ian sat at the bar, continuing to drink his beer, when another Cypriot came in and sat down by him. He was staggering a little and Ian figured he had drunk one too many already. Ian decided that he would not be of much use to him, so he finished his drink, paid for it, got up and walked out of the bar.

He walked some distance past Ledra Street and ended up in a tavern on Onasagotes Street. This one was crowded with Cypriots, who had stopped off on their way home from work. Ian had trouble finding a stool at the bar, but grabbed one, just as another man left.

He ordered a beer and started to talk to the men, on both sides of him. It turned out their names were Loukas and Yannis, and they both worked at the Nicosia International Airport. After a few casual discussions about the weather and troubles at the airport, Ian started to badmouth the British.

"You know I don't understand why the British are hanging on to Cyprus, except for the military bases. Why don't they let us join Greece?" Ian asked.

Loukas replied, "Don't say that too loud. It could get you in trouble. I agree with what you're saying, but it's dangerous to say it. You could go to prison."

Yannis joined in the conversation, "We have to be careful or we could lose our jobs. Good jobs are hard to find and we don't want to be placed on the DON'T HIRE security list."

"Well, I don't have a job with the British, so I don't have much to lose. I wonder how one goes about joining that EOKA organization. Maybe that's what I should do?" Ian continued.

Loukas whispered, "I certainly wouldn't talk like that, if I were you. I've heard, that to join them, you have to prove you're willing to carry out any orders given, including killing someone. Supposedly, it's an initiation rite, to be able to kill a British soldier."

"I'm not sure that I could do that," Ian replied. "I'll just forget about joining them and demonstrate in the streets. Have either of you heard the rumour that the Governor might visit the Old Town on Sunday?"

Both Yannis and Loukas shook their heads. "I've not heard that," Both of them replied.

"Well, maybe I'll go and demonstrate against him, if I can get up the courage," Ian responded.

The three of them started to talk about what was going on in the world, including the movement of American troops into Lebanon and the rumours of talks going on in London, concerning the Cyprus question.

"Well, I've got to go," Ian said. "Maybe, I'll see you both some other time."

Ian stood up and walked out of the tavern onto Onasagotes Street.

As Ian left, Yannis said to Loukas, "That was some Greek nut case. Maybe, he'll get himself killed by some British soldier."

Ian walked back down Onasagotes, until he ended up on the infamous Ledra Street. He found a small bar, in an alley, just off Ledra. It was full of young Greek Cypriots. Ian guessed that it would be too dangerous, for any Turkish Cypriot to go there.

He ordered a beer and had to stand for awhile, as all the stools and tables were taken. After about fifteen minutes, an older man stood up and walked out of the bar. Ian quickly grabbed the empty stool, before anyone else could get it. As he sat down, the Cypriot on his right started to speak to him.

"You were lucky to get that stool, you know. Friday and Saturday nights are a busy time here. What's your name? By the way, I'm known as Michalis."

"My friends call me Nico. If anyone else wanted this stool, they'd have had a fight on their hands," Ian replied.

"Well, Nico, it's nice to meet you. How are you doing today?"

"Things could be better, Michalis. I lost my job today at a warehouse run by an Englishman, because I made a derogatory remark, about the way the British treat us Greeks. I'll be glad when they pull out of Cyprus, and let us govern ourselves."

"Yes, I know what you mean. The British are the bosses, and we're the slaves."

"I often wonder if I shouldn't try and join the EOKA underground organization. Do you know anyone in it, Michalis?"

"Even if I did, Nico, I couldn't tell you. It would be too dangerous for me."

"I'd certainly like to talk to someone about it. What one has to do to join and what is expected of a member?"

"What I can suggest is that you go to the bar called the Sparta Club, located in an alley, close to the Dakis Restaurant, tomorrow night.   I understand that a few members of that organization sometimes go there on Saturday, to drink and commiserate about the British. That's all I've heard."

"I appreciate the tip, Michalis.   Maybe I'll go there tomorrow night and see if I find anyone there, who knows anything about the organization.   Let me buy you another beer."

"Thanks, I could do with another drink," said Michalis.

Ian had the bar tender serve both of them another beer. As they drank the beer, they talked about the current affairs in Cyprus and around the world.

When Ian finished his drink, he rose from the stool and said, "I'll see you around Michalis, and again thanks for the information."

Ian stepped out into the moonlit night, walked down the alley back to Ledra Street and then headed back to Salisbury House.   He'd had enough beer for the night and decided it was time to hit the sack.   He had trouble going to sleep, thinking about Aphrodite and the smirking Greek Cypriot. He couldn't erase the Cypriot's face out of his memory.

The next day, Ian rose later than usual, after a restless night of dreams, involving Aphrodite and the smirking Cypriot.   He went back to the Nicosia Old Town, to see if he could pick up any more lose information, concerning an attempt on the governor's life. Obviously, if there were any EOKA men around, they had learned the old American World War Two propaganda saying, "*Loose Lips Sink Ships*".

Ian visited a couple of bars early in the evening, without much more success.   He couldn't find anyone who seemed to know or admit to anything, about the governor coming there tomorrow.   So at about dusk, he went to locate the Sparta Bar in an alley off Ledra Street.   Initially, he couldn't find it and finally had to ask, in Greek, a man passing by, if he knew where it was.

"Excuse me, but can you tell me how to find the Sparta Club?"

The man looked at Ian, hesitated, and then in a low voice said, pointing down Ledra, "Walk in that direction, and the third alley on the right is where you'll find it. Please don't tell them that I told you." The man then hurried on up the street.

Ian did as the man said and turned right at the third alley off Ledra Street. He walked a few yards and came to a door, with a neon sign hanging over it. It read Sparta Club. He opened the door and entered a dimly lit bar, filled with half a dozen young men in their twenties, and a man who looked like he was close to forty. He had a ruddy face and a short stubby, black, Hitler style moustache. He was sitting at a small round table by himself, watching who came in and out of the bar.

None of the men sitting around the bar looked anything like the smirking terrorist that Ian had etched in his memory.

Ian went and sat down on an empty bar stool, next to a young Cypriot and ordered a beer.

"Hello, my name is Glafcos. I hope you like the beer that they serve here; it's a good local product. Are you a member of the organization?" the man said.

"I'm Nico. No, I'm not a member, but I'm thinking about joining it, if they'll have me," Ian replied.

"They're very particular who joins, and you have to pass a security check, as well as an initiation test."

"What does an initiation test involve? Is it like memorizing something or passing a written test?"

Glafcos laughed and replied, "They want to know, if you're dedicated enough. Generally to pass that test, you have to kill someone. I think that I've said too much already. You'll have to go and talk with Demetrio over there, sitting by himself. Be warned though, he's tough, and you can't fool him."

"Thanks, Glafcos, for the information. I'll go and talk to him in a minute, when I get my courage up. Maybe I should order another beer, before I go over to talk to him?" Ian said.

"Bar tender, bring me two beers," Ian said.

Ian gave one beer to Glafcos, saying, "It's been good talking with you."

Ian took a sip of the beer, rose from the stool and walked over to Demetrio, who was also drinking a beer.

"May I join you?" he asked.

"Only for a minute or two, I'm expecting a visitor soon. What do you want with me?" snapped Demetrio

"Well, my name is Nico, and I'm extremely upset with the way the British are running this island. I want us to have our own government and also to join the Greater Greece. I'd like to do something about it and thought that joining the EOKA organization, might allow me to be of use. I've heard that Dhigenis wants to force the British to leave, and I want to help in this endeavor.

"Have you ever killed anyone, Nico?" Demetrio demanded.

"Actually, I haven't."

"Before the organization will accept any candidate, they have to proof they're ruthless enough, to do as they're told," the man challenged

"I can take orders," Ian declared.

"I'll tell you what, Nico. You stand on Ledra Street tomorrow around 2:00 pm and, if you like what you see happen, come back and see me next Saturday. We can then talk some more. Leave now, as I'm expecting my visitor any moment," Demetrio ordered.

"Thanks for your time, Demetrio. I'll be back next Saturday."

Ian rose, gulped down the remainder of the beer and exited the Sparta Club. He walked down the alley and entered Ledra Street. He walked a few yards, turned and looked in a shop window. As he did so, in the window that acted like a mirror, Ian saw a young man walk by and proceed up the alley, towards the Sparta Club. For a brief moment, Ian saw the man's reflection in the window, and he could have sworn that it was the other terrorist, without a smirk on his face.

Ian thought, "*Is that the man Demetrio is waiting for?*"

As Ian walked up Ledra Street to get a taxi back to Salisbury House, he started to analyze what Glafcos and Demetrio had told him. After a lot of thought, it finally dawned on him that maybe the man, he just saw going into the Sparta Club, was going to try and kill the governor tomorrow. If he succeeded, he would the pass initiation test, and thus be admitted into the EOKA organization.

When he reached his room at Salisbury House, he took his Browning out and made sure it was clean and loaded. He felt he might need it tomorrow.

The next morning, which was Sunday November 2nd, Ian went down to breakfast and found Captain Phillips there, talking with John and Roger. He related to the captain what he had learned on his night out, and what he thought was going to happen this day on Ledra Street.

"Captain, I'm ready for any eventuality. I know what this terrorist looks like, assuming he's the same one that was on Ledra Street, when Aphrodite was killed. I'll walk ahead of the governor, scanning the people lining the pavement, to see if I can spot him."

"Ian, if you do see him and have to shoot at him, make sure there're no other people that could be hit. Killing or wounding innocent bystanders will not be looked upon lightly, by the authorities."

"Yes captain, I'll be careful. Nothing would rile up the Greeks more, than a British soldier shooting one of them. It would set back the peace process, by a least a few months."

After breakfast, Ian went back to his room, checked that his Browning was loaded and proceeded through the tunnel, from Salisbury House to the safe house. He ordered a taxi and told the driver to drop him off close to Ledra Street. He wandered the streets and alleys around the area and, after a couple of hours, stopped at a café for a light lunch.

At 1:30 pm, after he had finished his lunch, he went to the top of Ledra Street. There were quite a few people walking down the street looking in the stores, some of which were closed, since it was Sunday. It seemed that many of them expected some event to happen, since they were just standing around.

Ian kept walking down the street, looking at the people on the pavement, to see if he recognized anyone. He didn't see a single person that he had seen before. There were soldiers walking up and down the Street in pairs, carrying rifles, and looking for any security threat.

At 2:00 PM, a small convoy entered the Old Town. It was comprised of two Land Rovers, filled with more soldiers armed with Sterling SMGs. There was a black Daimler sedan, sandwiched between the two Land Rovers. In the car was seated the Governor-General of Cyprus, Sir Hugh Mackintosh Foot, accompanied by two plainclothes security officers.

At the top of Ledra Street, the convoy stopped and the governor got out, followed by the two security personnel. The governor started to walk down the street, shaking hands with as many people as he could. He stopped and talked to any shop keepers that had their stores open. The security officers kept back a little from the governor, but they kept a wary eye out, for any suspicious movement by the spectators.

Ian was walking down the pavement ahead, and to the right, of the governor. He was looking for the young terrorist he saw the night before, in the reflecting shop window. As they approached the Dakis Restaurant area, which was half way down the street, Ian finally saw his man. He was just standing on the pavement opposite to the one Ian was on, behind two other bystanders. In his left hand he had a brown paper bag, while his right hand was inside the bag.

As the governor approached the Dakis Restaurant area, the man got a smirk on his face and pulled his right hand from the bag. In his hand, he was holding a revolver. Ian would never forget that smirking look as long as he lived. He knew then that this man was a terrorist who was intent of assassinating the governor, just as his partner had murdered Aphrodite a few days before.

Ian drew his Browning automatic from beneath his loose shirt and stepped off the pavement onto the street surface. He yelled at the man, in Greek, "Drop your pistol and raise your hands". The few people in the immediate area saw the gun in Ian's hand and quickly scattered. The terrorist turned to see who was yelling at him, and saw Ian, whom he immediately recognized from the day of Aphrodite's death.

"Go to hell," he yelled back at Ian.

The terrorist aimed his gun at Ian and was about to fire, when Ian pulled the trigger on his automatic. The bullet ripped into the man's left arm that caused a lot of pain, but did not take him down. As the terrorist was hit, he fired his gun and the bullet went harmlessly into the air. He then aimed the revolver at Ian again. Ian shot at him twice more, in quick succession, and the man dropped to the street. He quivered for a few seconds and then lay still.

One of the governor's security men rushed up, to see what was going on and what all the noise was about. From experience, they recognized the sounds as gunshots. At the same time, two soldiers who were just fifty yards down the street turned around and ran back up. They asked to see Ian's ID, and after he showed it to them, they checked the man lying on the street. It only took a few seconds, for them to realize that he was dead. Ian explained to them what had happened, and they seemed satisfied. A police officer arrived a little later and talked to Ian, taking down details.

The man was taken away in an ambulance, and the governor continued his stroll down the street, amid a few cheers from the generally silent crowd of spectators.

Demetrio was standing off to one side in the shadow of a doorway, saw what transpired and recognized Ian from the night before. He figured that he had just lost the newest member of the organization, and that Ian would not be back the next Saturday, to ask about joining EOKA.

At the end of his stroll down Ledra Street, the governor came over to Ian and thanked him for being alert.

"Who's your CO?" the governor asked Ian.

"Its' Colonel Baker, sir, of the Intelligence Corps," Ian replied.

"Very well, I'll make sure you receive a commendation for your service today."

"Thank you, sir," answered Ian.

The governor then turned and went back up the street to his waiting vehicle, followed by the security men.

Ian walked down Ledra Street and found a taxi to take him back to the Salisbury safe house.

As he rode there, he thought to himself, *"At least I have exacted revenge for Aphrodite. Of course, it doesn't bring her back, but I can rest a little easier now."*

Back in his room, he started to write a report on the day's activities for the captain. He couldn't concentrate too much and put it aside until later, when he would feel up to it.

He lay down on his bed and went to sleep. It was the best sleep he'd had, since Aphrodite was murdered.

He awoke twelve hours later and headed down to breakfast. As usual, the captain and John were already there along with Roger. Ian joined them and the talk revolved about the attempt on the governor's life. No mention was made by the others, about the death of the terrorist, and Ian certainly didn't want to bring it up.

After breakfast, Ian got cleaned up and headed down to the conference room, for the usual Monday morning staff meeting. He looked at the clock outside the room and noticed he was ten minutes early, so he didn't expect many of them to be there yet. He opened the door, entered the room and immediately was greeted by a round of applause. He was surprised and embarrassed. Everyone was seated around the table, including the colonel.

"Come on in and sit down, Mr. Black," ordered the colonel.

"Yes sir," replied Ian, as he went and sat down in his usual chair, next to Captain Phillips.

"Gentlemen, the first order of business concerns a piece of paper that I just received this morning, from Government House. It is a letter from the Governor-General, Sir Hugh Foot, suggesting that a note of commendation be placed in Mr. Black's file, for his meritorious service on Sunday, the 2nd of November, 1958. It states that he saved the life of the Governor–General of Cyprus, by acting quickly in removing the threat of violence against his person. Mr. Black, this letter will now be added to your service file. I'd like to thank you, for all of us, in saving the governor's life. If he had been assassinated, it would have set back the peace process for a considerable length of time."

"Sir, I was only doing my duty, as a British Army officer."

"That may be, but this letter is going in your file anyway. If I didn't place it there, I would be disobeying an order from the Commander in Chief of the Cyprus armed forces. Now let's get on to other business.

We still have to find Grivas and bring him to justice, before the treaty is written and ratified. I figure we have about three months to get him, or then it'll be too late. So I want all of you to think about ways to achieve this goal, and let me know your ideas at the next meeting.

Unless there are any other matters that need to be discussed today, this meeting is adjourned."

Ian was about to leave the conference room, when Captain Phillips asked Ian to stay behind for a moment.

After everyone else had left, the captain said to Ian, "I received a call from the Nicosia Chief of Police this morning who stated that, although you were dressed in civilian clothes yesterday, you had the right as an army officer to use a weapon on the street. He questioned why you had to fire three shots, and I explained that the man was still up and a threat, after the first shot hit his arm. You were, therefore, justified in putting two more shots into him."

"Captain, to be honest, I could have finished him off with one more shot, but I wanted revenge on what his partner did to Aphrodite."

"Mr. Black, I didn't hear that and I'd better not hear that again. You had to fire two more shots to remove any threat to the governor. Do you understand?" the captain challenged.

"Yes, sir." replied Ian.

The captain then smiled and said, "Thank you again for what you did for the governor and the peace process. Now let's go to my office and have a private drink of scotch, to seal our secret agreement. This discussion never happened, right."

Ian nodded and followed the captain to his office for that drink.

22

Mole Search

At the next staff meeting, the colonel reminded all of them, concerning his previous order, that he wanted ideas for tracking down Grivas.

"Who wants to start out?" he asked. "How about you Mr. Black, you always seem to have ideas about almost any challenge?"

"Colonel, I've three ideas that may warrant more investigation and hopefully lead to Grivas, before the treaty is signed.

First, we captured some terrorists in the Troodos Mountains raid, and MI5 should have interrogated them by now. Hopefully, we have gleaned some useful information from them. Maybe not an address where we can find Grivas, but certainly some clues, as to which town or village has the safe house, he's hiding in.

Second, we retrieved some documents in the raid that amongst other things, pointed to a potential problem in the Limassol Police Force. We ought to check more into that. If I remember correctly, one name that was mentioned was Pachykostis. It's probably a first name or a pseudo name. Also, in those captured documents, Charles Foley, the Times of Cyprus editor, and Gabriel Gabrielides (Gabby), a Nicosia electrical contractor, were mentioned as friends and supporters of the organization. We ought to check them both out. Gabby is viewed as a friend of the British, but

271

maybe he's a double agent. In addition, Charles Foley is known as a liberal who is against the British Army and what it stands for.

Third, we can continue going to hangouts in the Old Town and try to obtain information, as to his whereabouts. This could be risky, especially at night, since any one of us might not return. Already, this chap Demetrio at the Sparta Club knows what I look like. However, he could be a source of information, if we followed him around and see who he talks to.

Finally, maybe we could create some kind of sting operation that would smoke Grivas out of his hiding place. The more often he moves, the more likely he is to make a mistake and be discovered. To be honest, I don't have an operation in mind at the moment, but I'll keep working on it. We need to know what his likes and dislikes are, so we can come up with an attractive lure. It will be like going on a fishing expedition."

"Ian, those are some splendid ideas, but we'll need assistance from MI5 and SIS. I'll contact our friends in MI5, to see if they have any idea what Grivas's affinities are; women, gambling, power, bloated self-importance, etc. Also, I'll see if they have a Greek speaking agent to go and talk to Demetrio next Saturday, at the Sparta Club, whom he won't recognize. In addition, we need their help in further investigating the backgrounds of Charles Foley and Gabriel Gabrielides," responded the colonel.

"What about the Limassol police situation and this chap Pachykostis?" Ian asked.

"I want Captain Phillips and yourself to start looking for this person and find out who he really is, if that's possible. Alright, captain?" responded the colonel.

"We'll get right on it, colonel," the captain declared, nodding.

"Mr. Snell, I want you to tour the Turkish areas of town, to see if you can determine where those arms went that were landed the other day at Dhavlos."

"I believe I can do that, sir," replied Roger.

"Very well, I believe that's all for the day. Let's get going and, if we can, obtain some solid leads on this terrorist. We'll meet again in a week, unless something comes up that requires an earlier get together."

After the meeting adjourned, Captain Phillips asked Ian to come to his office.

"Ian, I'll be busy the rest of the day on another matter, so why don't you visit the Nicosia Police Department and talk to the British superintendent. Tell him I sent you and ask him what the best way is to investigate police officers in a department, without them actually knowing they are being scrutinized. Tomorrow, we'll drive down to Limassol and discuss the "leak" issue with the British superintendent down there."

"I'll do it right away, captain," Ian responded.

He went to the motor pool, checked out a car and drove to the police headquarters located on the outskirts of the capital. The building was surrounded by security, since police stations were attractive targets to EOKA. Ian showed his ID to the sentry at the gate, drove in and parked in a visitors spot. He entered the building, where both Greek and Turkish police officers were supervised by British police officers. This mixture of different nationalities provided for a powder keg, when the communities rioted against each other. The Greek officers were often EOKA sympathizers and the Turks were on the British side, which they used to their advantage.

Ian was directed by a policeman to the Chief Superintendent's office, down a long hallway on the second floor. A secretary went into the chief's office and, in a few seconds, came out saying, "He'll see you now."

Ian went in and met a small British man with a moustache.

"I'm Lieutenant Ian Black with the Intelligence Corps and Captain Phillips suggested I come and discuss with you some methods ways for investigating police officers."

"How is Captain Phillips? I haven't seen him for a while. I suppose he's busy. By the way, I'm Edward Blake and I'm the Chief Superintendent for Central Nicosia, under the Commissioner. Exactly, what can I do for you?"

Ian responded, "Captain Phillips is fine. He's extremely busy today or otherwise he would be here with me. We are concerned that the police force in Limassol has been infiltrated by an EOKA sympathizer that is leaking information about our hunt for Grivas to the organization. We have a name that might be a first name or a pseudonym. We're wondering if you're able to give us any hints on how to go about an investigation of the entire force, without raising any alarm among them."

"You're talking about a force of 150 police officers and men, so it would be hard to run a complete investigation on all of them. Obviously, you can forget investigating any British or Turkish officers, which leaves you with probably about one hundred Greek officers to perform a background check on."

"Do you think it would be possible to just have the British officers bring us the personnel files to an office with no windows, so we can go through them in secrecy?" Ian asked.

"Probably, you would have to be very explicit with your request to the superintendent and make sure no Greek or Turkish officer hears your request. I would then go through the files fairly quickly to see if there is any match to the name you have, even if it's only a partial one. If not, you may be lucky enough to narrow the search down to a few people. You must be prepared for a long and exhausting search which may not bring any results."

"Thank you for your help, superintendent. We'll let you know if we have any success, since it might help you in the long run with all the Greeks you employ. Hopefully, you don't have any EOKA double agents in your force."

"I'm glad to have been of service, lieutenant. Good luck." answered Superintendent Blake.

Ian left the Nicosia police central office and drove back to Salisbury House, arriving there just in time for a cup of tea.

After eating dinner in the Officers' Mess, Ian decided to walk down into the Old Town and visit a few cafés and taverns, but not on Ledra Street. The purpose was to see if he could pick up any tips, on the whereabouts of Grivas. After about three hours, he drew a blank and figured he was not going to get any information that night. Ian walked back down the streets he'd come on, exited the Old Town and returned to Salisbury House. On the way, he saw a fight going on between a Greek and a Turk, and could guess what it was about. He did not interfere, but as he was walking out of the town, a police car raced by him, on the way to the disturbance.

In his room was a note from Captain Phillips, *"We'll meet for breakfast tomorrow at eight o'clock and then drive to Limassol."*

The next morning Ian met Captain Phillips for breakfast and told him about his meeting with Superintendent Blake, at the Nicosia police headquarters.

"He thought that there would be a hundred files to go through, and maybe we'd be able to filter them down a few possibilities. He added; if we're lucky."

Captain Phillips responded, "Maybe, since we have the name Pachykostis, we will be lucky and find a file with that in it, as a nickname or something."

"Let's hope so," Ian agreed, nodding.

They went down to the courtyard, after they finished breakfast, and climbed into a plain Ford that was waiting for them. The captain had already checked it out from the motor pool.

They drove out of the Salisbury House gate and headed for the road to Limassol. It took them about one hour to go the fifty miles and, by 1000 hours, they were pulling into the Limassol police headquarters. The captain led the way to the Chief Superintendent's office in the back of the building. He had already met the British police officer before and knew him quite well.

His secretary ushered them into his office.

"Captain Phillips, how nice it is to see you again. It's been quite a while, since we last met."

"Yes it has, superintendent. I'd like you to meet Lt. Black. He's attached to the Intelligence Corps, and reports to me and Colonel Baker. I believe you've met the colonel."

"Yes, indeed, what can I do for you?" asked the superintendent.

"We believe that you have a mole in your department who tells EOKA and Grivas, when we are going to conduct operations against them. We'd like to look at your personnel files on Greek Cypriots, to see if we can glean any information that matches the one name we have. We have to do this in secret, so as not to scare off the person, if we discover who it is. We want him to lead us to the big fish. We don't believe that a Turk would be helping EOKA. Our guess is that you have about one hundred Greek Cypriots in your department."

"One hundred and two to be exact. This is not many when one considers the population of Limassol is about 42,000, where the Greeks represent over eighty percent. Anyway, I have just the room you can use to go over the files."

"Thanks, we'll appreciate that. Is it possible for a British person to gather the files and bring them to us? We would prefer that no Greek or Turkish person be involved, so no one will know what we're doing here."

"I'll make arrangements for the files to be brought to you by my secretary. She's English and very trust worthy. If you follow me, I'll take you to the room that you can use," the superintendent said.

They followed him down the hallway to a large conference room with no windows. It was ideal, since it contained a large table on which they could lay out the files.

Soon, the secretary started to bring the personnel files to the room and stacked them on a small table in the corner.

"Let's get to work, Ian," the captain said, as he picked up the first file. "Let's see, we're looking for is a file that has the name Pachykostis in it or something like that, right?"

"Yes, that's correct, captain," Ian responded, as he picked up his first file.

They started to slowly go through the files. It was laborious and time consuming work.

After two hours, the superintendent came in to see how they were doing.

"It's not easy to go through a hundred files, is it?" he asked jokingly. Continuing, he asked, "Do you want some lunch? There is a small café just down the road. I'll walk with you if you would like."

"That would be nice, thanks," the captain replied.

The superintendent locked the conference room door and led them out of the building. They walked down the street, about 150 yards away, to a small Greek café. He treated the captain and Ian to lunch, and afterwards they had some strong coffee. As they were sitting there, there was a large bang and a plume of smoke rose into the sky.

Someone had thrown a bomb at the police headquarters. All three of them ran back up the street. The smell of cordite was in the air, and there were several policemen running around. Soon a fire truck and ambulance arrived. The major damage seemed to be some broken windows, and the front door of the building was blown in.

Superintendent Clarke shook his head, and said, "They're always throwing bombs at us, just to keep us on edge. Luckily, so far, none of them have been very serious. We've suffered very little in the way of wounded personnel."

He took them up to the conference room, unlocked the door and let them in.

"I have to go and see how much damage has been done, and I'll need to make arrangements to have it all repaired. I'll see you later."

Ian and Captain Phillips went back to work, looking at the files.

At close to four o'clock, Ian was looking at his fortieth file, when it popped out at him. The name on the file was Kostis Efstathiou, also known as Costas Efstathiou. He was a Chief Inspector in the police department.

"Was it a coincident that the first name was the last part of the of the pseudo name?" he thought.

"Captain, come look at this file. The first name is Kostis and he appears to be a large man. In Greek, pachy means large, massive or dense."

Captain Phillips came over to look at the file.

"It looks like a good possibility," he responded. "Let's finish up the few remaining files, and then we'll take the ten, or so, best possibilities and set them aside, including of course this one."

At 4:30 pm in the afternoon, they had gone through the 102 files and found twelve that looked somewhat suspicious, including the file on Kostis Efstathiou.

"Okay, Ian, let's call it a day. We'll gather up the ninety files that don't look questionable and give them back to the secretary. We'll also give her the other twelve and ask her to hold them. We'll come back tomorrow and spend a considerable amount of time studying them."

"That sounds like a good idea, captain. My eyes have about had it for the day, going through all the files," replied Ian.

They gathered up the files into two separate piles and handed them to the secretary, for safe keeping. They bade farewell to Superintendent Blake, telling him that they'd return tomorrow. They then drove back to Nicosia and Salisbury House.

The next morning they drove down the road to Limassol and headed for the police headquarters. There, workmen were busy replacing the windows and the front doors that had been blown out by the bomb.

Ian and the captain went to Superintendent Blake's secretary and retrieved the twelve files.

"Here they are gentlemen. Please be careful with them, as I have to replace them intact, as soon as you're finished with them."

"We'll get them back to you, before the end of the day. Is the superintendent in?" asked the captain.

"He's out at the moment, but when he returns, I'll let him know that you're in the conference room," she responded.

They carried the files to the conference room and divided them into two piles; six each.

Then Ian and the captain poured through all the information contained in them; people they knew, contacts, what cases they had been on, etc. By lunchtime, both of them had gone through all twelve files and made a note of the suspicious ones. There were three of them, all with the first name of Kostis.

After lunch, they took the three files and studied them again.

"Captain, the one that stands out the most to me is Kostis Efstathiou. He is a large man and seems to know the Gabrielides family, who actually wrote a recommendation to the department to hire him. In addition, it seems that he is also an acquaintance of Charles Foley, the editor of the Cyprus Times. Pachykostis pseudonym would fit him, since he does have a large frame."

279

"Ian, I think you're onto something. Let's go and find the superintendent, and see how much he knows about this officer."

They left the conference room, carrying the three files, and went to see Superintendent Blake. They found him in his office.

"Come in, gentlemen," he insisted. "What have you found out?"

The captain responded, "Well, we've narrowed it down to one officer by the name of Kostis Efstathiou, also known as Costas Efstathiou. There are several troubling details about him and he's fairly high up in the organization that allows him to get around, without much oversight. What do you know about him?"

"Not much. He was already on the force, when I arrived here, and he seems to perform admirably. His performance reviews have always been good, as far as I recall."

"Who does he report to?" the captain asked.

"He reports to another British officer, Chief Inspector Tom Butler. Would you like to talk to him?"

"If he's available now, we'd certainly appreciate the opportunity," the captain replied.

"Let me check," said the superintendent, as he picked up the phone.

"Tom, this is the superintendent here. Please come to my office right away," he requested.

"I'll be there immediately, sir," Tom replied.

In a couple of minutes, Tom Butler walked into the office. He was a tall, young man in his thirties, and he had been in Cyprus about three years.

"What can I do for you, sir?" he asked, as he looked around the office.

"Tom, I'd like you to meet Captain Phillips and Lieutenant Black from the Intelligence Corps."

They all shook hands and the superintendent outlined why they were there. "They believe that there is an EOKA mole in the department. He's in your outfit, and they want your opinion. His name is Kostis Efstathiou."

"He was on the force when I took over the detective division. I've had no problems with him. He operates alone quite a lot and seems to be out of the office, a considerable amount of time each day."

The captain replied, "At this point, we are not accusing him, but his background looks questionable. What we would like to do is place a twenty four hour a day tail on him. We want to know who he sees, who he talks to and where he goes. If he is a mole, we don't want to arrest him, until we know all his contacts. This has to remain a secret between us, for now. The intelligence Corps does not have any experts in tailing a person, so we will probably be asking the SIS to help in this matter. Is that okay with you?"

"Most certainly, I don't mind a bit. Please keep me informed, on any information you think I should know. Other than that, as the old saying goes; I know nothing, see nothing or hear nothing."

"Thank you Tom, you may go back to work now. Thanks for your cooperation, in this matter," said the Chief Superintendent.

As Tom left the office, Captain Phillips said to Superintendent Blake, "Well that about wraps up the matter for now. We'll keep you informed, about the tails and what they discover. Thanks for all your help. We'll leave now, as I believe that we've taken enough of your time."

Ian and the captain walked out of the police headquarters, just as the workmen were finishing their task of replacing the windows and doors, damaged from the bomb attack. They drove back to Nicosia, feeling gratified that they may have found the mole. Only time would tell, if Kostis Efstathiou truly was the mole.

23

Police Connection

The next day, after they arrived back from Limassol, Captain Phillips and Ian went to see Colonel Baker in his office, to report on what they found out in Limassol.

"Colonel, we've looked through approximately one hundred police department personnel files, during the past two days, and narrowed our investigation down to one individual, who could be the mole. He goes by the name of Kostis (Costas) Efstathiou, and he almost exactly fits the profile of the person we're looking for. The nickname of pachykostis seems to fit him to a tee. In fact, he is a chief inspector with the Limassol police and is a large man," explained the captain.

He continued, "In addition, he was recommended by the Gabrielides family, when he applied to join the force, and also seems to be an acquaintance of Charles Foley, the editor of the Cyprus Times. On top of that, he also appears to know Polycarpos Georghadjis; the Cyprus Chamber of Commerce clerk who organized up to twenty police officers to become informants in the past."

"I must agree that your information does point to a possible mole in the Limassol police department. He may even know where Grivas is hiding out. What do you suggest we do with this individual?" asked the colonel.

"Sir, I believe the best course of action would be to have a twenty four hour tail placed on him, to determine where he goes, who he talks to and what he does with his time. The problem is we don't have anyone in our organization who's experienced in following someone, such as this. You can bet he keeps his eyes open for a tail. Therefore, perhaps we could ask your contacts in SIS, to determine if they have an experienced person or persons to track this Kostis Efstathiou," Ian proposed.

"Captain, what do you think about this idea?"

"I agree with Mr. Black's suggestion, colonel," replied the captain.

"Very well, I'll contact my SIS sources to determine if they can help us in this effort," the colonel responded. "I'll let you know what the status is, as soon as I have been in touch with them. Thank you both for your hard work and for the information you've provided."

A few days later, the colonel called the captain and informed him that the SIS was placing a twenty four hour tail on Kostis Efstathiou, for a period of approximately two weeks.

****

Three weeks later, the colonel asked the captain and Ian to come to his office at 1400 hours, on the following day. Captain Phillips and Ian walked to the colonel's office and entered together. There was a man in his forties, dressed in civilian clothes, sitting by the colonel's desk. The captain and Ian saluted, and after the colonel signaled for them to do so, they sat down in the two vacant chairs.

The colonel started out by saying, "I'm sure we're all aware that the information, that we're about to talk about, is very sensitive in nature and, how we came about it must never be discussed by my organization. Is that clear?"

"Yes, sir," both the captain and Ian responded in unison.

"Good. I'd like you to meet Maurice, who's here to give us some feedback on the tail."

"Good afternoon, gentlemen. As the colonel said, my name is Maurice and I'm from the SIS." Maurice said, looking at the captain and Ian, who both nodded.

Maurice continued, "As per the colonel's request, a twenty four hour tail was placed on the Limassol Chief Inspector named Kostis Efstathiou. I'm glad to report it was well worthwhile, since I'm sure you are aware that it takes considerable resources to accomplish such a tail. It turned out he spends a large amount of his time outside the office. He appears to frequently visit a small white, stone house in an alley close to the Curium Palace Hotel, and only about 100 yards from the Limassol bypass, Pluto Street. We checked the ownership of the house and it belongs to a Marios Christodoulides, who works at the Ottoman Bank, along with his wife, Eli Christodoulides. We've had the house under surveillance and have identified two people who visit there, on a fairly regular basis, as Maroulla and Dafnis Panayides. According to our intelligence group, these individuals may be couriers for EOKA and, if so, their job is to move correspondence around the organization.

Besides performing in his regular duties as a police officer, Kostis does visit cafés and restaurants fairly regularly, where he meets many young men that look suspicious. In fact, a few of them are on our suspected EOKA list, including this courier Maroulla.

The bottom line is that we feel you may be onto something with this Kostis chap, and he needs watching some more. However, our resources are stretched to the limit on other activities. In addition, I feel there may be a high value target at this house. I suggest that your organization set up a permanent surveillance on this house. I'll forward the actual address of the house and a detailed map of the area to you, colonel."

"Maurice, thank you for that report and the hard work you've put into the round-the-clock surveillance, on this chap," the colonel responded

"You're welcome. I wish that we could be of more assistance. Good day," Maurice said, as he left the colonel's office.

"Don't forget, you've never met or talked with Maurice. I can't be more emphatic about that point. Understood?" demanded the colonel.

"Yes, sir," replied the captain and Ian together.

Ian thought, *"I bet Maurice is not his real name, anyway."*

"You know colonel. This may be the break we've been looking for, in the search for Grivas. It's possible that this white block building is a safe house, and this Maroulla chap is the courier between Grivas, Kostis and the EOKA organization. I believe we should watch this house twenty four hours a day, to determine if Grivas is there. If we could obtain possession of a house across the road and move in, it would be fairly easy to watch the house, without being seen," Ian suggested.

The captain added, "If we can determine that Grivas is actually there, we could plan a raid on the house, and maybe capture him alive. A house across the road would be useful to have as a base, where we could plan and implement the operation. The raid could be scheduled to take place, when the couriers are visiting the premises and the owners are also home. Maybe we'd end up catching some senior terrorists in one raid."

The colonel responded, "I agree and I'll make arrangements to obtain a building close enough to this house, so we can set up an around-the- clock surveillance on it. From there, we'll be able to plan our raid at the appropriate time."

24

Politics Trumps Military

On the second Monday, after the 1959 New Year, Colonel Baker called a special staff meeting, of the Intelligence Corps Special Unit.

"I hope that you've all had a great New Year's celebration. Now, however, it's time to get down to work. The army has located a house, four lots down and on the other side of the road, from the home of Marios Christodoulides. This will be ideal for us to use as a stake out location. It has great visibility of the house in question, and there's a back alley that will allow us to enter it, without being seen from the target building.   The owner is not aware as to who is going to be in it, and he has been sent on a four week, all expenses paid vacation, paid by the British Army."

"When can we move in, sir?" asked the captain.

"We've taken immediate possession of the single story premises, and we can move in immediately. The place does have an attic in the roof, with a small window in the front that overlooks the target house. Arrangements have been made to move in some additional furniture. You'll not be living in comfort, but it'll be up to British Army standards," the colonel responded with a smile.

"Colonel, since we don't know if there are any hidden cells or rooms in the house we're be watching, would it be possible to contact all building contractors to determine if any of them have worked on the target house and what work they accomplished?" asked Ian.

"That's a good idea," answered the colonel. "We'll have the Corps of Royal Engineers look into the matter to see if they can find any contractor that's worked on the house and grounds. Does anyone have any other ideas or suggestions?"

"How about if we obtain as many photos, as we can, of the key EOKA members and post them on a wall in the watch house?" asked Roger. "Then, every time we see one of them go to the house, we could place a mark by their photo and/or name. This way we could build up a tally, of who goes to the house."

"That's another good suggestion, thank you, Roger. By the way gentleman, we have to move quickly on this and capture Grivas soon. I have information from a reliable source that the negotiations in Zurich are going well, between Greece, Turkey and the UK. We may only have a short time to grab him."

"Colonel, the night of Friday, the 6th of February, will be moonless, and I suggest we aim to raid the house on that night. I believe we'll need the support of a few regular army troops, to seal off the road to the house, and to cordon off the rear garden. This will insure that he doesn't escape the area, even if he gets out of the house. Of course, this assumes he's in there. Since, we preferably want to capture him alive, we'll need some tear gas grenades to drive him out of the building, so we can grab him without killing him. To support this action, it would probably be useful to have a Matador searchlight lorry on hand, just in case we need the light to temporary blind the person or persons that come out of the house, after the tear gas has been thrown in," suggested Ian.

The colonel responded, "Why don't you prepare a plan of attack for the night you indicated and develop a list of equipment, you'll require to achieve success. Next, sit down with Captain Phillips and refine it, and then he can bring it to me for approval. Okay with you, captain?"

"Yes colonel, I believe that would be the best way to handle it. We'll need two radios, one as a backup, in the watch house so we can communicate with you directly," replied the captain.

"Let's get moving," ordered the colonel. "I want you to go to the house that we've obtained, and set up "shop" there. The additional furniture and equipment will be arriving shortly. I don't believe I need to stress that this is an important mission and stealth is critical, so as to not scare the target away."

The meeting ended and they all prepared to go to Limassol, to check out the watch house and the view of the target house.

Two days later, the furniture arrived, and the Intelligence Corps team consisting of Captain Phillips, Lieutenants Ian Black and Roger Snell, along with Sergeant Bingham were ensconced in the watch house. The equipment had also arrived, including several sets of binoculars, a telescope with a tripod, tear gas grenades, communications gear, and photographs of the suspected key individuals in the EOKA organization.

In addition, weapons of all kinds, including two bazookas and Sterling SMGs, were also delivered. Food was provided three times a day, along with water and other provisions, by an unmarked van at the back of the house. The people in the target house never saw any of the movements by the Intelligence Corps, since the watch house had the alley behind it.

On the first day the men were at the watch house, Captain Phillips held a meeting and explained the ground rules.

"The four of us will be divided into two teams of two. I'll team up with Sergeant Bingham and Lieutenants Black and

Snell will team up together. At all times, we need one of us watching the house from the attic window. In order to make it easy on us, we'll serve four hours on and then twelve hours off and interchange every other day. In addition, to eliminate boredom, two of us will take time off for two hours each day and go into town. However, I don't think I have to remind you that Limassol is basically eighty percent Greek, so keep your wits about you, when you're walking around."

On the first morning at 8:30 am, Ian who was at the window called out to those in the main part of the house, "Marios Christodoulides, the owner of the house just left, I assume, to go to work at the Ottoman Bank, but his wife did not leave the home with him."

At around 11:00 am, Roger who was on duty reported, "There's a man walking down the road towards the house and he's carrying a large folder. He just knocked on the door and a small woman opened the door and let him in. I'm not sure, but I believe the man is Maroulla Panayides, the EOKA courier, and the woman who let him in was probably the owner's wife, Eli."

At 11:30 am, Roger announced, "The same man is leaving and heading down the way he came. He certainly looks like Maroulla Panayides to me."

There was no more activity until around 4:30 pm. Ian reported down to the main room, "I believe Marios Christodoulides is walking down the road to the house. I assume he's coming home from work at the bank."

That evening, Colonel Baker called on the radio to Captain Phillips. "Captain, I just received some information from the Corps of Royal Engineers. They found a Turkish labourer, who works for a small Greek Limassol contractor. They were contracted by the home owner, Andreas Papadopoulos, to do some modifications in the kitchen, a couple of years ago. At that time, the target house was empty.

As they were working in the kitchen, the Turk noticed that a large stone slab in the centre of the floor was not cemented in. He asked Andreas what was below it, and was told there was a shelter built by the previous owner of the house. He had it built as a hideaway, in case the Germans invaded Cyprus during World War Two. The Turk lifted up the stone and looked down into the hole and the hide. To him, it appeared it went beyond the kitchen into the back garden. He assumes it's still there. This is all the information I have received, but it might be a great place for Grivas to hide. If troops raided the house, they might never find the hide, unless they knew it was there."

"That's valuable information to have when we raid the place, colonel," replied the captain.

"How's the watch going?" the colonel asked.

"Maroulla Panayides came to the house this morning and stayed for half an hour. He carried a folder in and out of the house. This chap is supposed to be a courier for EOKA, but who knows for sure. However, why would he come to this house for just thirty minutes? He was let in by the wife of the owner Eli Christodoulides. The only other activity was Marios Christodoulides going to work in the morning and coming home in the late afternoon."

"Keep up the good work; I'll talk to you tomorrow, captain."

That night, it was very quiet and no activity was seen across the road.

The next day, Sergeant Bingham was on duty and at ten o'clock in the morning, a man came down the road.

"Captain, there's a man approaching the house and he's looking around, as if he's afraid there's a tail on him. I'm not sure, but I think it might be Demos Hjimiltis, the suspected Limassol EOKA town commander. Right now, he's being let in by the owner's wife."

"That's good information, sergeant. Keep watching, and let me know if anyone else appears. I can also watch from down here, on the main level," replied the captain.

About thirty minutes later, the sergeant called down again. "Captain, there's a woman coming the road now in a hurry and is going to the target house. According to our photo gallery, I believe it might be Nina Droushiotou who is a special EOKA courier and the fiancée of Demos Hjimiltis who entered the home awhile ago."

"Keep an eye out and let me know, when either of them comes out," the captain replied.

It was two hours before front door opened.

The sergeant called down, "The woman is coming out alone, and I don't see the man. Oh, wait a minute, he's now coming out, but walking down the road in the opposite direction to the woman. He'll be passing this house in a few seconds."

The sergeant thought, *"They either had a long meeting with Grivas, if he's truly in there, or they've had a secret rendezvous."*

"He's gone past this house now and is proceeding down the road towards the Curium Palace Hotel," the sergeant continued.

The rest of the afternoon was quiet, until Marios came home from the Ottoman bank, where he worked.

That evening, Marios and his wife left to go out to eat at a local café. The sun had already set so the dark night had settled on Limassol. Captain Phillips went up to the attic to keep a look out on the house across the road. As he was watching it, he saw a faint light come on and a shadow moved across the curtains in the front window.

"That's strange," the captain thought. *The Christodoulides went out a while ago and haven't come back yet. Who could that be in the house?"*

He watched as the shadow crossed the curtain about three times and then the dim light went out.

"Was that Grivas moving around in there?" he wondered.

The next day when the colonel called in, the captain mentioned it to him.

"Colonel, I saw something strange last night, as I was watching the house. A dim light came on and I saw a faint shadow on the curtains, and yet the owners of the house had gone out on the town. Obviously, there is someone else in the house, besides the Christodoulides."

"Well, keep watching and when I get down there in approximately ten days, we'll discuss all the issues and develop a strategy to raid the place; assuming there is an agreement, amongst all of you, that it seems likely Grivas is hiding out there."

****

For the next ten days, they watched the target house and made note of who came and left. The procedure was basically the same. They all took turns watching the house, and it turned out the visitors were always identical. This seemed to indicate that the person in the house was a high value target, even if it wasn't Grivas; if the visitors were whom they thought they were.

****

On Monday, the 2nd of February, the colonel drove down to the watch house and held a meeting to discuss the raid.

The colonel started out, "We previously agreed that the 6th of this month was the ideal date to raid the premises, since it'll be a moonless night. The sun sets at 1720 hours on that day, so that any time after 1800 hours will be ideal for the operation. Do you all still agree?""

"Yes, sir." they all replied in unison.

"Do we know how many people are in the house?" asked the colonel

292

The captain replied, "We don't know for sure, but everyone who has gone in has come out. In the evening, the only people in the house are the owners and at least one other person based on the shadow we perceived crossing the curtains. Do we have any idea how large the hide is?" the captain asked.

"According to the Turk who looked into it a couple of years ago, the hide could only accommodate three people comfortably. Therefore, if we can somehow get rid of the owners, we would only have at most three terrorists to contend with," declared the colonel.

"I have a suggestion, sir, on how to get rid of the owners, on the evening of the raid," said Ian. "Marios Christodoulides, the owner, comes home from the bank, where he works, at around 1630. Before he enters the road, where his house is situated, a Limassol police car, with two British officers in it, could stop him, tell him he is under arrest for some crime, like financial wrongdoing, and take him away.

Then later, the same two officers in the police car could pull up at the house, one would get out and knock on the door. He would inform the wife that her husband was in trouble, and he needed her to come with them right away. Like any good wife, she would probably be eager to go help her husband.

She would be taken to a location, where there could be a couple of intelligence officers who are good at interrogation. They could offer leniency for her and her husband, if she would just tell them how many people are in the house, and the hide that we know about. In order to save her husband, I bet she would spill the "beans". Then, we would know before the raid, exactly what we would be up against; whether there are one, two or three people in the hide."

"That's all well and good, Mr. Black, but how do we get the people in the hide to come out, without guns blazing?" the colonel asked.

"May I answer that, colonel?" queried the captain.

"Of course, go ahead."

"Two of us could slip into the house quietly. Even if they heard us, they would think that we were the two owners of the house. We would then go to the flagstone and slowly pry it up, far enough to slip a tear gas grenade down in the hole. Fairly quickly, they would push up the stone to get out of there. They would be blinded by the gas, and we could nab them," the captain answered.

"What if there's an exit, from the hide, into the rear garden, and they use that to escape?" asked the colonel.

"We would station two men in the garden with SMGs, in case there is a second entrance to and from the hide." Roger replied.

"If I may offer another suggestion, sir, I recommend that we have one Matador searchlight lorry on standby down a side street away from the house, just in case it is needed to light up the area. In addition, it might be wise to have a few soldiers at each end of the road, to block off anyone from approaching on foot or by car," Ian said.

"What if they come out of the hide with guns blazing?" questioned the colonel.

"After we've thrown the tear gas grenade into the hide, we'll signal for two more soldiers to come in the house, in case they're needed. The hope is that we can take him alive," the captain replied.

"Let me summarize the resources we'll need for this operation, from what I've heard. First, we need one Matador searchlight lorry. Second, we'll need the assistance of probably twenty experienced soldiers. Third, we need two Limassol British police officers with Limassol police cars. Finally, we'll need two experienced intelligence officers who are good at getting information out of a reluctant witness. Is this correct?" asked the colonel.

"Yes sir," answered the captain. "That about sums it up."

"Captain, will you now lay out the timeline for this raid, so I can see if it makes sense?"

"Yes colonel, the following is the schedule, as we envision it.

1630. An British police officer in a car stops Marios and takes him away to a cell in a SIS safe house.

1700. An British police office drives up to the house and takes Eli to supposedly visit her husband in jail.

1730. Eli is taken to the SIS safe house and is interrogated by the two experienced interrogators.

1745. Any telephone cables to the house are cut.

1800. The Matador lorry arrives along with twenty soldiers.

1815. Six soldiers go to each end of the road and seal it off

1845. Two soldiers go into the rear garden.

1900. Mr. Black and Mr. Snell enter the house and throw the tear gas down the hole. At the same time, electricity is cut off to the house. Two soldiers enter the house in case they're required.

1930. By this time or sooner, Grivas and anyone else down in the hide will be in custody or dead. Hopefully, they'll be captured alive.

"Captain," said the colonel. "This timeline looks achievable and plausible to me. I'll time my arrival here at 1830, in order to witness the actual raid. Let me think about this plan and I'll get back to you within a day.

By the way, Mr. Black would have to organize the arrival of the Matador. You, captain, would have to arrange to have the twenty soldiers arrive here, at the same time as the lorry, and also arrange for the British police officers from Limassol to pick up the home owners. As I see it, I'll have to arrange for help from SIS, with the safe house and two interrogators. Is this correct?"

"If you agree, that is correct, sir," replied the captain.

"That's all for now," the colonel said. "I'll let you know my decision tomorrow. I will be discussing the plan with General Mastin, my CO, to make sure he is in agreement."

****

The next day, the colonel radioed the watch house and talked with Captain Phillips.

"Captain, we've an agreement for the operation to continue from my CO, so go ahead and make the necessary arrangements for the Matador from the 188th, the British police officers from Limassol and the twenty soldiers from the Lancashire Fusiliers. I'll arrange with the SIS to allow us to bring the owners of the house to one of their safe houses and for two of them to interrogate the owner's wife."

"We'll get right on it, colonel."

The captain found Ian up in the attic, watching the house.

"Lieutenant, the colonel just told me that we have a provisional go ahead for the raid. Get hold of the 188th and request that they provide one Matador searchlight lorry. Make sure they understand it must be parked on a side road, not too far from here, at 1800 on this Friday, the 6th. I'll be gone for some time, since I have to go to the Limassol police department and also make contact with the Lancashire Fusiliers."

"I'll have Lieutenant Snell and Sergeant Bingham watch the target house, while I make contact with the 188th. It shouldn't take long, since Major MacArthur and I are well acquainted with each other," Ian replied.

"I'll see you later," replied the captain, as he left the watch house.

Ian called Major MacArthur, and asked if the 188th could provide a Matador for a key operation. After he explained to the major what the raid was all about, his former CO enthusiastically agreed to send one lorry to the area.

296

ON HER MAJESTY'S CYPRUS MISSION

When Captain Phillips explained what the operation was all about to the Limassol Chief Superintendent Blake and the Lancashire Fusiliers CO, everyone was eager to support such a worthwhile operation. The captain explained in detail what they were expected to do. The fusiliers volunteered to send an officer to the watch house, to make sure his soldiers conducted themselves, according to the plan.

Superintendent Blake of the Limassol police was more than willing to provide the two British officers. He called them into his office and Captain Phillips explained what they had to do, and that he would inform them where to take Marios and Eli Christodoulides, when he had the address.

When the captain returned to the watch house, he held a short meeting with Lt. Black, Lt. Snell and Sgt. Bingham.

"It's very important that we watch the house closely for the next three days, until the raid, to make sure every visitor to the target house, also leaves the house. We have to be sure what we'll be up against, when we raid the place," he ordered.

****

The day of the raid finally arrived and the men in the watch house arose early to make sure everything was prepared. Ian Black cleaned, oiled and loaded his Browning automatic, just in case he had to use it later. They got the tear gas grenades out of the box and made sure that they all knew how to use them. They laid out the tear gas masks, so they could quickly put them on, if required.

The bazookas were placed on the floor, and they were all given instructions on how to operate them by Captain Phillips.

"Hopefully, we won't need to fire them, unless we're attacked ourselves," he declared.

By three o'clock in the afternoon, everything was prepared. The weather was fairly good for February, a little chilly and no rain. They had watched the house all day, and only one visitor arrived and left. It was the special courier Nina Droushiotou. Her boyfriend, Demos, did not accompany her.

At 1630, Marios Christodoulides left the Ottoman Bank where he worked and started to walk home. Before he reached the street where he lived, a Limassol police car containing two officers drew alongside him. One of them got out and went up to him.

"Are you Mr. Christodoulides?" asked the British police officer

"Yes, I am. Why do you ask?" he replied.

"Do you work at the Ottoman Bank?" asked the officer.

"Yes, I do. I've worked there for ten years."

"I'm sorry to inform you that you're under arrest," responded the officer.

"Me, what's the charge? I've done nothing wrong," Marios said, surprised.

"We'll see about that. You've been accused of embezzling bank funds. Until this is cleared up, we'll have to hold you. Put your hands behind your back."

Marios complied and the officer placed handcuffs on his wrists. He then led him to his car and placed him in the back seat. They drove off down the road and, in ten minutes, arrived at a nondescript house in a quiet neighborhood. One officer got Marios out of the car and led him to the door. After he rang the front doorbell, a tall burly man appeared who Marios inside, down some stairs, and placed him in a cage in the basement.

Marios screamed, "What the bloody hell is going on here?"

The man shouted back at him, "Shut up or I'll give you a reason to scream." The man then went up the stairs to the main part of the house and closed the sound proof door into the basement.

At 1700 hours, the same Limassol police car driven by the two British officers pulled up outside the Christodoulides home. One officer knocked on the door and a small woman opened it.

"Are you Eli Chistodoulides?" the officer asked.

"Yes, I am," she said, as she looked past the officer and spotted the police car at the kerb. "What's the problem, officer? I'm expecting my husband home any minute now."

"That's the problem, ma'am. Your husband is in trouble and he needs you right away. I've come to take you to him."

"I'll come right away," she said. "What kind of trouble is he in?"

"It has something to do with bank funds, I believe."

She closed the front door and followed the officer to the car. There, he opened the rear passenger door and helped her get in. He then closed the door which had been fixed so it couldn't be opened from the inside. They drove off to the safe house about fifteen minutes away.

As they got closer to the house, Eli said, "This isn't the way to the police station. I know where it is. Where are you taking me?"

"We're taking you to an alternate police station. So keep quiet, if you know what's good for you and your husband."

The woman tried to open the door at the next stop sign, but the door handle wouldn't move.

"Let me out," she yelled.

"I will in a minute," one officer said. "Stop yelling. It won't do you any good."

Finally the car pulled up outside the safe house, and one officer opened the passenger door. He dragged her out of the car, as she struggled. She fought him all the way up to the front door. When she saw the burly chap who opened it, she quieted down slightly.

The chap pulled her in and took her to one of the back rooms, where there was another man waiting. They sat her in a chair and tied her wrists to the arms of the chair.

The first man said, "You can make this easy on yourself or you can make it hard. The sooner you tell us what we want to know, the quicker you'll be released. Your husband has been accused of embezzling funds at the bank. What do you know about that?"

"I know nothing. He's never stolen anything in his life."

"How about EOKA, maybe he has stolen money for them?"

"Not that I know of, we don't even know anyone in EOKA."

"Do you want to see your husband again?"

"Of course, I do."

"Very well then, how many people live in your home?"

"Just my husband and I, no one else lives there. It's a small place."

"How about the hide below the kitchen, is there anyone in there?"

She gasped and began to shake. "How do you know about that?"

"Never you mind, how many people are hidden down there?"

She realized she was caught by her previous question. "There are sometimes two people down there."

"Who are they?"

"They'll kill me if I tell you. I only agreed to allow them down there, because my husband told me to."

"What are their names? The sooner you tell us, the sooner you get out of here and see your husband again."

"If I tell you, will you promise not to tell my husband or anyone else?"

"We can't make a blanket promise. However, we'll not tell EOKA or your husband. That will be up to you to decide."

Eli Christodoulides thought for a minute. *"If I don't tell them, I might not see Marios again. If I do tell them, maybe it will stay a secret. I guess that I have no choice, but to gamble."*

She trembled, as she gave them what they wanted to know, "One of them is Grivas, also known as Dighenis and I don't know the name of the other man. He's helping Grivas by typing his orders and his memoires."

The second interrogator rose and undid the rope that bound her wrists to the chair. He said, "Now that wasn't so hard, was it?"

The burly man went out of the room for a few minutes and got on the radio to the watch house

"This is Captain Phillips."

"Captain, this is Maurice. We managed to obtain the information you required in thirty minutes. We've determined that there are two people in the hide. One is Grivas, but we don't have a name for the other one."

"Thanks for the information. We now know what we can expect, if there is any trouble. Thanks for your help in this matter."

"You're welcome. Goodbye."

The burly man came back into the room and said to her softly, "We'll keep you here now and take you home at ten o'clock.

"What about my husband?" she asked.

"He'll be taken back to your house about thirty minutes after you arrive there. Don't worry he's safe."

"I'm sorry we can't let you go yet. Would you like something to eat or drink?"

"Just some water, please."

While all this was going on, at 1745, the twin pair of telephone cables were cut to the house by Sergeant Bingham, the communication expert from the Signals Corps.

At 1800, the Matador searchlight lorry arrived and parked down another road, ready in case its services were needed. A few minutes later, a lorry with twenty soldiers from the Lancashire Fusiliers rolled up behind the watch house and the soldiers got out. Six of them went to one end of the road and six went to the other. They sealed the road off to the Christodoulides house. No one would be able to get in or out.

At 1830, Colonel Baker arrived at the watch house and went in. He ordered Captain Phillips to assemble, with the other three men, in the main room.

"Gentlemen, we're all in the British Army and we have to obey the orders from our superior officers. They in turn serve at the discretion of the PM. Just before I came here, I received a call from General Mastin, and he gave me an order for us to stand down. As of now this operation is ended, and we'll not be raiding the Christodoulides house as planned. To give you some background information, I can tell you that the negotiations in Zurich are going extremely well and are almost concluded with an agreement. It was felt by the politicians in London that the death or capture of Grivas would make him a martyr, and would start up the violence here again. I know how this must be disappointing to all of you, who have worked so hard. However, when you took the oath in joining the army, you said that you would obey all the lawful orders of your superiors. Are there any questions?"

Captain Phillips asked, "Is it okay if we release the Christodoulides now and have them taken home?"

"Tell your contact to do that in thirty minutes. Also, inform the soldiers at the roadblocks and the Matador that their services are no longer required. I'll see you all tomorrow in a staff meeting at the usual location. Good night. Again, thanks for your hard work."

The captain called Maurice on the radio and told him the news. He asked him to release Marios and Eli separately to the police officers about thirty minutes apart, so they could be taken back to their home.

On the way back to Nicosia, Ian thought, *"As in many cases, politicians overrule the military. It happened in Korea with General MacArthur."*

The next day, the colonel held a staff meeting and again explained the issues around the decision.

Five days later, an agreement to settle the Cyprus issue was signed in Zurich. Under it, Grivas had to leave the island and not return, until the island was independent.

25

The Agreement

Archbishop Makarios III, head of the Greek Orthodox Church in Cyprus and leader of the political arm favouring enosis, had been exiled by the Cyprus governor, to the Mahe Island in the Seychelles, on the 9th of March, 1956. He had been sent there, because of his continuous defiance of the British/Cyprus anti- sedition law.

After one year, his exile had been revoked, but he had been forbidden to return to Cyprus. He travelled to Athens, where he had been received as a hero. There, he worked tirelessly for the next two years on the idea of Enosis, which most Greek Cypriots supported.

In the latter part of 1958 and early 1959, talks took place in Zurich between Greece and Turkey, over the future of Cyprus. On the 11th of February, 1959, the conference was concluded between the two countries and an agreement was reached. Then, Archbishop Makarios flew from Athens to London, to participate in a London conference, gathered for the purpose of finalizing the agreement. Eight days later, another conference was held at Lancaster House in London, attended by all concerned parties including Britain, Greece, Turkey, Archbishop Makarios and Dr. Fazil Küçük. Finally, by the 19th of February, 1959, the final details had been negotiated and agreed upon. The result was the formation of an independent Republic of Cyprus, with a constitution that was called an oddity, by the United Nations mediator.

However, Makarios believed this was the best deal he could get, even though EOKA, the military arm of Enosis, was not in favour of it.

Under the agreement, there were twenty seven points that defined how the Republic of Cyprus would operate. The constitution called for the president to be always from the Greek community and the vice president from the Turkish community. The basic flaw in this agreement was that the vice president had the right to veto any fundamental laws passed by the House of Representatives, and on any decision made by the Council of Ministers. This started the process of ethnic segregation and nationalism.

The judicial system set up by the constitution was also flawed and set in motion a biased judiciary. Even a minor disagreement, between a Turk and a Greek, required that the trial be conducted by a Greek and Turkish judge.

In towns and villages, where there were people of both nationalities, there had to be separate municipalities, which proved to be impracticable. Questions arose as to the makeup of the police force and civil service jobs.

Based on all of the problems raised by the terms of the agreement, the state could not function correctly, raise taxes or perform basic services. The UN Mediator was proved correct; the constitution was an oddity.

Besides the agreement between all parties which set up the constitution, two treaties were also passed and these created more problems, than the agreement ever did.

First, the "Treaty of Guarantee" had two parts and five articles which above all said that the three powers, the United Kingdom, Greece and Turkey, had the right of unilateral or joint action for the purpose of reestablishing the state of affairs created by the present treaty (Article IV). This Treaty obviously allowed any of the three countries to come to the island with armed forces. This meant that Cyprus was not truly independent.

Second, the "Treaty of Alliance" allowed Turkey and Greece to station contingents of their armed forces on the island. This was another infringement of the rights of an independent nation and against the principles of the United Nations charter.

The Republic of Cyprus managed to function smoothly initially, but the agreements and treaties were flawed. They did, however, allow Britain to get out of Cyprus virtually unscathed, except for the four years of the Emergency.

26

Emergency Ends

Immediately after the London Zurich agreement was signed on the 19th of February, Colonel Baker called a staff meeting, to discuss ways to prevent attacks on Archbishop Makarios's life.

"Thank you for coming at such short notice. As you're aware, under the terms of the Zurich agreement, Makarios has been given authorization to return to Cyprus. However, there might be certain elements within the EOKA terror group, as well as some Turkish Cypriots, who don't like this agreement. It's our duty to prevent anyone from sabotaging this agreement, before it goes into effect.

I see a two part plan that needs to be put in place. First, we need someone to go to London, and then return on the same Olympic flight that Makarios will be on. The purpose would be to prevent any threat on his life, and also to find out as much intelligence as we can from him; in other words, his contacts in Cyprus now and in the past.

"Ian."

"Yes, sir."

"You are herewith volunteered to go to London, and then return with Archbishop Makarios, on the same flight. As I speak, arrangements are being made for your flights and hotel reservation. I just explained your duties a few moments ago. The reason you were picked is obvious; your command of the Greek language. Do you have any questions?"

"Just one, sir, since I'll be entering England with my Browning automatic, I'll need a pass to allow me to enter and leave without any problem. Will I be provided with one?"

"That pass is being worked on, along with the flights and the hotel," replied the colonel. "As for the rest of us, we must keep our ears to the ground, in order to hear of any potential plots. I must remind you all, regardless of what we personally think about the UK government giving Grivas a pass to get off the island, we are duty bound to obey orders and let him go."

The colonel adjourned the meeting, saying, "Captain Phillips, I want to see you and Mr. Black in my office, before he leaves for England."

"We'll be there, colonel," Captain Phillips replied, looking at Ian, who nodded.

On the 22ndof February, the day before Ian flew to England, he and the captain went to see the colonel in his office.

"Colonel, we're here as instructed. Ian leaves tomorrow on the BEA flight to London."

"Mr. Black, I wanted to see you, before you left, to make sure there are no misunderstandings, as far as your duties are concerned. Your primary duty is to make sure no harm befalls the archbishop, on the flight back to Nicosia. You are not responsible for him in London, nor in Nicosia, after local security has taken over. Your secondary duty is to try and get information from him on the flight, as to the people he has been in contact with for the past two years. Until we haul down our flag on the 16th of August, 1960, our job is to prevent any violence or armed attacks in Cyprus. Knowing who his contacts have been, may be the key to preventing any attacks. One side issue, if photographers take pictures of the archbishop, it would be best if you're not in any of them."

"Colonel, I completely understand my duties and I'll carry them out to the best of my abilities."

"That's good, Mr. Black. One other point, it would be best that your gun is not visible, unless you actually have to use it. I hope you have a good trip and I'll see you back here on the 1st of March."

Ian went to the Nicosia airport the next morning and flew out on Cyprus Airways, operated by BEA. His flight in a Vickers Viscount turboprop took him to Athens, Rome and on into London, arriving in the evening, on the same day. He called his parents, as soon as he landed, and told them he would be there, in Richmond, later that evening. He took the underground from Heathrow to Richmond and walked to his parent's home.

They were up, waiting for him.

"We're glad to see you, son. What brings you to London?" his father asked.

"I'm here to travel back on the same plane as Makarios, in order to make sure no harm befalls him, on his London to Nicosia flight. I'll be here a couple of days, and then I'll be staying in London near Heathrow airport."

"We're glad you could make it," replied his father. His mother nodded in agreement and hugged him.

Ian's parents were happy that he had some time to visit. He told them about Aphrodite, and how she was killed. He did not tell them that she was pregnant, since this would have upset them more.

After two days, he said goodbye to his parents and returned to a hotel on the grounds of Heathrow Airport. He had a first class ticket on the Olympic Airways flight to Nicosia that was going to take Makarios back to Cyprus, after stopping in Athens.

On the day of the flight, Ian got dressed in a dark civilian suit, strapped on his gun under the jacket and headed for the airport. He passed through immigration, after showing his gun permit and passport, and entered the Douglas DC6B aircraft. Archbishop Makarios was already on board with a few friends, and Ian sat three rows behind him, in an aisle seat. The aircraft had a range of about three thousand miles, and therefore it could easily make the 1,500 mile flight to Athens, without a stop for refueling.

They took off on time but, after one half hour, the plane turned around and went back to Heathrow. The port outer engine (#1) was running rough, and the pilot did not want to take any chances. They landed safely and, after about an hour, a relief DC6B aircraft taxied up. The passengers were transferred and they took off again. This time there were no problems, and they proceeded on course for Athens, at roughly the 315 mph cruising speed. The flight took about five hours to complete, and then there was a one hour layover in Athens. From Athens, Nicosia was another five hundred and seventy miles, or two hours of flying time.

In the air, Ian was able to listen to the conversation between the archbishop and his friends, without them knowing he was fluent in Greek. He picked up the names of a few acquaintances' of Makarios that would need to be checked out. Towards the end of the trip, the archbishop rose from his seat, in order to stretch his legs. He walked back through the first class cabin and spotted Ian sitting there by himself. The rest of the cabin was empty, except for the archbishop himself and his entourage.

"Good afternoon. I'm Archbishop Makarios," he stated, offering his hand. "May I ask who you are, sitting all by yourself in first class?"

Ian rose and shook the archbishop's hand, saying in perfect Greek, "Your Excellency, I'm Lieutenant Ian Black of Her Majesty's British Army, returning to Cyprus for further duty."

"It's nice to meet you, lieutenant. Your Greek is very good, if I may say so. Do you have any duties on this aircraft? Normally I wouldn't have thought the British Army would fly you first class," he said, with a smile.

"To be honest Your Grace, I'm here to insure no harm befalls you between London and Nicosia. The British Government would not be happy, if something should happen to you."

"I hope you have a pleasant flight. Don't worry, my friends here will make sure nothing happens to me," he replied. He went and sat down in his seat, turned around to look at Ian and gave him a slight wave.

After the flight from London to Athens, and then Athens to Nicosia, they finally landed in Nicosia in the late afternoon on the 1st of March, 1959.

Two thirds of the Greek Cypriots turned out to greet Makarios on his triumphant arrival at Nicosia. He returned as a conquering hero, even though he could not deliver on enosis. By then, the Greeks were tired of all the violence and saw independence, as a way to finally have peace. They were mostly naïve and did not read what the United Nations Mediator Dr. Galo Plaza wrote about the agreement, where he described it as "a constitutional oddity."

The agreements left much to be negotiated, and upon his return, Makarios had his work cut out for him over the next nine months, trying to figure out how to implement the terms of the agreements. Many holes in the agreement had to be filled, and this was not easy with the two major ethnic parties in Cyprus, at odds with each other.

27

Murderer Escapes Justice

On the days leading up to the 9th of March, 1959, Georgios Grivas (nom de guerre - Dighenis), the chief architect of terror in Cyprus, while lodged in the hide of the safe house, wrote a letter to his followers supporting the ceasefire. He was not totally in favour of the ceasefire, and thought that Archbishop Makarios had given away too much, in order to get the agreement. He realized, however, that the threat of dividing the island into Greek and Turkish parts was worse, than having a Republic of Cyprus. The main point of disagreement was over the fact that enosis (union with Greece) was off the table. Cyprus would become a republic, and it was forbidden to join Greece. In fact, Greece was not really in favour of a union with Cyprus anyway. Grivas announced the ceasefire on March 9th and came out of hiding. He then stayed at Gabriel Gabrielides house for the next week. Gabriel was an EOKA sympathizer, who was never caught by the British troops. They thought he was on their side. Ian Black had been following leads about him, for a few weeks, but could never confirm his allegiance to the terrorists cause.

On Friday, the 13th of March, Colonel Baker called Ian on the phone. "Mr. Black, will you come to my office as soon as possible. I need to discuss with you an important task, and I believe that you're the best officer to carry it out."

"I'll be there right away, sir." Ian replied.

In a few minutes, Ian knocked on Colonel Baker's office door and entered, after hearing the colonel say, "Come in".

Ian gave the normal brisk salute to the colonel, who was seated on the corner of his desk, with his legs crossed.

"Take a chair," he said, after returning Ian's salute. "I have a major task for you to do. Due to a personal tragedy you suffered last October, you may not want to fulfill this duty. However, you are the best person to carry it out.

I'm sure you're aware that, under the terms of the London Zurich agreement, Grivas is obligated to leave Cyprus on the 17th of March, and cannot return until the 16th of August, 1960, after Cyprus becomes a republic. I have arranged for you to be part of his escort to Nicosia airport. Lieutenant Colonel William Gore-Langton, of the Coldstream Guards, will head the official escort party.

Accordingly, since you are fluent in Greek, you may be needed to conduct some translations. Your presence at this "farewell" has been approved by all concerned, including General Darling. I suggest that you have your sidearm with you. We wouldn't want any Turkish Cypriot trying to get one last shot at Grivas. I want you to make sure that he gets on the Royal Hellenic Dakota aircraft and leaves Cyprus on schedule at 1000 hours."

"Colonel, I'll do my best to insure no harm comes to him. Do I need a special pass to get through the security to Grivas and to get to the airport?" Ian asked.

"Your service ID card will be sufficient, as all security personnel have been informed about your duties." responded the colonel. "One final word, please be mindful of Colonel Gore-Langton's position as chief escort officer, and use your excellent common sense as to when you should speak up. When the press photographers take pictures, you should hang back a little, so that you are not prominent in any of them."

"Is there any special information you would like me to try and obtain from Grivas?" Ian asked.

"If it's possible, attempt to find out where he's been hiding the past few months and who some of his friends are in the Greek Cypriot community. We've also heard several rumours that the editor of the Times of Cyprus, an Englishman, has been of use to Grivas in avoiding capture. In addition, try to confirm that "Gabby" is actually on the EOKA side, instead on Britain's."

Ian replied, "I'll do my best to get Grivas to *spill the beans,* sir." He then saluted and left the colonel's office.

Monday, the 16th of March, was Grivas's last night in Cyprus, since the next day he was to be flown to Greece with some other terrorists, as part of the London-Zurich agreement. On Tuesday morning, the 17th of March, Ian rose early so he could get over to the hotel, where Grivas was being lodged and guarded. His duty, along with some other high ranking British officials, was to escort Grivas to the Nicosia airport in order to make sure he left the island for good. While the group of terrorists was collecting under the watchful eye of the British troops, two planes approached Cyprus from the northwest.

"Nicosia, this is the Camp Pomos radar site. We have two bogies on the screen about sixty miles out, coming in from the northwest," the camp radar operator called in to Maritime headquarters at 0730."

"Thanks, Pomos. Nicosia Airport also has the aircraft on their radar, and no further reporting of these two targets will be required. We've been expecting these two planes from Greece," replied the headquarters duty officer.

As the aircraft approached the Cyprus coast, Nicosia and the British military in Cyprus were placed on high alert. The two Douglas manufactured Dakotas (C-47s) belonging to the Royal Hellenic Air Force were scheduled to land at Nicosia Airport at exactly 0800.

The pilot of the first Dakota radioed the Nicosia control tower. "This is Royal Hellenic Air Force RHAF 437, approximately 30 miles out, requesting permission to land."

314

The Nicosia tower replied "RHAF 437, you have permission to land on runway three two. The wind is out of the northwest at three miles per hour. Switch to ground control frequency of 121.90 Mc/s, after you land".

"Nicosia, this is RHAF 437. We will land on runway three two as requested."

Then, two minutes later, the second Dakota RHAF 445 radioed the tower, in a similar fashion, and received permission to land.

Both RHAF planes were then advised that there was a RAF Javelin jet taking off right then, to escort them into the Nicosia area.

As soon as both of the RHAF planes had landed, taxied and parked, British troops surrounded the planes to make sure only authorized people entered or left them. The portable stair ramp was rolled to the exit door of the lead plane. The Greek General Paparodu and two officers walked down the ramp and were greeted by a British Army captain and two soldiers carrying SMGs. They were escorted to the airport terminal. The British soldiers, who surrounded the planes, wanted to make sure no explosives were smuggled on board, by persons wanting to eliminate Grivas. The refueling tanker came up and added fuel to the planes, for the return trip, under the watchful eyes of the troops.

In the meantime, Ian entered the Ledra Palace Hotel at 0730 and found Grivas, surrounded by armed guards, in the restaurant having breakfast, with some of his comrades. Grivas was a sixty year old man, who measured five foot four inches in height and was slight in build. Ian Black, on the other hand, stood a little over six feet. Ian gave him a *half* salute, as he didn't want to honor him, but he did call him colonel. Ian was dressed in his best uniform, with Intelligence Corps flashes prominently on his shoulders and his Browning automatic on his side.

Ian spoke in Greek the entire time he was with the Grivas party.

"Good morning, colonel. Would it be appropriate if I join you for a cup of coffee?" Ian didn't want to appear too deferential or condescending. His purpose here was to keep an eye on Grivas and, more importantly, the people around him.

"Certainly lieutenant, draw up a chair. You may sit by me if you'd like. I see your name is Ian Black. I believe I've heard of you. Your Greek is very good. If I didn't know you were English, I would say that you were a Greek. Are you the same Lieutenant Black that's given my group a hard time over the past few months?"

Ian responded, "Yes, I believe I am, colonel. It was my job to hunt you and your leadership down. Did you know that we'd been watching you for days, before the London Zurich agreement, at the house in Limassol? We were about to raid the building when the word came down about the agreement, and we were told to stand down. You were lucky not to be captured."

Grivas replied, "This Island was originally part of Greece and it will be again someday. I was born here and plan to die here. You might have raided the house in the centre of Limassol, but you wouldn't have taken me alive."

Right here, Ian basically confirmed what they knew about Grivas's whereabouts at the beginning of February. He was holed up in the hide at the house that they were watching.

Ian asked Grivas, "Where were you born in Cyprus? Was it near Famagusta?"

Grivas responded, "Well, as a good intelligence officer you should know that already. I'm sure the dossier on me has my birthplace of Trikomo listed in it."

"How about another cup of Greek coffee, lieutenant?" asked Grivas, as he laughed a little and looked at his EOKA friends, who had smirks on their faces.

At that moment, a Cypriot came in and whispered something in Grivas's ear.

Grivas then said, "I've just been informed that the RHAF aircraft from Athens have arrived at Nicosia airport and are refueling for the flight back. I suppose we have about another forty five minutes, before we have to go to the airport. I'm sure all the Nicosia citizens will be out there, to cheer me on."

"Yes, I would like another cup of coffee." Ian replied.

Grivas indicated for one of the waiters to pour Ian some more of the Ledra Palace coffee.

Grivas asked Ian, "Where did you learn to speak Greek so well?"

Ian responded, "Well, I attended Harrow school just outside of London and we had a Greek national teaching up-to-date Greek, rather than classical Greek."

"Aha, so you're a public school chap; upper crust and all that." replied Grivas.

"Yes, I guess I am. I also read the Times of London and the Times of Cyprus. Do you ever read the Cyprus Times?" Ian asked.

Grivas responded, "Yes, I have occasionally read the Cyprus Times. The editor, Charles Foley, is a good friend of the Greek Cypriots. He thinks the British have no right to hold on to Cyprus."

Grivas then stopped, and it dawned on him that he had said too much. He should not have mentioned Charles Foley's name. Ian picked up on it and continued the conversation.

"Yes, Charles Foley is somewhat liberal and has written several editorials, criticizing the British soldiers and the way Cyprus is being run." Ian said.

Grivas looked at Ian and slightly nodded, but didn't say anything. He then turned to his EOKA friends and started a conversation.

A few minutes later, Grivas turned back to Ian and introduced him to Gabriel Gabrielides (Gabby), who sat to Grivas's right.

"Ian, this is my good friend Gabby. Have you ever met him?"

Ian responded, looking at Gabby "Yes, I've had a drink or two at his establishment, before and after hours. I've heard recently that he has a secret room, behind the bar."

Grivas laughed and said, "There're all kinds of rumours that float around Nicosia. You don't want to pay too much attention to them."

Ian noticed that Gabby winced a little, when he mentioned the secret room behind the bar. At this point, they were interrupted by a group of British officers who had entered the hotel.

At 0915, Colonel Gore-Langton, together with other high ranking officers, walked into the hotel and came over to the table, where Grivas was seated with his friends and Ian. The colonel didn't salute Grivas, since he lost his right arm during World War Two. Ian rose and did give Colonel Gore-Langton a good British Army style salute. The colonel nodded at Ian and greeted him with a good morning.

The colonel said in English to Grivas, "Dighenis, it's time to go to the airport. We have transport outside the hotel front door, ready for you. As you're probably aware, it's about eight miles to the Nicosia Airport, and it will take us about fifteen minutes, with all the traffic cleared out of the way." Ian translated it into Greek, in case all the Cypriots did not understand.

Then, the colonel said to Ian, "I want you to go in the lead Land Rover and take us to the airport. As we proceed down the road, make sure there're no potential problems or demonstrations. If there are, signal us to stop. I don't expect any issues however, since the road is already lined with troops, all the way to the airport."

"Yes, sir, I'll stay alert the whole trip," replied Ian.

Slowly, all of them rose and went to the front entrance of the hotel. There waiting, in the hotel circular driveway, were five vehicles. In the front of the convoy was a Land

Rover, next came two enclosed automobiles, then another Land Rover, and finally a three ton Bedford lorry, loaded with armed British soldiers. Colonel Gore-Langton led Grivas to the first automobile, and they both climbed into the rear. The three other EOKA Cypriots went to the second automobile. Lieutenant Ian Black went to the lead Land Rover and sat by the driver. The other escort officers went and climbed into the other Land Rover.

Ian checked that everyone was in their vehicles, and then he told his driver to head out. The convoy left the Ledra Palace Hotel and headed southwest towards the Nicosia International Airport. As they went along the outskirts of Nicosia and then headed down the airport road, Ian noticed that all the troops lining the route had their backs to the road. The British did not want to give Grivas any thoughts that this was a parade in his honor. In fact, he was being driven to the airport, so he would go into exile. There were some crowds on the streets giving him a cheer, but the British troops kept them well back from the road. Ian Back was ready with his Browning, just in case some Turkish Cypriot decided to try and assassinate Grivas. The two soldiers in the back of the Land Rover, who were armed with Sterling SMGs, were on full alert. There were British Military Police at every intersection to control the traffic and permit quick passage for the convoy. The convoy finally reached the airport grounds that had been sealed off by troops, to prevent any demonstrations pro or con.

At 0940, the convoy pulled up by the two Royal Hellenic Dakotas that were parked on the tarmac, close to the terminal. The troops jumped out of the lorry and set up a cordon around the vehicles and aircraft. The passengers in the two cars got out and gathered at the bottom of the steps, leading up to the Dakotas. Colonel Gore-Langton spoke briefly, with Ian translating, to Grivas and the EOKA Cypriots. General Nicholas Paparodu of the Greek Army and three other Greek officers came out of the terminal, followed

319

by some more EOKA terrorists that were being released, and joined the group. The Greek officers had flown in on the flight from Athens to escort Grivas and his EOKA entourage back to Greece.

At 0948, two British RAF Gloster Javelin FAW 7 fighters taxied out, one behind the other, and stopped close to the main runway at Nicosia Airport.

"Nicosia tower, this is RAF Javelin XH301 requesting permission for immediate takeoff."

The controller replied, "XH301, you're cleared for takeoff on runway three two and you may climb to your assigned altitude. The wind is five mph out of the northwest and there are no aircraft in the immediate area."

The first jet roared down the runway and climbed into the clear, blue sky. The second Javelin, XH352 repeated the same takeoff pattern, two minutes later.

The roar of their Glosters' jet engines interrupted the conversation among the people standing near the Dakotas, for a few minutes. The jet's noise also provided cover for a Turkish Cypriot baggage handler, to emerge from luggage area and run towards the officials. The British officials, Grivas and the EOKA terrorists were watching the fighters take off and had their backs turned to the terminal.

As the Turkish Cypriot ran towards the group, he pulled a revolver out of his jacket, cocked it and let off one shot. As he did so, he shouted in bad Greek "Dhigenis, μπορείτε μπάσταρδος, δεν θα αναχωρήσει από την Κύπρο στη ζωή." In English, it was "Dhigenis, you bastard, you will not leave Cyprus alive." The bullet went wide of the target, since he was too far away and running. Ian Black heard the shot and, out of the corner of his eye, saw the movement of the man running. He turned to see what the commotion was about. He saw the Cypriot running towards Grivas and pulled his own Browning automatic, from the holster on his right side.

Ian quickly shouted at the Cypriot "Halt, Stamata, Dur." The man kept running and Ian realized that there was not much time to take care of the threat. The Cypriot did not stop, so Ian took aim and fired. The bullet hit him in the chest and he dropped to the tarmac. As he was falling, the Cypriot let off one last shot, into the air. Grivas, hearing all the commotion, turned and hid behind the Greek General Paparodu.

Ian ran over to the Cypriot and determined he was still alive. He signaled for the airport ambulance that was standing by, in case of any emergency, to come and pick the Cypriot up. The medics placed him on a stretcher and drove him to a local hospital, accompanied by two British soldiers.

Ian had saved the British from an embarrassing situation. It would have been bad publicity if Grivas had been killed, while under British protection. On the other hand, there were many British soldiers, including Ian, who would have loved to have seen Grivas assassinated. If he had been killed, there would have been riots and probably a civil war in Cyprus. The major civil war didn't take place until thirteen years later.

The Javelin jets, that had just taken off, climbed out of the Nicosia area and headed into the direction of Athens; the route that Grivas would be taking.

Why they did that has been a subject for debate? One reason that Grivas espoused was that they were an escort in honour of him. The other more plausible answer was that they were there to make sure Grivas actually left Cyprus airspace. Either way, it really didn't matter.

Finally, at 0953, Grivas, together with all the EOKA men and Greek officers, split into two groups. They climbed the stairs and entered the two Dakota aircraft. They settled into their seats and the main doors were closed by the flight attendants.

At 1000 hours exactly, the engines on both Dakotas were started up and the aircraft taxied away from the terminal. They stopped close to the runway and the pilots checked their engines by revving them up; with the brakes on. After their engines were checked and determined to be operating normally, the pilot of the first one called traffic control.

"Nicosia tower, this is Royal Hellenic Air Force 437 requesting clearance for immediate takeoff and vectoring towards Athens, Greece."

"Royal Hellenic Air Force 437, this is Nicosia tower and you're cleared for takeoff on runway three two. The wind is six miles per hour out of the northwest. Climb to 5,000 feet, level out and wait for further instructions. Be aware that there are two RAF Javelins in the area, but should pose no threat to you. They are monitoring this frequency."

"Roger, Nicosia. Taking off and will level at 5,000 feet," replied the first Dakota RHAF437.

RHAF437 rolled down the runway, climbed up to the assigned altitude and headed northwest towards Athens

Then the pilot of the second Royal Hellenic Air Force transport, Dakota RHAF445, repeated the same takeoff procedure two minutes later.

Inside the two planes were the EOKA terrorists, plus a few Greek officers. Ian Black believed that they were all murderers and terrorists, but Greek Cypriots thought they were freedom fighters. As the Dakotas left Cyprus airspace, the two Javelins that had escorted the aircraft as soon as they took off, peeled away and flew back towards Nicosia airport.

The first RAF Javelin pilot called into the Nicosia tower.

"Javelin XH301 requesting permission to land on runway three two."

Nicosia tower "Javelin XH301 permission granted. Wind is out of the northwest at five miles an hour."

At that moment, the second Javelin XH352 started to have engine trouble.

"Nicosia tower, this is Javelin XH352. I request immediate landing instructions. The engine is flaming out. This is an emergency."

"XH352 you have permission to land immediately. XH301. Please go around. We have an emergency."

The Javelin XH352 came in with a dead stick and made a hard landing. The fire truck and ambulance raced out to the plane but they weren't needed. Then the second Javelin came in for a smooth landing.

Everyone breathed a sigh of relief.

Mission accomplished with Grivas out of Cyprus for good, while the British still controlled the island.

After the planes left the airport, Colonel Gore-Langton said to the assembled British officers and officials.

"Well, thank goodness that's over. Hopefully we'll never see that vaudeville rascal again. Let's go have a drink in the airport lounge and celebrate."

As they walked to the bar, Colonel Gore-Langton said to Ian.

"Mr. Black, you are an excellent shot with that Browning. I thank you for saving the day and I'll give you favorable mention, when I relate the incident to your superior. Although, between you and me, in some ways I wish the Cypriot had made it and got rid of Grivas. However, the prime minister and the other politicians, who labored so hard to get the Zurich agreement, will be ever thankful to you."

"I must admit sir that I was tempted, for a second, to let him do the "job", or do it myself. My fiancé was shot and killed last year by an EOKA terrorist. Then, I thought better of it." Ian responded.

"I'm sorry to hear about your fiancé. Please accept my condolences."

At the airport bar, they all raised their glasses and the colonel said, "Rule Britannia. God Save the Queen." They all raised their glasses in unison and downed the scotch in one gulp.

28

Staying The Course

On the next day, after Grivas left Cyprus in accordance with the Zurich-London agreement, Colonel Baker called a staff meeting in the conference room at Salisbury House. In attendance were Captain Phillips, Lieutenant Black, Lieutenant Snell, Sergeant Bingham and John of MI6.

"Thank you all for coming, on such short notice," said the colonel. He then continued, "As you're aware, the leader of EOKA and many of its senior members have now left the island. Nonetheless, this doesn't mean that there aren't still some terrorists remaining here; either in the open or undercover.

For the next nine months, this organization will still be operational and our major task, except the hunting for Grivas, will be basically as before. Specifically, we must prevent the shipment of arms into Cyprus, by either the Greeks or the Turks. Probably by January 1960, however, this section of the Intelligence Corps will no longer exist, and our duties will be taken over, by other parts of the army. Until then, we must be on alert for any information that suggests arms shipments are on the way here.

We'll hold monthly meetings, and more often if necessary, to coordinate our intelligence activities. One of the major problems, or issues we face in this regard, is the fact that the Greeks have access to the remaining hidden

EOKA arms, while the Turks have very little in the way of armaments. Therefore, we can predict that the Turks will try to smuggle in arms, to equalize the situation. Ethnic cleansing, in all the towns and villages, can be expected to be attempted, by both sides. We have to be attuned to this situation and head it off, as best we can, until Britain is no longer responsible for the administration of the island. I'll now open this meeting up to any questions or suggestions you may have."

"Are there any specific towns or villages that are more likely to experience ethnic cleansing or nationalism?" asked Lieutenant Snell.

"No, not really," replied the colonel. "Any municipality that has a wide disparity in Greeks and Turks is likely to witness the minority being pressured to leave. In those towns and villages that have almost equal nationalities, you will probably see some violence, and they will be divided into two distinct areas or ghettos."

"Can we still expect the Greeks to try and smuggle in arms, even though they have the remainder of the EOKA arms?" Ian queried.

"Most certainly, both sides will try to get the upper hand in the conflict that is almost bound to happen in the future. I'll emphasize again, we must be alert to smuggling from both Turkey and Greece," the colonel responded.

"If you develop any intelligence about arms shipments or riots that are about to break out, let Captain Phillips know and he'll contact me. As I said earlier, we'll meet again in a month, unless there's an urgent need to meet sooner. This meeting is now adjourned." The colonel rose and left the room.

Captain Phillips instructed all of them to go out into the towns and villages, in plain clothes, and attempt to find out about potential arm shipments and/or riots.

****

For the next few months, Ian visited towns and villages around the island, trying to glean information on possible arm shipments. All he ever picked up was gossip and rumours, but no firm details. None really panned out.

In the middle of July, however, Ian went to a town near Morphou to check out a rumour that there was the possibility of a Greek arms shipment coming in, at the end of the month. He went to a bar to have a beer and talk to a few Greeks sitting there. However, all they were talking about was how the Turks were trying to drive the Greeks out of the town.

Ian asked one of them, "Why don't you stand up to the Turks?"

"We try to, but they outnumber us in this town so that they're always cracking more of our heads, than we are of theirs. The police don't do much about it, because they are split along ethnic lines. In addition, the British Army stationed in Morphou doesn't seem to be eager to get in the middle, unless there is major fighting."

Suddenly, there was a commotion and some loud noises coming from outside the bar. They all rushed out into the street and witnessed a riot going on, between the two rival nationalities.

"See what I mean," one of the Greeks, from the bar, said to Ian.

Ian was pushed along by the crowd and soon he was in the middle of the melee. He had to fight a few Turks to get out of the middle and reach the edge of the crowd.

Suddenly, a Turk came up to him and placed a gun in his ribs.

"Come with me quickly. I'm taking you hostage." The man said loudly in Turkish, and then whispered the same words in English.

Ian turned and, just as he was about to shoot the man with his gun, he recognized that the Turk was none other than Lieutenant Roger Snell.

Roger led Ian away from the crowd, took him to his car and drove off down the street, away from the crowd that was still fighting. Roger stopped a few streets away, and they both gave a sigh of relief.

"That was close, Ian," said Roger. "I didn't know what else to do, to make it look real and get you out of there. I'm sorry I had to pull a gun on you."

"You're lucky I didn't try and shoot you," Ian said. "For a moment I was planning to do that, until I recognized you."

"I'll take you to pick up your car. From there, we'll both drive back to Nicosia and have a stiff drink."

"I agree to that," Ian responded.

Both of them did run into a few more riots between Greeks and Turks over the next few months, but there was not much they could do about them, except report them to Captain Phillips.

This type of activity went on continuously, until October 1959.

****

At the beginning of October, Lieutenant Snell picked up some gossip in a small Turkish town, on the north coast, that a shipment of arms was expected to arrive from Turkey in the middle of the month. He checked out the report in a couple of other Turkish towns, close by, and decided there was a distinct possibility that the rumour was true.

He returned to Salisbury House and went to see Captain Phillips.

"Captain, I've picked up some solid intelligence that there'll be an arms shipment from Turkey, by a ship named MV *Deniz*, on or around Monday, the 19th of October. They will try and land the arms in a small sandy cove, on the north coast, east of Kyrenia. There will be almost a full moon on that night that will make the landing easier for them, but also better for us to catch them in the act."

"That's good information, Mr. Snell. I'll mention it to the colonel and contact the Royal Navy, to determine which ship is on patrol that night. I'll get back to you within a day."

Captain Phillips called the Royal Navy headquarters and found out that the HMS *Burnaston* would be on patrol that night, in the area where the landing was expected to take place. The minesweeper was under the command of Lieutenant Commander Smith, with First Lieutenant Robin Hogg as second in command.

Later that day, Captain Phillips contacted Lieutenant Snell and asked him to come to his office.

"Mr. Snell. I've determined that the minesweeper *Burnaston* will be on patrol off the Cyprus northeast coast on the 19th of this month. I've told Captain Smith about the possible arms shipment by the MV *Deniz* from Turkey. He has agreed that you and Mr. Black may join the *Burnaston* in Famagusta on the morning of the 19th of October. He felt your fluency in Turkish will be a key asset, if they have to stop and search this vessel. He asked that you both be on the wharf at 1100, on that day."

"Thank you, sir. Shall I inform Ian or will you do that?"

"I'll contact Mr. Black and tell him of my decision. When you get back from the patrol, write a full report and submit it to me. That'll be all."

Later that day, Captain Phillips met Ian at dinner and told him of the decision, to send Roger and him on the *Burnaston*'s patrol.

"Please keep an eye on Roger and make sure he doesn't get into trouble, like you seem to do," the captain said with a grin.

Ian replied smiling, "I'll do that, sir."

****

On the morning of the HMS *Burnaston* patrol, Ian and Roger drove from Salisbury House to the wharf at

Famagusta. They showed their military identification cards to the MP at the gate to the dock. They then found a vacant spot and parked the car.

At 1100 hours, the *Burnaston*'s cutter came and picked them up at the wharf. When they clambered up the swaying ladder of the minesweeper and set foot on the deck, they were met by First Lieutenant Hogg. He had a sailor show them to a small cabin that they could use, while on board. He told them that the captain would like to meet with them, as soon as they had stowed their gear.

At noon, the crew weighed anchor and the HMS *Burnaston* proceeded out to sea. There wasn't any storm in the weather forecast, and Ian hoped that neither the ship's radar, nor the Plakoti radar, would go off the air; as happened a year ago. Maritime headquarters sent out a Shackleton search plane to see if it could find the Deniz, and the pilot was given instructions not to get to close, so as to scare them off.

The *Burnaston* cruised eastward up the coast, rounded Cape Andreas, and then headed westward towards Kyrenia. At around 1800 hours, the minesweeper turned around and slowly headed back to the east, for the cape. They received a report from Maritime headquarters that a Shackleton had spotted a vessel heading towards Cyprus from Turkey. They did not know the name, because the pilot didn't want to get to close.

The Plakoti radar picked it up later and then the *Burnaston*'s radar detected it. The MV *Deniz* kept coming towards Cyprus and after dark anchored in a cove between Cape Plakoti and Cape Andreas. The *Burnaston* slowed to a crawl and proceeded to the same cove.

"Turn on the searchlight," Captain Smith ordered, when they were within a few hundred yards.

The crew turned on the light and illuminated the MV *Deniz* with the twenty inch searchlight. The crew on the *Deniz* started to run around the deck. They hadn't even launched any boats yet, to take the arms to shore. They could hardly throw them overboard, since the *Burnaston* was too close.

Captain Smith ordered the boarding party to go over to the *Deniz* and had the ship's crew man the Bofors 40 mm gun, in case the *Deniz* tried to flee.

The boarding party reached the Deniz and clambered on board. They rounded up the Turkish crew on the front deck and held them at gunpoint.

Lieutenant Snell interrogated the *Deniz* captain in Turkish, while Ian and a couple of the boarding party searched the crew for hidden arms. Two of the crew had separated themselves slightly from the rest and Ian searched them first.

The first man looked Ian straight in the eyes and gave him a wink, as he was patted down.

"*That was strange*," Ian thought, and then he went on to the next man who also looked Ian straight in the eyes; however he didn't wink.

After the entire crew had been searched and nothing was found, the boarding party searched the holds and found two dozen crates of arms.

Lieutenant Snell addressed the *Deniz* crew, "You're all under arrest for attempting to smuggle arms into Cyprus. This is against the United Nations agreement between nations concerning the transportation of arms into another country, without its permission. You're going to be taken to Famagusta and turned over to the British authorities, to be tried in the courts."

The one man, who winked at Ian, turned to the *Deniz* captain and said in Turkish, "None of this would have happened, if you'd listened to me. It's your fault entirely."

Lieutenant Snell commanded the man to keep his mouth shut. The *Deniz* crew was then placed in an empty hold and it was locked tight.

Captain Smith sent Lieutenant Hogg over to run the *Deniz* with a few of the *Burnaston* crew. Both ships then proceeded around the cape to Famagusta and, on the way there, they were joined by another Navy ship that was sent out to help them.

When they reached Famagusta and tied up, a squad of British troops came on board, to take the prisoners away. As the *Deniz* crew came out of the hold, the man who had winked at Ian stumbled and crashed into another crewman. They started to fight, and then his friend joined in, followed by some of the other crewmen.

The soldiers stopped the fighting. A civilian, who was standing by the sergeant in charge of the troops, whispered in the soldier's ear, "Separate those two from the rest and send them to an isolation cell."

The sergeant ordered the troops to take the two men and put them in a cell by themselves. The rest were to be placed in one large cell.

That was the last Ian saw of the two men. Captain Smith approached Lieutenants Black and Snell on their departure and said, "Thanks for all your help, lieutenants, on this patrol. Maybe we'll meet again someday, although these patrols will not last much longer."

After they bade farewell to the captain, Roger and Ian went down the gang plank, connecting the minesweeper to the wharf. They found their parked car, climbed into it and headed back to Nicosia.

When they returned to Salisbury House, Ian called his CO and inquired, "Colonel, may I come and see you about a sensitive and strange matter. There is something I would like to discuss about the Turkish ship, the MV *Deniz*, which we stopped off the coast of Cyprus."

"Certainly, I'll see you right away. Come to my office."

Ian walked down the hallway and came to Colonel Baker's office and knocked on the door.

"Come in," said the colonel.

Ian entered and gave him a salute.

"At ease, Ian, please take a seat. What can I do for you?"

"Something happened last night that was strange, after we stopped this Turkish ship. There were two men in the crew that looked a little out of place. I didn't say anything at the time, because I wasn't sure. Thinking back on the incident, I'm sure I was correct. Roger Snell and I patted down the crew of this ship to make sure that they had no arms on them. This one man looked me straight in the eye and winked, just before I patted him down, but he said nothing. I then went to the next seaman who also he looked me straight in the eyes, but he didn't say anything either.

The rest of the crew either looked down or away when we searched them. On the way back here, it dawned on me. The seaman, who winked at me, I had seen before. He came out of Percival's office in Beirut, when I was waiting to see him. I know it was him. In addition when we arrived back in Famagusta with the Turkish prisoners, these two seamen got in a fight with the others sailors. The sergeant in charge of the troops had them separated and taken away to isolation. I'm now wondering if these two seamen were actually British MI6 agents."

The colonel responded, "Let me check into all this and I'll get back to you. In the meantime don't say anything to anyone, even those in our organization."

"Yes sir," replied Ian

The next day, the colonel called Ian and asked him to come to his office.

He entered and saluted as usual.

"Ian, what I'm going to tell you must not go beyond these four walls. Those two men are in fact British secret agents and were gathering information, on the arms Turkey is shipping to Cyprus. In that regard, you and I have not had this conversation, and you will forget everything about it. Actually, it hasn't taken place. Is that understood?"

"Yes, sir!"

"By the way, the tasks you and Mr. Snell did on the patrol were excellent. I received a sincere thank you from Captain Smith. I'll see you at the next staff meeting. That's all, Ian."

Ian saluted, left the colonel's office and wiped the winking chap from his memory. Ian's time in Cyprus was slowly winding down. He knew that once the Republic of Cyprus came into existence, his services would no longer be required in Cyprus.

****

On the 25th of October, Ian purchased a dozen yellow roses and took them to the cemetery in the northern part of Nicosia. It was the first anniversary of Aphrodite's death on Ledra Street. He laid them on her plaque and said a silent prayer for her. It was a sad day for him, because he had lost his one and only true love.

Watching him, from the shadow of a large tree, was a young Greek man. After Ian left the cemetery, the man walked over to the grave and laid a bouquet on the plaque. It was Minervo, Aphrodite's older brother. He also laid some flowers on his younger brother's grave and his father's marker.

29

Ta-Ta and Cheerio

On Sunday, the 13th of December, 1959, the election for president and vice president took place in Cyprus. Archbishop Makarios III, who was the obvious favourite among Greek Cypriots, won with 66.8% of the vote. His opponent in the election was John Clerides who received just 33.2% of the vote. There was only one candidate for vice president, Fazil Küçük. Under the terms of the new Cyprus constitution, the president had to be a Greek Cypriot and the vice president was mandated to be a Turkish Cypriot. They would both take office on the 16th of August, 1960.

At the end of December, 1959, Ian was ordered by Colonel Baker, to come to his office and talk about his future, now that Cyprus was going to become a Republic in August.

"Ian, as you are aware, Makarios will be sworn in as president, in August, and the British Army will be winding down its presence on much of the island. Britain will shortly be negotiating, with Makarios's future government, the rights to bases it has and wants to keep; mainly, the Akrotiri Royal Air Force Base and a base at Dhekelia. In addition, an agreement will hopefully be made to keep the GCHQ electronic intelligence listening station at Ayios Nikolaos that would be connected to the Dhekelia base. The question is what do we do with you? I assume you want to stay in the army?"

"Yes, sir, my thoughts have been to stay in the army and hopefully in the Intelligence Corps."

"I was expecting you'd say that. If you'd like, I can make arrangements for you to attend the Intelligence Corps special school in England, to get some advanced intelligence training. It lasts for about a year, and you'll also attend language classes to study French, German and Russian. How does this sound to you?"

"I'd like that very much, sir. I already know German, so I'll be able to concentrate on the French and Russian. May I ask what you'll be doing?"

"I'll probably be given a desk job somewhere, until I retire. Maybe our paths will meet again. I'll put you in for this school in England and, as soon as I hear anything, I'll let you know."

In early January 1960, Ian was informed by the colonel that he had been accepted into the advanced intelligence training school and would be leaving shortly for England. He would have a couple of weeks off, before he had to attend the school, which would give him the opportunity to visit his parents.

Also In January, Archbishop Makarios, the future president of Cyprus, had to fly to London to continue the negotiations with Britain, about the ceding of the military bases in Cyprus to Britain.

The day before Ian left Cyprus, he decided to drive to the cemetery where Aphrodite was buried. On the way, he stopped at a flower shop and purchased one dozen yellow roses. He then drove on to the cemetery and walked to her gravesite. He laid the bouquet of roses on the plaque and stood there, praying for a few seconds. He then said in a low voice, "I'll be back. I don't know when, but I'll be back. I'll love you forever, Aphrodite."

Later that day, he said his goodbyes to Colonel Baker and Captain Phillips, cleaned out his office and packed his bags. He returned his faithful Browning automatic to the armory, since he couldn't legally take it back to England.

The next day, he went to the airport to take the Cyprus Airways plane to London. Cyprus Airways was being operated by BEA (British European Airways), until it had the manpower and equipment to operate itself. As he waited for the plane, Archbishop Makarios came into the waiting area, followed by three bodyguards and a couple of advisors. As he walked through the waiting room, he looked over and saw Ian sitting there. He stopped, turned and walked over to him.

"Don't I know you from somewhere?" he asked in Greek.

Ian rose from his seat and replied, "Yes Your Excellency, we met on the flight back from London ten months ago."

"Ah yes, now I remember. You're name is Ian Black and you're a lieutenant in the army. Are you also on this flight?"

"Yes Your Grace, I'm being reassigned, since the British Army is winding down most of its operations here."

"Are you flying first class, as before?"

"No, sir, I was given a special ticket, to make sure I was up front with you."

"That's a pity. I thought we might have a conversation together to pass the time, between any discussions with my advisors."

The archbishop then said goodbye and went through the lounge to the aircraft.

A few minutes later, the cabin class was called and Ian entered the aircraft through the front door and walked through first class to the rear of the plane. As he walked through, the archbishop, who was seated in the front of the first class section, nodded at him.

Ian went into the rear, placed his carry on in the rack above his seat and sat down.

Just before the plane taxied out to take off, a good looking stewardess came up to Ian and said, "Sir, please gather up your belongings and follow me."

"Have I done something wrong?" Ian asked.

"Sir, please do as I ask quickly and follow me. The plane is about to take off."

Ian gathered his belongings and followed her through the curtain and into the first class cabin.

She said, pointing to an aisle seat, "This is your seat for the rest of the flight."

Ian looked around and up in front was the archbishop who winked at him, and then he turned back to look to the front.

The plane took off for London on time and, as the island of Cyprus vanished from view, Ian thought about all that had happened, since he arrived on the island almost two years before. Foremost in his mind was that the fact he was leaving Aphrodite behind, lying buried in the ground. With a heavy heart, he pondered that, if events had turned out differently, she might be sitting by him on this flight.

During the flight, the archbishop sent one of his bodyguards back to Ian.

Looking at Ian, the man said, "His Grace would like you to come and sit by him, to discuss the future of Cyprus. There's an empty seat up there, next to His Excellency."

"Of course, I'll be right there." Ian replied, as he placed the book he was reading in the pouch on the back of the seat, in front of him.

Ian rose, went up to the front of the first class section and sat down in the empty seat, by the archbishop.

"Thank you for coming, lieutenant. What unit were you assigned to in Cyprus?"

"I was in the Royal Artillery and assigned to the 188th Radar and Searchlight Battery. Later, I was transferred to the Intelligence Corps."

"Aha, you were in the Intelligence Corps. No wonder they sent you to accompany me back from London to Cyprus. Well, never mind, that's all over now. You speak excellent Greek. Where did you learn it?"

"I went to school at Harrow and we had a Greek teacher, who was actually from Greece. He taught us modern Greek, not the classical format."

"Well, let's get down to business. You seem to be a bright young man. What do you think of the agreement that I managed to obtain with Britain, Greece and Turkey?"

"Sir, anything I say will be my personal view, and I won't be speaking for the British Army or the government."

"I understand perfectly, lieutenant."

"I believe you received the best agreement that you were going to obtain. If the agreement had been delayed much longer, we would have grabbed Colonel Grivas, and your bargaining power would have been greatly diminished. We were actually ready to arrest him, when we were told to stand down. Of course, all that is over now, so I'm not really giving away any secrets."

"What do you think of the constitution, and what the major problems will be going forward?"

"Well, sir, I believe the UN Mediator had it correct when he called it an *Oddity*. The Turkish minority is going to be able obstruct any legislation you put forward, and the government will come to a standstill. I know you wanted enosis with Greece, which actually would have caused an immediate civil war. Now, with a republic, you still have a problem with the minority. To be honest, I believe the best solution would have been the partition of the island into Greek and Turkish sectors. You could have held onto most of the island. As it is now, if a civil war comes, and I believe it will, Turkey is much closer to Cyprus, and they will be able to send troops here a lot easier, than Greece will be able to. When that happens, the Turkish Cypriots will be able to

338

carve up a bigger slice of Cyprus, than their numbers warrant."

"Your insight lieutenant is very good. I've been thinking along the same lines as you. So what do you recommend I do; now we are at this point?"

"Your choices are limited, sir. What I'd do is try to work with the Turkish leadership hoping they can bring the general population of Turkish Cypriots along with them. It would be like threading a needle, with a very small eye. If you can't achieve that, then I'd prepare for a civil war, within three to ten years. I wish I could be more optimistic, Your Grace."

"Well, thank you for your opinion, lieutenant. I believe that I'll get some rest now and think about what you've told me. If I don't see you again, I hope you have a great life in the army. Oh, by the way, I'm sorry about what happened to Aphrodite Palas. Goodbye."

Ian got up and returned to his seat, wondering how he knew about Aphrodite. He never had another word with the archbishop.

When the plane reached London, the archbishop and his advisors were immediately whisked away by British Government officials.

Ian took the Underground to Richmond station and walked to his parent's home on the hill. They were waiting for him, as he had called them from the airport.

"Welcome home, son," they both said in unison, as they both gave him a big hug.

He was home for two weeks before he had to report to the Advanced Intelligence Corps School, and enjoyed every minute of it. During the next two weeks, he told them about his exploits in Cyprus and his assignment to the Intelligence Corps School. He also connected with some old friends from the day school that he used to attend in Kew.

It felt good to be home again, visiting his parents, since he didn't know when the next opportunity would arise.

RICHARD AND BARBARA OSBORN

He had to report by Friday, the 29th of January, to the Intelligence Corps training facility located at Maresfield in East Sussex. Upon graduation, his probable assignment would be to Germany, as this part of the world was starting to heat up. Nikita Khrushchev, who was First Secretary of the Communist Party of the Soviet Union, was upping the ante in the cold war.

EPILOGUE

On the 16th of August, 1960, Cyprus became a republic with a Greek Cypriot president and a Turkish vice president. The British Union Jack was hauled down for the last time on the flag pole at Government House and the Governor-General, Sir Hugh Macintosh Foot, relinquished power to the new president and the new government.

Immediately thereafter, the flag of the new Republic of Cyprus was hoisted up on the same pole, and what was called Government House became the Presidential Palace. Archbishop Makarios III was sworn in as president and Fazil Küçük was sworn in as vice president.

However, all this was just a recipe for disaster. Centuries of distrust by the Greeks and Turks for each other was not going to vanish in a week or year. It will probably take a long time, if ever.

Three years later, in December 1963, President Makarios proposed thirteen amendments to the Cyprus constitution that in effect would limit the ability of the Turkish Cypriots to block legislation. The Turkish minority saw this whole idea of changing the constitution as a threat to them. The UK, Greece and Turkey wanted to send a UN force to keep the antagonists apart. This didn't happen and between December 21-26, riots broke out between the two sides. The Greeks had arms from the EOKA campaign. The Turks had few arms and this placed them at a disadvantage.

The Turks blockaded the road from Nicosia to Kyrenia and, in retaliation, the Greeks took approximately seven hundred Turks hostage.

By 1964, one hundred and ninety-three Turkish Cypriots and one hundred and thirty-three Greek Cypriots had been killed with many more missing and presumed dead. The

341

idea of a partition was raised again and Turkey prepared to invade the island. However, Turkey at the last minute was persuaded by President Johnson (LBJ) not to invade. LBJ threatened to not support Turkey, if the USSR threatened any of their territory. The Turkish Cypriots then started to build enclaves and ejected Greeks from them. The Greeks did the same thing, and thus a de facto partition was accomplished by the two major nationalities.

In 1967, more fighting took place between the two Cypriot rivals, but peace efforts by Makarios and Küçük helped calm the atmosphere. Unfortunately, this didn't last long. Centuries of hatred can be hard to overcome.

In 1974, the whole situation boiled over again. A coup in Greece, led by a military junta, changed the whole equation. They were in favour of Enosis. EOKA-B, with the new Greece government's assistance, planned a coup against President Makarios, and he had to flee the island with the help of the British that still had bases there.

Then, in July 1974, the Turkish military invaded the island and by August held forty percent of the island. Since Turkey was considerably closer to Cyprus than Greece, it was easy for their military to win in the northern parts of the island. It was finally agreed to partition the island and the UN built a monitored Green Line. People from the south could not go to the north and vice versa.

The Turkish Republic of Northern Cyprus (TRNC) was declared independent in 1983, but it is only recognized by Turkey. The international community considers TRNC territory, as the territory of the Republic of Cyprus. This continues to this day.

One side effect of this partition is that a person wanted by any of the "western" countries for financial malfeasance or other crimes can hide out in the TRNC. This is because that, since most countries don't recognize the TRNC, there are no extradition treaties between them.

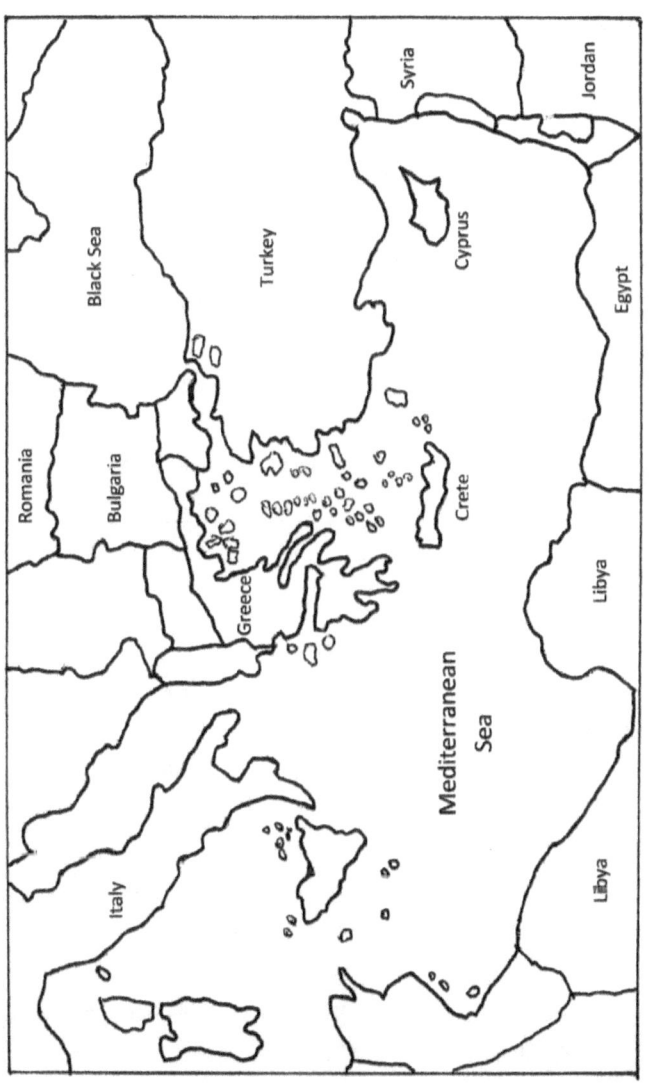

Eastern Mediterranean

CYPRUS People March 1958 to August 1960

Actual People

Cyprus Governor ....Sir Hugh Mackintosh Foot (1907-1990)

Royal Artillery 188th CO......Major MacArthur (unknown)

EOKA Leader .... Georgios Grivas (Dighenis) (1898-1974)

Greek General .... General Nicholas Paparodu (unknown)

Greek Religious Leader ... Archbishop Makarios III (1913-1977)

British Prime Minister ...... Maurice Harold MacMillan (1894-1986)

Lieutenant Colonel .... William Gore-Langton (1914-2003)

Cypriot Businessman ...... Gabriel Gabrielides (Gabby) (1910-1973)

Cyprus Times Editor ...... Charles Foley (1909-?)

HMS Agincourt Captain ... Erroll N. Sinclair RN (unknown)

Fictional People

Lt. Colonel Baker	Intelligence Corps
Captain Phillips	Intelligence Corps
Lt. Ian Black	Intelligence Corps
Diana Palas	Nurse, mother of three children
Minervo Palas	Aphrodite's older brother
Aphrodite Palas.............................	Nurse
Andreus Palas................................	Aphrodite's younger brother
John (Andrew Dinglefoot)	MI6
Percival	MI6
2nd Lt. Roger Snell	Wiltshire Reg., fluent in Turkish
Sgt. Kenneth Bingham	Communications, Signal Corps
HMS Benton Captain..................	Curtis Abney RN

BRITISH ARMY OFFICER RANKS

Officers: Field Marshal

General

Lieutenant General

Major General

Brigadier

Colonel (1 crown and 2 pips)

Lieutenant Colonel (1 crown and 1 pip)

Major (1 crown)

Captain (3 pips)

1st Lieutenant (Lt)   (2 pips)

2nd Lieutenant (2Lt) (1 pip)

If the second lieutenant's surname is Smith, he will be addressed as Mr. Smith by senior officers. Similarly, a first lieutenant is addressed as Mr. Smith.

A second lieutenant generally stays at that rank for 1-2 years before automatically being promoted to first lieutenant.

Promotion to Captain and above is by passing the promotion exam. Normal time to make Captain is five years.

British pronunciation of Lieutenant is "Leftenant"

GLOSSARY

HUMINT	Human Intelligence
SIGINT	Signal Intelligence
MI5	Protects UK national security from espionage
MI6	UK equivalent to the CIA
SIS	Secret Intelligence Service
AYIOS NIKOLAOS	British /US Communication Intercept Station
SAS	Special Air Service
AAC	U.K. Army Air Corps
RAF	Royal Air Force (British Air Force)
RHAF	Royal Hellenic Air Force/Greek Air Force
NICOSIA	Capital of Cyprus (Lefkoşa to Turks)
KYRENIA	Port town (Girne to Turkish Cypriots)
4 Mk 6	Search Radar developed by Marconi of Canada
CO	Commanding Officer
OIC	Officer in Charge
LORRY	English word for truck
BOOT	English word for trunk of a car
HELLO	English word for greeting (American Hi)
BOOKING	English word for reservation
KERB	English for curb
JACK TAR	Sailor

This page intentionally left blank

THE AUTHORS

Richard Osborn

He was born and raised in England, and educated at King's School, Canterbury. He is a veteran of the British Army Royal Artillery and the United States Air Force. He is a graduate of California State University at Los Angeles and of the Thunderbird Graduate School of International Management. Later, he worked at General Dynamics, Aeronutronic Ford, Hughes Aircraft and Tektronix. He is a licensed pilot and has conducted numerous seminars for Tektronix Inc. in the Far East and Europe. Now he is writing fiction and non-fiction in Knoxville, Tennessee.

Barbara Osborn

She was born and raised in Virginia. She attended art classes at the University of Georgia and studied art history at the University of Tennessee. She has travelled extensively in Europe and the Mediterranean. After living in England for awhile, she came back to Knoxville, Tennessee remarried and retired. Currently, she and her husband are co-writing fiction novels.

ON HER MAJESTY'S CYPRUS MISSION

AVAILABLE NOW

Ian Black is transferred to Berlin after graduating from the Advanced Intelligence Corps Academy. He arrives just in time to be involved before and after the construction of the Wall. He befriends an East German politician's mistress and assists a Czechoslovakian ice skater in her defection to the West. Ian follows the Russian troop movements in the East.

On Her Majesty's
BERLIN MISSION

An **Ian Black** *Novel*

ACHTUNG!
Sie verlassen jetzt
WEST-BERLIN

RICHARD *and* BARBARA OSBORN

BRITANNIA-AMERICAN PUBLISHING
ISBN: 978-0692780855

RICHARD AND BARBARA OSBORN

AVAILABLE NOW

After resigning his commission in the British Army and going to the United States, Ian Black meets with General Carter in Washington. He is offered a commission in the USAF and works in the Air Force ISR Agency as a Captain. Due to his experience in Berlin, he is transferred to the USAFSS Section H during the Vietnam War.

BRITANNIA-AMERICAN PUBLISHING
ISBN: 978-1981773022

AVAILABLE NOW

The Osborns' explosive novel delves into whether the President, Edward Tuckwell, is able to remain in office after two terms, using a false flag operation. The climax shocks the nation and calm finally returns to Washington, after the tanks knock down the White House gates.

BRITANNIA-AMERICAN PUBLISHING

ISBN: 978-0692503379

RICHARD AND BARBARA OSBORN

AVAILABLE NOW

This book by Richard Osborn delves into the blunders and appeasements of the last one hundred years and what effect they have had on the *Western* world. At the end of each chapter, the author analyzes the blunder and who was responsible for causing it.

TWILIGHT

FOR
THE

WEST?

A CENTURY OF
BLUNDERS AND APPEASEMENTS
BY NAÏVE, NEOPHYTE POLITICIANS
1914-2014

RICHARD OSBORN

United States Air Force Veteran
British Army — Royal Artillery Veteran

BRITANNIA-AMERICAN PUBLISHING
ISBN: 978-0692418413